VAL VEGA:
SECRET
AMBASSADOR
OF EARTH

VAL VEGA:
SECRET
AMBASSADOR
OF EARTH

Ben Francisco

a_vb

aventura
books

Published by Aventura Books LLC, Brooklyn, NY.

Cover illustration by Luis Carlos Barragán.
Cover design and interior graphics by Todd Cooper, All-D.

ISBN: 979-8-9892709-0-3

First Edition: February 2024

10 9 8 7 6 5 4 3 2 1

*For my parents, Janet and Carl, who are skilled
in the art of naming.*

TRANSCRIPT OF SUBSPACE MESSAGES

between Umberto Olmeda (Ambassador of Earth) and
Pash-Ti of Phasmus V (Licensed Observer of Primitive Worlds)

Galactic Standard Date 43A3.71

ObserverPashTi: Ambassador, this was the second attempt on your life this month. It pains me to articulate, but you must develop a prudent succession plan.

AmbUmb: we already have one

ObserverPashTi: I said prudent. That child hasn't even completed the basic schooling rites on Earth, as barbaric as that educational system may be.

AmbUmb: 15 is the official age of maturity for a terran. she's eligible and there's no one as qualified. Punto.

ObserverPashTi: It's been difficult enough convincing the Great Powers to take you seriously as ambassador of Terra. Even for a primitive world, Terra has a horrid reputation. The ecological self-destruction. The violent divisions. The intolerable humidity.

AmbUmb: well, Earth may have its shortcomings, but we do have salsa. the Yankees. RuPaul's drag race.

ObserverPashTi: This is no time for levity. Your personal feelings are clouding your judgment.

AmbUmb: <Galactic standard signal for indignant hurt> my personal connection to her has nothing to do with this! she did better on the xenoreactive scenario than anyone else on Earth who's taken the test—even me! i've never met a single sentient with greater capacity for empathy for those who are different from her.

ObserverPashTi: Her potential is significant, but even you have said she tends to be indecisive—and there is no room for indecision amidst the complexities of interstellar politics.

AmbUmb: you don't know her like i do. my decision is final. Valeria Vega will be the next ambassador of Earth.

CHAPTER I

I HATE MULTIPLE-CHOICE QUESTIONS, because I can always see a way for every answer to be right. My answer sheet is a mess of As, Bs, Cs, and Ds all crossed out and replaced and crossed out again, frenzied scribbles of an alphabet in distress. I wish they'd just let you answer "all of the above" for every question. I'm sure to get a record-breaking low score on the SATs.

Will is sitting cross-legged on a big pillow on the floor, chewing on their pencil, which means they're anxious. Kate is sitting on the other end of my bed, her face buried in her long blonde hair, her fingers gliding across her laptop.

Kate closes her laptop with a typical-Kate decisive clack. "I so have this. I got nearly every one right on verbal." This whole practice session was her idea, even though she's way better at this stuff than Will or me. I'm curious about everything from black holes to evolution, but the SATs and all the classes at my high school are all about regurgitating other people's ideas instead of actually learning.

"And you, William?" I say. "Are you also headed for the Ivy League?"

Will runs their purple fingernails through their curly black hair and stretches out their long legs. Will's my best friend and has been hanging out in my room since we were seven, but lately when they come over all I can think about is how close I am to those adorable lanky legs. "I'm hoping film schools recognize film is a visual medium, not a verbal one," says Will. "And you, Val?"

"Well, if you doubled my score, then I'd be doing great."

"You guys really should take Kaplan," Kate says.

Will and I look at each other. Neither of our families can afford Kaplan. For Kate, money's as accessible as air, so it never occurs to her there are things some of us can't afford. But if I say that, it'll just embarrass all of us in different ways. So I just say, "The SATs are culturally biased anyway. Like, what does a passage by Edith Wharton have to do with anything in real life?"

Kate makes air-quotes with her fingers. "'Culturally biased' or not, you need the SATs to get into any good college, basically. You two need to get your acts together. You've got, like, no ambition."

"Well," says Will, "not all of us can grow up to be president of the United States."

"Actually," Kate says, "lately I'm thinking I need to think bigger."

"What's bigger than president?" Will says with a laugh. "Pope?"

Kate folds her arms around her SAT workbook. "Excuse me for having ambition. It's so not-cute to have no goals in life. Especially you, Val. At least Will has this whole movie director dream, even if it's totally unrealistic. You don't have *any* goals."

Will clenches their teeth that way they do when they're hurt but don't want to show it. I don't care when Kate insults me, but I can't stand it when she demeans Will's dreams like that. She even used to do that during the two-month drama when they dated last year, which is how she and I ended up being friends, or at least friends-in-law. I have the urge to call her out, but that will only escalate things, so I resist with gentle humor instead. "You're probably right that I'm a hopeless cause. That's why I plan on mooching off Will when they're a famous filmmaker. Luckily, they're not going to have to solve for X or interpret some 19th-century passage to make all the awesome films in their head."

Will smiles at me and bites their lip in appreciation, which gives me a little flutter.

"Whatever," Kate says. "Mooching is totally not a plan."

There's the familiar sound of a car rolling into the gravel driveway—tío Umberto's Toyota Camry. He's been away in Istanbul for weeks. He's the only person I can really talk to, and half the time he's traveling for work, either with no time or no signal.

"My uncle's home," I say. "BRB, please carry on the scintillating SAT excitement without me."

I bound down the stairs and find Mami and my little brother Miguel in the kitchen. The three of us nearly crash into each other on the way to the back door.

The door swings open and tío Umberto walks in, rolling his purple suitcase behind him, loaded up with shopping bags. "Saludos!" he says, with a tip of his purple fedora.

"Umberto!" Mami greets him with a hug and kiss on the cheek. "Por fin vuelves!"

"I'm back, and I come bearing gifts!" tío Umberto says in Spanish. We all gather around as he fishes in his bags. He pulls out a Federico García Lorca play for Miguel; a singing key-finder keychain for Mami ("Not that you ever lose your keys"); a book on the Treaty of Paris for my big brother, Timoteo ("He can pick it up when he comes home from Harvard"); and a miniature stuffed soccer ball for me.

I toss the soccer ball into the air a couple times. I'm way too old for stuffed toys. Must be a last-minute airport purchase, because tío Umberto's gifts are usually more thoughtful.

He taps me on the shoulder. "So you ready for the SATs?"

"Um, maybe I could do a gap year with you in Istanbul?"

Tío Umberto laughs. "I'm sure you'd be exceptional in my line of work. But maybe you should stick out school a bit longer."

Mami invites Will and Kate to stay for dinner. Kate doesn't speak Spanish, so I have to play interpreter any time she and Mami talk. Things end up splitting into two conversations in two languages: Kate talking with Uncle Umberto in English and Mami and Will talking with Miguel in Spanish about the spring musical. Will's family is Chinese-Peruvian, and Will is trilingual, which is easily as sexy as their lanky legs. I'm sitting between Kate and Will, and I dip in and out of both conversations.

"So exactly which NGO do you work for?" Kate asks Uncle Umberto. She has these moods where she's all into having adult conversation. "I do Model UN, you know."

"That's lovely," says Umberto. "My work is ... complicated. Let's see. Take Puerto Rico as an example. Are you familiar with Puerto Rico's status—as a U.S. territory?"

"Of course," Kate says. "I think it should be a state." Kate always has an opinion.

"Well," says Umberto, "my organization helps give voice to pla— uh, places like Puerto Rico. The territories, the colonies, the small places that usually don't get a seat at the table."

"Seems like you're not doing a very good job," Kate says. "Because they still don't have a seat at the table."

Umberto laughs. "Well, it's certainly slow-going. But I've always been drawn to underdogs and lost causes."

After Mami serves flan for dessert, there's a knock at the front door. "It's one of those people from your work," Mami tells Umberto as she comes back to the kitchen.

"Ah." Umberto gets up with a grimace. "I'll be back in a moment."

I can see the front door, partially blocked by the mound of jackets on the coat rack. One of Umberto's co-workers is standing there, in a red leather jacket and tight jeans. I've met him a few times—his name is Johnny, and some quirky last name that sounds made-up.

"Johnny," Umberto says, "it's late."

"I know, boss," Johnny says. "But with everything going on, I thought ..." He looks past Umberto, toward us. For a second, his eyes meet mine. My cheeks go red, and I look down at my plate, embarrassed to be caught eavesdropping. I spoon a slice of flan but keep listening. Johnny says, "Maybe we could chat somewhere a little more private?"

"I don't think that's necessary," Umberto says.

"Okay," Johnny says. "Well, you know there's been a huge ... *tick* problem lately. Not to brag, but I'm really good at handling ticks. So I thought I could hang out a bit, check for ticks, spray some pesticides. Then stay the night in case any *ticks* come back."

"My *tick* problems were far away," Umberto says, stern. "You know, out in the woods."

"Boss, there have been two tick outbreaks in the past month. Don't you think we should be a little cautious? I really don't want you getting Lyme disease."

Kate gives me a "what-the-hell?" look. I guess she can't help eavesdropping either. I reply with a shrug. It's obvious "ticks" are a code for something. I wish tío Umberto would tell me more about his work. I'd love to go with him on one of his trips, to learn more about other cultures all around the world. He promised to take me with him some day, but that day's never today.

I go to get more flan and glance toward the door again. Johnny is staring at Umberto as if listening—but Umberto's not even talking. "Whatev!" Johnny finally says, pointing at Umberto's fedora. "You could never have stopped it, not with that pea brain of yours!"

It's weird for Johnny to insult tío Umberto when he's Johnny's boss. Why are they so stressed? Their work is in international relations, and lately the whole world always seems on the brink. But they work on cross-cultural understanding, nothing dangerous. I think.

"Johnny," Umberto says, inching the door closed, "this is inappropriate. Go home."

Umberto comes back and drapes his napkin on his lap. "Sorry about that. Now back to my important date with this flan!"

"What's the deal with that guy?" asks Kate, never one to be diplomatic.

"Things have been stressful at work," Umberto says. "And we did have a problem with, ah, mites on our last trip. Johnny can be over-protective."

Miguel licks the flan from his spoon. "All the people at your office are weird."

"Johnny's from … a remote island," Umberto says. "Weird depends entirely on where you are and where you come from."

✧ ✧ ✧

SATURDAY NIGHT, KATE'S PARENTS are out of town, so of course she has a party. A bunch of seniors come who I don't even know—Kate overachieves at party-throwing just like she does in school. I'm sitting on the couch, holding a Heineken, talking with Kate and a few other girls. Getting drunk isn't my thing, but if I don't drink at all, then everyone will ask why not and shove more drinks in my face. It's easier just to nurse one beer all night long.

I'm half-paying attention to Kate and the others talking about prom. Across the room, Will is talking to Des, leaning into her. I wish Will were leaning into me. But I can't even join the conversation, because Des will get passive-aggressive with me. Now Des is leaning into Will too, a mutual lean. A mutual lean seems so appealing, yet so unattainable. It's inevitable they'll get together, and maybe there's some cosmic justice in that, a penance for what I did to Des.

Kate elbows me and points her chin at Des and Will. "Des still isn't talking to you, huh?"

At least she thinks I'm staring at Des and not Will. Kate's the last person I want to know about my crush on Will. They're still exes, and even if Kate's been all BFFs with me lately, she still doesn't feel like a true friend. Not like Des was. "Nope, Des still hates me."

"It wasn't even your fault, mostly," Kate says.

"Easy for you to say. You're the hero of the story."

"I just thought she should know. I don't like when people keep secrets." Sometimes it's like Kate's trying to make me feel even worse about things with Des.

Kate gets up to get another drink. Will and Des extricate themselves from their mutual lean, and Will comes over, dramatically collapsing next to me on the couch. A few strands of their curly hair graze my jeans, and it takes all my effort to keep my breath steady. "I'm going crazy over Des," they whisper. "Do you think she likes me too? You must have some idea."

"I'm not the expert on Des that I used to be, Will." How can they know me so well but be so clueless about how I feel about them?

"You've got to make up with her. I can't stand having my two favorite people not talking to each other." I grin at that, though the smile fades when I realize I'm probably a distant *second*-favorite.

Will's eyes dart to the fireplace. "What was that? Oh my God, it's a snake!" A flash of dark green slithers from the fireplace to the television stand.

"There's a fricking snake in the house!" someone shouts, and there's a chorus of yelps. In seconds, everyone but me evacuates the couch.

"Fricking wuss," some guy says to Will. "It's just a snake."

"Give it a kiss then, if you're such a fan of snakes," Will retorts. I love the way they're never mean but never take crap from anyone.

Most people have run out of the room, except a few of the senior guys standing behind the couch, trying to look cool—but keeping a notable distance from the snake.

"What if it's poisonous?" one says.

I look at the snake from my lone vantage point on the couch. It's less than two feet long, olive green with two blotchy yellow stripes running along the length of its body. I'm kind of addicted to documentaries and amateur nature videos, so I recognize it right away. "It's just a garter snake. It's not venomous."

"Snakes are *so* scary," says some senior girl I've never met, clearly trying to get attention with this damsel-in-distress routine.

"I'll take care of it," says one of the boys, his speech slurring. Great, now a drunken prince is coming to the rescue.

I get up and pull the poker from by the fireplace, and slowly walk toward the snake. "Oh shoot," someone says, "Val's going to impale it!" There are a few drunken laughs.

"I've done this before," I say, which is not technically true, but I've seen someone else do it—twice, if you count YouTube. I hold the poker out near the snake's head, then go behind it while it's distracted. I try to be quick but gentle, picking it up with one hand at the middle of its body, then lift the front part of its body with the poker. For a few seconds, I hold it like that, level, letting it get accustomed to where it is.

"Ranger Val's got it under control," says a member of the drunk-guy chorus.

The snake slithers through my hand in my relaxed grip. I wrap my other hand around it further up its body. I let it slither back and forth between my left and right hand as I rotate my grip between the two. That's right, get comfortable, little snake. It's just like being in a tree, always with somewhere else to climb.

"So gross," says the damsel.

"It's probably more scared of you than you are of it," I say as I walk around her, carrying the snake toward the back door.

"She's such a freak," someone says as the door shuts behind me. Apparently it's freaky to not be freaked out by a harmless snake.

There's a brook behind Kate's backyard, which is probably where the snake came from in the first place. I hold it up in the moonlight. Up close, its scales are intricate, and its bright black eyes stare back at me. It's funny so many people are scared of snakes. People and snakes have most body parts in common, except for limbs and scales and a few other things. Maybe I should be a zoologist. I did okay in bio last year. But that would require a college degree, and a decent score on the SATs, which is about as likely as Will asking me to prom. I point the snake toward the brook and let it go.

When I get back inside, Kate and Will are in the kitchen, Kate hovering by the back door, Will leaning over the fridge. "What'd you do with the snake?" Kate asks, sounding not-thrilled about having a snake in the house during her parents-out-of-town party.

"Let it out by the brook," I say. "It was probably just confused."

Will emerges from the fridge and pops open a White Claw. "Val Vega, you're my hero," they say. I jab them softly in the chest, but they shrink away. "Just wash your hands before you touch me, okay?" they say with a smile. "Because that was hella gross."

Great, now I'm Val Vega, snake-handler, least sexy person in school.

As it gets later, the general drunkenness increases. Will and Des are sprawled on the couch, their bodies pointed in opposite directions, but their heads only inches apart, speaking to each other in hushed tones. The party has definitely ceased to be fun, so I text tío Umberto to see if he can pick me up. It's late, but he's a night owl and always says he'd rather I wake him than risk driving with someone who's even a little bit drunk.

Umberto texts back right away: *your chariot is en route!* :)

Over on the couch, Des has fallen asleep—clearly in no condition to drive. She was Will's ride too, so they both have no safe way home. I walk over to them.

"Hey, Will," I whisper. "My uncle's on his way. We could give you guys a ride."

Will looks over at Des. "I ... think that's a good idea. I'll wake up Des."

That's my cue to leave them alone. While I'm searching the pile of jackets on Kate's bed, I hear Des shout, "No way!" My stomach twists. Des is so angry she doesn't even want a ride home from me.

I walk back to the living room and find Will helping Des to her feet. I take a deep breath and walk over to them. "Des, I'm really—"

"Shut up," Des says, pointing at me with a drunken sway. "We're coming with you. But it's your uncle who's helping me. Not you, Two-Face."

"Okay," I say. It's been two months since she said my name. All I am to her is Two-Face.

We walk outside and wait on the front porch, Will with an arm around Des, who's chewing gum, loudly. I stand in awkward silence with my best-friend-slash-unrequited-crush, while they hit on my former-best-friend-who's-not-speaking-to-me.

It's a relief when tío Umberto pulls up a few minutes later. He salutes with a tip of his fedora. I hop in the front seat and ask if we can give Will and Des a ride.

"But of course," Umberto says. "Great to see you two."

We pull onto the twisting roads. The only sounds are the hum of the motor and the occasional bubble bursting from Des's mouth.

"Haven't seen you in a while, Des," says Umberto. "How are things?"

"Fine," Des says.

Silence again. Des's gum-chewing gets so loud I can hear it from the front seat. Uncle Umberto shoots me a quizzical look. I shake my head at him with a clenched-teeth face. Thankfully, he gets the drift. We drive another few minutes in silence.

Umberto pulls up in front of Des's house. "First stop, Madame Desiree's abode!"

"I'll get out here too," says Will. "It's a short walk. Thanks, Mr. Olmeda!"

They get out of the car, Des leaning on Will for support. I feel a pang of jealousy—of both of them. If only I could figure out a way for everyone to get along with everyone else, then everything would be better. Des and I would be friends again, and Will would realize I understand them in a way no one else can.

Uncle Umberto pulls the car back onto the road. "Des didn't even say good-bye. Was that just because she was drunk?"

I slump in my seat. "She doesn't talk to me, like, ever. I kind of deserve it."

"What happened?"

I look out the window, torn between embarrassment and desperately needing to talk to someone. Will is too wrapped up in their crush on Des. I can't talk to Des because she's the problem, and Kate's never been someone I go to for advice.

"There are a few people—some of the girls on the team," I say, "who said Des was really moody. Like she'd be happy one second and the next she'd be angry. Someone said it was like she had multiple personality disorder, and they started counting her personalities. They'd even do it in front of her. We'd be at the diner after practice, and Des would say something, and somebody would go 'Seven!' or '23!' And Des had no idea what was going on."

"And you participated in this?" There's disappointment in the softness of tío's voice.

"Of course not," I say. "But I didn't *tell* her. One time she even asked me what the deal was with all the numbers, and I acted like I didn't know. Then Kate told her what was going on, and that I knew about it, and Des sent me like thirty texts saying she couldn't believe I'd do that to her, and that I was a terrible friend. And she blocked me on, like, everything, and now all she ever calls me is 'Two-Face.' And to be honest everything she said is true. I lied to her. I do act like a different person depending on who I'm with. I'm two-faced."

"It sounds like a hard situation," Uncle Umberto says. "What do you think you should have done?" He's doing his Socratic thing, which is totally not what I was hoping for.

"I probably should have told her what was going on. Or told the others to stop. Or both."

"And why didn't you?"

"Because I knew it would just hurt her feelings, and the team would say I snitched, and everyone would be pissed at each other, and it all seemed like more trouble than it was worth."

"Then I think 'two-facedness' is a misdiagnosis of the problem. You have some exceptional gifts, Val. When you're with someone, you imagine yourself behind the eyes of the other person. You see the world from their perspective and meet them there—even if that perspective is vastly different from your own. But our greatest gifts can also be our greatest liabilities. You saw that Des was going to feel hurt, and you saw there would be strife on the team, but you didn't go a step further and do something about it. The problem is you took the path of least resistance. And that path, though the easiest, is often not the one that gets you where you need to go."

Umberto's cell phone rings, his favorite Gloria Estefan merengue beat. "Sorry," he says. "It's work, I have to take this." He gets work calls at all hours of the day. It must be morning by now in Istanbul. He nestles the earpiece onto his ear and says, "Yes, Patrece? ... I know, they were rumbling about that before."

The car picks up speed as Umberto listens. "Increíble," he says, slapping the steering wheel. "Then say we'll set them up with seats near the ceiling." Umberto scoffs. "Well, it's not like we can change their physiology. I'm not letting this derail us, not now. ... Then we'll build them an alcove!" He yanks off the earpiece, barely slowing as he turns the corner.

"Um, you have to build an alcove for someone?" I ask.

Umberto chuckles. "Luckily, I don't personally have to build it."

I think back to that weird conversation he had with Johnny. These people making these demands—are they connected to the "ticks" that Johnny was worried about? "Is everything okay, tío? I know your job is stressful, but lately it seems even worse."

Umberto slows down. "I have a big meeting coming up, a major negotiation that I'm mediating. If it goes well, it will make a real difference in many people's lives. If it doesn't ..." His voice trails off as we come to a red light, and he takes off his fedora to reveal his thinning hair. "You're so young, Valeria. There are things I have to tell you. This might not make much sense now, but a time is coming, sooner than I'd like, when you may have to leap into a whole new set of challenges. You'll find realities that are wondrous—but also harsh."

"What are you talking about?" I say. "I know life is hard. You don't have to tell me that."

Umberto squints at the road ahead of him. "Right. We'll talk after the SATs. I don't have to leave until a week from Wednesday."

"You're leaving again?" I slump deeper into the seat. "I hate it when you're not here. You're basically the only person on the planet who understands me."

Tío Umberto pats my knee. "Well, that's not so bad. That means you might still find plenty of people who understand you on other planets."

✦ ✦ ✦

KATE SLEEPS OVER THE NIGHT BEFORE the SATs for some final cramming. I wish it were Will or Des, but it's good to have someone to study with. In the morning she wakes up before everyone else and even makes omelets for everyone, impressing Umberto and Mami.

The test is a disaster, my answer sheet filled with scribbles that will probably invalidate half my answers even if I got them right. At least it's over.

There's no sign of Umberto's car, and Kate and Will both get a ride with Des's parents, which is awkward, so I just avoid all of them and go sit at the picnic tables and doodle. Tío Umberto promised to take me out for ice cream as my reward for surviving the SATs. It's a ritual we've followed on special occasions since my First Communion. We'll have cookie's 'n' cream ice cream cones with chocolate fudge and chocolate sprinkles. The chocolate sprinkles are essential. We'll talk about the Yankees, then go home and stream a movie.

After ten minutes, I dial Umberto. No answer. I redial. After four rings, it picks up. At first I think it's a bad signal, but then realize that strange sound is actually a high-pitched sob. "Hello?" I say. "Tío?"

"O Dios mío." It's Mami's voice. "Dios mío," she says over and over, in between sobs.

"Mami?" I say. "Qué pasó?"

"Ay, m'ija," she sobs. "Umberto está muerto. Mi hermano está muerto."

But we were going to get ice cream, is the first stupid thought that goes through my head.

Then a planet tilts inside my heart. It can't be true. Tío Umberto can't be dead.

CHAPTER 2

ARTICLE 9

ARTICLE 9 — Enacted in the wake of the Sufri Uprising and ensuing Fourth Galactic War, Article 9 of the Third Treaty of Centron granted recognition to thousands of primitive worlds, including representation in the Interstellar Assembly by special ambassadors who have "a voice but no vote."[1] In most cases, the native populations of these worlds remain unaware of the interstellar community's existence — or that sentients from other planets secretly live among them …

Excerpted from **WIKI GALACTICA**

MAMI PULLS INTO AN EMPTY SPACE in the parking lot of the funeral home, utterly failing to line up the car with the white lines. As we walk across the lot, Mami grips my hand tight, the way abuela always used to. For a second, I wonder if Mami has somehow transformed into abuela, because that's how everything seems now, like the universe is conspiring in every way possible to pull the rug out from under me.

"I'm so sorry for your loss," the guy at the funeral home says at the door.

"He says he's sorry about Uncle Umberto," I tell Mami in Spanish. She nods through tears as he ushers us into the sitting room. I hold Mami's hand and interpret as the funeral director writes down our info and asks about scheduling for the wake and the funeral. Interpreting for Mami is so familiar that it's oddly comforting.

"Another important matter," the funeral director says, "is the selection of a casket."

The funeral director hands Mami a catalog, thick like an art portfolio. Mami looks at it, lets out a high-pitched sob, and drops the book to the floor. "No puedo más!"

I don't translate that for the funeral director, just give Mami's hand a firm squeeze.

"I'm so sorry," the funeral director says, putting a box of tissues in front of us.

I hold Mami as she sobs, and I wonder why I'm not crying too. It's like Mami and I are a single entity: my mother is the part that expresses our grief, and I'm the part that does everything else.

I bend over to pick up the catalog and lay it on my lap. I thumb through it, surprised that caskets are so expensive. Mami is always cost-conscious but she'd never get one of the cheapest ones—they're too simple and unadorned, and Mami would want better than that for her brother. The mahogany ones are elegant, but the prices are over the top. Then I see one that's deep purple with silver lining. It reminds me of tío Umberto's fedora and has a bit of his flair. It's not the cheapest, but it's on the less expensive side.

"How about this one, Mami?"

"Ay, Val," she says, looking up and smiling through her tears. "That's perfect. This is the one we want."

We talk through prayer cards and other details of the wake. When we get up to leave, the funeral director catches my eye and pats me on the arm. "Lo siento," he says, with a thick American accent.

"Thanks," I say, Mami leaning on me as we walk out the door.

✦ ✦ ✦

THE WAKE IS THE NEXT DAY. I loosen the collar of my black button-down shirt. At least Mami didn't make me wear a dress, but my formal pants and shirt are almost as uncomfortable. Miguel and I are standing in the parlor, on the far end from Mami and the casket. Mami is sitting a few feet from Umberto's body, where a receiving line has formed. Our cousin is up front with Mami, arms flailing. "He was so young," she says. "And so flaquito! How could someone so skinny have a heart attack so young?"

"I feel like we're in a telenovela," Miguel says. "All we're missing is the dramatic background music."

I chuckle. "Totally."

Will and Desiree walk in, dressed in black and grey. They're both here—together. I'd have too many feelings to count, if my heart weren't too numb for feelings. Will waves awkwardly, then comes up and wraps me in a hug. A few days ago, my heart would have raced feeling the warmth of their body surrounding mine, but now we're just two empty bodies pressing into each other.

"I'm so sorry," Will says, pulling apart from me.

Desiree holds out a plate of homemade M&M cookies, her old specialty. "I brought these for you and your family." I take the cookie tray and hold it like it's a newborn baby. For the first time in weeks, our eyes meet without instantly dashing away from each other. "I'm sorry about your uncle, Val."

My name. She actually said my name. "Thank you, Des, that means a lot to me." For the first time, I feel a sniffle coming on—but I can't cry yet, I need to take care of everyone else. I focus on finding a place for the cookies on the credenza.

"We should talk," Desiree says. "Not now, but. When I heard about your uncle ... Yeah, um, let's talk. When you're ready."

"I'd like that," I say, a tangle of appreciation and sorrow in my throat. Des and Will hug me again, then walk toward Mami.

Miguel taps me on the shoulder and points to the door. "Check them out. The telenovela is over and it's time for Cirque du Soleil." Umberto's co-workers are walking in. Patrece stands a full six-and-a-half-feet tall, her arms almost long enough to reach her knees without bending. Wasala is three feet tall, her head barely reaching Patrece's waist, and her movements are oddly fluid, like she's double-jointed everywhere. Then there's Johnny, who came by the other night. Instead of his usual red leather jacket, he's wearing a perfectly fitted jet-black suit. I'm no good at designers, but it looks expensive, an Armani or something. As Johnny walks in, he snatches off his sunglasses with a dramatic flourish.

"So they're eccentric," I tell Miguel. "They were tío Umberto's friends."

They come over to us. Patrece shakes my hand, and I feel a sudden rush of cold—not from her hand, but from the air around it, like opening the door of a freezer. Has it gotten colder outside?

"My condolences to you and your family," Patrece says.

"Condolences to everybody," Miguel says. "Condolences to the whole fricking world. It's a worse off place without Uncle Umberto."

"That's truer than you know," Wasala says. "Umberto's passing will be felt in many spheres."

"I'm not much of a people-person," Patrece says. She says "people-person" the way people with a severe allergy to cats say they're not cat-people. "But Umberto was exceptional. He was one of the most impressive beings I've ever had the honor of knowing."

"Plus, he had a magnificent sense of fashion," Johnny says. "These past few decades, very few people have been able to work a fedora, but Umberto pulled it off effortlessly."

I want to be nice to these people because I know they cared about Umberto too, but am I supposed to be comforted by the eulogizing of his fedoras? I can't wait for them to leave, so I can be alone with my family, the people who really knew tío Umberto.

"We knew Umberto with a depth you might not guess," Wasala says, and it's creepy how what she's saying is like an answer to my thoughts. "We worked with him for years, through crises and triumphs. He possessed a remarkable ability to maintain his composure in the midst of adversity. He consistently exceeded expectations for a—" She's cut off by a wide-eyed glance from Patrece. "For someone of his background," Wasala finishes.

"We really must move on to pay our respects to Umberto's corpse," Patrece says, shepherding her colleagues away.

"Background?" I say. "Why would Turkish people have issues with Puerto Ricans?"

"Islanders," Wasala says, as Patrece leads her to the casket. It's almost cartoonish, a near-giant dragging a little person along behind her. "Terrible prejudice against islanders of any kind."

They're certainly a weird bunch, but tío Umberto always says—said—that weird depends entirely on where you are and where you come from. Part of me wants to know more about them, more about that other world in Istanbul where Umberto spent so much of his time.

The three of them hover at the casket. Wasala looks up at Patrece with a questioning glance. Then Johnny crosses himself and kneels to pray. Funny, I wouldn't have guessed he was Catholic. The others follow Johnny's example. Patrece holds her palm completely flat as she makes the sign of the cross, like a series of gentle self-slaps. Wasala's motions are the opposite, an excessively fluid dance of her hand. Johnny stands, and the others follow. Just as they're leaving, Patrece reaches into the casket and touches Umberto at the neck. What the hell? Mami has been touching tío's body all day, but it's just weird for a co-worker to do that.

Then something glints in the casket. Did Patrece drop something inside? I walk over to the casket. For less than a second, a gentle green glow pulses through the veins of Uncle Umberto's neck. I lean in to look more closely, but Umberto's neck looks normal now. It happened so fast—could it have been a trick of the light?

That weird conversation about the ticks. Umberto's weird phone call in the car. Tío Umberto having a sudden heart attack even though he was completely healthy. And now a strange green glow in his body. Could Umberto have been involved in some sort of international espionage? Something that made someone want to kill him? Or, if he was a spy, maybe he faked his death and is really still alive?

I stare at his body, and realize I'm letting denial and wishful thinking carry my brain to ridiculous fantasies. Tío Umberto is gone, and I just have to accept it.

"You okay, Val?" Miguel says, coming up behind me.

I shake myself out of my stampede of wild thoughts. "I'm fine."

"Timoteo just texted. His bus was delayed but finally got in. He'll be here any minute."

Timoteo will be devastated when he sees the body, and I need to be there for him when he does. I turn toward the door. He's walking into the parlor, wearing his only suit. He flashes Miguel and me a weary smile. He walks toward us, then comes to a halt. He hunches over, his eyes wide in disbelief as he stares at tío's body. A sob chokes out of his throat.

I'm already striding across the parlor in steps as long as my short legs can manage. I wrap my arms around my big brother and let his weight fall onto me. He's so tall that I'm holding him just above the waist, my head buried in his jacket. Neither of us says anything. I just stand there, propping him up and holding him tight as he sobs.

✧   ✧   ✧

TIMOTEO IS CALMER by the time he gives the eulogy. It's the thing I admire most about my older brother. Ever since he came out a few years ago, he's had this special way to find power in his own vulnerability. He talks about how Uncle Umberto was the world's biggest Yankees fan, how he often spoke of the Yankees' victories and losses in colossal proportions. "All is well in the galaxy," he would say. "The Yankees won today." And everyone in the church laughs this exhausted laugh, like laughter's the only way they can get a break from all their tears.

Then he talks about the way Umberto loved to travel, the way he could make friends with anyone in any place in any language. At the end, Timoteo says, "I've never been a big baseball fan like tío Umberto. But the Yankees beat the Cardinals today, four to one. And if Umberto were here with us now, I know that he would tell us that all is right in the galaxy." Mami lets out a sob, and I squeeze her knee.

At the end of the service, the priest announces that Umberto's other nephew is going to share a song. Miguel walks up to the podium. "This is a song from the show I did last spring. Umberto came to all my shows— if he wasn't out of the country—and this was one of his favorites."

He sings a cappella, "Who Am I?" from Les Misérables. When he sings, "If I stay silent, I am damned," his voice chokes on the word "damned," which never happens to Miguel on stage. But he gets his composure back as the song goes on, until he booms out the final chorus, his voice filling the church. He wipes away tears and says, "Thanks for teaching me to always be who I am, Uncle Umberto." It's nothing but sniffles and sobs in every pew. I was so much closer to Umberto than any of these people. But I still haven't shed a tear.

There's a tap on my shoulder—Johnny in the pew behind us. "You gonna sing a little ditty for us too? Maybe a speech or a poem?"

"That's not really my style," I say.

"That's a shame," Johnny says. "I was psyched to hear what you had to say." As the organ music plays, Johnny gets up and takes his place at the side of the casket. Mami asked him to be one of the pallbearers, along with Miguel, Timoteo, three of Uncle Umberto's ex-boyfriends, and two primos—all guys. Together they lift up the casket and slowly carry it down the aisle. Johnny carries the weight effortlessly, but Miguel's and Timoteo's arms are trembling. It's silly that Mami only asked guys to be pallbearers, especially since I've been able to beat both my brothers at arm-wrestling since I was fourteen. But I don't need to be up front. I'm an invisible pallbearer, carrying more of the weight than anyone can see.

✦ ✦ ✦

OUR HOUSE IS TOO SMALL and too messy, so Mami tells everyone to meet at the Valley Diner afterward. The cousins alone fill up half the seats. I'm sitting with my brothers in a booth near the entrance when Umberto's co-workers come in, the last group to arrive.

"It's a five-minute wait," the hostess tells them. "Your name?"

"Johnny," says Johnny. "Johnny Excelsior."

The hostess lets out a snort. "All right, Mr. Excelsior. We should have a table for you in just a few minutes."

Patrece says, "Must you use that ridiculous name?"

"You don't even know," says Johnny. "Johnny Excelsior is what I am."

"This is why I detest being in public with you in foreign places. Can you try not to draw any unwarranted attention, Johnny?"

Why is Patrece worried about drawing attention? Maybe Uncle Umberto's NGO really was a cover for something else. What *was* that green glow on Umberto's neck?

My train of thought gets interrupted by Timoteo and Miguel, talking about how when we were kids, Umberto used to grab us by the wrists and spin us around. But I don't want to reminisce. I want to think about anything but tío Umberto, because every time I think of him it feels like someone stabbing my stomach from the inside.

I get out of the conversation by going to the restroom. I'm washing my hands when Wasala comes in. "Hello, Valiant One," she says.

Does she mean me? That's what "Valeria" literally means, but the only one who's ever called me that was tío Umberto. I just say, "Hey," and pull out a paper towel. Wasala's still standing there, hovering, as much as a three-foot-tall person can hover.

"Patrece or Johnny haven't spoken to you yet?" Wasala asks.

"About what?" I say, wondering what they could possibly have to talk to me about.

"Indeed," Wasala says. "That's just as well, I suppose. Have to allow you time to grieve."

It seems like all of Umberto's co-workers speak quirky or cryptic as their first language. Now I'm really curious and want to know what she was going to say.

"Everything in time, dearie," Wasala says. "I see, you know. I see how much of the weight you carry. And I worry even more weight is about to fall on your shoulders. But some are asked to bear much because they have the strength to hold it."

Okay. They certainly are a melodramatic bunch of peace activists from Istanbul. "Okay, um, thanks for the tip," I say, and walk out the door.

✧ ✧ ✧

I JUST WANT TO COLLAPSE by the time I get home. But I can't sleep, so I pull out my phone. With the funeral and everything, I haven't even looked at my email since Umberto—since the SATs. I scroll through dozens of condolence messages. I don't even want to open them— condolences are pointless. Then, further down in my inbox, I see the name "Umberto Olmeda" in the From column and I let out a yelp.

He must have sent it just before he'd died. My hands tremble as I click on the message. The top of it says, "This is hilarious!" followed by a forward of a joke-news article with the headline, "Construction Delayed for Train Station under Volcano." It's totally typical of tío's bizarre sense of humor—quotes of locals talking about how the volcano was perfect for a train station, such a great tourist destination, and they'd never expected the magma to pose so many challenges. Uncle Umberto always used to send me articles like that. It must have been one of the last things he did before he died, the last thing I'll ever hear from him, and it's not even a very funny article.

That's when it hits me. Tío Umberto is gone, and I'll never get to spend another moment with him. From deep in my lungs, a sob rises up. It moves through my windpipes like an enormous stone rolling through a narrow crawlspace. Finally, the sob escapes from my mouth, but it offers no relief. More sobs come, each one like a stone struggling to roll out of my insides. It just keeps going, like an endless supply of rocks on a lonely stony shore. I cry until my sobs turn into pebbles, small enough that I can whimper myself to sleep.

CHAPTER 3

SYNTHETICS

SYNTHETICS – One of the five <u>Great Powers</u> of the Galaxy, the Synthetics are an ancient society of non-organic sentient lifeforms that pre-existed all present-day organic civilizations.[1] Most Synthetics reside in the outer globular clusters and avoid contact with organic cultures, making reliable information on their culture limited.[2] ... The majority of Synthetics that interact with organics are children or adolescents by Synthetic standards, no older than a millennium...

Excerpted from **WIKI GALACTICA**

THE DAY AFTER THE FUNERAL, I stay home from school and spend the day with my brothers. After all the funeral expenses, Mami is even more worried about money than usual and has to go right back to work cleaning houses. Timoteo, Miguel, and I go through tío Umberto's collection of books. Timoteo takes the poli sci stuff, Miguel takes the plays, and I take the philosophy. We all want the science fiction and fantasy, so we split those up one by one. The books make us reminisce, especially the ones he read to us as kids, like Narnia and *The Little Prince*. We chuckle and then we sniffle and then we sob, and then we're all exhausted.

I volunteer to make dinner, since Miguel made omelets and Timoteo made lunch. We need groceries, and the house is getting suffocating, so it's a good excuse to get outside.

Just as I'm about to leave, the doorbell rings. It's Kate, holding a pile of papers. "Hey," she says.

"Hey," I say. It was nice of Kate to come by, but I don't have the wherewithal to invite her in for a longer visit, so I just hover at the door.

Kate clutches the papers to her chest. "I'm really sorry about your uncle. I was going to come to the wake, but my dad was being a jerk and made me stay home to study."

I summon the energy for a smile. "No worries."

"I brought my notes from the past few days," Kate says, "and the homework and such. I mean, not that you should be thinking about school, but I figured at some point you'll need it."

"Thanks, Kate." I take the stack of papers and set them on the chair by the door. "I could probably use the distraction, actually."

"I'm brilliant at distractions," Kate says. "I can help you study later if you want. Pinker gave us a pop quiz on *Julius Caesar* today."

I swat away a fly. I've left the door open too long. "That is so not surprising. And I'm so completely behind on the reading."

Kate brushes her long blonde hair behind her ears. "Listen, is everything really okay? I just keep thinking about how that guy came to your house the other night, and was saying weird stuff to your uncle about ticks, but they were obvi talking about something else, and now all of a sudden your uncle is dead, and I'm thinking like what if he got caught up in something sketchy with all his international work, like what if it was spying or terrorism or something."

I stare at Kate, trying to take in her long, intense ramble, disoriented that her wild fantasy of international espionage is so similar to my own wild fantasies yesterday. Part of me wishes it were true—because then maybe Uncle Umberto could still be alive, maybe he faked his death as part of some secret spy plot. But I'm not one for wishful thinking.

I lean into the door jamb, let my weight fall into it. "Thanks for worrying, Kate. But it was just a heart attack. I'm pretty sure Umberto wasn't doing any spying. His job was mostly boring meetings."

"Yeah, I'm sure you're right," Kate says. "It just really shocked me. And if it shocked me, you must be in, like, extreme shock."

"It's natural to be shocked," I say. How am I the one reassuring her? "Honestly, I'm fine. Thanks for bringing the homework."

I say good-bye and then hop on my bicycle and ride toward the supermarket, making a mental list for my vegetarian lasagna, a family favorite. Mami loves it, and so does tío Umberto.

So *did* tío Umberto, I correct myself. Every stream of thought leads back to him.

Tomato sauce, mozzarella, a loaf of bread. I chant the list in my mind, a supermarket prayer to distract myself from the emptiness in my chest.

A fly buzzes in my ear. I'm riding down hill pretty fast, but it stays on me like it's stalking me. Flies have a vendetta with me today.

The loud drone of a motor comes from behind. A hot-rod red motorcycle with a sidecar pulls up beside me. The driver is wearing a red jacket that perfectly matches the motorcycle. It takes me a few seconds to recognize it's Johnny. For a moment, I wonder who the kid in the sidecar is. But then I realize it's not a kid, it's Wasala.

"Hey there," Johnny shouts, slowing the motorcycle to ride in tandem with me.

"Hello, Valiant One," shouts Wasala.

"Hey guys," I shout back. We stop at a traffic light, and the din of the motorcycle quiets enough that we don't have to shout. "I didn't know you were still in town. Or that you drove a motorcycle."

"Oh, I get around by many modalities of transportation," Johnny says with a wink. I'm not sure what to make of that.

"No one knows what to make of Johnny, dearie," Wasala says. "But there are things we must tell you about Umberto. Things you must keep secret from everyone, even your family."

My heart skips three beats. Could there be something to all the conspiracy-thinking? Could the secret be that tío Umberto is still alive? No, I have to stop with these fantasies—it must be something simpler. Maybe they don't realize tío Umberto has been out to the whole family since I was a kid. "Um, we all know Umberto's gay."

"No, no," Johnny says. "Nothing as trivial as human constructions of sexual identity. Although the recent rapid shift in human sexual mores is totally fascinating!"

Then the fly that's been buzzing around flies straight toward Johnny and disappears into his ear. Johnny doesn't even flinch, as if he doesn't care a fly is wandering around his ear canal.

"Um, Johnny," I say. "A fly just flew, like, right in your ear."

"Oh, that was no fly," Johnny says. "That was a lil nanocam. Didn't want to intrude on your grieving rituals, so we've been keeping an eye on you to wait for the right moment to give you the tea."

Nanocam—that must stand for nanocamera. But that would be major advanced tech. Could my whole spy fantasy actually be true?

"Oh, dear no, not spies," Wasala says.

"She thinks we're spies?" Johnny says. "That is so fun and kind of weirdly almost right."

"We're not spies, Johnny!" Wasala says. "We're doing this all wrong. Can we go somewhere more private?"

How is everything Wasala says is an exact answer to what I'm thinking? Is she like some super-genius at reading facial expressions?

Wasala looks up at me from the sidecar. "Human facial expressions can be surprisingly difficult. But please—we've much to explain and little time to do it."

Human facial expressions? Now my brain is searching for possible explanations. Espionage. Some weird reality-TV prank show. Secret society of telepathic little people who Umberto was trying to help empower. Two delusional co-workers of Umberto's? Or maybe Wasala's creepily intuitive, like tía Irene?

"Light's green," Johnny says, revving the motor. "And we've got a lot to cover."

I point at the supermarket across the street. "We can pull over here. I was about to go shopping anyway."

Johnny salutes and cruises ahead, pulling his motorcycle into the parking lot of the supermarket. I pedal close behind. As I get off my bike and kick out the kickstand, Wasala walks toward me. "This really isn't the proper place. We have a full orientation ready for you back at the office, Madame Ambassador."

I bend over laughing as I close my kryptonite lock. The Umberto-has-some-delusional-co-workers explanation is looking more likely. "Um, I'm a high school student. And I'm pretty sure you need a decent score on the SATs for a career in diplomacy, which is definitely not happening any time soon. I need to do the groceries."

Wasala scuffs her shoes on the pavement. "Verbal communication is so maddeningly slow." She scans the parking lot, which is vacant except for a few empty cars.

A dozen flies converge on Johnny from all corners of the parking lot and land on his palm. "The coast is clear," he says. "No one within earshot."

This is ... getting weirder.

"Then we do it here," Wasala says.

Johnny leans toward me over his motorcycle. "We don't really work for an NGO, and neither did your uncle. Umberto was the secret ambassador of Earth in an interstellar council of planets."

Wasala looks up at me, her eyes wide and serious. "You are your uncle's successor, Valiant One. You are the new ambassador of Earth. You must come with us to our Interstellar Embassy in Istanbul, and from there you must go to Hosh to save my world and complete the mission your uncle left unfinished."

Okay. This is even wackier than any of my theories. But if Johnny and Wasala are delusional, that doesn't explain the mind-reading. Or the fly-cam things. Or why Umberto always spoke of them as friends he respected. But none of what they're saying makes sense. How can Earth even have a space ambassador when we've barely made it past the moon?

Wasala turns back to Johnny. "She's still skeptical."

"Isn't she allegedly, like, the most open-minded person on the planet?" Johnny says.

Wasala lifts her nose in the air. "Indeed, that's why her reaction is so … subdued. She's trying to reason it out. Some of her questions are quite sensible."

"Um, I'm standing right here," I say.

"We gotta break out the big guns," Johnny says. "I'm going to whip up a holosphere."

"Agreed. We need the privacy regardless."

Wasala walks toward Johnny and beckons for me to follow. I stay a few cautious steps behind her, until the three of us are clustered a few feet apart. Johnny spreads out his palms and the lights of his motorcycle turn on—but not with normal light, with a light that holds the entire rainbow in a single beam. The lights fly out of the motorcycle and swirl around us, forming stars and nebulae. Suddenly the supermarket and parking lot are gone. There's no floor, no walls, just the three of us floating in a sea of stars. For a second I'm dizzy, my body looking for an anchor. I kneel down. The ground looks like it's made of stars, but feels like the rough concrete of a parking lot.

I stand back up and look at the star-scape all around me. I hold up my hand in the air. The projection of stars isn't hitting my hands, and there's no mist or wall where light could land. "How on earth are you doing this?"

"This technology ain't from Earth," Johnny says. "And neither are we."

"So you're ... aliens," I say, my brain unable to find another explanation.

"If by aliens you mean in the geocentric sense of sentient beings not native to Earth, then yeah," Johnny says. "I'm Synthetic."

"Johnny can control photons at the quantum level," Wasala explains. "From within this sphere, the three of us are seeing this star-scape. From outside of it, any passerby would just see three people having an ordinary conversation outside a Terran food market."

I turn around and walk a few steps away from them. Suddenly, the star-scape disappears, and I'm back in the parking lot. I look back, and Johnny winks at me. Wasala waves with wiggling fingers. I turn around and abruptly cross back into the sea of stars.

I take a deep breath and think. They're from outer space. Tío Umberto was Earth's ambassador, so he *worked* in outer space. There's no other explanation, so it must be true. And if anyone would be an outer-space ambassador, it would be Umberto.

But if that's true, then anything is possible. Maybe tío Umberto is still alive. Maybe his death was faked, maybe ...

Wasala walks toward me, her lips trembling. "Umberto's mind has gone silent. I saw for myself at the wake. I'm so sorry, dearie. He was our friend, too, and we miss him terribly."

"Yeah," Johnny says. "Umberto was one of a kind."

My eyes tear up. Their sympathy feels so much more authentic than so many other people's—and they're not even ... people. I look up at the stars around us and think of all the times tío Umberto and I looked up at the sky and wondered at the stars together. Suddenly their beauty is a cruel betrayal. My jaw tightens and my breath speeds up. Why didn't he tell me? Why did these two get to be part of this whole other life he had, and not me?

"I saw in his mind how badly he wanted to tell you," Wasala says. "But interstellar law forbade it."

Wasala really is hearing everything I think, all the pain and grief I haven't shared with anyone. She has no right to all these feelings I haven't even figured out myself.

"I'm sorry," she says. "I know most mind-deaf keep private thoughts. But I can't turn off my telepathy any more than you can turn off your ears."

"Okay," I say, sniffling with anger. "Then give me something back. Use your telepathy to share a memory of Umberto in outer space or something so I can understand this whole other life of his."

"It doesn't work that way," Wasala says. "Telepathy is just another kind of sensory input. I hear your thoughts, but I can't transmit mine. You either have it or you don't."

I wipe my eyes and slow down my breathing, try to turn off my heart and turn on my brain. I look at Johnny and Wasala. "If you're aliens, then how come you look so human?"

Johnny spreads his arms and points at his chest with his thumbs. "This snatched bod is only my latest look." The motorcycle hums to life and drives itself in circles around us. A swarm of flies emerges from Johnny's sleeves and whizzes through the air in formation, spelling out

E-X-C-E-L-S-I-O-R. "The flies, the motorcycle—they're all a part of me as much as my ripped abs and slick black hair."

Okay, the motorcycle and the flies are pretty convincing, though the quirky narcissism is not what I'd expect in an android. "So you're like ... the droids in *Star Wars*."

Johnny rolls his eyes as he sucks all the flies back into his sleeves. "Do *not* get me started on all the inaccurate depictions of synthetic life in Terran pop culture! But I love *Star Wars*, even if that last one was pretty mid at best. But we really should get you—"

I interrupt Johnny, poking him in the cheek with my keys and pressing hard. "Hey," he says. "That low-key hurts."

"If you're Synthetic, why would it hurt?"

"Because I made this body that way," Johnny said. "Pain receptors provide useful info. That's why you have them."

That seems convenient, but I guess it makes sense. "And you?" I say to Wasala. "You can read minds, but Johnny can't do that. You're not Synthetic. You're something else."

"Indeed, dearie." She taps her wrist. For a few moments, Wasala is like a Picasso painting, her face a scramble of a human's and a raccoon's, her body a jigsaw puzzle of clothing and brown fur. Then the puzzle is complete, and a new Wasala is in front of me. Her fur is the color of mahogany. She has a long snout and whiskers, and two black splotches around her eyes. The ears atop her head are pricked up attentively. She looks a bit like a meerkat, except she has six limbs, not four—the two extra limbs sticking out of the middle of her body.

A series of snorts and chirps come from Wasala's nose and mouth, followed by English words that don't at all match the movement of her face. "It does get exhausting walking on my hind legs," she says, dropping to four legs. "And the Salfren translation software is quite effective, though it does take some getting used to when it's not matched with a holographic face." She walks toward me on her lower four legs, her torso remaining upright, almost like a centaur.

She's kind of adorable and reminds me of a stuffy I had as a kid, of Timon from *The Lion King*. I have the urge to pet her—then my cheeks flush. She can hear everything I'm thinking!

Wasala takes a few more steps toward me. "Oh, it's quite all right, dearie. We Hoshans are an affectionate people." She leans her torso forward so that her head is just a few inches from me. I gently touch her head. Her fur is short and soft, more like the fuzz of a peach than the fur of any animal I've encountered on Earth.

Wasala upturns her snout and lets out another few snorts. "Well, I do try to keep myself fresh."

I'm touching the fur of an actual alien from another actual planet. Goosebumps dance along my skin. I can't believe I'm getting to have this experience, to see this amazing being in front of me—and that tío Umberto has had this experience too.

I take my hand away from Wasala. Tío Umberto is gone now. When things were hard, he was the one who took care of my mother and my brothers. And now I'm the only one who can do that. "I have to get the shopping done. You can come in with me if you want."

I walk out of the stars and into the Shop-Rite.

✧ ✧ ✧

I PUSH THE CART through the aisles of the grocery, again chanting the shopping list in my mind. The tomato sauce is right there in aisle four like always, which is comforting.

Johnny tugs on the cart. "We can't dilly dally. You've got to meet with the Levinti ambassador in less than 38 hours."

I put the tomato sauce in the shopping cart and roll past Johnny. "First I have to make dinner. Anyway, how can Earth be part of some federation when we've never even made it past the solar system?"

Johnny puts a bag of marshmallows in the cart, and I take it out. "Now you're asking good questions! Earth is what we call an Atomic World."

Wasala—back in her human disguise—looks up and down the empty aisle and whispers, "Too primitive to have interstellar travel."

"Basically, y'all are basic," Johnny says.

I push the cart to the next aisle, Johnny and Wasala trailing close behind. I feel like a mom with two alien kids in tow. "And no one on Earth knows all this except the ambassador."

"Exactamundo," Johnny said. "Whenever possible, the existence of the interstellar community is not revealed to the general population of the primitive worlds."

I search through the cheese bins for the mozzarella. "But why would the other planets even want Earth in their federation?"

"The theory goes that the primitive worlds should have a voice to protect their interests," Johnny says, "but really it was just a political compromise after the whole Sufri revolt."

The what revolt? This is all so much information all at once.

"It *is* a lot of information," Wasala says. "If you'd just watch the orientation holo, then you'd know I designed a whole special section on the primitive worlds and Hoshan history."

Johnny nods as he fiddles through the string cheese. "She worked really hard on it."

I grab two hunks of mozzarella. "Okay, but basically the whole idea is to protect planets like Earth from being exploited?"

"If only it were that touchy-feely," Johnny says. "This representation thing is just the latest way the Great Powers are using the primitive worlds as a football. The Galaxy is a rough playground."

The Great Powers. I've overheard Uncle Umberto use that exact phrase on dozens of whispered phone calls. This is real.

"It is quite real," Wasala says. "I don't think you understand the urgency of the situation. If we don't complete the treaty negotiations on Hosh, my entire world will be plunged into war."

Treaties—planets at war? How can I possibly do this? "Hosh is where you're from?"

"It's complicated," Wasala says. "It's where my parents are from."

"And I guess we'll, like, take a spaceship there."

"Don't be silly," Johnny says. "That would take forever. We'll take the Subway."

Of course, the subway. Why not take a subway to another planet? It's weird that all of this isn't shocking me more.

Wasala peers over the shopping cart, her nose lifted, and I can picture her snout lifting beneath the hologram. "Yes, your nonplussed reaction would be shocking if you were anyone but you, dearie. That's why you were selected to be the ambassador. You handle unfamiliar situations with aplomb. The xenoreactive test revealed that."

"You scored through the roof, TBH," Johnny adds.

"What test?" I say. "I'm terrible at tests. There must be a million people who'd be better ambassadors than me. My brother, Timoteo. He'd be a great ambassador!" I pull out my phone. "Let's ask him."

"Your uncle did not designate your brother as his successor," Wasala says. "He took the test, too, and did well for a Terran, but not as well as you."

I put two baguettes in the cart. "When did I take this test?"

"The xenoreactive scenario," Johnny says. "We use it to help identify ambassadors on the Atomic Worlds. Remember, when Umberto brought you to the office, and you sat in the chair and he strapped that headset on you?"

I remember a blur of creatures that seemed like monsters until I looked more closely and realized there was nothing hostile in their non-human posture. "That was, like, a year ago. He said it was some intercultural study. *That's* why I'm supposed to be ambassador?"

"Yup. You're quite an atypical human, really. Kinda like your tío." Johnny grabs a nectarine and takes a bite. "Mmm. Nectarine-y."

"You eat?"

"I can eat," says Johnny. "I don't *need* to eat. Food's a totally inefficient energy source."

"You know you have to pay for that," I say.

"Obvi," Johnny says, licking the juice off his lips. "I've studied Terran capitalist customs extensively. I'm a sociologist, and humans are my specialty."

They keep saying Terra and Terran. Umberto used to say that too. When his phone would drop a call, or the computer would freeze, or the car was running out of gas. "Terran technology," he would mutter. For years, he did that, ever since I was a kid. For years, he's been the ambassador, and he never told me. He wanted me to take over this whole ambassadorship, and he never told me, never did anything to prepare me. I squeeze the handlebar of the shopping cart, angry at him for leaving me alone with all this.

Wasala reaches up to touch my hand. "He thought he'd have more time. But he knew you could do this. He saw what I see in your heart. You're the only one who can complete the work he started."

I loosen my grip on the cart and let out a breath. As I lead us toward checkout, Johnny chomps off another bite of nectarine. "There's so much more," Wasala whispers. "As ambassador of an Atomic world, you have a voice but no vote in the Interstellar Assembly. Most sentients will see you as a third-class citizen."

"More like fourth-class," says Johnny.

"Can you slow down a bit?" I say, unloading the groceries for the cashier. "I need some time for all this to sink in."

"Okay," says Johnny, "but hurry up with the sinking. Levinti are not patient." He holds up the nectarine pit to the cashier and says, "This is all I'll be purchasing today, ma'am."

The cashier glares at him. "How am I supposed to weigh it if it's in your stomach?"

"My apologies. The nectarine was calling out to me. But I checked the weight before I ate it, and it was exactly 4.7 ounces." The cashier looks at him incredulously. Johnny whispers to me, "This is the tragedy of primitive capitalist mores, they erode all trust."

"How about you charge us twice for the tomatoes," I say to the cashier, and she nods.

I walk out the sliding doors with a Synthetic and a telepath, each of us carrying a paper bag of groceries. It's so unreal and yet so ordinary. Is this what Uncle Umberto's life was like for all these years, holding a universe of secrets in his heart?

"So," I say to them. "You want to come over for dinner?"

CHAPTER 4

WHEN I WALK INTO THE HOUSE with Johnny and Wasala, my brothers look up from the couch and shoot me raised-eyebrow looks. I respond with a sheepish smile. "Look who I ran into at the supermarket."

Timoteo pulls me over and whispers, "Mami's already super-stressed, and you invite guests over? You know she'll hate that."

Of course whispering does no good with Wasala. She walks toward Timoteo and me, saying, "We promise not to be an imposition."

Maybe this wasn't such a good idea. Some part of my brain thought that inviting Johnny and Wasala for dinner would be a win-win: delay this overwhelming interstellar-ambassador thing and make dinner for my grieving family. "I thought it'd be nice for us all to have dinner together," I tell Timoteo. "They lost Umberto too."

Timoteo presses his lips together, then leans over to clutch Wasala's shoulder. "I'm so sorry. It must be so weird for you all. Going back to that office without Umberto there."

Johnny takes off his sunglasses. "Yeah. Nothing's the same without Umberto."

Everyone nods at that, the stark reality we all share, even if we're literally from different worlds. Suddenly, my strange group dinner idea doesn't seem strange to anyone. Wasala joins Miguel on the couch to help him run his lines for *Into the Woods*—and she actually does a pretty good witch. Johnny and Timoteo follow me into the kitchen to help with dinner.

As I unload the groceries, Johnny takes off his red-leather jacket, revealing a snug white t-shirt that shows off his muscles. Of course Johnny's "snatched bod" is perfect—he made it that way, just like his shiny motorcycle. Timoteo gapes as Johnny drapes his jacket over a kitchen chair. I contain my laughter to a smirk at my little secret that my big brother has the hots for a Synthetic alien. The three of us get along easily, grating cheese and cooking up the sauce. Johnny chops vegetables like he's on Iron Chef. It's funny which human things he's mastered, and which things he's clueless about.

Mami walks in just as we're about to set the table. At first, her face is startled at Johnny and Wasala's presence, but then she shifts into host mode. She tells Timoteo to get the nice dishes from the top shelf of the pantry.

Johnny and Wasala shift to Spanish for Mami without skipping a beat. Johnny can probably speak any language, and Wasala's translator must process Spanish as easily as English. Johnny's Spanish is especially impressive—he speaks with a perfect Puerto Rican accent, down to skipping d's and s's in all the right places.

As we move to the table, I realize none of our chairs will work for Wasala's short height. I grab two pillows and stack them on her chair so she can easily reach the table. "Ever anticipating the needs of others," Wasala whispers to me as she hops into the chair.

As the rest of us sit down, my mother says, "Johnny, what you told me at the funeral was so moving. Would you like to say grace?"

"It would be my honor," Johnny replies, bowing his head, and I say a silent prayer, asking God to please help Johnny not be completely inappropriate. "Wondrous God, thank you for being with us during this time of tribulation. For as the Lord tells us in the Book of Revelation, 'Do not fear what you are about to suffer. Behold, the devil is about to throw some of you into prison, that you may be tested, and for ten days you will have tribulation. Be faithful unto death, and I will give you the crown of life.'"

I look up and catch Miguel covering his mouth to hide a chuckle. Mami is blinking at Johnny, uncertain whether the prayer's over. Only Timoteo and Wasala still have bowed heads.

"Amen," I say.

"Amen," the rest of the family echoes.

As we serve ourselves, Wasala takes a small bottle from her purse and pours sauce on her lasagna. Johnny's synthetic body can probably process anything, but maybe Wasala can't eat human food. Maybe the sauce has an enzyme or something to make it edible. "I don't mean to be rude," Wasala says, spreading the sauce. "This looks delicious, but being from Turkey, I'm used to a different ... palette."

Mami nods. "All my mexicano friends always use lots of hot sauce whenever I cook them Puerto Rican food. I've learned not to take it personally."

Johnny says how delicious the food is, then there's an awkward silence. Maybe this was a mistake. None of us really know each other, and we obviously can't talk about space ambassador stuff—which I kind of prefer, because just thinking about it overwhelms me. Then Timoteo says, "So, Johnny, what exactly do you do at the Institute?"

"Oh, I pitch in on a bunch of things, but my main job is our sociological research."

"What's your specialization?" Timoteo says.

Miguel groans, eating with one hand and texting with the other. "It's time for the Timoteo podcast!"

"Don't disrespect your brother, Miguel," Mami says. "And stop texting at dinner."

Timoteo quizzes Johnny and Wasala about their work at the Institute. Miguel's not all wrong—sometimes Timoteo does act like he's hosting a podcast. Johnny talks about his sociological research on "primitive capitalist societies" and "1980s music," and Wasala talks about her work on climate change. I think back on all the phone conversations and meetings I overheard Umberto having over the years. It's coded, but there's a seed of truth in their cover story. They really are studying and protecting the "voiceless territories," it's just that all of Earth is one big voiceless primitive society to them.

Wasala cuts Timoteo short and turns to me. "Actually, we're somewhat short-staffed now and could use some help at the Institute. We were hoping Val might do an internship with us." I guess that would be my cover story—if I do the ambassador thing. I guess they can't say a 16-year-old is taking Umberto's place as executive director. Suddenly the lasagna on my plate looks less appetizing. I can't imagine lying about an "internship" when I'm really going to other planets. How did Umberto do this? Why didn't he tell me the truth?

"What kind of internship?" says Timoteo.

Johnny waves his fork in little loops. "Oh, you know, errands, traipsing around, that sort of thing. What do you say, Ms. Vega?"

"No sé. Val has her homework and sports, and I need her help with—" Mami gets cut off by a knock at the front door. "Were we expecting someone?" As she walks to the door, Johnny and Wasala side-eye each other like they just got caught playing hooky.

Mami opens the door, and Patrece is standing outside, her tall frame filling the doorway. I wonder what her real body looks like—her species must be much taller than the average human. My way-too-polite mother welcomes her and even apologizes for starting dinner without her.

"Thank you so much for your hospitality, Ms. Vega," Patrece says, bending slightly to step through the doorway. She holds up a two-liter bottle of sparkling water. "I brought a beverage to accompany dinner, of course."

Mami takes the bottle of Perrier and blinks at it. "How lovely." If I do end up being ambassador, I'm going to have to give these aliens some tips on the subtleties of Earth culture.

Everyone scoots around the table to make room for one more, and Timoteo sets a place for Patrece while I get another chair.

Patrece sits down, her body folding awkwardly into the too-small chair. "I apologize for being late. My colleagues' text message invitations must have been disrupted by a poor signal."

Wasala purses her lips. "I'm terribly sorry, Patrece. We meant to text you right away."

"We ran into Val at the supermarket," Johnny says, "and it was all totes spontaneous."

"Indeed," Patrece says. "The two of you have been quite spontaneous recently." She takes a small bottle out of her briefcase and pours some sauce on her lasagna, just like Wasala did—though she offers no explanation. It *must* have some sort of enzyme or technology that makes Earth food digestible for them.

Wasala taps me on the knee and mouths, "You're so smart," which I would find affirming if I weren't too busy wondering why Patrece is being passive-aggressive with Wasala and Johnny, and why she didn't come with them to talk to me in the first place. I guess that strikes a chord, because Wasala purses her lips and looks in the other direction.

"Hold on a sec," Miguel says. "Does this intern thing mean Val gets to go to Turkey?"

Johnny scoops up more lasagna. "We'll definitely need her for a trip or two."

Patrece stiffens her long back and looks at Johnny and Wasala with narrowed eyes. "I suppose it was another moment of spontaneity that led the two of you to discuss the potential internship without me."

"Someone had to tell her!" Wasala snips back at Patrece.

"I'll do an internship if I get to go to Turkey!" Miguel says.

"Me too!" Timoteo says.

"Sorry, boys," Johnny says, giving Timoteo a wink. "Only one slot open at the moment."

"Oh," Miguel says, taking out his phone again. "Only *Val* gets to go to Turkey."

"This entire discussion is premature," Patrece says. "We are indeed short-handed and in need of assistance after the loss of Umberto. However, both Val and her mother will need to consider the matter, of which I am personally quite unconvinced. Val must still fulfill her schoolwork and other obligations, and it may be that this difficult time is not optimal for an undertaking as intensive as an internship."

"Yes, it is a hard time," Mami says. My skin tightens, and I'm not sure if it's the stress of Mami depending on me or having to be a space ambassador or just all the things.

Wasala leans toward my mother and says, "Or perhaps working at the Institute could help Val to process her grief and better understand the powerful legacy her uncle has left behind." She must be reading my mother's mind. Reading my thoughts is one thing, but I don't want her using her telepathy to manipulate my mother.

Mami stares at her plate. "Bueno, if she keeps up with school ..."

"Um," says Timoteo, "if you guys need an intern, don't you think, like, the Harvard poli-sci major might be a bit more useful than a high school student?"

Johnny smacks his teeth. "Don't underestimate your sister, Timsito. She's got skills."

"And yet," Patrece says, "Timoteo is correct in noting her lack of experience."

It's overwhelming. Everyone arguing about me right in front of me, all the double-meanings, my family not even knowing what the conversation's really about, Wasala reading people's minds, Patrece totally against me for no reason ...

"I don't even know if I want to do it!" I snap. I push my chair away from the table and stomp into the kitchen with my half-empty plate. My appetite's completely gone. I scrape the rest of my food into the trash and leave my dish to soak in the sink. This dinner was a terrible idea. I wish I could just end it now, but Mami is sure to insist everyone stay for dessert.

I walk out to the backyard and take a few deep breaths, try to let the cool night air calm me down. The stars are coming out. Looking at the stars used to make me feel wonder at the possibility of what might be out there. But now the stars have a new, weighty reality to them. Those three aliens inside are all *from* those stars. Umberto has *been* to those stars. The idea of going there, going out into the Galaxy like Umberto did would be ... amazing. And terrifying.

Behind me, someone clears their throat. I turn around and see Patrece, holding up two small bowls of rice pudding. "I told your mother I'd like to have a word with you about your 'internship,' and she suggested I bring you dessert."

"I'm not really hungry," I say.

Patrece holds up one of the bowls, balancing it on her long fingers. "And this is not really food for me." She sets the two bowls down on the back stoop and pulls a small silver cylinder out of her briefcase. "Let's dispense with pretense and discuss this in private."

She presses the cylinder, and it projects a gradient of gentle blue all around us, like we're standing inside a screensaver—another holosphere, I guess. Standing in the middle of the blue, where Patrece just was, is a giant greyish-white stick insect standing upright. Her body is a long stalk, with three spindly legs and two long arms that almost reach the ground. Her face is noseless, hairless, and lipless, but has two eye-stalks that extend upward and wriggle like antennae. Two penny-sized holes in the sides of her thorax heave in and out like gills. Her physiology is even more amazing than Wasala's. Instinctively, I reach out, curious what her skin feels like. Patrece responds with a series of abrupt whistles. Just like with Wasala, a translation follows, her mouth eerily still, like a movie where the sound track is off sync. "Never touch me without permission."

I pull back my hand. "I'm sorry, Patrece." Her spindly limbs almost look like icicles. I remember her cold hand at the wake. Looking like a pile of giant icicles would be useful camouflage in an icy climate. "Your planet's colder than Earth, isn't it?"

Patrece lets out more whistles. "Umberto was correct that you're a quick study, if nothing else. Yes, Terra is quite hot and humid for my taste, among other shortcomings. And my real name is Pash-Ti. It was inappropriate of Johnny and Wasala to speak to you without me. Allow me to offer a more realistic assessment of your situation. Hosh is on the brink of war, and it was only thanks to Umberto's skillful mediation that there was a slim possibility of peace. It's true that you're the appointee to be the next ambassador of Earth, but there's no reason you must accept the position. If you do, your inexperience would doom any prospect of renegotiating the treaty. There is an alternative candidate who is far more prepared."

"Would that be you?" I say.

Pash-Ti's blowholes let out a high-pitched screech, like the whistle of a demanding tea kettle, which gets translated as laughter. "The likelihood of you asking that question is inversely proportional to the depth of your knowledge. Only a Terran can represent Earth. That is the logic, what little of it there is, behind the politically dubious system of appointed representatives for primitive worlds. My only interest is assuring that this sector of the Galaxy is not plunged into chaos simply because a young girl from an Atomic world has been placed in a situation far beyond her ken."

"You're not like Johnny or Wasala," I say. "You act like you're the ambassador's boss."

"My formal title is Observer of Earth. The ambassador has authority over the embassy, but the Observer of a primitive world tracks its progress for the Interstellar Council."

"So you're kind of our babysitter."

A few soft, low whistles. "That metaphor would not be entirely inaccurate."

With long, spindly white fingers, Pash-Ti pulls a small cube out of her briefcase. The air above the cube lights up with a string of glowing words. "Sign this document and you need not concern yourself with these matters. You can return to your life, finish high school, and enjoy the final years of your youth."

The words are English, followed by a column of unfamiliar characters—several different types of characters, maybe three or four translations. "I, Valeria Vega, hereby resign and waive my responsibilities and privileges as ambassador of Earth, now and forevermore. In so doing, I understand that the alternate shall immediately assume the title ..." It goes on about all the responsibilities being waived and the maintenance of strict confidentiality.

"Standard language of interstellar law," Pash-Ti says. "You need not concern yourself with the details. You may sign with your thumbprint or standard Terran signature, as you prefer."

But I've already read it, and two details do concern me. The first is the word resign, and the second is that if I sign it, I'm not just giving up being ambassador for now, but forever. "I'm already the ambassador," I whisper. My breath is short, as if the air were shallow.

Pash-Ti adjusts her weight, leaning back on her third leg. "Technically, the title passed to you at the moment of Umberto's death."

I stare up at Pash-Ti's face, at her eyestalks that are two feet higher than my eyes, at her greyish-white skin. I wonder if it's actually skin or more of an exoskeleton. I felt overwhelmed when Johnny and Wasala first told me I was supposed to be ambassador of the entire planet, but Pash-Ti's smug smack-down almost makes me want to do it. That, plus seeing her in her real form, and Wasala in hers, and learning there are Synthetics like Johnny—it all makes me want to see what's out there, to be part of this secret Galaxy that made up so much of tío Umberto's life.

Before I can say anything, Johnny and Wasala burst into the blue gradient surrounding us. Johnny points at the holographic words hovering between Pash-Ti and me. "I knew it! Really, P.? Ten minutes with our new ambassador and you've got her resignation letter out?"

"This is so rude," Wasala says in clicks and chirps, now back in her true furry form. "This is exactly why Johnny and I went to her without you."

Pash-Ti steps forward on her front leg and leans toward Wasala, towering over her even more than in their human guises. "It's my role to recruit the new ambassador. It was *you* who violated protocol."

"Ah, you were dragging your feet like a Centarian sandslug," Johnny says.

These three alien diplomats are arguing like my brothers. "What's up with you three?" I say. "Shouldn't you, like, be on the same page about this?"

"Indeed," Pash-Ti says. "We are divided on this matter because my colleagues—and Umberto before his tragic fate—failed to see that you are not ready for this. You are a child. The only reason you're even eligible to be ambassador is because the protocols of the Terran embassy were enacted hundreds of years ago, at a time when the average human life expectancy was barely 37 years and a female your age would in all likelihood have already been married off like property. Your dubious appointment is one of history's odd accidents."

I can't argue with anything Pash-Ti is saying, but the way she's tearing me down makes me want to find some hole in her argument. "So how come the law is still the same? If the age cutoff is obsolete, why haven't they changed it?"

Pash-Ti laughs again, that harsh whistle followed by recorded laughter. "Because no one has bothered to update it. Because not one real ambassador in the Interstellar Assembly cares one iota about anything on this backwater world of yours."

"Age schmage," Johnny says. "She's as ready as any Terran can be."

Wasala strides toward Pash-Ti on four legs, and for a moment they look like two creatures in the most interesting zoo ever. "Her mind is uniquely malleable. That will be a great asset as mediator."

Pash-Ti lets out a series of shrill whistles. "I acknowledge she has potential. That's why her heart rate remains unaltered even though she's in conversation with three alien beings, a realignment of her understanding of reality that would overwhelm the average Terran. But her malleability is also a deficiency. Imagine how the Etoscans will manipulate her around the Tumasra issue. How the Levinti will make an intellectual snack of her! And how will this child handle the next inevitable attack from the Hosh-Unam Front?"

"Okay," I say, "I'm not a kid. And I'm getting tired of all the conversations about me when I'm right here in the same, um, holo-sphere thing." But I have to admit Pash-Ti makes it all sound overwhelming, especially the string of names I don't know, and the thing about an inevitable attack. This is all way over my head.

Pash-Ti presses something on the cube, and the projection of letters disappears. She extends a long white arm toward me. I'm not sure what to do, so I hold out my palm and take it. "It would be helpful if you sign the document." Pash-Ti says. "Or you may simply do nothing—you seem to be rather good at that—and at midnight tomorrow I may appoint an alternate on the basis of your absence."

The cube still has a slight glow to it—which reminds me of something that happened at the wake. I put it in my pocket and stare up at Pash-Ti's eyestalks. "What did you put in Umberto's casket?"

Pash-Ti's boney white shoulders hunch forward. "What do you mean?"

"You were fiddling with his body, and then there was this green glow on his neck."

"WTF?" Johnny says. "Did you for real inject Umberto's body with a nanoprobe?"

Pash-Ti snaps back at Johnny with a shrill whistle. "I was merely looking for evidence of what or who may have been involved in Umberto's murder."

Murder? The blue gradient around me abruptly gives me vertigo, like all of a sudden I've fallen into the sky.

Wasala reaches toward me with an upper claw. "I'm so sorry, dear. Pash-Ti is so abrupt. We don't even know for certain if Umberto was murdered."

"You expect her to be ambassador, and you haven't even told her this?" Pash-Ti says. "Of course he was murdered. He was doing his job too well. The Etoscans, the Levinti, the Hosh-Unam Front—they all want war! And his skillful mediating was making war look just as unreasonable as it is. That's why he was killed."

"But he died in his bedroom." I say, wishing I could bargain my way back to normalcy. "They said it was a heart attack. How could he have been murdered—by aliens?"

"I hate to say it," Johnny says. "But Pash-Ti's probably right. It was probably a nano-sassin, delivering a poison designed to mimic a human heart attack."

Wasala lifts her long snout. "It would have to be quite advanced to get past the ISS security protocols."

"Since the murder took place on a primitive world, of alleged natural causes," Pash-Ti says, "there will be no investigation."

"So," Johnny says, "your nanoprobe find anything?"

Pash-Ti lets out a few short whistles. "Unfortunately, the assassin left no trace."

I'm listening to everything they say, the alien sounds and the English translations—but all I can think is—if someone killed tío Umberto, that means he didn't just die. It means someone *took* him from us.

Wasala gently scratches my arm with her upper claw. "Yes, they took him from us all." She turns to Johnny and Pash-Ti. "I think we've overwhelmed this poor Terran enough for one day."

Pash-Ti de-activates the holo-sphere. The blue is replaced by our ordinary backyard, and she and Wasala return to their human disguises. "Simply sign the resignation letter. You needn't concern yourself with these matters."

Johnny sidles up to me as we walk toward the back door of the house. "Or you could call me tomorrow and get off this hunk of rock. My Earth phone number is EXCELSIOR-7. Don't forget the C. Call me any time. I mean that for reals—sleep is boring."

Pash-Ti harrumphs as she walks inside, and I wonder what harrumph sounds like in her real language of whistles. "I don't even know how to decide this," I say.

"I totes get that," Johnny says, "but we've got to meet with the Levinti ambassador in less than thirty-six hours. So you need to get in gear by midnight tomorrow to make it in time."

As Johnny follows Pash-Ti indoors, Wasala reaches up and touches my face. I feel her claw beneath the hologram. "I know this is all overwhelming, even for a mind as open as yours. Interstellar politics, a secret history, and murder of a family member are a lot to digest. It's hard to know what to make of it all. But your uncle knew. He trusted you more than anyone in the Galaxy. He knew you were the one to finish what he started, to bring peace to my world."

I wonder if Uncle Umberto really thought that. I wish I could talk to him. He's the only person I can imagine helping me figure all this out, and now he's gone, leaving a mess of a Galaxy behind him.

CHAPTER 5

AMBASSADOR UMBERTO OLMEDA

AMBASSADOR UMBERTO OLMEDA – ... Ambassador Olmeda attained an exceptional level of respect for an ambassador of a primitive world. ... He was the initial mediator for the negotiation of a "New Hoshan Treaty" to address the conflict between the Etoscans and Levinti regarding control of Hosh[1] ... After seven other candidates for mediator were rejected, Olmeda emerged as an unexpected "consensus choice" due to his amicable relationship with all four parties.[2]

[Suggested addition from Contributor 12B17: Multiple observers have noted that the Etoscan and Levinti representatives also likely believed they would more easily be able to maneuver a mediator from a primitive planet with no political influence. Response from Editor 412: Suggestion declined. Please provide at least three validated sources to support claim that "multiple observers" believed this to be the case.]

Olmeda died just weeks before the scheduled formal treaty negotiations. His death is suspected by some to be an assassination ...

Excerpted from **WIKI GALACTICA**

THE NEXT DAY, MAMI MAKES MIGUEL and me go to school, because she's worried about us falling behind. Part of me is relieved to be back in familiar territory. High school is the worst, but at least I know what I'm in for.

I still have no idea whether to do the ambassadorship. One moment I think Johnny and Wasala are right, that if this is what Umberto wanted for me, then I have to do it—for him and for everything he believed in. But then I think of Pash-Ti, of her piercing high-pitched whistle of laughter, and that everything she said about me being unprepared is totally right. I can't take care of my family and my own life if I'm trying to solve some interstellar crisis that's way out of my league. How could I possibly handle this job if it got Umberto killed—who was the smartest, most amazing person I've ever known?

I muddle through a morning of awkward condolences. Pinker gives me the pop quiz on *Caesar* that Kate warned me about, though I'm pretty sure I still failed. I tried to read it last night, but put it down when political assassination turned out to be a disturbing trigger.

It's an "A" day, so Des and I are the only ones from our crew who have lunch together. The past few weeks, I've dreaded A-day lunches, the two of us avoiding each other by sitting with different sets of people who aren't true friends. But today Des comes up to me with her brown paper-bag lunch and says, "It's getting spring-like. Want to eat outside?"

I smile for the first time all day. "I definitely want to eat outside!"

It's barely spring—sunny but chilly—so not many people are outside. We take one of the picnic tables. We catch up on gossip and our latest binge-watching, and Desiree seems to understand, implicitly, that I want to talk about anything but Umberto.

Halfway through lunch, Des says, "It's good to have you back, Val."

"Same," I say. "I really missed you. And ... I know I've said this before, but I'm really sorry for what I did."

Des nods through tears. "It was hard. When Kate told me what happened, and that you knew about it. Even though you weren't one of the main perpetrators—just the fact that you knew and didn't tell me—it hurt so much."

"I know," I say. Am I crying because of Desiree or my uncle or because there's an interstellar crisis and I have no idea what that even means? "I really messed up. I talked with Uncle Umberto about it—a little before he died. He said I take the path of least resistance. That I didn't tell you because it was too hard. But sometimes the hard way is the right way. And I really wish I'd done the hard thing and just told you what was going on even though I knew it would hurt."

"Your uncle was pretty fierce with the wisdom," Des says, and puts her arm around me.

We sit like that through the rest of lunch, side by side, our knees touching. Her miniskirt shows off her beautiful legs, almost as beautiful as Will's legs. Is it weird that my two best friends are the two people I find most attractive? I guess I'm more sapiosexual than anything. They'll probably get together anyway, and I'll be doomed to third-wheel status for eternity.

But having Des back as a friend again—my oldest friend, my best friend since kindergarten—makes me feel like one thing, at least, is right in the world. Or in the Galaxy, as tío Umberto used to say. He always approached life with an ironic wink, but now I'm realizing just how many layers of irony hid beneath so much of what he said.

I think back on what tío Umberto told me in the car. Is declining the ambassadorship the right path? Or just the easier path?

✦　✦　✦

AFTER DINNER I GO TO MY ROOM to catch up on homework, but it's impossible to concentrate. I check the time on my phone. Just a few hours left before the deadline. Pash-Ti is right about everything. I am indecisive. I am "especially good at doing nothing." I'd make a horrible ambassador.

But then there's what Johnny and Wasala said, that Umberto had been sure I was the only one who could carry on his work. If I say no, will I be letting him down? Why didn't he ever talk to me about this? How could he leave me to figure all this out on my own?

I stomp across my room, my muscles tight. I want to kick something. On the floor by my bed is the stuffed soccer ball that Umberto before he died. The last gift he'll ever give me. He's gone, and all he left me is a stupid stuffed soccer ball! I dig my fingers into its black pentagons and white hexagons and fling it against the wall.

A female voice comes from the soccer ball as it bounces off the wall and lands on the floor. "Fingerprints recognized: Valeria Vega, ambassador of Earth. Playing message."

The hexagons of the soccer ball light up the room like a dozen miniature searchlights. The lights converge on one spot only a few feet below the ceiling, forming a shape of dark purple that soon becomes a fedora. The lights flow downward, rendering a familiar brown face, a dark purple blazer, black pants, black shoes with silver buckles—until all of him is there, right there, standing in front of me with a smile more alive than anything I've ever seen.

I choke back a sob. "Tío Umberto?" I reach out, but my hand passes through him, becoming tinted with the same shade of purple as his blazer.

"Hi, Val," Umberto says, and I step back so I can look at his face. "I guess if you're watching this it must be nice to see me again. I guess I'm dead now. Sorry about that. I hope by now I've had the chance to tell you about the aliens so this isn't a complete surprise."

"That would have been nice," I say, crying and smiling just at the sight of him.

Umberto goes on, "Well just in case, I'll start from the beginning. For more than thirteen years—nearly all your life—I've been the secret ambassador of Earth. I remember, when you were a little kid, sometimes in the summer I'd take you out to the park to watch the stars. We'd walk through the dark forest, and I was always surprised that the shadows never frightened you. Then we'd sit in the clearing and spread out our blanket and lie down and look up, and more than once you asked me if somewhere out there, on those tiny points of light, we might someday discover life. Now for the first time I can answer you truthfully. I have been to some of those stars, and there is life on the planets that circle them. But we're much too late to discover them, because centuries ago *they* discovered us.

"I'm afraid they weren't terribly impressed with us. They see us as savages, primitive not only in our technology but in our way of life. My first few years as ambassador were so ... disappointing. My head was filled with naïve optimism. I thought it would be like *Star Trek*, exploring strange new worlds and seeking out new life. But the Galaxy is just as much of a mess as Earth. Most of the time I couldn't even get the new life to talk to me."

Umberto looks at his shoes for a moment, adjusting his fedora, then looks up with a mischievous smile. "So I spoke louder. My entire career as ambassador, I've worked to gain respect and recognition for the primitive worlds. Everything has culminated in the negotiations on Hosh. If we get this right, then Hosh could have more freedom and autonomy than ever in its history. And that would set a precedent that even primitive worlds must be treated with dignity.

"But if we fail, our sector of the Galaxy will be plunged into interstellar war. When the Great Powers agreed for me to mediate these negotiations, I suspect they were trading wagers on how badly I would fail. The Etoscans and Levinti talk of peace, but I know both are secretly preparing for war. And I've learned things—things I'm fearful to tell you even on this recording. Twice now there have been attempts on my life." Umberto looks to his left, then takes off his fedora and rubs his hand through thinning hair. "Whoever's trying to kill me seems to know my every step. I shudder to think it, but I fear that someone here in the embassy is a spy. Pash-Ti has been my closest confidante for years, but she's a Levinti sympathizer and lately trust is short between us. Wasala is a Hoshan in exile herself, and this conflict is so personal for her I can't be certain where her loyalties lie. Remember to steer your thoughts when you're near her. And Johnny—Johnny is Johnny, but he's oddly sympathetic with the Hoshan autonomists. Never forget that he was originally a Synthetic war machine. Any of them could be the one who betrayed me. That's why you must be the next ambassador, Val. You're the only one I'm sure I can trust.

"Johnny, Pash-Ti, or Wasala would all be dangerous adversaries, so I've left you with a weapon. In your phone, in the games folder, I've hidden an app called Set to Stun. It has two settings—a stunner to render unconscious Wasala or Pash-Ti or any other organic being of similar size, and a neutralizer to temporarily disable a Synthetic like Johnny. It's easy to operate—just point and shoot. I'm fortunate that one of the most clever software designers in the Galaxy owed me a favor. She helped me camouflage the weapon in the primitive Terran circuitry of your phone, so that no interstellar technology will detect it. Now steer your thoughts and forget that you have it until you're certain it's time to make use of it.

"You must go to Hosh, Val, and mediate the talks in my place. Do what you do best—listen to all the parties involved, get inside their alien shoes and figure out what they really want. And even though they're not an official party to the talks, you must speak to the Outlanders as well—to Ferus especially. I trust him. Find Ferus—or, if you can't, I suspect he will find you.

"I'm sorry to put all this on your shoulders, Val. I can imagine how overwhelming it must be, and I know there's a part of you that will want to run away from it all. But even if you don't have faith in yourself, know that I have faith in you. You have never been afraid of the unknown. Most people see something they don't understand and shirk away in fear, but you reach out with empathy. That is true courage, Val. Your courage will guide you through the Galaxy."

Umberto smiles at me, and then the hologram fades, the darkness working its way up his body until there's nothing left, and I'm sitting alone in my room.

I wipe the tears away. There's no way I'm going to let tío Umberto down, and there's no way I'm going to let a ruthless killer destroy everything he'd been fighting for. Minutes ago, this choice felt impossible. I grab my phone, my body moving faster than my brain. Pash-Ti doesn't know me. I *can* take action. It just takes me some time to figure out which action is the right one.

The deadline! What time is it? 11:15 pm. There's still time! I dial E-X-C-E-L-S-I-O-R-7.

"Hey," Johnny says, though it's hard to hear him over the melody of "Like a Prayer" in the background. "Did you decide?"

"Yes. I'm ready to take a trip on the Interstellar Subway."

"I knew it!" Johnny says. "I'm there in 9.2 minutes."

I hang up the phone and look at it. I open up the Games folder. There it is—Set to Stun. It looks easy to use, just like tío Umberto said. Johnny and Wasala seem so ... harmless. And Pash-Ti might be aggro, but not a killer. I can't imagine any of them killing tío Umberto. I hope it *wasn't* any of them, and I hope I never have to use this weapon. I close the app and try to do what Umberto said—forget it exists.

I open my closet. What's the appropriate attire for an interstellar ambassador? I'm no master of a hundred lewks like Will, but I don't want to offend any of the aliens. I shoot Johnny a quick text: *Dress code?* For a brief second I wonder if Johnny is text-capable, but then my phone vibrates. Of *course* Johnny is text-capable.

U can go nude 4 all aliens care. Attire highly culturally relative.

Well, that takes the pressure off but is decidedly not-helpful. When Umberto went on his trips, he always wore his purple fedora and matching blazer. Formal but flashy. Very Umberto. I'm not so flashy, but I like the idea of being a bit formal and a distinctive. Ugh, I don't want to wear that same black shirt I wore for the funeral. But I do have a nice white blouse that's also pretty formal, but looser and more comfortable.

Now—pants or a skirt? I hate wearing formal pants almost as much as I hate wearing skirts. Can I just wear jeans? I can imagine Mami's endless diatribe if she found out I wore jeans to a formal meeting. But Johnny said no one would care what I'm wearing, and I'll feel much more comfortable and confident in jeans. I compromise by pulling on my best and newest pair of dark blue jeans.

Then I pull on a pair of grey boots with flat heels. They look pretty formal but are also comfortable and practical: decent for running and good for any terrain—hopefully even alien ones. Umberto always said, in a crisis, you get as far as your shoes can take you.

I look at myself in the mirror. I need a final touch. Last year for Christmas, Umberto gave me a newsie cap, which I almost never wear. The cap has a pattern of grey, black, and purple checkers, and has a bit of Umberto's flair—including the touch of purple. I pull it over my head. It matches the boots and keeps my hair out of my face. I'm usually more of a baseball-cap kind of girl, but I'm not about to wear my Yankees cap to outer space. It feels right to wear something that Umberto gave me.

I put a few pillows under my blanket in case anyone peaks in the door overnight. Then I quietly slip outside.

Johnny is waiting on his motorcycle out front. I follow him on my bike, and we ride a few blocks to what Johnny calls "the New Jersey consulate," the office that Umberto would use for work when he was in town. I've been there a few times, and it looks pretty much the same—just an ordinary office. But then Johnny leads me somewhere I've never been—the basement.

"How exactly are we getting to Istanbul?" I ask. "Didn't you say we have to hurry?"

"Patience, young one," says Johnny, in a parody of an old wise man's voice. To the air, he adds, "Gravity express, tickets for two."

There's a rumble from the ground beneath us, and a giant silver bullet, about the size of an elevator, rises up out of the ground. In the bullet's side, a door shimmers open, revealing two seats inside. Johnny gets in and sits down in one of the seats. Thin threads of silver emerge from the walls and wrap themselves around Johnny's waist and chest in a tight net, like a spider's web. I follow Johnny's lead and sit beside him. A similar web wraps around me. It hugs my body tightly and is cool to the touch, not sticky at all. The smooth, curving walls are silver on all sides, except for a small transparent window in front of us.

"Hey," Johnny says, "You ever do that Drop of Doom ride at Six Flags?"

"Um, I think I did that one once."

"Perfect." Johnny winks.

The giant bullet shoots into the ground. My stomach leaps up. There's nothing but darkness all around us, and it feels like we're falling to the center of the earth.

CHAPTER 6

HOSH

HOSH — A primitive planet orbiting an orange star in the Orion arm. Hoshans, the predominant native sentient species, are the Galaxy's only known lifeform capable of <u>telepathy</u>.[1] The planet was discovered and colonized by the Levinti. During the Second Galactic War, the Etoscans arrived on Hosh, beginning a 1,000-cycle conflict between two of the five <u>Great Powers</u> for control of the planet.[2] Both the Etoscans and Levinti have recruited legions of telepathic spies and agents from the local population, rendering the planet the most valuable military strategic asset of any primitive world in the Galaxy.

<u>Article 17</u> of the <u>Third Treaty of Centron</u> divided Hosh between the Etoscans and the Levinti, establishing a fragile détente that has lasted more than 1,500 cycles.[3] With Article 17 set to expire this cycle, many interstellar political scholars predict the conflict will re-escalate, placing Hosh at the center of a renewed war between two of the Galaxy's most powerful empires …

Excerpted from **WIKI GALACTICA**

OUR BULLET-SHAPED VESSEL is still accelerating, like a roller coaster that never stops picking up speed. Through the front window, in the bullet's headlight, a smooth metallic tunnel stretches ahead, a blur of silver whooshing past. Other than the acceleration flattening me against my seat, the ride's surprisingly smooth. "Is this magnetic or something?" I ask.

"Partly!" Johnny says. "Welcome aboard the Gravity Express. Frictionless tunnel direct from NJ to Istanbul. Very direct. No need for propulsion—gravity is carrying us there."

"I definitely noticed the gravity," I say. "Who built this?"

"Oh, little side project of mine a couple decades ago. It was getting tedious dealing with Terran airplanes, Customs, and the like. Fourteen hours to go a few thousand miles! I'm not one to criticize primitive cultures, but *that* is savage."

I remember from a documentary that the Lincoln Tunnel took years to build and cost millions of dollars, and that was only a mile and half long. This must be a thousand Lincoln Tunnels, and Johnny made it single-handedly, a "side project." He was originally a Synthetic war machine, Umberto's message warned. I shudder at how easily Johnny could take down an entire army, then shudder again knowing he might be the one who betrayed my uncle. If only there were some way I could be sure I can trust him—but what am I supposed to say? So, Johnny, my uncle's posthumous hologram said you're a war machine—what's up with that? For now I have to stay quiet and figure things out on my own.

My stomach lurches again. "Um, why build this huge tunnel? Why can't the embassy just be in New Jersey?"

"Because the Interstellar Subway Station's in Istanbul," says Johnny, his voice casual, like we weren't falling through the Earth at hundreds of miles a second. "You can't just load that onto a U-Haul. This whole scarcity thing you've got going on Earth is very old-school. On any civilized planet you can get anything you want, made to order at the molecular level. But the Subway? That's a tunnel through gravity-space-time. You need the energy of a black hole, quantum threads to guide you through subspace, a direct link to a planet's gravity well, plus exotic matter so the whole thing doesn't fall apart. Even with dozens of fabulous me's, it'd take decades and a whole bunch of imports to move Earth's Subway or make a new one. And no way the Interstellar Transit Authority would commit those kinds of resources for a backwater Atomic World."

My stomach stops lurching. We must have stopped accelerating. "Are we almost there?"

"Halfway!" Johnny says. "Now we're not falling anymore, just coasting."

"Oh," I say, picturing how the tunnel works. "So we, like, passed Earth's gravitational center, and even though we're going in a straight line, now it's like we're going uphill instead of downhill."

"Exactamundo!" Johnny says. "And with no friction, inertia will take us the rest of the way. Every planet ought to have them."

As the bullet slowly coasts to a halt, Johnny announces, "Last stop, Terran Interstellar Embassy, Istanbul!" The netting around us retracts and the door opens. I follow Johnny out.

I half-expect to come out onto the bridge of a starship, but it's another ordinary office. The carpet is an innocuous shade of blue, and the overhead lights have a dull fluorescent glow. Paintings and photographs dot the walls—mostly ordinary landscapes and portraits, but one glows with a phosphorescent pattern that changes by the second.

Through the windows, the faint light of dawn falls on a row of pastel-colored buildings—colors that remind me of Viejo San Juan. But just a few blocks away, the dome and minarets of a mosque peek out above the rooftops, something I've never seen in Puerto Rico.

"Wow," I say. "We're really in Istanbul. This is the farthest I've ever been from home."

"You're about to go a lot farther, kid," Johnny says.

"We're in Istanbul's historic district," I say, remembering a documentary on the Hagia Sophia. "These buildings must be hundreds of years old. The embassy—the Interstellar Subway—the aliens—they've been here for centuries, haven't they? That's why the Subway is in Istanbul. When the aliens came, this was the capital of the Roman Empire, like, one of the centers of civilization. The Subway's been here since Istanbul was Constantinople."

Johnny starts snapping his fingers, singing some song about how Istanbul used to be Constantinople.

"Huh?" I say.

"Your generation has no appreciation for the great works of the 1900s." Johnny says.

There's a sound like a dog scurrying—I turn and see Wasala rushing toward us on all six legs, letting out a series of clicks and chirps. "I knew you'd say yes, Valiant One!"

I find myself smiling at the sight of her. Then I remember that I'm supposed to guard my thoughts around her. How am I supposed to do that?

Wasala stops a few feet from me and stands up on her hindmost legs. "Who told you to guard your thoughts around me?"

I intentionally turn my thoughts to Johnny, to our conversation on the Gravity Express. "No one. I just heard you can't trust anyone when it comes to interstellar politics."

"Well, that, sadly, is true," Wasala says, eyeing Johnny. "But it need not be. Trust begets trust, just as distrust begets distrust. But our time is short! We need to get you suited up, dearie." Wasala leads us down another corridor, walking on four limbs, the lower part of her body waddling on her short legs. "Closet," Wasala says, and the wall shimmers open, revealing a closet lined with tiny cubbyholes. Wasala stretches up on her two hindmost legs to reach into one and pulls out a wallet-sized blue pouch with a subtle sheen. "Where shall I attach it, Valiant One?"

"Attach?"

"The suit needs to be integrated with something on your person," Wasala explains. "For example, Pash-Ti's suit is integrated into her briefcase, mine into my palms."

"Where did Umberto have his?" I ask.

"His fashion-forward fedora," Johnny says. "Where else?"

I take off my newsie cap. "Then put it here."

"Perfect," Wasala says. She tugs on the pouch, and the thin blue fabric expands, enveloping my cap. Then it contracts suddenly, tightening around the cap and taking on its exact shape—the fabric so thin now that it seems more like tinted Saran Wrap than cloth. It turns a deeper shade of blue, then bubbles, like boiling paint. The blue slowly sinks into the cap, which goes back to its ordinary pattern of black, purple, and grey checkers.

Wasala hands the cap back to me. It's warm to the touch. I put it on, and a thin, transparent film seeps out from it and spreads around me—like a giant soap bubble. The bubble closes around the shape of my body, leaving less than an inch of distance from my skin. It gets even thinner until it's nearly invisible.

"An ultra-thin semi-permeable membrane," Wasala explains. "It'll carry your atmosphere with you wherever you go. You mostly won't notice it, and it'll work even when you touch objects or other people. I've got mine active now." Wasala holds her claw up to the light. A thin bubble glints around Wasala's fur, just barely visible in the places where the light catches it.

I remember the rush of cold I felt when I shook Pash-Ti's hand. It must have been a suit just like this. "Just so, dear," Wasala says. "Pash-Ti basically walks around with a freezer around their skin."

They? Have I been getting Pash-Ti's pronouns wrong?

Wasala crinkles her nose at me. "Oh, grammar. Pash-Ti's species is eusocial, with multiple genders, sort of like ants or bees on Terra. They don't really fit the binary genders of Terrans or Hoshans, but Pash-Ti mostly uses female designations on Earth, to blend in." That makes me think it's more accurate and respectful to use they, at least when we're off Earth. "Now, listen, we just need to set up your interface. What would you like? Contact lenses with eye-mouse? Holographic touch-screen? Or I could set up a primitive interface similar to a smart phone if you prefer something more familiar."

An eye-mouse sounds hard to get used to, but a smart phone sounds boring when holographic is one of the options. "Where would the holographic screen go?"

"Wherever you like."

"How about here?" I say, gesturing to the underside of my forearm.

"That should work," Wasala says, pressing a small remaining piece of the blue fabric into my arm. A glowing screen lights up across my inner forearm, like a luminescent tattoo.

"That is very cool," I say.

"Gracias, Valeria," says a baritone voice in my ear. "Estoy aquí a sus órdenes."

"Oh, it also has an auditory interface," Wasala adds. "Only you can hear it, unless it needs to talk to someone else. Umberto set the default for Spanish, but you can switch it to English if you prefer."

"Um, English would be good," I say.

"Then English it shall be," the voice says.

"You should give it a name," Wasala says. "So it knows when you're talking to it."

"Okay," I say, thinking of my cap. "I'll call you Checkers."

"A noble name," the suit replies.

"So the suit has all the basics," Wasala says. "Communication system, Salfren multisensory translation software, Wiki Galactica access, atmospheric and gravity adapters, defenses from your more basic nano-assassins and weapons."

Johnny said a nano-assassin might have killed Umberto. If Umberto had a suit like this, why hadn't it protected him?

Wasala scratches behind her ear. "I've wondered that too. I doubt Umberto would have been careless enough to turn his suit off, even on Earth, after the other attempts on his life. More likely the defenses of the suit were simply insufficient. I'm afraid the primitive embassies don't get very state-of-the-art tech. Johnny and I have done our best to update things here, but this suit's defenses—or Umberto's—could easily be evaded."

"Then what good is it?" I ask.

"Quite a bit of good, I should think," Checkers says. "I may be a few centuries old but there's wisdom that comes with age."

"Um, is the suit—intelligent?" I ask.

"Sort of," Johnny says. "But not compared to say, me. It has to have baseline artificial intelligence just to run the Salfren translation software, but it's more like a pet than a person."

Checkers lets out a surprisingly human harrumph, and this time he projects his voice so everyone can hear. "I may not be as sophisticated as a true Synthetic, but I take pride in my work."

"Touchy much?" Johnny says.

From behind us comes a sharp-pitched whistle. I turn to see Pash-Ti's intimidating seven-foot tall grey form striding toward us. "You should have heeded my counsel, Ambassador Vega, rather than this Synthetic dilettante. But since there is nothing I can do to prevent this disaster in progress, I suggest we make haste for your meeting with the Levinti ambassador. Tardiness for your first meeting will only reveal you for the unskilled novice that you are."

Johnny rolls his eyes at Pash-Ti. "It must be, like, so exhausting, living in that hard head of yours. But I agree on the making haste part. Elevator!" On the wall opposite the closet, an egg-shaped door irises open. I follow Johnny and Pash-Ti into the elevator.

Wasala doesn't follow. "May Synchronus guide you," she says, as the elevator closes.

"Wasala's not coming?" I ask. The elevator descends—it's the opposite of the gravity bullet, smoother than any elevator on Earth. "Wouldn't it be useful to have, um, a native?"

Pash-Ti looks down at Johnny, letting out two shrill notes. "Have you briefed her at all?"

"Yeah, no, we didn't exactly get to the full orientation yet," Johnny says.

"As if her inexperience weren't sufficiently disastrous, now she'll be arriving at this first meeting with no proper preparation." Pash-Ti turns from looking down at Johnny to looking down at me. "Wasala is of Hoshan descent but is forbidden to set foot on Hosh because she is the daughter of Legionnaires. The issue of homecoming for Legionnaires and their descendants is one of four key areas of dispute in the negotiations which you are now to mediate."

The door opens, and we step out onto a platform. A massive tower looms above us, a shimmering shade of green. I'd pictured the Subway as looking like the New York Subway, but it's more like an underground skyscraper.

As soon as we set foot on the platform, Pash-Ti and Johnny rise into the air, as if a sudden gust of wind had whisked them up but missed me completely.

"Tell the suit to take you to level five!" Johnny says from above.

"Um, Checkers," I say.

"I heard," Checkers says, and then my feet are no longer touching the platform. As I levitate up, there's no wind, no force pushing me upward. It's more like I'm suddenly lighter than air, and it's only natural for my body to float higher, the same way that when underwater, your body is tugged to the surface.

Whoa, I am totally flying!

As I glide up, I see that each floor is smaller than the one beneath it, with a set of doors appropriate to its size. The first level was big enough to fit a small family of dinosaurs.

The suit takes me to the fifth level of the tower, through a door that's nine feet high, nicely sized for humans and even for Pash-Ti. As I land, three seats extend up from the white floor, one for each of us. Pash-Ti sits in the tallest—which is more like a stool, allowing all three of their legs to hang comfortably over the sides. When I sit down, my chair shapes itself to the contours of my body. It's possibly the most comfortable chair I've ever encountered.

"Computer, make the jump to Jupiter," Johnny says. "Mmm, you might feel a bit odd for a few secs."

Are we leaving now? I think.

Did I say that out loud? Everyone's sitting so still. How long has it been since Johnny spoke? A second? Minutes? "Are we—leaving?" I say, the words like rocks.

"We left, kiddo," Johnny says, his fingers moving quickly across the console. "Welcome to Jupiter."

"The temporal and psychological disorientation you're experiencing is normal," Pash-Ti says. "Leaping through gravity-space-time has a dissociative effect on most lifeforms. Fortunately, the effect diminishes once your physiology has experienced it several times."

"That was so fast," I say.

"From Earth you can practically spit on Jupiter, but this is just a quick stopover. Computer, initiate jump to Hosh-Tor, standard sequence." He looks back at me. "We needed Jupiter's deeper gravity well to get us out of the solar—" Johnny's lips freeze mid-word. I look down at my hands. Am I frozen too? I feel suddenly, deeply, that tío Umberto ought to be here instead of me, that I've betrayed him by taking his place.

"—system. You okay, kiddo?"

"I think—so," I say. The world isn't frozen anymore, at least. "Are we there?"

"Hosh is pretty close to Terra," Johnny says. "But it takes more than a few seconds to get there."

Pash-Ti points a spindly white finger at me. "And in our limited time we must brief you as much as possible given the circumstances." They launch into a long monologue about interstellar diplomacy and Galactic Wars, with Johnny interrupting to disagree every couple minutes. I ask lots of questions, trying to absorb about a hundred names and alien empires and treaties all at once, hoping I can remember enough to get through this first meeting. More than anything, what's clear is that the Etoscans and Levinti have both been exploiting the Hoshans for thousands of years for their telepathic abilities. These "Great Powers" act like they're so advanced, but they sound like they do all the same messed-up things as humans do.

"The Treaty of Centron reified a delicate balance of power on Hosh," Pash-Ti finishes. "The Etoscans would retain control of the Northern hemisphere, including the site of the Tumasra phenomenon, which is considered sacred by the Etoscans and believed to be linked to telepathy. The Levinti would maintain control of the Southern half, including the planet's sole Interstellar Subway Station. But that provision expires in just one month."

"Which has everybody in a hissy," Johnny says. "The Etoscans and Levinti both want control of all of Hosh. If either of them got control of the entire planet, they'd eventually have exclusive control of all the telepathic agents in the Galaxy—which would make them the dominant power in the Galaxy."

"Our best hope is to negotiate a new Hoshan Treaty that simply maintains the status quo," Pash-Ti says.

"But Umberto wanted more than that," I say. "He wanted Hoshans to have more autonomy."

"Yeah, Umberto had a way of always seeing how things could be better," Johnny says.

"Perhaps in Umberto's skillful hands, we might have achieved incremental steps toward Hoshan autonomy." Pash-Ti extends their eyestalks toward me. "In the current context, it will be a success if we avert a full-scale Fifth Galactic War."

I slump in my chair, hoping I can be half as good a mediator as Umberto.

"Almost there," Johnny says. "Making the final jump from Hosh-Tor to Hosh."

"We've barely scratched the surface." Pash-Ti leans their tall grey torso toward me. "In any diplomatic meeting, focus on your goal. The main goal of this meeting is to assure the Levinti ambassador that despite Umberto's death, negotiations will continue as planned. The negotiation terms indicate that the Terran ambassador will serve as mediator, but much of the role is ceremonial. If she asks any substantive questions, let me answer."

"Or me," Johnny says.

Time seems to freeze again, and then the Subway doors open. We all step off to the station platform. Above and below us, the platform and ceiling are made of a thick, crystal-clear material. Through it, I can see dozens of levels above and below us, like ten Penn Stations layered on top of each other, every floor filled with furry Hoshans scurrying in all directions. After we get off, the tower disappears with a flash and a tremendous ripping sound.

"No time for sight-seeing," Johnny says, tugging at my jacket. Pash-Ti is already ahead of us, taking long strides alternating weight between their center leg and two outer legs, like a human racing on crutches. They lead us through a crush of furry Hoshans, toward a row of what look like giant soap bubbles.

As we approach one of the bubbles, it envelops us. The floor of the bubble is soft beneath my boots, like a plush carpet. Pash-Ti says, "Valeria Vega, Ambassador of Earth, and staff, to meet with Doctor Ambassador Kantroponar, Levinti ambassador to Hosh."

The bubble takes us up in a diagonal path through the air. Enormous floating structures shaped like peach pits crowd above and below the clouds of a deep orange sky. Each structure is speckled with cavernous windows, like the holes in Swiss cheese. Chills rush across my skin as I look across the alien city. I'm actually on another planet!

"Don't gawk," Pash-Ti says, looking down at me. "Always address her as Doctor Ambassador. Titles are of the utmost importance in the Levinti Scholocracy."

"The Levinti embassy is near the Station," Johnny says. "We'll be there in a sec."

Pash-Ti's eyestalks draw inward. "Which is several minutes too late."

The bubble swoops into one of the giant seed-shaped buildings, setting us down in a chamber more impressive than Earth's most magnificent cathedrals. The ceiling is hundreds of feet high, a pattern of luminescent colors dancing across it.

Floating in the air just above us is what looks like a massive jellyfish. Its bell-shaped body is a translucent shade of white, as big as a blue whale. It has five tails—or fins?—spaced evenly apart around the sides of its body. I can't find a face. How do you have a conversation with someone without a face? A row of shimmering blue spheres runs around the entire circumference of the bell. Are they like giant jewels—or could they be eyes? I wonder how a brain could process seeing in all directions at once.

The Levinti's body expands, its skin stretching like an inflating balloon. It rises a meter higher into the air. A pattern of green and yellow light flash across its skin. The beautiful dance of lights must be the Levinti's native language. But then the translation from Checkers comes in my ear, and the words are more harsh than beautiful.

"You have arrived three minutes late, Terran."

CHAPTER 7

LEVINTI

LEVINTI – One of the five <u>Great Powers</u> of the Galaxy, the Levinti Scholocracy encompasses 472 star systems.[1] Academic research, teaching, and government are all unified in Levinti society, with the 118 academies of the Scholocracy each directing various aspects of Levinti planets and colonies.[2] The Academies of Colonial Administration, Interstellar Transit, and Military Studies are among the most influential, although recently the Academy of Interdisciplinary Efficacy has been rising in prestige ...

Outsiders sometimes describe Levinti cultures as matriarchal, but that is erroneous, since all Levinti eventually transition to biological females in the final phase of life ...

Excerpted from **WIKI GALACTICA**

THE LEVINTI AMBASSADOR HOVERS above us. The lighting gets dimmer, and it takes me a second to realize that's because we're in the Levinti's shadow, which is as big as an Olympic swimming pool. The Levinti is so enormous, so amazing, and I have so many questions. Is it like an organic blimp, with hydrogen or helium or some other gas inside its body, making it lighter than air? Is it from a gaseous planet like Jupiter? I wish I could float up and touch it to see what it feels like, but that's probably not proper ambassador behavior.

Another pattern of green and yellow light flashes across the Levinti's skin.

"Have you an explanation for your tardiness?" Checkers' translation of the phosphorescent patterns is a female voice that's different from the voice he uses for Wasala. It seems like Checkers invents and assigns different voices for different aliens to help me keep track of who's speaking. The translated voice reminds me that Kantroponar is not an "it." I look at the giant floating squid above me and let my brain take her in as a full, sentient "she."

She's angry that I'm only three minutes late? Okay, so Levinti culture really is anal retentive about punctuality. My perpetually-late Puerto Rican family would not do well with them. But tío Umberto always said that an apology costs you nothing but can mean everything to the offended person.

"I apologize," I say. "I was only just appointed to the ambassadorship, and came as quickly as I could."

A phosphorescent green pattern flashes across Kantroponar's skin. "You did not come quickly enough. The fact remains that you are late for our appointment, derailing not only my schedule but that of my staff, creating a cascade of inefficiencies."

I imagine the situation from Kantroponar's perspective. She's an ambassador for one of the most powerful species in the Galaxy, and I'm from a "primitive" planet that nobody cares about. It probably annoys Kantroponar just to have a conversation with me. I'm like a rookie breezing in late for a meeting with the best coach in the league. I need to make a bigger apology—to show her I know I'm just a rookie and she's big-time.

Pash-Ti steps forward to say something, but I speak up first. "I'm truly sorry, Doctor Ambassador. Your time is extremely valuable, and it was disrespectful of me to arrive late, to inconvenience you and your staff, and to upset your important schedules. I'm new to these duties, and still learning, but that's no excuse for my mistake. Please accept my humble apology."

Kantroponar hovers silently for a few moments, her dangling tendrils swaying slightly. Several of the tendrils are adorned with rings, jewels that glow with phosphorescent colors much like the Levinti's language. "Your humility is … appropriate. With such humility, perhaps you will one day earn the prestige commensurate with the ersatz title you now bear."

A note flashes across the holoscreen on my wrist: *Prestige is an approximate translation for the Levinti concept of respect resulting from scholarly achievement and devotion to the Levinti Scholocracy.* That's helpful to know, and it's a relief that Kantroponar seems to be easing up about the lateness.

Kantroponar floats away from me and seems to pause in reflection. Beyond her looming body, there are two other figures in the room. A much smaller jellyfish-like creature hovers just behind her—only slightly larger than a human being. Its skin is partially transparent, while Kantroponar's is white, when she's not talking. Is it a Levinti child? Is this bring-your-kid-to-work day?

On the far side of the room, a Hoshan stands, wearing a blue armband on their upper right limb. Wasala's tail is thin and naked like a mouse's, but this Hoshan's tail is fluffy like a squirrel's. On the Subway trip, Johnny mentioned that male Hoshans have fluffier tales, so I guess Hoshans have two biological sexes, like humans. I wonder if some of them don't fit the binary, like with humans?

Two of the Hoshan's claws are a flurry of motion, as if typing on an unseen keyboard. He turns to look at me. Is he here to spy on all our thoughts? Is he listening to my thoughts right now? His head cocks to one side. I guess that's a yes.

Kantroponar's skin lights up again, a glowing rainbow tapestry, faster and more complex than the patterns before. "Let us turn to the matters at hand. The death of Ambassador Olmeda and abrupt transition to a new mediator has raised significant concerns about the viability of the treaty talks. It was never optimal for a primitive to play the role of mediator. We only agreed out of respect for the wishes of the Hoshan representatives, and because Ambassador Olmeda had demonstrated such exceptional proficiency in the Nevachen crisis. You have yet to demonstrate such skill. Indeed, you have yet to demonstrate anything at all."

Pash-Ti steps forward. "Respectfully, Doctor Ambassador, Ambassador Vega may be new to the position, but the agreed-upon guidelines for negotiation stipulate that the Terran ambassador serve as mediator, not that it be Ambassador Olmeda specifically."

Kantroponar's body inflates slightly and rises a few feet higher into the air. Another note flashes across my holoscreen: *Levinti instinctively inflate and ascend when angry, or to express confidence in the superiority of their own argument.* "Perhaps the point was unclear in some other translations of the document, rendered as they were in the less precise terms of non-Levinti languages. However, in the definitive, Levinti version, the present-status case of the noun ambassador clearly indicates that the agreement applies only to the Terran ambassador serving at the time of its signing, Mr. Olmeda."

Johnny holds out his palm, and a stream of lights project upward from it, creating an enormous, life-sized holographic projection of a Levinti in the air above him. A pattern of green and yellow flashes across the holographic Levinti's skin as Johnny speaks. He must be speaking in the Levinti language at the same time as English. "Respectfully, there's nothing in interstellar law that suggests Levinti translations are more definitive than any other language. Also, the present-status case is used for only four of nine references to the Terran ambassador in—"

Kantroponar cuts him off with a dance of red and lime lights. "Your counsel is not sought in this matter, warlord." Checkers' translation of her voice captures the tone as well as the words—harsh and impatient. "It is only by the generosity of my prestige that you are permitted on these premises. Do not overestimate your welcome."

Johnny purses his lips and closes his palm, the giant hologram disappearing with a flash.

Kantroponar points an anaconda-sized tendril at me, decorated with rings the colors of sapphire and ebony. "Despite the dubious legal standing of your position, we are open to continuing negotiations, so long as you uphold all assurances made by your predecessor."

I'm not sure how to answer that. Pash-Ti said our whole goal of this meeting was to keep Kantroponar on board with the negotiations even though the mediator job got switched from Umberto to me, so it seems like I should go along. And it seems safe to follow whatever Umberto agreed to. "I stand by everything my predecessor said."

"And when I say all of the prior ambassador's assurances," Kantroponar says, "that includes his recent promise that he would seek fair and free access to Tumasra for all interested in the scientific study of its unique phenomena."

Pash-Ti lets out two sharp notes. "I'm surprised to hear of this, because the Terran embassy has no record of such an agreement."

"Ah," Kantroponar says. "Ambassador Olmeda made this assurance on his most recent visit to Hosh, just before his untimely death. He likely didn't have the opportunity to formally report it."

"Will you stand by your predecessor's word, Ambassador?" Kantroponar says. Pash-Ti starts to reply, but Kantroponar cuts them off. "I would hear from the ambassador herself."

Suddenly the Levinti's shadow seems even darker—and a little bit cold. Maybe Kantroponar is just lying to take advantage of me, the rookie primitive ambassador. Or maybe she's telling the truth, and Umberto didn't tell the others about this new deal with the Levinti, because he knew someone in the embassy was a double agent. The only thing I can think of is to get Kantroponar talking some more. "I'm new to all this, Doctor Ambassador. Could you tell me more about the assurances you're looking for?"

"Indeed," Kantroponar says. "All of this new information must be quite overwhelming for one born to an uncivilized planet like Terra. Allow me to elucidate. Tumasra is the site of a unique storm found nowhere else in the Galaxy. There is evidence it is linked to telepathy, which is likewise found nowhere else in the Galaxy. It presents a tremendous opportunity for learning—and above all else, the Levinti are committed to learning. But for 1,500 years, the Etoscans have permitted no Levinti to enter Tumasra. All we seek is the establishment of a permanent center at Tumasra for scientific inquiry!"

Even from the little Johnny and Pash-Ti told me on the Subway ride, I can tell the Etoscans would not be thrilled about this idea. "That seems reasonable, Doctor Ambassador, but I understand the Etoscans have concerns about protecting a site they consider sacred."

The Levinti inflates herself to an even greater size and rises a dozen feet higher into the air. "The Etoscans would claim that a mound of waste was sacred if it suited their purposes! Their religious pretensions are nothing but a shield for their own interests."

"Well," I say, "I can understand your frustration."

"Frustration?" Kantroponar says, inflating even more and floating even higher. Checkers' translation takes on an even harsher tone—increasingly exasperated. "You speak far above your prestige, Terran. It's becoming apparent that your lack of knowledge will make a farce of these negotiations."

Now Kantroponar is hovering several dozen feet above us, and we all have to crane our necks to look up at her—even seven-foot-tall Pash-Ti. Last year, my brother Miguel told me where the word upstaging comes from—when an actor moves upstage, forcing the other performers to look back instead of to the audience. Miguel said when another actor did that to him, he would move upstage too, so they were still at the same level.

Kantroponar is asserting her superiority, literally. If I were another Levinti arguing with Kantroponar, I'd probably just float higher too, to stay on her level. Too bad humans can't fly. But I do have ...

"Checkers," I whisper, "can you anti-grav me up so that I'm on the same level as Kantroponar? And can you not translate this?"

"Of course, Madame Ambassador," says Checkers. "And I'll assume you don't want me to translate your commands unless you instruct me otherwise."

I lose my balance for a second as I rise into the air, but quickly straighten myself back out. Checkers brings me up until I'm at the same level as Kantroponar, hovering only a few feet away from her. From this close, Kantroponar's white skin looks smooth and slightly slimy, like a squid's. I can see my own reflection in the blue spheres that dot the circumference of her bell-shaped body. Now I'm pretty sure they're eyes—each one as big as my head, several of them looking right at me.

"I meant no offense," I say, trying not to be intimidated by having a conversation with a giant alien while floating several dozen feet above the floor. "And I don't mean to speak above my prestige. It seems reasonable that you want to study Tumasra, but I'm not sure it's my role as mediator to take your side on the issue."

Kantroponar inflates again. The Levinti's skin becomes thinner and more translucent as she expands and rises even higher. "Your role is to assure that these negotiations remain fair and balanced. At the very least, fair access for the ongoing study of Tumasra must be discussed in the formal talks."

"Checkers, bring me up again?" I say.

"At your service, Madame Ambassador," Checkers says, and takes me up to Kantroponar's level.

"So you just want it to be up for discussion," I say.

"Yes!" Kantroponar says, and she rises again, so high now that she nearly reaches the ceiling of the cavernous room. "A half-day of the talks devoted to parameters for ongoing study of Tumasra."

This time, I don't even have to give Checkers the order—he immediately lifts me up to the ceiling with Kantroponar.

"Well, that seems reasonable," I say, hoping I'm not making a mistake. "I'll do what I can to make sure the study of Tumasra is a topic of fair discussion."

"Excellent," Kantroponar says. Drops of bluish-green color rain across her skin. "And we seem to have argued our way to the ceiling! Thank you for your time, Madame Ambassador. You may leave."

How ... abrupt. Checkers slowly lowers me to the floor, landing me gently beside Johnny and Pash-Ti. As we turn to leave, Kantroponar huddles with the smaller Levinti and the Hoshan. Kantroponar's many-ringed tendrils entwine with those of her smaller counterpart. The gesture between the two Levinti is odd— maternal yet almost romantic.

"That was great," Johnny says, patting me on the back. "For a Levinti to say that you argued your way to the ceiling is practically like being acknowledged as an equal."

"That was a terrible mistake," Pash-Ti says, all three feet padding on the floor as we walk out. "Umberto had already settled the Tumasra issue, with both Levinti and Etoscans agreeing that the Levinti would be allowed temporary visitations, with only the schedule to be determined in the formal talks. Now you've committed to re-opening the matter, and the Levinti will renew their demand for the establishment of a permanent base at Tumasra, which is anathema to the Etoscans. Your ignorance is already derailing the negotiations and bringing us closer to war."

"Whoa," Johnny says. "Ease up, Pash-Ti. It's not ideal, but we can make it work. The important thing is that Val established a bit of credibility."

"She established that she is easily manipulated," Pash-Ti says, quickening their pace. "We must put more distance between ourselves and Kantroponar's Hoshan agent to assure that we are out of his range."

Pash-Ti leads us down a whale-sized corridor, in long strides that alternate between their middle leg and outer two legs. They guide us to a small alcove that juts off the side of the corridor. "This should be far enough. Though I suspect your thoughts have already betrayed just how vulnerable our position is."

"So that Hoshan behind Kantroponar—he was there to spy on our thoughts?" I say.

"Yes," Pash-Ti says. "Throughout the meeting, he was transcribing your thoughts—and mine—and transmitting them to Kantroponar. Fortunately, Hoshans cannot read the thoughts of Synthetics like Johnny, and I steered my thoughts carefully. But I doubt you did the same."

I think back on what my thoughts could have given away. "I don't even know enough to give anything away."

"Precisely," Pash-Ti says. "Your thoughts undoubtedly revealed your lack of knowledge, which is why Kantroponar knew to press her advantage and won a significant concession from you on Tumasra within minutes."

I thought I'd done so well, using Checkers to float up to Kantroponar's level. But Pash-Ti's right—I've already messed things up, undoing the progress tío Umberto had been making. I scuff the smooth yellow floor with my boot and walk away from Pash-Ti and Johnny, toward a floor-to-ceiling window on the far side of the room.

Through the window, I have a clear view of the city I only glimpsed before. The floating, peach-pit-shaped buildings seem to be moving in a set pattern, like a miniature train set making its way around the tracks. Each building is dotted with holes of various sizes, like Swiss cheese. I must be looking out from the inside of one of those holes. Less than an hour ago, the sight of this alien city gave me goosebumps. Now it's just overwhelming, reminding me there's no way I can live up to tío Umberto's expectations of me.

Johnny sidles up to me and gives me a friendly nudge with his elbow. "Don't let Pash-Ti get you down. It's true the Tumasra thing was kinda sub-optimal, but we'll make it work. And I meant what I said. Floating up to Kantroponar's level was an awesome implicit clapback— and diplomacy is all about the implicit communication."

I nod, hoping that's true, but still not sure if I can trust him. Maybe he wants me to fail.

Nearby, a Levinti swoops down into one of the buildings, disappearing into a window on one of the middle floors. They're not just windows, they're doors, so the Levinti can enter and exit from any level, which makes sense for beings that could fly. Dozens of Levinti are floating back and forth between the towers, as are aerial pods that must have Hoshan passengers.

"This city is made for floaters," I say, thinking out loud, "for beings that move through the air, not on the ground. This is Hosh—but this city seems made for the Levinti."

"This is the Southern capital," Johnny says, "so there are more Levinti here than anywhere else on the planet. But pretty much the whole continent looks like this. Actually, pretty much all the Levinti colonies look like this. Oh, colonization! Levinti-towns everywhere!"

Pash-Ti joins us, their tall frame nearly as tall as the window-door. "The Levinti, the Etoscans, the Sufri—all of them have subjugated and assimilated primitive worlds for their own benefit. Terra may be fortunate that it was never of strategic enough importance to be conquered before Article Nine was introduced."

It's the same as all the exploitation and unfairness that happens on Earth. I understand, more than ever, what Umberto was trying to do. I want to do the same thing, to be an ambassador who makes the Galaxy a better place for Hosh and Earth and all the primitive worlds. If only I had a clue how to do that.

Pash-Ti goes on, bending their long torso forward, so that their eyestalks are almost at the same level as my eyes. "Ambassador, I do not wish for us to operate at cross-purposes. I merely ask that you learn from this. Do not make commitments when you know not their full implications. Do not take actions when you know not their consequences. Now let us return to Terra and complete your orientation so that, for your next meeting, you'll be properly prepared."

From Pash-Ti, that almost seems generous. And they're right. "Thank you, Pash-Ti. I don't want to—"

"Hold up," Johnny interrupts. He's staring intently, as if his eyes were lenses zooming in on something—which, they just might be. "Someone is watching us."

I follow Johnny's eyes to the building closest to us. A silver pod emerges from the level right across from us and zips into the bustling aerial traffic.

"It's a Hoshan agent! Come on, Val," Johnny says, pointing a thumb at his back. "Hop on."

Pash-Ti lets out a shrill. "This is exactly what I'm talking about. We are diplomats, not agents of espionage. Prudence must guide our actions ..."

Pash-Ti is probably right, and I'm still not sure I can trust Johnny, and Johnny's probably about to do something opposite-of-prudence. But whoever's spying on us now was probably spying on Umberto before. This agent might know the truth about who killed Uncle Umberto—might even have been involved in his murder. And whoever killed Umberto was also trying to sabotage the negotiations. Figuring out who killed him could also be the key to saving Hosh.

"I'm sorry," I say to Pash-Ti. "I do want to learn and be prudent and everything—but I've got to know who's been spying on us—and on Umberto." I hoist myself onto Johnny's back and wrap my arms around his shoulders.

"Hold on tight," Johnny says and launches out the window-door. He soars, Superman-style, as if his fists are engines pulling us higher into the air. The wind whips across my back, and I cling tightly to Johnny as we speed into the orange sky.

CHAPTER 8

HOSH-UNAM FRONT

HOSH-UNAM FRONT – The Hosh-Unam Front is a network of Hoshan terrorists demanding the immediate expulsion of all non-Hoshan sentients from Hosh.[1] The extremist ideology of the "Hosh-Unam" claims that the Etoscans and Levinti have corrupted Hoshan culture with their alien influences and that Northern and Southern Hosh are "destined to be one and free."[2] Their violent tactics disregard the nonviolent values that characterize the traditional Hoshan culture they purport to represent.

[Suggested from Contributor 1277B: This entry inaccurately implies that the Hosh-Unam Front is the sole group advocating for the Hosh-Unam. There are other groups and individuals, particularly those in the Outlands, that believe in reunification and autonomy for Hosh but who use nonviolent methods. Suggest noting this distinction for clarity. **Response from Editor 791:** *The Hosh-Unam Front is the only group of notable scale and influence advocating the Hosh-Unam. Suggestion declined; Contributor 1277B is blocked to prevent further disruptive contributions that legitimize violence.]*

Excerpted from **WIKI GALACTICA**

I HOLD ON TIGHT to Johnny as the wind whips through my hair. Above and below us are a dozen layers of pods and floating buildings and the occasional Levinti, the bustling flow of an aerial city that's humming and whooshing all around us, so big it makes New York seem sleepy. The farthest pods below look like tiny specks. Good thing I'm not afraid of heights.

The silver pod we're chasing is barely distinguishable in the traffic, and it's fading into the distance. "We're losing him," Johnny says. "These aerodynamics are totally sub-optimal. Why don't we switch it up and you take a seat?"

The lower part of Johnny's legs has been replaced by the stern of a small aerial pod, complete with a seat for one. "That looks a lot more comfortable," I say, and shimmy down Johnny's back, then carefully buckle myself in the seat. As we fly, a thin, hot-rod red scaffolding extends upward from Johnny, into the rough outline of a pod. The spaces between the scaffolding fill themselves in until I'm in an aerial pod complete with a forward window. Johnny's human body is nowhere to be seen.

"Johnny," I say, "you're a Transformer!"

Johnny's voice comes from a speaker above, singing, "More than meets the eye," in a robotic tone. "Now we'll catch him."

I lost track of the spy's pod while Johnny was transforming, but then I see one the same shade of silver, only about a soccer field ahead of us. "Is that them?"

"Yup." Johnny zig-zags around two Levinti arguing in the air. Now the pod is only half a soccer field away. If we catch this Hoshan agent, it could be my first chance to get some real clues about what happened to Umberto—and maybe the key to figuring out who's been trying to sabotage the peace talks.

Suddenly, the silver pod nose-dives, cutting through ten layers of aerial traffic and disappearing into the clouds below.

"Whoa!" Johnny says. "I did *not* see that coming. Hold tight!"

Our pod dives too, dodging other pods racing past us in all directions. We pass the traffic and then the clouds. A purple and brown landscape stretches beneath us.

"Did we lose it?" I say. "I guess they came down here to get away from all the Levinti monitoring systems in the city?"

"Maybe," Johnny says as our pod descends toward a cluster of old stone buildings overgrown with purple vegetation. "But we were trailing that pod close enough that my own scanners tracked it here." Johnny lands us a few dozen feet away from a tall, crumbling building that's covered with purple vines. The silver pod is in front of the building, and the Hoshan agent is curled up on a brown stump beside it, as if waiting for us. Her tail is thin and pale, like Wasala's, so I guess she's female—or at least assigned female at birth.

"Is she—armed?" I say.

"I disabled her pod and weapons, but these buildings are made of thick minerals that my scanners can't get through, so we should be careful. I contacted the local Hoshan police. They'll be here soon, but we should have a few minutes to question her ourselves." A hatch opens on the right side of the pod. "You hop out. I'll be right behind you as soon as I reincorporate my human body. Just stay near me so I can protect you if anything goes down."

"Okay." I say, noticing it's already normal for me to wait for someone to reincorporate his body.

I unbuckle myself and hop out of the pod, keeping a close eye on the nearby Hoshan, still curled up on the stump, no more threatening than a housecat lounging on the couch. Why isn't she running?

We're surrounded by crumbling brown stone buildings, overrun by purple vegetation everywhere. It's the ruins of an abandoned town. This must be where the Southern Hoshans lived before the Levinti came, literally uprooting them to live in the clouds above.

The Hoshan returns my gaze and gestures upward with her fist, then extends both thumbs, moving them in circles. A note flashes on my forearm-screen: *Hoshan Southlanders communicate through a sign language invented and taught to them by the Levinti.* The Levinti have a visual language, so they must have taught Hoshans a visual language too.

"Indeed this was once our home." Checkers' translation of the hand-signals comes in a clipped alto voice. Checkers definitely assigns distinct voices for everyone he translates, which is helpful. The Hoshan looks at the ruins around us. "After the Levinti invaded, they slowly ripped us far from the ground, forcing us to live in the air, as they do. One of infinite crimes against my people."

She's responding to my unspoken thoughts, just like Wasala does. So unnerving. The way she's talking—is she part of the militant group that Johnny and Pash-Ti told me about?

"Militant is a subjective word—and inaccurate," she says. "I'm simply a believer in the Hosh-Unam and am willing to fight for it." Another note flashes across my arm: *The "Hosh-Unam" refers to a unified and autonomous Hoshan state, supported by extremists as the one true destiny of Hosh.* Autonomy for a planet that's been colonized doesn't exactly seem extremist to me. I wonder if the Hosh-Unam really is only supported by extremists—and exactly who authored these little notes. All the info I'm getting, even from Wiki Galactica, could be biased. "Of course they're biased," she says. "They're written by our oppressors."

"Why were you spying on us?" I ask.

The Hoshan points her whiskers up and signs. "We just want to get to know the new mediator who holds the fate of our world in her hands."

I look behind me. Johnny's nearly done transforming himself, which makes me feel a little bit safer. I take a step closer to her. "What do you know about the murder of my uncle?"

"I know little," she says. "But I do know that your familial's murderer has hidden well. Our network is vast, and none of us have caught even a glimpse of the murderer's thoughts. That means the assassin was either someone whose thoughts we can't see or who never gets close enough for us to see their minds. Or someone well-trained in thought-steering, a rare skill among off-worlders."

That doesn't narrow it down much. Telepathy doesn't work on Johnny, and apparently Pash-Ti is trained in thought-steering. Wasala has never been on Hosh, so it could be her, too.

I catch myself, realizing the Hoshan is watching my every thought. I wish *I* were trained in thought-steering.

The Hoshan traces her middle two fingers in a series of concentric circles. "You mind-deaf aliens really believe your thoughts are private possessions. What does it get you, this notion of privacy? Instead of a web of connections, you live in a web of duplicities. That was the first violence of our oppressors: they taught us to keep secrets."

"Well, you sure seem to have taken to the secrets thing," Johnny says as he steps past me, back in human form. As he says the words in English, he also signs them—and he's grown an extra thumb on each hand for the purpose. "Secrets are the specialty of the Hosh-Unam Front."

She cranes her neck toward Johnny. "We've learned to deal in secrets because we must."

"Then fight for the Hosh-Unam through diplomacy instead of violence," Johnny says.

"We've been excluded from every diplomatic negotiation that ever considered Hosh's fate. The Hosh-Unam does not belong to the Levinti, nor to the Etoscans."

"Yeah, but most Hoshans disagree with you," Johnny says. "That's the real reason you have to resort to violence."

"I imagine you could teach me much about violence, warlord."

Johnny stands silent for several beats. The Levinti ambassador called him the same thing, and my uncle said he was a war machine. What has Johnny done in his centuries-long past?

"I renounced violence a long time ago," Johnny says.

"With all other tools stripped of us, violence is the only one we have." The Hoshan leaps off of the stump. Abruptly, three Hoshans emerge from the building beside the Hoshan's pod—another female and two bushy-tailed males, the one in the middle with a long neck. Behind them fly five machines shaped like six-winged dragonflies.

Instinctively, I take a step back, and Johnny gets in front of me. "Don't hurt her," he says, his fists transforming into tiny red bots that form a protective circle around us.

The long-necked one lets out a series of clicks, which Checkers translates, "We came prepared for you, warlord."

The Hoshan woman to his right holds up what looks like a miniature satellite dish and aims it right at us. I duck, but it's way too fast. It releases a pulse of light in a wide, blinding arc.

I blink. Bright shadows blur my vision, but it doesn't hurt. Did it miss me?

The bright after-images fade. Johnny is on the floor beside me, immobile, surrounded by tiny red bots that are just as lifeless. I almost check for a pulse, but then realize Johnny doesn't have one. I can't do CPR for a Synthetic.

My own breathing is suddenly shallow. My body feels heavier, like a boulder is strapped to my back. Is this a panic attack? No, it's more than that. The blast affected me somehow, too.

Maybe I can get Checkers to use his anti-gravity to fly me out of here, take me back to the Levinti city. "Checkers?" I say, but there's no answer.

All four Hoshans surround me. I gasp for air.

That blast of light—it didn't hurt me, it hurt Checkers. It must have been like an EMP or something, knocking out any technology—like Checkers, or Johnny. I'm miles beneath a floating city on an alien world, surrounded, completely helpless—too much gravity and too little oxygen. I never should have jumped on Johnny's back. My head floods with dizziness. I fall to my knees.

The long-necked Hoshan stands over me, letting out a series of harsh clicks. But no translation comes in my ear. Instead, the English translation comes from one of the dragonfly-machines, rough and scratchy, like an old intercom system. "Yes, not quite enough oxygen here for your sensitive Terran system, I'm afraid."

He reaches into a satchel at his side and pulls out what looks like a small black mask. A ventilator? He leans over me. With surprising gentleness, he lifts my head and straps the mask to my face. I take a deep breath, oxygen filling my lungs. My lightheadedness fades.

"I'm truly sorry it had to be this way," the dragonfly translates for the long-necked Hoshan as he stands up on his hindmost legs. "But you are the arbiter of the grotesque chattel-market that will shape the fate of my world. It's time you learned the truth. My name is Marrow, and I am the leader of the Hosh-Unam Front."

Fear fills my body. I just got to this planet, and now I'm on my own with the leader of a group of underground rebels. I thought they didn't have any advanced weapons, but they just managed to knock Johnny out—maybe even kill him.

Marrow prowls toward me on all six legs. "Our positronic pulse did no permanent harm to the Synthetic warlord, nor to your synth-suit. A blunt weapon, but effective. We only want to talk."

I sit up and lean against a boulder for support. I'm still catching my breath and feel weighed down by Hosh's gravity. "If you just want to talk, then why'd you ambush us?" My eyes land on the Hoshan female just behind Marrow, the one we chased here in the pod. This was their plan all along. They wanted Johnny to see that Hoshan spying on us, so they could lure us here—lure *me* here.

She signs, and a dragonfly-bot above her broadcasts the translation. "Apologies for the deception. Since we're not granted the privilege of an audience with our mediator, we'd no choice but to arrange one for ourselves."

She's signing, but Marrow has been speaking in clicks and barks. Does that mean he's from the North, like Wasala is?

"Yes, the Hosh-Unam Front is true to our name," Marrow clicks. "In our ranks Hoshans from North and South are united, just as we dream it shall someday be for all of Hosh."

I sit up fully. My body is adjusting to the heavier gravity, but even if I were at full strength, I have nowhere to run. With Checkers disabled, my only hope is that Johnny's message got to the South Hoshan authorities—that they'll get here soon.

"We're aware of the Synthetic's transmission to the collaborators," Marrow says. I really need to figure out this thought-steering thing. "His homing beacon was disabled by our pulse as well. It will take some time for them to find us. Time enough for a history lesson." Marrow shifts to four legs, walking in that centaur-like Hoshan way, slowly circling me. "Before the invasions, all of Hosh lived in harmony in the Hosh-Unam. There were no secrets. There were conflicts, undoubtedly, but they were open and direct, in the Hoshan tradition of *vasek antom*."

"Then the invaders came." Marrow saunters, lightly clawing at his whiskers, his manner oddly leisurely, almost professorial. It's hard to believe he nearly suffocated me only moments ago. "First the Levinti, then the Etoscans. We became pawns in their wars. They took the brightest among us, the most farsighted telepaths, and exiled them to the stars to serve as their warrior-slaves. They split our world in two, as if we were nothing but crops to be harvested."

Johnny and Pash-Ti said something similar, though I still don't understand why Hoshans never used their telepathy to organize a rebellion. "Rebel we did!" Marrow says, all four upper arms spread wide. "We rebelled again and again, but each time we were overwhelmed, our telepathy insufficient to overcome weaponry millennia ahead of our own."

Marrow clicks away, the dragonfly-shaped bot following close behind him, translating his words. "And what happened after every revolt? The leaders were publicly tried and humiliated for their so-called crimes, while any traitor was exalted with high rank. With each successive rebellion, our oppressors became more insidious in their manipulations. Anyone reporting so-called seditious activity was rewarded, becoming the well-groomed pets of our oppressors. Until it became a crime to even think with fondness of the Hosh-Unam!"

Marrow's story of Hosh isn't so different from the one I've already heard. It's not like the Etoscans and Levinti deny they're exploiting Hoshans. It's not so different from the history of Puerto Rico or so many places on Earth. Colonizers always say they only want to help their colonies, and people always find a way to rationalize the systems that benefit them.

Marrow steps closer. "Yes, your predecessor told us of the regions and peoples of your world that have been colonized and exploited. He understood our cause, as I see you do. As mediator, you must demand I participate in the talks on behalf of the Hosh-Unam Front."

Could I even do that? Should I? Some of what Marrow makes sense, but he's also way too sure of himself, like there's no room for anyone's perspective but his. And Johnny and Pash-Ti said the Hosh-Unam Front has *killed* people, even the fellow Hoshans they say they're fighting for.

Marrow leans into me, glaring. "Would you believe two offworlders rather than learn from Hoshans ourselves?" he asks, and has a point. "We minimize loss of life whenever we can. Our use of violence is nothing compared to that of our oppressors. Peace, freedom, unity— these are the pillars of the Hosh-Unam Front. Peace is hollow if it comes without freedom. I met with Umberto personally, and he understood. He assured me I would represent the Hosh-Unam Front in the talks. Do you stand by his word? Do you stand with my people or against us?"

Did Umberto really meet with them? Pash-Ti is right, everyone is taking advantage of my ignorance. "Marrow, I don't even know if I could do that if I wanted to. My power is mostly ceremonial. I'm from a primitive planet too. You must know that."

"Still," Marrow says, "you are the official mediator. You could refuse to participate unless they include us."

"Aren't the Hoshans already being represented?" I say. "By the leaders of the North and South?"

Marrow grinds a hind claw against the floor. "Have you heard nothing I've said? Trimana and Charism are nothing but well-fed pets! Hoshans' very minds have been enslaved! That's why we must use every tool we have to cut the chains from our minds."

I stand up, Hosh's gravity weighing on my legs, but it's good to be reminded that I'm almost twice their height. Tío Umberto was always against violence—I can't imagine him trusting Marrow. I have to figure out another way to have the autonomists be represented—maybe by the Outlanders that Umberto mentioned.

"The Outlanders are weak-minded fools, just like you—filled with ideals but unwilling to make the sacrifices they demand." Marrow and the other three Hoshans and their five bots form a circle around me. "The so-called peace talks can't go far if they lose another mediator."

I back away. The mask is taut against my face, holding in my fast, hot breaths. I clutch my messenger bag to stop my hands from trembling. Desperately, I look for somewhere to run. Maybe I can hide in the ruins until help comes.

The Southland female signs, "We know these ruins as we know our own fur."

Two of them pounce on me so fast I don't have time to dodge. One is on my leg, claws digging into my skin. The other is on my back, the scratchy fur of two arms in a chokehold around my neck. With a third arm, he reaches for my mask. I swat his hand away but can't shake him off my back.

Suddenly, their grip loosens. All four Hoshans' ears prick up.

Marrow lets out a series of clicks. "The Southern collaborators are arriving," the dragonfly drone translates in its scratchy voice. "Think hard on all I've told you, Ambassador. Every moment that you continue these talks you are *complicit* with our oppression. If you don't stop them, then countless lives will be yours to account for! The Hosh-Unam must live—free, one, and forever!"

Marrow motions to his lieutenants, and all four of them scurry into the ruins, the line of dragonfly drones buzzing close behind.

In the sky above, three dots approach.

Nearby, Johnny sits up, rubbing his temples.

I extend a hand to help him up. "Are you okay?"

Johnny stands up. "Yeah, I'm okay, just took me a while to reboot. They hit us with a positronic pulse. I didn't think they even had that kind of tech. But how are *you* doing, Val? I'm so sorry—I was supposed to be protecting you."

I haven't even had time to think about how I am. "I'm shaken up, but okay. They cut off my air—they disabled Checkers!"

"I'm well again, Madame Ambassador, and at your service," Checkers says.

"Oh, yeah, I sent in some microbots to reboot your suit's little brain too," Johnny says.

"I appreciate your assistance, Mr. Excelsior, though I could do without the insults," Checkers says, projecting his voice. "I'm terribly sorry I wasn't able to assist you, Madame Ambassador."

My adrenaline is fading, exhaustion taking hold. I take off my ventilator, and it's like my face has been let out of a cage.

The three dots have turned into pods. They land nearby, their sides marked with phosphorescent patterns that look like Levinti words. From each pod, a pair of Hoshans emerges, each landing on all six legs. They have green armbands on their upper right limbs and carry thin silver batons. They must be like Hoshan police. They move with such fluid, silent coordination that it seems choreographed. Two of them approach Johnny and me, while the other four charge into the ruins— where the Hosh-Unam Front fled.

The two approaching police point their batons at Johnny. My body tenses. One—the captain?—makes a series of hand-signals. "Why did you pursue the insurgents yourselves instead of calling us?"

Johnny signs and speaks in response. "I signaled as soon as we saw the first one. I chased her because I knew you couldn't get to us fast enough."

The police captain holds up five fingers and makes a series of sharp gestures. "The two of you should never have interfered in the first place. You'd have us believe that the primitive Hosh-Unam Front escaped from a Synthetic warlord?"

Johnny gestures back, his face stone-still. "They had a positronic pulse. It caught me off-guard and knocked me out until just a minute ago, when I re-activated my homing beacon."

The two police officers exchange glances of surprise. I guess they didn't know the Hosh-Unam Front had that kind of tech, either. If they have access to new weapons they didn't before, could the Hosh-Unam Front be the ones responsible for Umberto's death?

The other four security officers emerge from the ruins, whiskers furrowed in frowns. The captain looks at me and signs, "We've lost them in the catacombs beneath the ruins."

"We have questions for you, warlord," another Hoshan says. "Come this way." Clutching Johnny by the arm, she leads him toward one of the pods.

"Remember," Johnny says, looking back as they pull him away, "you're an ambassador in the Interstellar Assembly with diplomatic powers!" The Hoshans push him into the pod.

The next thing I know, I'm surrounded by the other four Hoshans, who suddenly seem intimidating despite their small stature. They lead me into a pod that's larger than the others I've seen—the equivalent of a truck, I guess. Two of them crawl into the front section of the pod, and two sit in the back, on either side of me. They're all silent. Silent to *me*, but not each other.

The pod takes off, and I have no idea where we're going. I'm not sure if I'm being escorted, interrogated, or arrested.

CHAPTER 9

THE HOSHANS LEAD ME down a dark corridor, the ceiling so low that my cap skims against it when I don't crouch. I ask where we're going, again, and they just answer with silence, again. Are they police, or some other kind of agent of the South Hoshan government? Is all this silent treatment and hostility just because Johnny and I tried to confront the Hosh-Unam Front before they got there?

There are seven of them now, surrounding me on all sides—seven shadows, each a foot shorter than me. They march in unison, seven pairs of claws clicking on the hard floor with each step. Their silent coordination is beautiful ... and intimidating.

We pass a row of doorways that barely reach my shoulders. This miniature world is so surreal it makes me think of *Alice in Wonderland*, which tío Umberto used to read to me when I was a kid. I loved it but sometimes got irritated with Alice. There's no way I'm drowning in my own tears.

Two Hoshans grab my wrists and tug me through one of the doors. I duck to avoid knocking my head against the archway. Inside, it's a bit brighter, like a bedroom lit by a nightlight. Maybe Hoshans are nocturnal and see better in the dark. A lone Hoshan female is curled up on a bowl-shaped chair, her long pink tail curled up behind her. There's another bowl-shaped chair across from her, and one of the guards shoves me toward it. The chair is too low for me, forcing me to squat so all the pressure is on my lower back.

Who is this Hoshan woman in front of me? A detective, a political official? Johnny told me to remember I'm an ambassador with diplomatic powers. "My name is Val Vega. I'm the ambassador of the planet Earth."

She says nothing.

I'm exhausted and hungry, and the pain in my back is getting worse. It's been hours since we left Earth—it must be 4:00 a.m. in New Jersey by now. I sit up straight, using only the edge of the chair. Not exactly comfortable, but at least the pressure on my back is less. And it makes me feel taller, more in control.

"I'm happy to talk to you," I say, "but it would help if I knew who you are and what's going on." Still silence. She doesn't even nod. Maybe I need to be more direct. "I'm an interstellar ambassador with diplomatic powers. I hope you know any attempt to detain me would be a violation of interstellar law." I hope I sound more confident than I feel, then realize she can hear me thinking about my lack of confidence. God, telepathy is unnerving.

I desperately need help. Even more information would be useful, but Johnny is probably being held in some other dark room, and who knows where Pash-Ti is. Those are literally my only two friends on this planet—and I'm not even sure if they're friends. I look at my arm. I do have another resource.

"Checkers, where am I?" I whisper.

"You're back in the capital of Southern Hosh, in a facility of the Hoshan foreign affairs office, Madame Ambassador." It's a relief hearing Checkers' soft, measured voice in my ear. "According to my files, the Hoshan across from you is Trimana, administrator of Southland Hosh."

"Can she do this?" I whisper. "Can they hold me against my will—legally, I mean?"

"As an interstellar diplomat, you're generally protected from prosecution by local governments," Checkers says. "However, when you and Johnny pursued the Hosh-Unam Front, you arguably violated interstellar law by involving yourselves in a matter of local jurisdiction. I'm afraid they're within their rights to hold and question you, Madame Ambassador."

Why didn't Johnny warn me about this? Maybe he never expected the Southlanders to be so intense. "Don't I get an attorney or something?" I whisper.

Trimana snaps her tail against her chair and shoots me an angry look. She glances at one of the guards, who comes to my side and reaches into a pouch at his waist, pulling out what looks like a square-shaped piece of cellophane. He presses it against my mouth. It's sticky and gossamer thin, like a film of glue stretched permanently between my lips. I try to speak but no noise comes out, though I can still breathe through my mouth without any problem. Instinctively, I reach for my mouth to pull it off, but two guards grab me, each taking one of my arms. They bind my wrists with a rubbery cord. I try to wriggle out of it, but pulling at the cord only makes it tighten. I collapse back on the chair, waves of fear and exhaustion pulsing through my body. It takes all my effort to fight back tears.

"I'm terribly sorry," Checkers says. "You do seem to be in quite a bind, Madame Ambassador. I know it's no longer possible for you to give me commands verbally, which I'd guess is the way your, ah, hosts, want it, but I'll try to answer your last question and anticipate any other information that might be useful to you.

"I'm afraid you don't have a right to a legal advocate at the moment. The Hoshans have the right to hold you under their own system of law for at least one standard interstellar day, or approximately 37 hours, to determine if your actions warrant investigation by interstellar authorities.

There is no concept of attorneys in the Hoshan justice system, much of which centers on the use of telepathic interrogation."

The Hoshan woman stretches her neck, leaning toward me, making me wonder if the telepathic interrogation has already started.

"I also don't recommend attempting to escape," Checkers goes on. "Despite your advantage in size, your Hoshan guards are armed with weapons that could easily immobilize you. The good news is it's unlikely they'll kill you, though they could bring charges against you, which could result in the loss of your ambassadorship, or, at worst, detainment away from Earth for months. My best suggestion is that you cooperate. I'm terribly sorry I can't be of more help."

Months in prison far from Earth? They can't really do that, can they? I taste something sour in my mouth. It must be coming from the adhesive thing. I desperately want to gulp, to swallow back my fear—but the adhesive could be toxic, so I resist my urge to swallow.

Trimana glances up at the guards, and they all leave, a brief march of claws clicking on the floor. Then her bright red eyes fixate on mine. I meet her gaze with my boldest stare, trying to show with my eyes that I'm not afraid. But then, Trimana can see through that. She can see all my doubts.

I try to speak again, pointlessly. No sound comes out of my mouth. I can't even groan. I'm so hungry, so exhausted, I could easily fall asleep if not for the panic making my heart race. I again fight the urge to swallow as I realize I might never see Earth again. I think of Mami, of Timoteo and Miguel, of how much they need me, that I should never have left them alone only a few days after Uncle Umberto died.

Umberto. I still feel a sharp stab in my gut when my thoughts turn to him, like my stomach is a bowl full of knives. Can the Hoshans see how my grief is blowing me apart? The nerve of these Hoshans—what right do they have to steal any thought or feeling as they please?

Trimana cocks her head to one side, as if listening more closely, which only makes me feel more exposed. Steer your thoughts, Umberto said, but he didn't give me a clue how to do that. I stop myself—I shouldn't think about Umberto. More than anything I should steer my thoughts away from him, away from the message he left for me, away from the fact that I think he was murdered by someone trying to sabotage the peace talks.

Trimana lifts her whiskered nose and sits up in her chair, almost cat-like, looking at me expectantly.

This is impossible! It's like trying not to think of an elephant! The more you try to avoid the thought the larger the elephant looms in your mind.

I wish I could go home, or—better yet—back in time, to a time when Umberto was still alive, and when all I had to worry about was interpreting for my mother and the SATs and Desiree's not-speaking-to-me and whether maybe at some point Will would finally notice I want to be more than just a sounding board for all their problems.

There have been times when Will was all I could think about, and now I've barely thought of them in days. I wonder if they'd be impressed if they knew I've been to another planet and spoken to telepathic aliens and Synthetics.

Trimana half-smiles, her whiskers curling up as if amused, and my cheeks go red. They're watching my every thought, and here I'm thinking about the stupid feelings I've caught for Will!

How do Hoshans live like this, with their every thought on display? I try to imagine what it must be like for them, what my world would be like if everyone could hear everyone else's thoughts. Will would have known that I had a crush on them at the same time as I did, and I would have known right away whether they felt the same way. My friends would never have made fun of Desiree behind her back, because there'd be no such thing as doing anything behind anyone's back. You'd know that the man next to you on the bus was thinking about his problems at work or something, and he'd know you were thinking about your dead uncle, and you'd have no choice but to share those thoughts. Strangers wouldn't stay strangers for very long, in a world without privacy. Just like that autonomist said.

Trimana's tail slowly lifts from her chair, pointing upward.

If only they'd take this high-tech gag off. If only I could just have a normal conversation with Trimana. If only I could talk.

But I can talk. I am talking. To the Hoshans, thinking and talking are one and the same. All right then. I won't guard my thoughts. I'll share them.

I look at Trimana, whose eyes are still tethered on mine. I sit upright as much as I'm able in the bowl-shaped chair. *Hello*, I think. *My name is Val Vega and I'm the ambassador of Earth. I guess you know that already. You must have known Umberto, I mean, my predecessor, Ambassador Olmeda. He died suddenly—I guess you know he died suddenly—so, to be honest, I had to step into being ambassador without a lot of time to get up to speed.* I feel a pang of grief and then the urge to repress it, to place a wall around my feelings, but I resist that urge, determined to open myself up the way Hoshans must do routinely. *Umberto was my uncle. It hurts every time I think of him being gone. I want you to know I'm here because of him. Because I know he cared deeply about protecting the rights of the Hoshan people, and he asked me to carry on that work for him. And I know you must know that's sincere since you can sense everything I'm thinking, right?*

Trimana stares at me a moment, red eyes narrowing in the dark. Then she sits up and lifts four hands and begins to sign. "Pleased to make your acquaintance, Ambassador Vega," comes the translation. "I am Administrator Trimana of Southland Hosh, domain of the Levinti Scholocracy. What exactly were you doing, pursuing those insurgents with the warlord?"

It's a relief just to have something break the silence of the room. I open my mouth to speak, then remember I can only talk by thinking. *One of them was spying on us. After my meeting with the Levinti ambassador, Johnny saw her watching us from that building nearby—I guess she was watching our thoughts, or my thoughts and Pash-Ti's thoughts, anyway. She drove off in her pod, so we chased her. We didn't know the Hosh-Unam Front would ambush us.*

"Still," Trimana says, "why didn't you contact the local police right away?"

We did, I think, *or at least Johnny said he did.* It all happened so fast—I was following Johnny's lead, trusting him, hoping the Hoshan agent might have answers about Umberto's murder.

"I would beware trusting the Synthetic former warlord," Trimana signs. "It is suspicious, is it not, that a being as advanced as he was so easily disabled by primitive insurgents?"

That thought had crossed my mind but I'd dismissed it. *Are you saying he conspired with the Hosh-Unam Front to set up the ambush?*

Trimana spreads four arms wide, then interlaces them in a pretzel-like shape. "Anything is possible in these dark times," she said. "It would explain much, if he were conspiring with the Hosh-Unam Front. A Synthetic warlord's assistance could explain, for example, how their weaponry has advanced so rapidly this cycle."

Could Johnny really be an agent of the Hosh-Unam Front? Could he be the one who helped have Umberto killed?

"Any number of factions hope to see these talks fail," Trimana says. "Any of them might have had your familial killed. Perhaps our interrogation of the Synthetic will reveal more."

I can't stop myself from wondering where Trimana's allegiances are, if she could have been the one who had him killed.

She snaps her tail. "That thought is as baseless as it is preposterous! It was the Voice of the North and I who first petitioned for Ambassador Olmeda to mediate the talks. We knew well his commitment to Hosh and to peace, and we knew the Great Powers underestimated his skill. We thought him our best hope for negotiating a new treaty. His murder brought us closer to war, which is the one thing, above all else, that I hope to avoid."

Then we have that in common, I think, trying to move the conversation in a more positive direction. *All I want is to carry on my uncle's work and help Hosh remain at peace.*

"Then tell me," Trimana says, "exactly what happened when you encountered the insurgents."

I let the memories wash over me, of how they ambushed us, of Marrow's threats.

She signs with quick urgency. "Marrow himself?" she says. "You met the leader of the Hosh-Unam Front and allowed him to escape?"

I didn't know. And I didn't even have oxygen or anything, there was nothing I could do.

"What threats did Marrow make to you?"

He demanded to be part of the talks, I think. *As representative of the Hosh-Unam Front.*

"Again with this madness," Trimana says. "I should hope you told him the four-party structure of the talks must be maintained."

I try to choose my thoughts carefully, but you can't just choose thoughts the way you can choose words to speak. Marrow and his lieutenants ambushed me, but some of what he said made more sense than I expected. More than anything it left me frightened ... and confused.

Trimana snaps her tail against the chair, then makes a series of rapid signs. "Confused? That violent, anti-social militant left you confused? You really are a neophyte. The Etoscans and Levinti are each hungry to conquer all of Hosh for themselves. They're simply looking for an excuse to do so. The Hosh-Unam Front, with their absurd vision of a unified, independent Hosh, will undoubtedly give them that excuse the moment they sit down at the table. Five-party talks are a sure road to war. So I ask you, will you limit the talks to four parties, as Ambassador Olmeda did?"

Marrow claimed the opposite, that Umberto had promised him a place in the negotiations, but I can't imagine him working with a violent group like the Hosh-Unam Front. But in Umberto's message he did say I should talk to the peaceful autonomists—the Outlanders. Does Trimana know about them?

My thoughts are in dangerous territory. I shift back to how I want peace the same as Trimana does, but it's too late—her tail is pointing sharply up and she's signing a series of rapid, aggressive motions. "The Outlanders are eccentric hermits, less dangerous than the Hosh-Unam Front, but just as deluded. Their participation in the talks would jeopardize peace almost as much as the Hosh-Unam Front. Yes, I myself saw in Olmeda's thoughts an occasional idealistic flight of fancy for the Outlands to be formally recognized. But ultimately he knew the true prize is peace, and that the only path to peace is limiting the talks to four parties. I ask again, will you stand by his commitment?"

Everyone's telling me what Uncle Umberto was committed to, and I hate that I don't even know enough to know what's true. I want to build some trust with Trimana and wish I could stop my thoughts from taking us into these minefields. But I also don't want to make the same mistake I did with the Levinti, promising something I can't deliver. *What you're saying makes sense,* I think. *But I'm just figuring all this out—I know you can see that's true. Can you tell me more about what you want out of these talks?*

"The peaceful, prosperous future for Hosh," the administrator says. I focus all my attention on Trimana, on both her gestures and the translation. I listen intently the way I do with my friends, without judgment or criticism, all my mental energy devoted to putting myself in her shoes. "And the way to prosperity is through the Levinti Scholocracy. The Levinti have been generous—unlike the Etoscans—sharing their technology with us and fostering our own scientific progress. The new treaty must outline a path for Southland Hosh to become an independent member state of the Levinti Scholocracy. Only then will we be a fully recognized and equal participant in the interstellar community. Homecoming must be allowed, for the *children* of Legionnaires at least. And the Etoscan blockade of Tumasra must end so that we can scientifically, finally study the link between the graphotonic storm and telepathy." She pauses and looks at me, red eyes glowing in the dim room. "Where did you learn to do that?"

Do what? I think.

Trimana climbs down from the chair, padding toward me on four feet. "Have you been trained in mental conversation?"

I don't even know what that is, I think.

"When Hoshans listen, we quiet our minds and focus our own thoughts exclusively on the thoughts of the other person. It's called syncing. Otherwise we would all be talking at once. You were syncing with me just now. Where did you learn that?"

Nowhere. I mean, I was just trying to listen closely to you.

Trimana pads closer, her red eyes inches away. "I've never met a mind-deaf who could sync without training in thought-steering."

I've never even left Earth before today, I think. *I didn't even know Hosh existed until yesterday.*

Trimana's whiskers twitch. "I'm not certain if you're a well-meaning neophyte or an adept confederate. In either case, I've learned all I need, for now." The guards re-enter the room. One removes the cord from my wrists, and another points a small tube at my mouth that vacuums up the gag.

It's a relief to be unrestrained, even if my mouth feels like I just left the dentist. I shake out my arms and stretch my mouth. I have the urge to spit out the sour taste left behind by the gag, but resist it, because a gesture like that might come off as offensive.

Trimana holds up a small cube. "This is the petition requesting your prosecution for interfering with internal Southland Hoshan affairs. I would hate to be forced to file it. It would be unfortunate if you were to attempt to invite the Hosh-Unam Front—or the Outlanders—to participate in the talks, or if you were to renege on your promise to Doctor Ambassador Kantroponar to re-open discussion of access to Tumasra. Whether or not you are as innocent as you claim, Ambassador Vega, you'd be wise to heed me."

The guards lead me out the door. I feel a wave of relief that they're letting me go, that I'll get to see Earth and my family again—then a wave of dread as I realize I'm already getting threats and ultimatums from every direction on a world I barely know.

CHAPTER 10

THE HOSHAN GUARDS LEAD ME into a room lined with the low circular pads that Hoshans use as chairs. Apparently they contacted Pash-Ti to come pick me up, which is humiliating, like they're my parent coming to get me at the principal's office. Pash-Ti is squatting with all five long limbs contorted on top of a pad that's three sizes too small, like a spider that's too big for its own web. The Hoshans march away, leaving us alone.

Pash-Ti stands. They bend at the thorax, leaning into me, but I'm not sure if it's to avoid the low ceiling or to intimidate me with those long eyestalks. "Ambassador Vega, you are a primitive child on an alien world embedded in a complex interstellar conflict of which you have little knowledge and virtually no preparation. And yet you jumped upon that Synthetic's back to pursue a telepathic Hoshan spy of unknown allegiance, endangering not only yourself but the fragile détente that keeps these negotiations in motion."

I look down at my boots. "I was just—following Johnny's lead."

"Indeed," Pash-Ti says. "You have a talent for following the lead of others. If you must follow someone in the future, I advise against following that adolescent Synthetic."

"Where is Johnny?"

Pash-Ti lets out a few flat notes. "Still being held for questioning."

"Is he in danger?" I say.

Still bending, Pash-Ti walks toward the exit, like a crooked white tree in motion. "The situation is of his own creation, and he must find a way to un-create it. For the moment, we must focus on other concerns and return to Earth. As Ambassador, you're required to fulfill your local cultural obligations as much as possible."

I follow Pash-Ti. My stomach growls. It must nearly be morning on Earth. "Is it required for my mom not to kill me? Because she'll totally kill me if she realizes I've been out all night."

✧   ✧   ✧

I SLEEP MOST OF the Subway ride home. I'm still groggy when we get to Earth, and I board the underground gravity train from Istanbul to New Jersey. Wasala comes with me. As the bullet-shaped vessel free-falls through Earth, the sudden rush of gravity jolts me awake better than three cups of coffee. I can't believe it was only hours ago that I travelled the other way. I can't believe I went to another planet!

"What was it like?" Wasala says. "On Hosh?"

I'm almost getting used to telepathy. *I've never seen anything like it,* I think, trying to shift to the Hoshan way, where thinking is the same as talking. *It takes getting used to, everyone sensing everyone else's thoughts. They all talk about honesty and openness, but so many of them seem to be guarding secrets.*

"Well, yes," Wasala says. "That sort of hypocrisy is rampant in the South."

So you're from the North?

"I've never been to my homeworld," Wasala says. The bullet slows. "Yes, we're at the halfway point, decelerating now. But, yes, my parents were from the North and volunteered for the Etoscans' telepathic Legion. I grew up off-world, on a base for Legionnaires and their families. All my life, Hosh has been like a mythic place, a place I only see through other people's minds."

Because there's no right to homecoming, I think. *Once a Legionnaire volunteers, they can never come home, and neither can their descendants. Did you sign up for the Legion like your parents?* I try not to focus on Wasala growing up in a family of spies.

"Spies makes it sound so dramatic, dearie! I wanted to but wasn't eligible." Sensing my next question, she goes on, "I'm telepathically nearsighted. Most Hoshans sense thoughts within 50 feet or so, but my range is only ten feet. A genetic disability. And since no one understands how telepathy works, there's no way to treat it."

I'm sorry, I think. *That must be hard.*

"So it is," she says. "Growing up on the base, with children of other Hoshan Legionnaires—it's hard to fit in when you can't hear conversations more than a few feet away. My North Hoshan name by birth was Wise Seer, but that only give the other children one more way to mock me, so I just go by Wasala."

I guess it's not just Earth kids who can be cruel. *But you don't have to see far to see wisely*, I think.

"You're kinder than most," Wasala says. "But since I couldn't join the Legions, there weren't a lot of options. So I volunteered for the interstellar diplomatic corps, thinking I could contribute something. But I ended up being assigned to Earth. Such an insult. Even the Interstellar Council didn't take me seriously because of my disability."

Is Earth so bad?

"No offense, dearie," Wasala says, "but Earth is an assignment you get when no one else will take you."

If you could, I think, *would you go back to Hosh?*

"Sometimes all my thoughts flow toward that," Wasala says. "It would probably be an adjustment, but my life now is so isolating, spending all my time with the mind-deaf. It's exhausting having to articulate all my thoughts with words. But homecoming is far from reach. It's one of the few things the Etoscans and Levinti agree on, because they both want their telepathic legions intact. Even Umberto couldn't get them to give any ground. It would take something cataclysmic for homecoming to be a reality."

If Wasala is so sympathetic to the North, could she be working with the Etoscans? Even with the limited range of Wasala's telepathy, she could easily have sensed whatever secrets Umberto uncovered.

Wasala makes a series of sharp clicks as the bullet coasts to a halt. "I may hold dear the values of the Etoscan Fellowship, but I know they're far from perfect. I'd never do anything to endanger my people's homeworld, and I'd never betray Umberto."

"It was just a thought," I say. "I'm sorry." But I can't help but wonder where Wasala was the night Umberto died, if she has an alibi.

Wasala hops out of the bullet, landing on all six legs. "I was at the Terran embassy, with Pash-Ti, on the other side of the planet. Johnny was the only one of us in New Jersey."

Does that make Johnny the most likely suspect? Maybe Trimana's right, it was way too convenient the way he led me right to the Hosh-Unam Front and then got knocked out. Could Johnny be secretly working for the Hosh-Unam Front?

"It's possible, though that would surprise me. I can't see Johnny's thoughts, but he's been a pacifist as long as I've known him." She reaches up to place a paw on my arm. "I understand your suspicions, Val, I do. Before he died, I saw in Umberto's thoughts that he was worried someone was spying on him. But I can't imagine Johnny or Pash-Ti killing him. We don't know for certain it was one of us. I've done my best to keep the safeguards on our Interstellar Subway station up to date, but interstellar software is ever evolving. It may be that someone found a way to get past them, and sent a nanosassin directly from Hosh."

Is there a way to check for that? I think.

"I've been poring over the logs every day, searching for a clue, but I've found nothing." Wasala stands on her hindmost legs to her full height. "But I shall redouble my efforts, Valiant One."

"Thanks," I say. I turn on my phone. Shoot, it's 7:40 a.m. I don't even have time to stop at home—I've got to go straight to school.

"Go!" Wasala says. "Your Terran duties matter too!"

I race out of the office, feeling whiplash at jumping back into my ordinary life after being in outer-frigging-space.

My phone rings—Mami, of course. How many times has she tried to call while I've been out of range? *Way* out of range.

"Hi, Mami," I answer, walking briskly to the rack where my bike is locked, trying to think of an excuse for where I've been.

"Valeria!" says Mami. "Gracias a Dios. I've been trying to call for half an hour."

Only half an hour? That means she didn't notice I was gone until this morning—for once, I'm in luck. "Lo siento, Mami. I went to school early to do homework at the library. And you know the reception's bad there, so I haven't had a signal."

"Bueno," Mami says. "Next time, text me. I can't cope with you disappearing on me. Not after everything that's happened."

"Sí, Mami." I tuck the phone back in my bag, feeling guilty for lying. As I bend over to unlock my bike, my head swims through another wave of exhaustion. "Ugh, if only I could shower!" I mutter. Five minutes of showering equals like five hours of sleep.

"A shower of sorts can be arranged, Madame Ambassador," comes Checkers' unexpected voice. "And your clothes could be laundered as well. Would you like me to do so?"

I toss my kryptonite lock into the bike basket. "Um, do I have to get undressed?"

"No, madam," Checkers says. "It'll only take a few moments."

"Um, sure, then, hit me." All across my skin, I feel a touch of cool dampness, as if my entire body is falling into a drop of dew. My hair and clothes are suddenly heavy with water. Then, just as quickly, comes a subtle warmth, like a cup of hot cocoa warming me up from the inside out. My hair, clothes, and skin are all dry in seconds. "Wow, thanks, Checkers. That was really refreshing."

"At your service, Madame," Checkers says. I hop on my bike and race to school.

I get to school with ten minutes to spare before the bell. I open my locker and realize half my books are at home. Lockers, books made out of paper—suddenly it all seems so inefficient, so ... primitive!

Desiree walks up and leans against the lockers. "You okay, chica? You look tired."

"Yeah," I say. "Been having trouble sleeping."

She rubs my shoulder. "I'll bet. But your outfit's cute. Maybe I can distract you with something completely different? There's something I've been wanting to talk to you about. It's a big deal and you were, like, the first one I wanted to tell, but I didn't because—"

"Because," I say, taking the few books I have out of my locker, "you were understandably mad and not speaking to me."

"Well, yeah," Des says. "But now we're all good, and I, like, need to talk to my bestie."

"The bestie is at your service," I say, but in the back of my mind I'm worried I know where this is going.

"So, I've been hanging out with Will a lot," Des says. Shoot, I definitely know where this is going. "And they're just so sweet, and so creative. And cute. And it's like, how have I not noticed this before? I like them. I like them like them." Des pauses. "Well?

"That's ... great," I say, closing the door of my locker, avoiding eye contact. Des isn't trying to be hurtful. She has no idea how I feel about Will. I've never had a chance to tell her about my crush either—we haven't been speaking for weeks. I'm definitely not telling her now, not when we're finally getting to be friends again. "I mean," I eek out, "we've all been friends forever, and you're both great, so obviously that's great."

"Well, yeah, that's why I'm asking you. Have they said anything about me?"

Des chews a few strands of hair, her eyes wide with eagerness. Why did we both have to suddenly realize how amazing Will is at the same time? But I can't disappoint her again, and it's not like I'll ever have a chance with Will. Trying to stop them from getting together now would be like trying to fight gravity. "I may know certain information I've sworn to keep confidential. So let's just say I think you should have a conversation with Will. And I have a feeling you and Will are both going to be very happy after that conversation."

"OMG, yay!" Des wraps her arms around me.

I hug Des back, hoping the gash in my heart isn't reaching my face.

Kate comes up to us mid-hug. "Hey. What's with the lovefest?"

Des bounces up and down, pitter-patter clapping her hands. "Val says Will likes me too!"

"Actually, I only heavily implied it."

"Are you really okay with it?" Des says to Kate. "Even though you two went out?"

"Girl, you can have him—them," Kate says. "I was the breaker-upper, remember? They're sweet, but I need someone more ambitious."

"You're ridiculous," Des says. "Maybe I can find Will before the bell. We should hang out this weekend—all four of us. It's been forever since we did that." Won't that be fun, watching Des and Will be cutesy with each other. Des walks away immersed in her phone, her attention shifted to her search for Will. "See you two at practice."

"So what's the special occasion?" Kate gestures at my silver jacket and checkered cap.

Oh, this is just my space ambassador outfit. For a sec, I worry I'm not steering my thoughts, then am relieved I'm not surrounded by Hoshans. "Just trying a new look. My uncle gave me the cap."

"Oh." Kate looks down. "So how are you ... I mean, did you end up doing the internship at his NGO? That seemed like a cool opportunity."

I'm not sure which is more annoying: people being overly sympathetic about my grief, or people like Kate who are totally clueless about it. "Yeah, I did. It's just something to do. But I don't really want to talk about it ... or my uncle."

"That's cool," Kate says. We stand awkwardly for a few seconds, both burying ourselves in our phones. Then Kate looks up and says, "I guess Des and Will are finally getting together. It's funny you told her the Will thing is mutual. You never did that for me."

"That was like a year ago," I say. "You and Will both made me swear not to tell anyone about your crushes, and I've apologized like a million times."

"Oh, come on, Val. Everyone knows there's an implicit exception if the object of a crush confesses to also having a crush on the holder of said crush. It's the same as with Des and the personality counting. You're always so passive, I can't believe you ever get anything done."

Pash-Ti and my interstellar profile would agree with her. Maybe that's why Kate and I have never really gotten close. I'm adaptable to the point of passivity, Kate is proactive to the point of insensitivity. "I'm definitely a work in progress," I say. The first bell rings. "Shoot, is it an A, B, or C-day?"

"B-day," Kate says, as we walk briskly down the hall together. "Ergo, I have history, you have study hall, and after that we both have trig. Ready for the test?"

I try to rub the sleep from my eyes. "Test?"

"Law of cosines and what-not. You forgot?"

"I've had a lot on my mind."

Will and Des are getting together. Aliens are on the verge of war. My uncle is gone forever. And there's no one I can even talk to. There must be some trigonometric formula for all the triangles of tension intersecting across my back.

✦ ✦ ✦

IN STUDY HALL, I open the chapter on sines and cosines, but my thoughts keep turning back to Hosh, to who killed tío Umberto. I fiddle with Checkers, mouthing some commands to him with my hand over my mouth. He sets up a holographic interface that layers on top of my trig textbook—with a privacy screen so no one else can see.

Checkers is amazing—he's got access to Wiki Galactica, the Terran embassy logs, tons of interstellar documents. First I check the embassy logs, which confirm that Wasala and Pash-Ti were at the embassy in Istanbul, and Johnny was in the New Jersey consulate, barely a mile away from our house. He was the closest to the crime—and Trimana was suspicious of him too.

As I start reading Johnny's file, a text from Will shows up on my holographic display: "OMG Des likes me too!!! First date tonight! All thanks to you! U R THE BEST, VAL!"

My stomach lurches. Will's just texting me because I'm their best friend, but it still feels like a rejection. I push down the feelings. I am *not* going to be that person crying in study hall.

If I can figure out what happened to Umberto, nothing else matters. I go back to Johnny's file. Johnny really was designed for war. The Synthetics basically think they're above interstellar politics. But like a thousand years ago, they got drawn into a conflict they didn't want to bother with, so they designed Johnny and a whole generation of "warlords" to beat down their opponents. At some point, Johnny became aware of the destruction he was causing and basically became a conscientious objector. He was cast out from Synthetic society and has been an eccentric Synthetic warlord-in-recovery ever since.

Wasala said he's a pacifist too. But his file also says he's sympathetic to autonomist movements on primitive worlds—like the Hosh-Unam Front. If he's really so advanced, how did the Hosh-Unam Front overpower him so easily? Was he really just unprepared—or was the whole thing a set-up? He delivered me right to Marrow, and then Johnny was conveniently knocked out for just enough time for Marrow to attack and threaten me.

Could Johnny be providing the Hosh-Unam Front with weapons so they can push out the Levinti and Etoscans? Could he do that single-handedly? Would he really be okay with that kind of violence? Could he really have killed Umberto?

My reading gets interrupted by a text from Desiree with dozens of happy emojis about her hang with Will tonight. My stomach does another somersault. It probably doesn't help that all I had for breakfast was a granola bar. How are they even sneaking these texts past their teachers without a secret interstellar hologram-projecting thing? I just can't handle this right now, so I have Checkers disconnect the hologram from my phone.

Wasala and Pash-Ti's files are much shorter. Wasala's just confirms everything she told me. If she's sympathetic to the Etoscans, could she secretly be helping them? But wouldn't she want to protect her planet from war?

Pash-Ti's species has multiple genders or roles, like Wasala said. Apparently Pash-Ti rejected their assigned role of caregiver, which resulted in Pash-Ti being cast out from their people. That means all three of the aliens working in the Terran embassy are basically outcasts or exiles. I guess Earth really is an assignment you get when no other place will take you.

Despite Pash-Ti's outcast status, they've had a long career in interstellar diplomacy—including attaining a degree at the Levinti Scholocracy's academy of diplomatic administration. Whenever Pash-Ti talks about the negotiations, they seem way more sympathetic to the Levinti. Could Pash-Ti be a Levinti agent undercover?

Nothing in their public files is obviously incriminating, but it does confirm one thing. Each of them is sympathetic with one of the three factions that's working for war. So if I figure out who the spy was working for, maybe I'll know who the spy *is*.

I can't believe I helped Will and Des get together.

✧ ✧ ✧

AFTER A HORRIBLE DAY of failing the trig test and falling asleep in history, I text coach that I can't make practice again and bike straight to the New Jersey office of the Terran embassy. No one else is there—Checkers says Pash-Ti and Wasala are in Istanbul, and Johnny's still detained on Hosh. I search all their offices. The corner of Wasala's office has a cushion and an altar with icons of Hoshans and aliens that look like elephants—Etoscans, I guess. She's definitely sympathetic with them. Pash-Ti's office is so immaculate it's sterile.

As I finish rifling through Pash-Ti's office, I get a text from Kate. "Where r u? U r team CAPTAIN, not cool 2 miss practice EVERY day."

Um, my uncle died, I'm dealing with an interstellar crisis, and trying to solve his murder, but, what*ever*, Kate.

Johnny's office has a high-quality Terran speaker system and, weirdly, a collection of Terran toys like Legos and Hot Wheels cars. I guess he really is a Terra-phile. But then, in a drawer under the shelves, I find a map—an old-school paper map of Hosh. Why would a Synthetic even need a paper map? With help from Checkers, I figure out it's a map of sites of known activity of the Hosh-Unam Front—including one near Tumasra in the North, and another beneath the Southland capital—where we just got attacked by them. That means Johnny knew we were heading into Hosh-Unam Front territory. Maybe Trimana is right and Johnny set me up. He suddenly seems like the most likely suspect. I use my phone to take a photo of the map and put it back exactly how I found it.

I scour Umberto's office last, hoping he left me some sort of clue, maybe something in code only I could understand. But I can't find anything. I wish he were still here, that he'd left me with more information, more hints, more—anything!

Then it occurs to me—if tío Umberto were to leave me a clue, he wouldn't have left it here, where Pash-Ti or Johnny or Wasala could easily find it. It would be much safer to leave it at home.

Luckily, no one is home when I get there. Mami's still working, Miguel has rehearsal, and Timoteo's probably at the library. I slip into Umberto's room. My brothers and I cleaned it up pretty well, but that was before I knew about all the interstellar stuff, so maybe I missed something. Mami even re-made his bed after they took away his body. The room is eerily tidy in its emptiness. Timoteo could easily sleep here, but he's been crashing on the couch. It's like we're all secretly hoping tío Umberto still might come back to it.

There's nothing in the desk other than a bunch of office supplies and his collection of coquí figurines. Umberto didn't have a tablet or use his laptop much. Probably because he was using a suit like Checkers for all that stuff. He did scribble notes to himself—in a tiny black notebook he used to carry around everywhere. But it's not anywhere in his desk.

I go into his closet and check his jackets. I find it in the inside pocket of his favorite purple blazer. My hands tremble as I thumb through the pages. His handwriting's atrocious, but I can make out most of the words—notes on everyone involved in the talks: the Levinti, the Etoscans, the Hosh-Unam Front.

On the last page, it says "Beneath Tumasra—impenetrable to scans. Could Ferus help?" in big letters. Tío talked about Ferus in his holographic message. He said to find Ferus and the Outlanders. It sounded like Ferus might be the only person I can trust. God, do I need someone I can trust.

I wipe my eyes to stop my tears from landing on the pages. I don't want to damage a single page of this treasure trove of Umberto's words.

"Checkers," I say, "pull up everything you have on the Hoshan named Ferus—and on Tumasra."

"I'll happily do so, Madame Ambassador," says Checkers, with an oddly wary tone. "First, however, you might direct your attention to the visitor just outside the window."

Outside the window, a squirrel is perched on the sill, looking right at me.

"That is no ordinary Terran squirrel," Checkers says. "It is a biosynthetic construct built by a primitive artificial intelligence."

The squirrel presses a paw against the glass, like it wants in. "Is it dangerous?" I say, though its posture seems friendly.

"It has no weaponry, other than its claws," Checkers says. "It says it has a message for the Ambassador of Earth."

Just in case, I pull out my phone and open "Set to Stun." If this thing could neutralize Johnny, it's got to be able to take out this squirrel-bot. I push up the window, my phone pointed at the squirrel.

The squirrel bounces into the room and onto Umberto's bed. Its eyes glow, projecting a hologram of a neatly trimmed Hoshan male. "Ambassador Vega, I pray to Synchronus this message reaches you," the hologram says. "I am Ferus of the Outlanders. I failed to help your familial in time, but I shall not fail again. I have attained the sample the Bright Warrior sought before his tragic demise. It is … most unusual. You must meet me in the safe haven of the Outlands so that I can give it to you, and share all I have learned with you. Umberto's notes will guide your way. Tell no one else in the Terran embassy of the sample, or of this communication. Your familial's suspicions were well-founded. Something illicit is hidden beneath Tumasra. Trust no one. Come soon, and come alone."

CHAPTER 11

> ENERGY SURGE NEAR TUMASRA from
> "unidentified source" — confirms my theory —
> and worst fears. Changes everything.
> But need proof!

- From the notebook of Umberto Olmeda

I STAY UP FOR HOURS re-watching Ferus's message and poring over Umberto's notebook and Wiki Galactica, trying to piece things together. So far I've figured out two things: (1) there was a suspicious quantum energy surge near Tumasra a few months ago, which convinced Umberto something was hidden beneath the storm; and (2) Umberto asked Ferus to get a sample from somewhere near the source of the energy surge. I guess Ferus finally did.

I find a map to the Outlands in Umberto's notebook, though it's super vague—on purpose, I guess, since they're in hiding. But even if I figure out how to get to the Outlands, how do I sneak away from Pash-Ti? And how am I supposed to commandeer a pod for myself?

I wake up in the morning still clutching tío Umberto's notebook.

It's another horrible day at school. I skip softball practice again, partly because Will is coming to cheer Des on and their cutesiness on Day Two of their relationship is already making me grind my teeth.

But mostly it's just that figuring out what happened to Umberto is way more important.

I take the gravity express to the Terran embassy in Istanbul. I watch the full orientation holo, which is actually super-useful. Then Pash-Ti and Wasala give me more background on Northern Hosh and the Etoscans, which is even more useful. But then my mind starts wandering to Ferus and the Outlanders, and Wasala wrinkles her snout at me, which reminds me how Ferus said I can't trust anyone and I still have no idea how the thought-steering thing works. I rush home for dinner before my thoughts give anything away to Wasala, especially about Ferus.

After dinner, I lie on the couch staring at the ceiling. All I can think about is Hosh and the secret that got Umberto killed. I wish I could get help from Wasala, or Pash-Ti, or Johnny if he were around. But one of them murdered my uncle. I can't trust them, and I'm facing a problem so titanic I can barely wrap my brain around it. I wish I could just talk through this with someone, like I used to with tío Umberto. My whole body aches to live in an alternate timeline where he mentored me before he died.

My cascade of thoughts is interrupted by a flurry of loud typing from the kitchen. I poke my head in. Timoteo is typing on his laptop at his usual hundreds of words per minute.

"Whatcha doing?" I say.

The cacophony of key-tapping stops for a second, though Timoteo doesn't look up from the screen. "Memo for negotiation class. Recommendations to the Secretary of State for facilitating multi-party talks in the Korean peninsula." His fingers return to their flurry.

"Oh." I walk back to the living room. An idea's coming to me. "Hey, Checkers?" I whisper. "Pash-Ti said I couldn't tell anyone about all the interstellar stuff, but then Johnny said something about an exception for Terran staff working for the embassy. Is that right?"

"That's correct, Madame Ambassador," Checkers says. "On primitive worlds, as many as three indigenous staff may be appointed by the ambassador."

"So I could appoint someone, like Timoteo, to be on the embassy staff?"

"Yes," Checkers says. "So long as the appointees received qualifying scores on the xenoreactive test. Timoteo has taken the test and qualified."

"Thanks, Checkers."

I go back into the kitchen. "Hey, Tim-Tim? Could you come into the living room a sec? I need to talk to you about something."

With a sigh, Timoteo picks up his laptop and walks into the living room, then sits down on the couch with the computer beside him.

I sit in the chair by the couch. "There's something important I have to tell you."

"Okay," Timoteo says, scrunched over his laptop, again typing furiously.

"This is important. Don't multi-task me."

"Fine." Timoteo types a few more words. "Okay. You have my undivided attention."

"Um, I'm not sure where to start."

"Please tell me this isn't a coming-out moment," Timoteo says. "Because, really, our family is way past its queer quota. And I just assumed you're pansexual or metasexual or whatever you kids are saying these days."

Timoteo can be so condescending, and so limited in how he thinks. I hope this is the right thing to do. "It's not that," I say. "Just listen for a second. Um, I've been to outer space."

After a few moments of silence, Timoteo says, "Is 'outer space' some new expression that means you've like been rolling on Molly or something? Please tell me you're not doing meth. Occasional light drugs are fine, but meth is seriously dangerous."

"No," I say, "Outer space, like another planet, in a totally different solar system."

"Okay," Timoteo chuckles, and puts his laptop back on his lap.

"You don't believe me."

Timoteo squints at the screen. "Well, you seem a bit geocentric for an interstellar traveler."

I sigh. Now I understand why Johnny and Wasala got impatient when they first told me about everything. I didn't even take that conversation seriously until Johnny made the holo-bubble. Too bad I don't have Johnny's powers—though I do have ... "Checkers?" I say.

"Checkers?" Timoteo says. "What's up with you? Checkers is boring. And I always win."

"Float me up to the ceiling," I tell Checkers.

"At your service, Madame Ambassador," Checkers replies.

I levitate in our living room, my feet hanging just above Timoteo's head. I might as well do this with a little flare. "The Earth is part of an interstellar federation, and for years, tío Umberto was our secret ambassador, and now I've taken his place. And I need your help."

Timoteo grabs the couch with both hands as if he needs it for support. "Okay," he says. "Now you really have my undivided attention, Val-Val."

✧   ✧   ✧

TIMOTEO LEANS OVER from the couch, strumming his fingers on the coffee table.

"Are you in shock?" I ask.

"No, in a weird way it makes sense. There's just one thing I don't understand." Timoteo takes off his glasses and rubs his eyes with a thumb and forefinger. "Why are *you* the ambassador of Earth?"

"What do you mean?"

"Come on, Val-Val," Timoteo says. "You know what I mean."

"No, I really think I don't, Tim-Tim."

Timoteo interlaces his fingers and speaks in his gentle yet super-annoying mansplainy voice. "Look, everyone knows you're smart. But if you were to conduct a poll asking who in our family was most likely to be an interstellar ambassador, a significant majority would say me."

My skin tenses with anger. I stand up. "Could you try to not be the most patronizing big brother in the world?"

"I'm not patronizing you," Timoteo says. "I'm just saying I'm the one with more of ... an ambassador profile! Why would you get to be the ambassador instead of me?"

My words come racing out. "I'll tell you why. Remember that thing tío Umberto had us all do around when we turned 15? He said it was a psychology test, and you had to sit in a chair, and it was like virtual reality, and there was this maze with all these non-humanoid creatures?"

"That gave me nightmares for weeks," Timoteo says.

"Well, that was the test for potential ambassadors," I say. "To see how we react to the weird and unexpected. And guess what, Mr. Perfect SATs, I did better than you! *That's* why I'm ambassador of Earth."

Timoteo stares down at the coffee table. "I thought I did well on that test," he mutters. "Tío Umberto didn't think I could do it?"

Behind Timoteo's glasses, there are seeds of tears in his eyes. The volume of my anger goes down. I've had such a tangle of feelings these past few weeks as I realized all the things Umberto never told me. Timoteo's dealing with all that now. At least Umberto left me that holographic message. At least I know for sure he wanted me to know all these secrets, eventually. Timoteo doesn't even have that. I sit back down next to him on the couch and wrap my arm around him. "I'm sure Umberto knew you would've been a great ambassador. When Johnny and Wasala told me about everything, the first thing I said was that it should be you."

"That's sweet of you," Timoteo says, wiping away his tears. He flashes a self-conscious smile. "By the way, Johnny is so hot. So, what is he, like, an alien reptile?"

"No, he's Synthetic," I say, "and, like, hundreds of years older than you."

"That makes him even hotter," Timoteo says. "Patrece and Wasala, they're aliens too?"

"Yup," I say. "Patrece's real name is Pash-Ti, and they're actually nonbinary. They're basically a giant grumpy stick bug. Wasala's furry and reads minds. And, listen, there's something else I have to tell you. Tío Umberto left me this message. One of them was spying on him— Johnny, Pash-Ti, or Wasala. One of them probably killed him, or at least helped kill him."

"Killed?" Timoteo says. I nod, and Timoteo sucks in a deep breath, as if he's hoping to find courage in the air.

"So we can't trust any of them. That's why I need your help. I need someone who's smart and who I can trust and who can help me figure all this out. I need you, big brother."

Timoteo hugs me tight. "A la orden, Madame Ambassador."

✦ ✦ ✦

TIMOTEO STARES at the row of cubicles. "This is the interstellar embassy?"

"Not exactly," I say. "This is sort of the New Jersey consulate."

"I was expecting something more ... sparkly."

I laugh. "I know. But wait till you see the gravity express and the Interstellar Subway."

Wasala comes out from the inner office, in her true form, walking on all six legs. Timoteo jumps back and shouts, "Ay Dios mío!"

Wasala stands up on her hind legs and lifts her snout in indignation. "I look nothing like a Terran rodent! Can't you see how well-groomed I am?"

Timoteo touches his palm to his chest and lets out a breath. "Wasala. You must be Wasala. I'm sorry. You look lovely, really."

Wasala snorts. She drops to her two hindmost pairs of legs and walks toward us. "So you've deputized your brother. You all sure like to keep it in the family. Pash-Ti is not going to be happy. But come along, Timoteo, the giant rat needs to get you suited up."

Timoteo and I follow Wasala, and she sets him up with a suit just like Checkers, which Timoteo names Majel in some obscure *Star Trek* reference. As soon as it's set up, Timoteo's eyes dart from side to side, looking *at* his glasses instead of through them. "This is awesome!" he says "I can make this thing do anything with just a glance!"

That's weird. Mine doesn't do that.

Wasala's left set of whiskers point up. "Should have gone with the eye-mouse, dearie." She flashes Timoteo a knowing look, and then looks up at me. "So, you even told your brother not to trust me."

Timoteo's gaze shifts from his lenses to me. "Sorry. I guess I'm not very good at thought-steering."

"That's all right," Wasala says. "It's true enough you have to be careful. We're in dangerous waters, all of us."

Pash-Ti enters from the stairway to the basement, eyestalks extending toward Timoteo. "Madame Ambassador, must you flagrantly disobey every directive you're given? It's strictly forbidden to reveal the presence of advanced aliens to primitives outside the embassy."

"Um, hi," Timoteo says, saluting Pash-Ti with an awkward wave. "I like your ... skin. It's grey. I mean, it's nice."

I stride over to Pash-Ti and look right up at them. "I haven't violated interstellar protocol. Timoteo is part of the embassy now. I've appointed him as my political advisor."

Pash-Ti's lanky frame looms over me. "Appointments to the embassy staff are made by the ambassador but must also be approved by the observer."

"Well?" I don't let my gaze stray from Pash-Ti's unblinking eyestalks. "Are you going to overrule me? According to interstellar protocol, the ambassador and the observer are supposed to work in cooperation, aren't they?"

"Indeed," Pash-Ti replies. "Which is why you should have consulted me first. However, Timoteo Vega did receive a qualifying xenoreactive score and has been listed for some time as a potential appointment to the embassy. I see no need to overrule you in this case. It would only divert crucial time and resources in the midst of a crisis. Has Mr. Vega been oriented?"

"Val covered a bunch of the basics," Timoteo says. "And I'm getting all kinds of helpful information from my awesome new suit."

"Then we should proceed with our preparations for our meeting with the Etoscans," Pash-Ti says, and leads us into the small conference room.

Timoteo and I sit in standard Terran office chairs, and Pash-Ti sits at their usual stool, allowing all three long legs to hang over the sides. Wasala curls herself up on a circular Hoshan chair.

"So," Pash-Ti says, "now that we've reviewed the basic background on the Etoscans, we need to discuss challenges likely to arise at this meeting. In particular, I remain concerned that the Etoscans will balk that the ambassador has imprudently reopened the subject of opening Tumasra to Levinti researchers."

I really hope I didn't mess that up as badly as Pash-Ti says.

"So what's the BATNA for each of these stakeholders?" Timoteo says.

Pash-Ti interlaces their long fingers and turns to Timoteo. "My translator is having difficulty with one of the morphemes in that utterance. Please explain."

"BATNA," Timoteo says. "Best Alternative to a Negotiated Agreement. The most important thing in any negotiation. If the negotiation fails, then what else can they do?"

"BATNA," Pash-Ti says. "A blunt but potentially useful tool of analysis. The BATNA, as you say, for the Levinti and the Etoscans is the same: violent conflict for control of Hosh."

"And if it came to that, who would win?" Timoteo asks.

Wasala stretches her torso up from her chair. "They're fairly evenly matched, in military power. But the Levinti have the stronger position. Both have Subway stations on Hosh-Tor, the nearby gas giant, but only the Levinti have a station on Hosh itself. I fear that gives them a major tactical advantage in terms of the transport line for swarms, weapons, and other supplies."

"Couldn't the Etoscans just build another station of their own?" Timoteo asks.

"That takes years," I say, remembering my conversation with Johnny. "So most planets only have one or two of them."

"And they could not build a new station without approval of the Interstellar Transit Authority," Pash-Ti says, "which tightly regulates the construction and control of all Interstellar Subway stations. It is the most powerful of any interstellar body—the only one the Great Powers have any deference for. The smooth and relatively peaceful functioning of a coordinated interstellar transit system is the foundation of the Galactic order, fragile as it may be."

"So the Levinti have the best BATNA," Timoteo says. "So we'd expect them to drive the hardest bargain, because there's no reason they can't walk, er, float away from the table."

"The Levinti do seem like they're playing hardball," I say.

"True," Pash-Ti says. "However, throughout the course of negotiations, the Etoscans have often proved just as uncompromising."

"But they must know they have the weaker hand," Timoteo says.

"They certainly seem overconfident," Pash-Ti says, "However, interstellar actors do not always behave rationally. There are militant factions among the Etoscans eager to see war renewed with the Levinti, regardless of the cost. As is true among the Levinti—who might prevail in the end thanks to the tactical advantage of their Subway station, but only after significant losses."

Timoteo strums his fingers on the table. "So if they're all so trigger-happy, why haven't they gone to war already?"

"Until the treaty expires, the war will not be a legal one." Pash-Ti says. "The Great Powers always prefer to make wars that are justified in the eyes of interstellar law. Both the Levinti and the Etoscans have a vested interest in the maintenance of a positive image in the interstellar community—particularly among the other Great Powers. Ideally, each would prefer for the failure of the negotiations to appear to be the fault of the other."

"Which is the only way we can shame them into keeping the talks going," I say.

"Indeed," Pash-Ti says. "Which is why in this meeting, we must tread carefully in responding to any demands the Etoscans make. You must express openness, but never make explicit commitments."

Timoteo nods, reading something on his glasses. "That's diplomacy."

The conversation goes on for over two hours. Timoteo asks a lot of questions and uses lots of negotiation concepts from school. He gets along with Pash-Ti more easily than I do, which makes me wonder if Umberto really should have chosen him instead of me, but I push that thought aside. It's a relief to have someone I trust in the room. I love Timoteo's geeky smarts when they're on my side.

✦ ✦ ✦

IN THE NEXT FEW DAYS, I fall into a new routine. In the morning, I bike to school, then softball practice after school. From there I go to the interstellar consulate, where I strategize with Pash-Ti, Wasala, Johnny, and Timoteo. Some days I skip softball practice and go straight to the consulate. I spend less time with my friends—even Will. Nothing is as important as Hosh. At night, it's back home for dinner with the fam, followed by long talks late into the night with Timoteo. He brought his sleeping bag into my room and told Mami the floor was better for his back than the soft cushions of the couch. It gives us an excuse for time alone every night.

Timoteo is useful in more ways than one. His cover story is that he's working with Umberto's NGO as the capstone project for his poli-sci major. Having Timoteo come to the office with me helps assuage Mami's worries about the locos from Umberto's office. She even agreed to let us take two more trips to "Istanbul:" one for the next round of meetings, and one for the official negotiations on Hosh—the latter of which luckily coincides with spring break.

The night before we leave for Hosh, Timoteo and I sit on my bed talking, looking through Umberto's notebook together. Timoteo thumbs through it the same way as I always do, like every page is a treasure. "I think you're right this thing about the quantum energy surge near Tumasra is important. The Tumasra storm creates all sorts of interference from scanners—so you could hide almost anything underneath it. That must be what Umberto was suspicious of."

"Johnny's map of Hosh-Unam Front activity," I say. "One of the locations was right by the energy surge near Tumasra. Maybe the Front is building a base there. And maybe Johnny's helping them get new technology, more advanced weapons for a deadlier attack. Maybe them ambushing me was all a set-up. Maybe the Southern Hoshans are still holding him because they suspect the same thing."

Timoteo shakes his head. "That's a little off. If Johnny and the Hosh-Unam Front are the culprits, why didn't Umberto just expose them, even without much evidence? The Front are outlaw insurgents and Johnny's an exile—neither have any interstellar clout. If Umberto needed proof for his theory, the realities of interstellar power dynamics mean one of the Great Powers was involved. The simplest explanation is that the Etoscans are secretly building up a storehouse of weapons— probably some weapons outlawed by interstellar law. They're trying to make up for the Levinti's tactical advantage if it comes to war."

"If that's true, then Wasala's the most likely agent," I say, "since she's the one most sympathetic with the Etoscans. We have to keep our distance from her before we leave tomorrow. But Umberto's message said he was suspicious of all three. It could be any of them."

Timoteo puts the notebook down. "We do need more data."

"Exactly," I say. "That's why, after our meetings on Hosh tomorrow, we need to find a way to the Outlands and find Ferus. He got a sample from whatever caused that surge. That could be the key to all this."

Timoteo is reading the inside of his glasses. "I'm not sure about this Ferus guy. It says here he's a wanted criminal."

"Well, all the Outlanders are," I say. "Anyone who resists colonization is a criminal in the eyes of the Etoscans and Levinti."

"It's not just that," Timoteo says. "This says he used to be in the Hosh-Unam Front! That he's a murderer!"

I read that too, but thought it had to be wrong. "I know, but there must be more to the story."

Timoteo pushes his glasses up. "More to the *killer* story? You're way too trusting, Val."

I flex my fingers, annoyed at his patronizing tone. "Don't believe everything you read in Wiki Galactica. "

"Sometimes you go way too far with the both-sidesism, Val."

"The Etoscans and Levinti are doing everything they can to repress the autonomists," I say, "even the nonviolent ones. We've got to talk to the Outlanders directly to understand what's happening on Hosh, and to figure out what happened to Umberto."

"Even if we find Ferus," Timoteo says, his voice tense, "and get information from him, we can't even be sure it's reliable."

"All I know is that tío Umberto trusted Ferus. That means *we* can trust him."

Timoteo clenches his jaw and shakes his head at me. For the first time, he looks at me like I don't deserve to be ambassador. "Really? That's the sum-total of your analysis on this question?"

"We need to find Ferus and the Outlanders tomorrow," I say, keeping my voice flat.

Timoteo stands up and spreads his sleeping bag out on the floor, avoiding eye contact. "Whatever you say, boss," he says, sharp edges of sarcasm leaking out between the syllables.

He's the only person I can trust, and now things even feel tense with him.

Chapter 12

ETOSCANS — Not exactly a theocracy — more like communitarian mystics. Synchronus — cool concept. Half deity, half quantum-physics. Internal divisions getting worse? "One True Synchronus" faction — fundamentalists, ethnocentric — seem to be rising in power. Typical.

- From the notebook of Umberto Olmeda

"Wow! Wepa! Wow!" Timoteo says, palms pressed against the window of our pod. Since there's no Interstellar Subway Station in Hosh's Northern hemisphere, we have to fly there from the Southern capital via pod. Pash-Ti's flying the pod, doing their usual silent stoic thing. While Timoteo gawks at the landscape below, I've been watching Pash-Ti work the controls, asking questions about how the pod works. Hopefully I'll be flying one soon myself, if we can find a way to get away to the Outlands.

We fly over an uninhabited area of forests, a canopy a bright shade of lavender instead of Earth's green. I wonder if photosynthesis works differently here.

"It's interesting there's so much purple in the vegetation, almost like photosynthesis works differently here," Timoteo says, which makes me smile. Timoteo and I don't have to be Hoshan to have our thoughts go in the same direction, which feels like a relief after our tense conversation last night. His first trip to outer space has put him in a better mood.

"Your hypothesis is correct," Pash-Ti says, their whistles coming across as mildly impressed but condescending at the same time. "Hoshan photosynthesis operates via bacteriorhodopsin rather than chlorophylls."

"Fascinating," Timoteo says, reading something on the inside of his glasses.

Seeing Timoteo see another planet for the first time makes me think of Umberto, how he saw all this, and who-knows-how-many other planets. Now I understand that glint he always had in his eyes. Umberto spent his time on Earth knowing that life was not a rarity. He knew our universe was one of abundant possibility.

But then he was taken from us, from the whole Galaxy.

Could it have been Pash-Ti who killed him? They're so abrasive, but I always know where they stand. Their advice is harsh but often right. They're starting to seem like the least likely suspect, and I'm starting to feel relieved about that.

We approach a city in the distance. From this far away, the floating, seed-shaped buildings meld into one vast aerial cityscape, and the synchronized movements of the towers make the entire city undulate, like a fleet of ships rising and falling with the ocean's waves.

Our pod descends toward the outskirts of the city. At the edge of the horizon, a dark cloud covers the lower half of the sky. As we get closer and land, I realize it's not a cloud, but a wall alive with motion, like a massive swarm stretching as high as a skyscraper.

"Are those insects?" I ask. "Like a plague or something?"

"Not insects," Pash-Ti says. "They're robotic. An army of military machines patrolling the border between the Levinti and Etoscan-controlled hemispheres of Hosh."

"All those are ... weapons?" Timoteo asks.

"In one form or another," Pash-Ti says.

"My God," I say. "There must be millions of them."

"You underestimate by several orders of magnitude. The swarms stretch around the entire circumference of Hosh, and many are invisible to your eyes and mine." Pash-Ti climbs out of the pod, arms first, their weight resting on their long arms for a moment as they bring their three legs to the ground. Timoteo and I follow.

I can't take my eyes off the enormous, terrifying swarm. Is this what Johnny looks like as a fully powered war machine?

We enter the dome. "Customs inspection," Pash-Ti says. "Guard your thoughts."

Two armed Hoshans meet us at the door. "Ambassador Vega of Terra and staff, seeking entry to the North to meet with the Etoscan ambassadors," Pash-Ti tells them.

"We know," one of the guards signs, with an air of impatience at the slowness of non-telepathic communication. "Authorization, please." Pash-Ti hands him a small rod no larger than one of their spindly fingers. The guard scans it and waves us through.

We exit through the opposite end of the dome, the low hum of the swarm permeating the air. The bots are a range of shapes and sizes— some as large as my fist, but most the size of locusts. Some have wings, like metallic insects, others look like miniature missiles.

The swarm parts, creating an arch a few feet taller than Pash-Ti. As we pass to the other side, another swarming wall stretches before us. "Another one?" Timoteo says.

"Did you think only the Levinti had an army?" Pash-Ti says. We walk toward the second swarm, crossing a hundred-yard stretch of barren earth.

"This is the Etoscans' swarm," I say, thinking aloud as we walk. "And if war comes—"

"Then within seconds, these two swarms will be locked in battle, and these hordes of machines will devour the cities and sentients on either side of the border. The Great Powers have had millennia to perfect the art of war. They are quite efficient at it."

We reach the second swarm. Hundreds of tiny machines part ways to create a path for us. My heart quickens, many of the tiny machines pointing at us as we pass.

✧　✧　✧

WE BOARD A GROUND VEHICLE for the final leg of the journey. It's like a big van, but has no wheels, its body resting directly on the ground.

"Why are we riding in a high-tech truck instead of a pod?" Timoteo asks.

"Etoscans avoid aerial travel whenever possible," Pash-Ti explains. "They have mechanoreceptors in their toes and communicate in part through bioseismic signals sent through the ground from their trunk and legs. They feel half-deaf in the air."

We pass red stone buildings that are only one story tall, and there's a roughness to the architecture that's almost primitive. They remind me of the ruins beneath the Levinti cities in the South—except not as … ruiny. The Hoshans of the South have followed the Levinti into the sky, while the Hoshans of the North have stuck close to the ground with the Etoscans.

"Though there are two Etoscan ambassadors, Speaker will do most of the talking," Pash-Ti says to me. "Follow my lead this time and don't make things worse." They turn to look down at Timoteo, whose head is swiveling in every direction. "And you remain quiet as well."

"I practically already have a degree in international political economy," Timoteo says.

Pash-Ti leans over him, eyestalks extending down toward him.

Timoteo presses his glasses against his face, fiddling nervously. "Yes, Mixter Pash-Ti, I'll be quiet, definitely." I really hope Timoteo turns out to be more help than liability.

I mentally run through everything we've been studying. The two Etoscan ambassadors are Speaker and Listener, which are their names as well as their roles. Apparently Etoscans change names a number of times in their lives. I wonder how that works when a bunch of them must have the same name, but I guess it's not that different from other humans being named Val.

Pash-Ti goes on, "It's likely they've heard that you've agreed to reopen discussion of Tumasra—and they may seek some recompense in return. If you must speak, don't agree to anything. If they make a direct request, simply say you'll need to review the matter. Diplomacy is the art of gracious delay."

"Okay," I say.

"Avoid all religious topics," Pash-Ti adds. "Their bizarre religion is a minefield. It's best to avoid the topic entirely."

I nod. Our vehicle glides to a stop in front of the Etoscan embassy.

A Hoshan meets us at the door and silently leads us down a corridor that's not Lilliputian like Hoshan spaces or gargantuan like Levinti spaces. It's just the right size for humans, the Goldilocks-chair of alien hallways.

We enter a large room cluttered with statues. Some look like elephants, and others have the familiar Hoshan shape of six-legged meerkat-like creatures. They're not made of stone—they're brown and rough, like tree bark. The sculptures meld seamlessly into the floor, which has the same rough texture.

One corner of the room is dominated by a sort-of grotto. Its irregular shape seems so natural that I wonder if it was extracted in its entirety from some cave and installed here, like a prefab house. A light trickle of water flows from the grotto's rocky peak into a small stone pool of water. The whole room is like the outdoors imported indoors— and maybe not the outdoors of Hosh, but of the Etoscan homeworld. It seems like the Levinti and Etoscans have one thing in common—they both like to remake their colonies in their own image.

Several Hoshans and two Etoscans are standing near the pool. I expected them to look like elephants, so I immediately notice how they're different from elephants. They have four legs and are elephant-shaped, but they're not grey. One has a white hide that looks smooth and hard, like bone. The other has similar smooth, hard skin, but dark red, like a red ant, or a giant armadillo. Exoskeletons, maybe? They have no tusks and are a bit smaller than elephants on Earth—about seven feet tall. Each is wearing an elaborate bronze headpiece, which tapers at the top. They have nodes and glowing lights—circuitry?—which makes me think they're not just decorative. Maybe the headsets connect them with a suit like Checkers.

But their trunks are the most interesting of all. Dangling from the tip of each trunk is a set of seven thin digits, like fingers. Their fingers just barely touch the floor, gently writhing, like the antennae of an insect exploring its terrain.

Timoteo stares up at the Etoscans, his mouth dropping open to form a quiet, "Whoa." Pash-Ti hushes him with a sharp look.

The red Etoscan lets out a low rumbling trumpet. "Welcome!" comes the translation. "I am Speaker, and this is my counterpart,

Listener. We're honored to see your eyes, Valiant One."

The eyes of both Etoscans gaze at me, eyes that are much more human than any other alien I've met. "The honor is mine to see your eyes," I say, mirroring Speaker's words.

Speaker shifts her gaze to Pash-Ti and Timoteo. "This is my ... advisor, Timoteo," I say. "You know, Pash-Ti, Observer of Terra."

Speaker's trunk turns toward Timoteo. "Your name is a weighty one, You Who Live in Awe of Synchronus." A note flashes on my wrist-screen: *Etoscans match foreign names to their own nomenclature, often translating names into their original, literal meanings—such as "Valiant One" for Valeria or "One Who Lives in Awe of God (or Synchronus)" for Timoteo.*

Timoteo reads something on the inside of his lenses and fidgets with his glasses. He must be getting the same note. "Um, yes," he says. "It is indeed a weighty name. And I do seek to, um, live in awe of Synchronus."

Pash-Ti steps forward with one long stride. "Perhaps we should turn our attention to our more formal agenda for today."

Taking no note of Pash-Ti, Speaker twists her trunk toward me. "We understand that your predecessor, the Bright Warrior, was a family elder of yours?"

Bright Warrior—that's the meaning of Umberto. Will the Etoscans consider it a good or bad thing that I'm related to him? Could they see it as nepotism? There's no way to hide it anyway, especially with Hoshans in the room. "Yes. He was my uncle."

A gentle, deep rumble comes from Speaker's trunk, shaking the ground beneath us slightly. "We feel his absence from this plane. We feel it deeply."

I take a deep breath. It's the first time any of the aliens have expressed any real sympathy about Umberto's death. "Thank you. I feel it deeply too."

"In times of loss," Speaker says, "we find solace in prayer."

Pash-Ti steps forward and says, "Honorable ambassadors, we do have time-sensitive matters to discuss regarding the coming talks, which convene in only nineteen days."

The Etoscans glance at them for a moment, then turn their attention back to me. The white one—Listener—speaks for the first time. "The Bright Warrior has told us your species prays half-consciously, through visions that come while you sleep."

Praying while you sleep? I look at my wrist but there's no note from Checkers. I think back on what I've read—that the Etoscans believe that the psychic world and the material world mutually shape one another, that they pray through immersive meditation that taps the unconscious.

They must mean dreams. Dreams must seem like a kind of prayer to them.

"Yes," I say. "We call them dreams."

"Of course, half-conscious prayers," Listener says, and I guess that's the closest the Etoscan language can get to the word for dream. "It's common for primitive species to only have the capacity for half-conscious prayer. Tell us, Valiant One, when you awaken, do you remember the prayers of your sleep?"

He asks the question the way adults ask each other, What do you do for a living? A test question, a way of sizing someone up. "Yes," I say, "I often remember my dreams."

"And what have you seen?" asks Listener. "What have you seen in your recent prayers?"

Usually that question wouldn't faze me. But for the past two weeks, all my dreams have been about Umberto. Should I tell them that? If dreaming—or praying—is so important to them, what will it mean to them that all my dreams are prayers of grief? Will they see that as primitive?

From the corner, I'm being watched by a Hoshan, wearing a headpiece much like the Etoscans. Whatever I say, they'll all know my thoughts sooner or later. "Lately I've been dreaming of my uncle, of Umberto—dreaming that he's still alive."

"Ah," says Speaker, "then you still speak with him in your prayers. It is well that you do." She says it as if my dreams were a comfort, when they're more like the twisting of a knife.

Pash-Ti's blowholes heave, about to speak again, but then the doors swing open, and five Hoshans march in, each carrying a bucket filled with a steaming liquid. They scurry to the grotto and pour the steaming buckets into the pool.

"Ah," Listener says, "it's time for our afternoon mist. Please honor us by joining our misting, Valiant One."

I look at my wrist-screen, hoping Checkers will help me out, which he does: *Many Etoscan cultures perform a daily ritual in which an herbal mist is absorbed through the skin, believed by Etoscans to facilitate communion with Synchronus. Physiologically, it stimulates the nuclei of the brain involved in REM sleep in humans, or the dream-like state Etoscans call prayer.*

"Excuse us a moment, honorable ones," Pash-Ti says, and pulls me back into a huddle with them and Timoteo. In hushed tones, Pash-Ti says, "It would be unwise to participate in this. The effects of the mist are unpredictable in humans."

"No way," Timoteo says. "That would be a total cultural insult."

"With all due respect to your new ... advisor," Pash-Ti says, "you should feign participation but have Checkers obstruct the mist from passing through the membrane of your suit."

Timoteo quietly scoffs. "That's still totally rude, like pretending to finish tía's dry mofongo by moving it around on your plate."

"Timoteo's right," I say.

"Indeed?" Pash-Ti says. "An analogy regarding Terran dining customs will determine your decision in this matter?"

I look back at the Etoscans, the grotto steaming around their silent figures. We've already kept them waiting too long. "Did Umberto do this?" I ask.

"Yes," Pash-Ti concedes, "but only after years of experience in the field, and in controlled dosages."

"Checkers," I say, "do you know how much of the mist Umberto would let into his suit?"

"I have that information on file," Checkers replies.

"Then do a third of that for me," I say.

Timoteo gives me a thumbs-up, while Pash-Ti's eyestalks extend in pointed irritation. I turn back to the Etoscans. "I apologize for the delay, esteemed ambassadors. I'd be honored to join you for your afternoon mist."

CHAPTER 13

SPEAKER PLUNGES HER TRUNK into the pool, then draws it out and releases a gentle, misty spray onto Listener's back. Listener reciprocates, spraying Speaker's back. The mist spreads out into the chamber as the two Etoscans turn to face me.

"Please," Speaker says, with a gentle rumble from her trunk, "allow me the honor of misting you."

"The honor is mine," I say. I'm not sure what to do, so I bow at the waist. A gentle mist sprinkles across my back, a warm, refreshing sensation of wetness on my skin. There's a faint scent—pleasant, but unfamiliar, like a mix of lavender and cilantro.

I stand up straight. "Thank you." The Etoscans are silent. They stand staring straight ahead, as if gazing at some unseen object in the distance. I mirror them, standing still and letting my gaze relax. The mist has spread throughout the chamber, wisps of vapor swirling among the life-sized statues of Etoscans and Hoshans. The room has no windows, and there's no visible light source, but light seems to permeate the room from all directions, like sunshine. A few feet away, the light catches the mist, creating a tiny rainbow, its colors bright and sharp.

But is there really a rainbow there at all? Or is that the effects of the mist? It's getting hot. Why is it so hot?

Timoteo squints at me. "You okay, Val?"

"Yeah," I say. "It's just ... did it get hotter all of a sudden?"

"No," Timoteo says.

From behind me, Pash-Ti says, "Be cautious. The mist will distort your perceptions and your judgment. You'd be wise to remain quiet until the experience passes." Pash-Ti's whispers carry their usual stern tone. But then, it's not really Pash-Ti's voice, but a translation of it. A translation of tone as well as words. The real words are the notes that preceded the English translation: harsh notes, like a cruel oboe.

The mist is thicker now. Where did the rainbow go? The mist darkens from grey to black, swallowing me up and surrounding me in darkness. I feel the urge to cry out, to grab for something solid. What if this is all a trap laid by the Etoscans?

My heart's beating faster. Have to stay calm. This is probably all a hallucination. I just need to confirm that none of it's real.

"Checkers," I say softly, startling myself with the sound of my own voice.

"Yes, Madame Ambassador?" comes Checkers' reply. My breathing relaxes at the sound of his gentle voice in her ear.

"Is everything okay in the room?" I mouth. "No danger?"

"No danger that I can see," Checkers says. "Your heart rate has increased slightly, but everyone is standing in silence and all seems well. Is there anything I can provide for you?"

"No," I whisper. "I'm fine. Just don't let any more of the mist through the suit, okay?"

"Of course, Madame Ambassador."

My heart rate eases. The darkness is less intimidating now.

My fear is replaced by curiosity. In the darkness, there are dim grey shadows amidst the black. The grey spreads and divides, like dark paint being unraveled into reds, blues, and yellows. The flowing colors form themselves into a hallway lined with orange lockers. It's a hallway at school, except the lockers are twice as tall as in real life, and the hall extends endlessly in both directions.

There's a single knock, a tap of flesh on metal. Then another knock, and another. I follow the sound. The knocking is rapid now, desperate. "I'm coming!" I say.

I follow the knocking to its source, locker number 237. That's so strange. That's my locker.

I spin through my combination and open the door. Tío Umberto is standing inside the locker—impossibly, at least eight feet tall—facing to the side. He's tapping the locker's inner wall with his keys. His facial expression isn't desperate, but inquisitive, as if he's testing if the walls are hollow. He pauses and turns to look down at me.

"Ah!" he says. "There you are, Valeria. Just checking for telepathic termites. Pesky little buggers!" He steps out of the locker and into the hallway. He pats me on the head. "Don't forget to wind your watch. You don't want to miss the train!" Then he dashes down the hall, his purple blazer flapping behind him.

"Wait! There's so much more I need to know!" I chase after him, but in seconds he vanishes beyond sight.

"You must be deep in prayer," says a disembodied voice. "Share your prayers with us."

It's one of the Etoscans—Speaker. Am I really still in that room with them? This all seems so real, this dream, this—prayer. It makes so much sense now. Of course dreams are prayers to the Etoscans. That's exactly what they are, the mind connecting with deeper truths. Or is the mist still skewing the way I see things?

"Yes," I say, wishing I could keep chasing after Umberto, feeling like my prayer is only half-finished. "I'm deep in prayer."

"Where have your prayers taken you?" says Speaker.

Pash-Ti warned not to say too much. "I'm on Earth." I'm about to say the words school and locker but I'm not sure those will translate easily. "In a place of learning. A place where things are stored in a place of learning."

"Ah," says Speaker, as her head materializes in the air in front of me, a red elephant's head hanging in an oversized version of the hallway of my school. I'm totally tripping.

The floating elephant head goes on, "It is auspicious to encounter a place of learning in one's prayers." They might not think it's auspicious if they knew what high schools on Earth are like. The rest of the Etoscan's body follows its head into the room. Then the entire scene changes, and I'm back in the chamber with the Etoscan ambassadors. I blink, my eyes adjusting to the light, my mind adapting to the sudden shift. The mist has dissipated—only a few wisps of it remain now. Both Etoscans stand over me, staring at me intently.

"What did you find," Listener asks, "in this place of storage in a place of learning?"

For a moment, I have trouble remembering—like the vague memory of a dream. Then it comes back to me.

"Careful," Pash-Ti whispers, coming up beside me. Their eyestalks point toward the Hoshan by the grotto. "They're watching more than just the words you say aloud."

I nod and try to steer my thoughts away from dangerous territory. But my mind is still so—well, misty. It's hard to steer my thoughts in any direction at all.

"I saw my Uncle Umberto," I say.

"Ah, yes," Listener says, "you said he'd been visiting your prayers. Even in death, he reaches out to guide you. Did he bear a message for you?"

My memory flashes to Umberto's notebook, to his holo-message. Even in my hazy mind, I know I should think of anything but that. I think of my mist-dream again, of Umberto standing inside the locker.

"He said something about not having a lot of time," I say.

"A prayer of urgency," Speaker says, lifting her trunk. "A prayer of urgency, learning, and visits from the dead. An auspicious prayer, especially for a primitive incapable of true prayer without the aid of the mist. Heed your prayers, Valiant One. The wisdom of Synchronus lies within them."

Listener takes several steps toward me, the floor rumbling slightly with each footfall. "Umberto was a family elder," he says. "Did he often play the role of Mentor in your life?"

"Yes," I say. "He taught me a lot, all the time."

"Undoubtedly," Listener goes on, "his tutelage prepared you for the role of ambassador."

I imagine an alternative version of reality where that happened, where Umberto hadn't been killed, where he'd taken me as his apprentice. I picture him showing me the embassy, giving me tips on how to use the synth-suit. The two of us, stepping off the Interstellar Subway side by side, Umberto watching as I walk on an alien planet for the first time. Umberto retired, fully bald but with no less vibrancy, advising me from an armchair as I carry on his work. It's so vivid, an entire history imagined in an instant. Is it the lingering effect of the mist that my mind's eye can race across time so fast?

I look over at Timoteo, who's standing quietly, his eyes soft with tears he's holding back. He must be thinking of Umberto too, of the Galaxy he never shared with us.

"I wish," I say, only half-aware I'm speaking out loud. "I wish I'd had more time to learn from him. He died before he had a chance to teach me as much as he could have." The Etoscans exchange low rumbles from their trunks that go untranslated.

The deep recesses of their eyes look so human. I don't know if it's the effect of the mist, or that they're the first ones to acknowledge that the loss of Umberto was a personal one for me, but I can't imagine them conspiring to have him killed. I have the urge to trust them, to ask them for their help in confidence. But I can't do that, and I can't confront them either, by asking for their alibis or something—being confrontational will only hurt the talks. If only there were another way to probe them for more information.

But before I can finish my thought, Timoteo steps forward. "Umberto was my familial as well," he says, his voice sharp. "Before he died, there was an unusual energy surge near Tumasra. He seemed concerned about it."

Listener lets out a deep rumble. "The Tumasra storm often emits unusual energies," he says. "I'm surprised Ambassador Olmeda would be concerned with such a minor matter."

Pash-Ti whistles a few sharp notes in my ear. "You must curtail this dangerous digression immediately."

On the other side of me, Timoteo's face is tight with a combination of anger and grief. I shouldn't have brought him into this. He's still too deep in his grief over Umberto and isn't thinking straight. He could ruin the talks with just one aggressive question.

Listener continues, his tone much harsher than the gentle one he was using earlier, the floor trembling beneath the rumbles of his trunk. "Why would Ambassador Olmeda—or you—even raise such a question? It's almost profane for a primitive ambassador to question matters related to an Etoscan sacred site."

This is extra defensiveness for a "minor matter." But Pash-Ti is right—I need to figure out a way to roll back Timoteo's implied accusation. "My apologies, honorable ambassadors. My advisor and I are still new at this and meant no offense." Something occurs to me that could serve as both explanation and deflection. "Ambassador Olmeda was quite anxious about the Hosh-Unam Front disrupting the peace talks. I think he was worried the surge may have been related to their recent acquisition of more advanced weaponry. That's probably why he was concerned."

Timoteo presses his lips together like he's holding back a flood of words. Listener and Speaker exchange glances and rumbles. "The Hosh-Unam Front is endlessly seeking to undermine the peace," Speaker says. "And we are investigating whether they had any involvement in the recent unusual surge. But we have re-doubled our security to assure that the terrorists disrupt these talks no further."

Terrorists. I don't like the violence of the Hosh-Unam Front, but it seems like that word is only used for the terror created by the ones with less power. Are those swarms on the border weapons of terror too?

"Honorable ones," Pash-Ti cuts in, "the ambassador apologizes for this needless digression, which, as she said, is simply a result of the newness of these Terrans to their roles. Above all, we wish to make sure that all is in readiness for the formal talks to begin in nineteen days. Have you any questions or concerns?"

"Indeed," Listener says, his white trunk waving from Pash-Ti to me. "We understand that you wish to widen the discussion of Tumasra in the talks."

"That has been suggested by other parties," Pash-Ti says flatly.

Speaker comes closer, stopping only a foot away from me. She moves with surprising fluidity, her back less rigid than I expected. Up close, thin ridges are visible along her red back, like the banded segments of an armadillo's armor. "You understand, Valiant One, that Tumasra is a sacred place, and must remain sacrosanct above all else."

"Of course," I say, feeling like I still have to recover ground with them. "Any discussion of Tumasra has to respect its sacredness."

"Then we're in agreement, Valiant One," Listener says. "With that assurance from you, we are open to allowing Tumasra to be discussed, with one other caveat."

Speaker raises her trunk, letting out a screeching trumpet. "Listen well, Listener," comes the translation, "and I shall speak, unless you would seek a new name this season."

Listener twists his larger white trunk—a sign of surprise?—and steps back. "I meant not to violate your name. By all means, speak."

Speaker points her trunk back at me. "We wish to host the talks here in the Northern Capital, at the prayer Citadel overlooking Tumasra."

"Really?" I say. That seems odd—almost like a conciliatory gesture, to invite everyone to a place they claim exclusive control of.

"As hosts," Speaker goes on, "we shall of course open the talks, with a ritual of welcome."

"Okay," I say, trying to figure out the catch. "We'd be open to that, but need—"

Pash-Ti cuts me off. "Your offer and suggestion are most gracious, honorable ones. The ambassador shall consider these proposals as our office works with all parties to finalize the agenda, and we shall reply within three days' time."

"We await your response eagerly," Speaker says, "and, as Synchronus carries us, look forward to hosting this important conversation. It has been an honor to meet you, Valiant One."

"The honor's mine," I say.

The three of us walk outside. The sky is a dark shade of purple, and beyond the valley of flat roofs of stone, the sun is setting. Two moons hang in the sky, one white and one brown, both smaller than Earth's moon—a dime and a penny instead of a nickel in the sky.

As we walk beyond the gates of the embassy, Pash-Ti turns to Timoteo. "It was reckless of you to raise the energy surge. This is why I told you to stay quiet. How did you even know about that?"

"We read about it in Wiki Galactica," I say, only half-lying, not wanting her to know about Ferus, or Umberto's notebook. "And we overheard Umberto having a conversation before he died, where he said something about a surge. In retrospect we figured out it was about that."

"He *was* concerned about it," Pash-Ti says. "Though I never understood why. But if you meddle in the same areas as Umberto was inquiring, it will only put you in the same danger as he faced."

Timoteo scuffs his shoe against the stone pathway. "Somebody had our tío *killed*. If we don't figure that out, we're still all in danger, and so are the peace talks."

"Our situation is challenging," Pash-Ti says. "But our powers are limited, and our primary goal must be simply to keep the talks in motion. Neither of you should ever raise a controversial topic that could jeopardize the peace." This time, I can't help but agree with Pash-Ti—Timoteo's question was way too risky. But the way the Etoscans reacted only makes me more certain it's important. Hopefully Ferus will have more answers. "Still," Pash-Ti goes on, "you recovered to some degree, and you did well in not acquiescing to their requests immediately, as you did with the Levinti."

"That request about Tumasra was suspicious too," Timoteo says. "Why would they want to have the talks there? I thought they didn't want the Levinti and the Southlanders anywhere near Tumasra."

"Indeed," Pash-Ti says, as we near our vehicle. "They would make no such offer unless it's to their advantage. The Etoscans speak as much through ceremony as through words. Perhaps hosting the talks at Tumasra is intended as a display of power, cementing their claim over the site."

"That would make sense," I say, relieved that we're shifting to a more constructive conversation—almost like we're the team we're supposed to be. "And what was going on with the two of them? I thought Speaker was supposed to do most of the talking, but Listener kept taking over."

"A circumstance that was duly noted by Speaker," Pash-Ti says. "I've heard of tension between them, but they must be at great odds for their conflict to be so evident in our presence."

Just as we're about to board our vehicle, a Hoshan scurries up beside us, running on all six legs. "Valiant Ambassador," she says, standing up on her four hind legs, "I have a message from Charism, the Voice of Northern Hosh. He awaits your audience at Tumasra."

"Um, right now?" I say.

The Hoshan spreads all four upper limbs, as if welcoming me with all of them. "Yes, he hopes to receive you."

I look up at Pash-Ti. Charism is the head of state of Northern Hosh, as well as its representative in the talks. But we weren't supposed to meet with him until later today.

"I'm uncertain why Charism is seeking this meeting earlier than planned," Pash-Ti says. "He is a ... strong personality, and well-liked by his people. He may wish for your meeting to be more public. Regardless, out of respect, we should accept this invitation."

I turn back to the Hoshan. "Okay. I'd be honored to meet Charism. Please let him know I'll be there shortly."

"I already have," the Hoshan says, and drops to all six legs to scurry down the stone road.

"How could she have told him already?" Timoteo asks as he gets in the vehicle. "I didn't think Hoshan telepathy had that long a range."

Pash-Ti enters the other side of the vehicle, bending their long limbs in a spider-like squat in the confined space. "It doesn't, except in uniquely gifted Hoshans." Pash-Ti enters a destination on the console, "but Northern Hoshans—especially important Hoshans, like Charism—often send messages via telepathic relay, along a chain of messengers."

I enter behind Pash-Ti, and our vehicle exits the embassy's grounds and drives along a stone road. After we meet with Charism, maybe Timoteo and I can find a way to slip away and look for Ferus.

Pash-Ti goes on, "You should know that Hoshan telepathy is stronger in the vicinity of Tumasra. The closer we get to it, the stronger their perceptions. They can sense thoughts from a greater distance, and with greater sharpness. They can see even some thoughts at the periphery of consciousness. That's why it was considered a sacred site even before the Etoscans co-opted it—Hoshans claim that Tumasra allows them to see into another's soul."

"And that's where Charism wants to meet me?" I say. "In a place where he can see my soul?"

"Etoscan and Hoshan religious beliefs aside, the soul is a quaint notion with little evidence to substantiate it," Pash-Ti says. "But you *will* be particularly exposed. Keep your mind clear and the meeting brief. We're nearly there already."

We crest a hill, and there's a whiff of a sulfur-like scent. The sun has fallen, but stars and moons still light up the vast valley of sandstone below us. Thousands of Hoshans fill the valley, a crush of undulating fur.

At the far end of the valley is a whirling storm of glowing orange-red embers, a tower of lava as tall as a skyscraper, stretching from a deep chasm below the valley up into a thick layer of orange clouds. Tumasra is even more awe-inspiring than I'd imagined.

CHAPTER 14

THE NIGHT IS LIT only by the stars and moons and the Tumasra storm itself, its orange glow lighting the valley like a giant bonfire. The sulfur-like scent gets harsher as we get closer to the storm. Pash-Ti, Timoteo, and I walk toward the edge of the tightly packed crowd of Hoshans that surrounds Tumasra. The Hoshans never speak a word, but their non-verbal communication is palpable. They weave gracefully around each other, never colliding. Often, as two Hoshans cross paths, their eyes meet and they clutch each other, claw against forearm, brushing one another's fur, then move on to do the same with someone else. Human waves and handshakes seem cold compared to this all-encompassing Hoshan intimacy.

We reach a point where the crowd gets so thick there's barely room to walk. "How are we going to find Charism in all this?" I ask.

Before Pash-Ti can answer, a passing Hoshan reaches up to clutch me at the elbow. "Fret not, Valiant Ambassador. Enter the *unam*, and we will guide you to Charism."

Now I'm confused—Unam like in the Hosh-Unam Front?

"No, no," the Hoshan says, her lips curled up in a cat-like smile. "Not the Hosh-Unam, just the *unam*. The loving spirit of the people."

The Hoshan moves past us. Pash-Ti's long arms are folded, their height and stony expression even more prominent in the crowd of Hoshans. Even the taller Hoshans are a good foot shorter than Timoteo and me—but Pash-Ti towers above them.

"No sense delaying," Pash-Ti says, and ventures deeper into the crowd. Timoteo and I follow, and the Hoshans part ways for us, with that same grace that seems perfectly choreographed. As we pass by, some Hoshans meet my eyes and gently run their claws across my forearm. At first it feels intrusive, but then I get used to it. I join in, returning the Hoshans' friendly scratches along the arm as they pass. *Hello*, I think as I look into their eyes, *warm greetings from the planet Earth! I'm Val, and thank you for the welcome!* I want to reciprocate their warmth.

Pash-Ti moves through the crowd impassively, folding their long arms so they remain out of reach of the Hoshans. Timoteo lets the Hoshans scratch at his sweater, but his shoulders tense up as they reach for him, and he doesn't reciprocate the gesture.

The crowd gets thicker as we enter the inner circle surrounding Tumasra. Even through the protective shield of my suit, the storm feels hot on my face. From this close, I can see that it's not like solid lava—more like thousands of pieces of red-hot shrapnel oozing in a slow and ceaseless spin, a magnetic tornado of embers as tall as a skyscraper. The storm makes no sound of wind, only a soft crackle. The scent of sulfur is so strong I have to fight the urge to gag. Beside the storm is a stony building that stretches the height of Tumasra, adorned with Etoscan sculptures. That must be the Etoscan citadel, where they want to hold the talks.

In a semi-circle wrapping around the edge of the cliff, hundreds of Hoshans lie across the ground, a sea of brown and red fur. Their eyes are closed, and most are curled up, all six limbs tucked under their bodies, kind of like dogs sleep. Some lie with a limb or tail extended, touching the fur of a nearby Hoshan. Their bodies heave together in a unison of breaths. It looks more like meditation than sleep. It seems like some sort of telepathic communion—or prayer, maybe?

Beyond the mass of Hoshans, there's a fountain and a bunch of Etoscans. They're misting each other, and several are lying on the ground, their trunks intertwined. That's strange. The Etoscans aren't telepathic, but it seems like they're imitating a Hoshan ritual.

A Hoshan emerges from the crowd, letting out a series of clicks. "The Etoscans have indeed emulated our unam pile ritual. They often say they've as much to learn from us as we do from them. Just as we journey here from around the globe, so do the Etoscans come to bathe in Tumasra's sacred heat, but for them it is a pilgrimage across the stars."

He's tall for a Hoshan—standing almost as high as my ribs—and his tail is the puffiest I've seen, almost as if it had a perm. This has got to be Charism.

"You've spotted me!" he says, lifting up his nose and flourishing one short, furry arm. "I am indeed Charism. Walk with me, Valiant One." He leads me away from the storm, back into the crowd, which parts wordlessly for us. I haven't seen Pash-Ti or Timoteo for a few minutes and crane my neck to look for them. Timoteo is a good twenty yards away, surrounded by a throng of Hoshans. Pash-Ti's wiry greyish-white frame is even farther.

"Fret not about your companions," Charism says. "The *unam* will care-take them."

I don't like being separated from them, especially Timoteo. The telepathic crowd must have steered the two of them away from me so Charism could meet me alone. Can I trust him?

Charism continues to walk deeper into the crowd, farther away from Pash-Ti and Timoteo. "Ah, trust. A fascinating concept. Like so many concepts, its very nature implies its opposite. To trust another being means, inherently, that you have some uncertainty about that trust, because you had to make the choice to trust them. Thus you do not trust them implicitly!"

We're getting even farther away from Pash-Ti and Timoteo, but I walk along with Charism, since that feels like the only option. I shift my thinking to the Hoshan way, where every thought is speech. *That's true. Right now, I'm walking with you, putting my trust in you that I'll link back up with my friends. I feel the warmth of everyone here—and that makes it easier. But you're right. I have to think about it, so it's not total trust, like Hoshans must have. It must be amazing to have your mind be open to everyone, their minds open to you. On my world, people spend their whole lives searching for that kind of closeness, and Hoshans have it every moment.*

"So charming," Charism says, "you choose not to speak aloud, to simply let your thoughts flow to me. Few mind-deaf aliens do that. They prefer the noise of their own speech."

That seems silly, I think. *If I could read people's thoughts I'd pay much more attention to what they think than what they say.*

Charism snorts and chirps. "So we do, Valiant One. It's quite odd to us that the gap between thought and speech is often wide. The minds of the mind-deaf are often like an animal of two parts, each tugging in different directions."

And you? I think. *Right now, are you sharing all your thoughts with me? Or are you holding things back like the mind-deaf? Sorry, that came out more blunt than I meant ... it's still new for me to think by talking.*

Charism lets out a high-pitched titter. "Fret not. We Hoshans quite enjoy directness. And, yes, I'm doing my best to share all our thoughts with you, though speech is slow and clumsy."

It's weird he said *our.* Is that like the royal we or something?

"I do mean we," Charism says, gesturing to the crowd around us.

"As Voice of the North, I speak for the *unam*. We all want to hear from our new mediator. The fate of our world is in your claws."

It's overwhelming thinking of it like that. The faces of the Hoshan crowd look up at me, noses upturned and eyes wide. I can almost see their minds listening. I thought they were walking in and out of Tumasra, but actually the crowd's attention is on *us*.

"Of course," Charism says. "The *unam* would know you better. What the people see here tonight, they will pass on to their loved ones, who will pass it to others, until it spreads across the whole of Northern Hosh."

The way he says it, it sounds like all my thoughts are being broadcast on the Hoshan equivalent of social media.

"We make little use of media," Charism says, "not here in the North. Broadcasts and media—such a hollow imitation of communication. We share our news through the unam, passed from mind to mind with all the depth that speech does not allow."

I imagine an entire hemisphere watching me—not just me, but my thoughts. Half a planet sharing the intimacies of my mind, things even my mother doesn't know, or my brothers, or Will, or any human. I guess that's part of being human, of being "mind-deaf." We can knock on the door of another person's mind, but we can't go in. We can only guess what's inside by glimpsing through the windows. I'm from a planet of island-minds.

"Just so!" Charism says, nodding. Several Hoshans let out a hiss, though it sounds approving, not negative. A note flashes on my arm: *Hissing is a Hoshan signal of approval or applause.* Charism leads us on. As we walk along, I hold my arm out, trading gentle scratches with Hoshan after Hoshan.

"We're impressed at your sense of perspective," Charism says. "Your thought-stream flows with our thought-stream. It's hard for us to grasp the existence of the mind-deaf, how your psyches carry on without companionship! You seem such lonely creatures."

We do get lonely, I think. *But we have moments of connection. We can build bridges between our island-minds, if we work at it.*

"Just so," Charism says.

We continue passing through the crowd, a wave of upturned smiles and friendly scratches following us as they go. The Tumasra storm makes the air hot, and the smell of sulfur is giving me a headache. Despite the discomfort, I'm enjoying getting to know Charism and the Northern Hoshans. This public meeting is overwhelming, but I'll take it any day over the way Trimana interrogated me.

Charism lets out another high-pitched titter. "Trimana interrogated you? I'll bet she used a gag and everything. You'll find we do things differently here. In the North we've no desire to imitate the subterfuge of the mind-deaf." The Hoshan crowd lets out a collective hiss, as if hundreds of them are speaking through Charism's voice. "In the North we're true to our roots. In the North the *unam* lives on!"

What does that mean? I think.

"It means we follow the old Hoshan ways that are unique to us in all the Galaxy. We still hold the unam-pile ceremony. We still, all who are able, make the journey to Tumasra every seventeenth cycle. Our leaders, like me, are not chosen by some academic committee, but by the *unam*, through the wisdom of our minds together. And, above all, we hide nothing from each other, as it has always been on Hosh!" Hundreds of Hoshan hiss in agreement.

What's made things so different in the South?

"The Levinti, of course," Charism says. "The Southlanders have been twisted by millennia of living amidst their silent, calculating minds.

And we have only sympathy for them! From the day the Levinti arrived, they used fear and intimidation to control our Southern siblings, to remake their culture in the mold of the Scholocracy,"

And the Etoscans? I think. *They haven't tried to make you more like them?*

"The Etoscans are different," Charism says, stopping on top of a hill near Tumasra, its scent and heat strong. I try not to let my throbbing headache distract me, to focus on Charism as he looks out on the crowd. "The minds of the Etoscans are open to us. True, they brought changes. New technologies. An understanding of the ways of Synchronus. But we chose those changes. And the Etoscans have learned from us as well! They recognize that our mind-sharing is a gift from Synchronus Itself, that Hosh is a sacred place, where the energies of Synchronus flow deep. While the Levinti believe they know all, seeking only to teach and never to learn."

Charism is looking more at the crowd than at me, as if, at some point, he shifted from casual conversation to political speech. What he's saying makes sense—but Trimana said just the opposite, that the Levinti are more benevolent, while the Etoscans withhold their technology.

Charism lets out a friendly titter. "I do tend to get carried away, when the spirit of the *unam* flows through me. And it is well that you seek to understand all sides. But beware the manipulations of the Levinti and their Southland puppets. It's true the Etoscans haven't shared their technology at as fast a pace as we might like. But they have shared deeper truths with us, only strengthening the *unam*."

You believe in the unam, I think, *but not the* Hosh-Unam. I immediately regret the thought, remembering Pash-Ti's advice to stay away from controversial topics.

"Here in the North we all hold the *unam* in our hearts," Charism says. "And many of us believe that the Hosh-Unam, the idea of a Hosh that is unified and autonomous, is a beautiful dream. But for centuries it's been a dream that can never be realized. We've become too different, North and South, to ever again be one. The Hosh-Unam Front claim to represent true Hoshan ways, yet they could be no more un-Hoshan in their methods. They train themselves in thought-steering and hide away in the most secluded parts of the planet to conceal their stratagems. They murder not only Levinti and Etoscans, but their fellow Hoshans. In the name of the Hosh-Unam, they violate all that the *unam* truly is."

But the Hosh-Unam Front aren't the only autonomists, I think. *I've been told there are also autonomists who are peaceful. That some seek refuge in a place called the Outlands.*

"A fringe minority," Charism says, "The Outlanders are not violent, but are still hermitic, hiding beyond the mainlands, afraid to share their thoughts with the *unam*."

My headache is getting worse, with Tumasra so close. Tumasra, I think, before I can stop myself. Trimana and the Levinti say they want to study the Tumasra storm.

"That is indeed what they say," Charism says, looking out across the crowd, again speaking more to them than to me. "And how we wish there were no gap between their speech and thought. The Levinti do not seek merely to study Tumasra. They seek a permanent base here in the heart of the North! A base from which they could launch a military strike, against which we'd be helpless to defend ourselves. They would do so here, in the most sacred of spaces!"

I nod, thinking back to the two swarms of deadly weapons poised to strike.

"Ah, yes," Charism says. "You have seen the swarms of war. Of those billions of weapons you saw, do you know how many are Hoshan-controlled?"

I didn't think any were, that they were all controlled by the Etoscans or the Levinti.

"Just so," Charism says. "Not one. Follow closely my stream of thoughts, Valiant One. I could do as Trimana did, make demands, posture as if I had some powerful gamepiece to play." He stands on his two hind legs, and holds out four arms, as if embracing the multitude. "But we have no such gamepiece. It is the Levinti and the Etoscans who control those swarms, and those are the only gamepieces of consequence. But if we of Northern Hosh could make demands, we would make only one, and that would be for peace. Our demand would be that those swarms never descend upon our land as they have in millennia past. Peace is all we seek."

Hundreds of Hoshans hiss in agreement, hundreds of pairs of eyes fixed intently on Charism. Their attention is so rapt, they must all be syncing with him.

Charism drops to four legs, and the energy of the crowd shifts. A few nearby Hoshans stay focused on Charism and me, seeking a friendly scratch from us, but most turn their attention to each other or Tumasra. I guess my telepathically televised interview is over.

Charism lets out his tittering laugh. "Just so."

There's something charming about Charism. Even if this meeting was as much for the crowd as for me, his authenticity is refreshing. I wonder what Umberto thought of him.

"The Bright Warrior was a remarkable being," Charism says, strolling away from the crowd's center, giving a friendly scratch and a smile to several Hoshans as they pass. "He is the only non-Hoshan with whom I've ever shared a moment of *vasek antom.*"

Marrow used that term too, but Checkers was disabled then. My arm lights up with the words: *Vasek antom is the Hoshan concept of strong disagreement leading to deeper intimacy.*

"So you really did meet Marrow," Charism says, snout upturned. "In any case, your computer's definition is utterly inadequate. *Vasek antom* is much more. It is the moment when you see—when you palpably feel—a deep difference between yourself and another. It is the moment in a relationship when your thoughts flow in opposition. For the mind-deaf this may lead to alienation, but not so for us. Even as our thought-streams run against one another, still they flow together. There is no greater intimacy than *vasek antom*. Your familial, unlike most mind-deaf, did not shy away from it."

I think he was murdered, I think, unable to stop myself.

Charism's ears prick up, more in seriousness than alarm. He ushers me down a stone path, farther away from the crowd. "Of course he was murdered. That thought is close to the surface of everyone's minds, though few dare to speak it."

Do you know who did it?

"Alas, I know little more than you. But I will say this." With his snout, Charism gestures toward Pash-Ti, still in the thick of the crowd on the far edge of the valley, like a giant grey statue surrounded by a mass of teeming rodents.

"Be wary of that one. They're skilled in the steering of thoughts. We've been watching their mind this while, and even here, in Tumasra, where our senses are sharpest, their closest thoughts are well-guarded from us."

I already know Pash-Ti could steer their thoughts—they told me as much. But I didn't know they were *that* good at it.

Pash-Ti's far enough away that now might be my best chance to steal away from them, get to the Outlands, though I have no idea how to do that. Charism's ears prick up and I realize I have to stop this train of thought—but it's already too late. I'm terrible at this thought-steering thing.

Charism tugs at my sleeve and pulls me farther from the crowd. "Come, Valiant One, there is a spectacular view of Tumasra atop this hill that you must see before you return home."

Charism leads me up a brown-stone path along a hill that takes us farther from Tumasra—and the crowd. We reach the crest and turn around. The view is spectacular—the Etoscan citadel, the bright orange storm of Tumasra lighting up the nighttime sky, the teeming mass of Hoshans surrounding it.

Charism stands on his hind legs and lets out a series of quiet clicks that sound like a gentle drizzle of rain. "Indeed, you are terrible at thought-steering, though at least only a few minds were in range when you revealed your interest in the Outlands. But here we're well beyond the range of even the most far-seeing of telepaths." He's right—the nearest Hoshans are specks in the distance now—at least a few hundred yards away. "Yes, here we may speak openly. Now what is it that you hope to accomplish with those Outlander hermits?"

I'm still not sure if I can trust Charism, but he seems genuine, and at least he hasn't gagged me. And he might be my only chance of getting to the Outlands. *My uncle left notes behind*, I think. *About a suspicious energy surge near Tumasra. I think it may have something to do with what got him killed, the key to figuring out who's trying to sabotage these negotiations.*

Charism pulls at his whiskers, contemplative and serious. "I sensed the Bright Warrior's suspicions about that surge, and I share them."

Maybe it's a sign the Etoscans are building up a storehouse of more weapons near Tumasra, I think. *Speaker and especially Listener seemed weirdly defensive about it.*

Charism snorts in frustration. "Listener is defensive about every trifle. But it's widely known the Etoscans are building up their storehouse of swarms—especially around Tumasra. They've no reason to hide it. Nothing in interstellar law forbids them from building weapons in territory that belongs to them."

It's strange to hear Charism speak so cynically about the Etoscans when he'd been praising them just a few minutes ago.

"I do believe the Etoscans have treated us better than the Levinti—that stream of thoughts was no deception," Charism says. "But I'm well aware that Etoscans like Listener see Hosh as little more than a breeding ground for their Hoshan agents. I have seen in his mind his hunger to conquer all of Hosh, much as he may try to disguise it. Thankfully Speaker is far truer to the path of Synchronus—and holds the higher rank. But listen—I have resources of my own and may aid your investigation. My own agents scanned the signature of that energy surge and found indications of quantum threading—technology used in highly advanced surveillance. I fear the Levinti may have already established a secret observation base in the caves beneath Tumasra. With quantum surveillance, the Levinti could study Tumasra's effect on telepathy just as they've always wished. And such an outpost would also provide them with an even greater military advantage should the peace talks fail."

But could the Levinti even hide an outpost like that from the Etoscans, right here in their own territory?

Charism looks out at the Tumasra storm. "Yes, I believe so. Tumasra's unusual properties interfere with every known scanning technology. The caves beneath Tumasra would be the ideal place for the Levinti to hide such an outpost—from the Etoscans and from interstellar observers. And if the Levinti did indeed build such a base, directly beneath the sacred site of Tumasra—it would change everything. They would be in violation of the Treaty of Centron and humiliated in the interstellar community. If that is what the Bright Warrior uncovered—it is most certainly a secret the Levinti would murder him to contain."

My head swims with all this information. This is a whole new theory I never even thought of. And Charism's right, it's the first theory that would explain why one of the Great Powers felt so threatened by Umberto. And it would make Pash-Ti the prime suspect. But then why were the Etoscans so defensive when Timoteo brought up the surge?

"Of that I am uncertain," Charism says. "I have sensed their paranoia grow in recent weeks, particularly Listener. Perhaps they share my suspicions but have been unable to find the Levinti outpost in the vast caves beneath Tumasra. You must understand, those caves are vast and dangerous—impenetrable to telepathic sight. They have often been a refuge for criminals and outcasts—including the Hosh-Unam Front. I can only imagine what Ferus and his Outlander friends had to do to obtain the sample you're seeking from him."

I haven't been able to stop by thoughts from drifting to Ferus, to getting the sample—but I'm surprised Charism even knows Ferus.

"Oh, yes," Charism says. "Ferus and I were friends once, before he was seduced by the Hosh-Unam Front, and then the Outlanders. His mind has always had good intentions, though his thoughts have often turned in misguided directions—which has made him one of Hosh's most wanted criminals."

Ferus may be seen as a criminal, I think. *But my uncle trusted him.*

"I know," Charism says. "I saw that trust in his mind more than once. I confess it wounded me—to see that, in some ways, he trusted the Outlander more than me. The Bright Warrior knew that circumstances prevented me from assisting him as much as I would have liked. A mistake I will not repeat with you. Listen with your whole mind, Valiant One. If Ferus has a clue to unlock the mystery of whatever's hidden beneath

Tumasra, it may be the key to salvaging the peace. You must find him. I have access to one of the few pods here in the North."

My heart beats faster with shock and hope. Is Charism really going to help me get to the Outlanders? Why would he risk so much to help me?

"I am a pragmatist, above all else, Valiant One. I will risk everything for peace." With his upper claw, he points to another brown-stone path leading down the hill. "Follow this path and turn right at the fork at the edge of the valley. That will take you to a small hangar beside my private residence." He takes a small, star-shaped metallic device and places it in my palm. "This card will give you access to both the hangar and my pod. Maintain your distance from any Hoshans you cross in your path or your thoughts will betray you."

I can't leave Timoteo behind, I think.

"I will have the *unam* guide him to you," Charism says, "under the pretext of the two of you visiting my home."

What about Pash-Ti? I think. *They'll be suspicious. And I can't bring them with us when they might be the traitor.*

"The *unam* and I can keep Pash-Ti occupied, for a time at least."

It's all so overwhelming. Even once I get to Charism's pod, I'll have to fly it myself and find my way to the Outlands. But I *have* to find them. It's the only way. Charism's whiskers curl up in a smile. "You're much like your familial, Valiant One. Open-hearted yet determined."

Thank you, I think. *Thank you more than my thoughts can even say.*

Charism gives me a friendly scratch on the arm, and I return the gesture. "Go, quickly," he says. "May Synchronus guide your path."

CHAPTER 15

OUTLANDERS — On Earth & many planets, there are always subcultures seeking to carve a new, different path. A way of living that rejects false binaries. A safe haven for those who are different. That's what the Outlanders are for Hosh—a hope for a better future.

- From the notebook of Umberto Olmeda

THE BROWN MOON IS RISING HIGHER in the dim night sky. Our pod flies over the ocean below, which stretches from horizon to horizon.

It was nerve-wracking getting to the hangar. I kept taking long detours around the path to avoid getting within even 50 feet of any Hoshan. Then, once I got there and found a confused Timoteo, I had to figure out how to operate the pod—which turned out to have a slightly different interface from the one I'd seen Pash-Ti operate. I finally managed to get it working with some help from Checkers. We turned off our suits' location trackers before we left ... Hopefully, Charism has convinced Pash-Ti we're off meditating or something.

Timoteo is sitting beside me in the two-person pod. He still thinks we can't trust Ferus but has limited his protests to passive-aggressive snipping. He squints at the map to the Outlands scrawled across two pages of Umberto's notebook.

"Are you sure you're reading that thing right?" I say.

Timoteo squints at the notebook. "Well, sis, Umberto scribbled like a doctor writing prescriptions, and we're flying over miles of alien ocean with no landmarks, and my sense of direction has been known to fail me on the 10-minute walk from my dorm to class, so, um, no."

I turn a dial to increase our speed. Once I got the pod activated, the interface has turned out to be pretty intuitive.

The brown moon rises higher, followed closely by the smaller, silver moon, which Hoshans call the daughter of the larger moon. After over an hour, I wonder if this was a mistake. I just hope we find Ferus and that his sample will finally give us some answers.

The big moon is directly over us when Timoteo says, "Hey, what's that?" He points toward several small shadows flying across the sky. From a distance they look cigar-shaped, and for a second I think they're pods. I make a slight right toward the shadows. As we get closer, I see they're only about the size of eagles—way too small to be pods. A blurry set of wings carries the long, scaly creatures through the air, like living helicopters.

"I can't believe I'm seeing actual alien animals!" Timoteo says, reading on the inside of his glasses. "They're similar to Earth's birds in some ways, but their method of flying is totally different—more like a bumblebee or dragonfly, or—"

"Flying like that must take a lot of energy," I say. "They must need some place to stop and rest, which means we can't be too far from land. From the Jutting Archipelago."

I slow down to make sure we don't miss anything. I feel a glimmer of hope that we might be close. I just hope my instincts are right that we really can trust Ferus, like Umberto did.

Then I see something on the far horizon. Many somethings. At first I think it might be a long convoy of oddly-shaped barges. As we get closer, I see that each object is bowl-shaped, held high above the water's surface by a single column beneath its center. The bowls are all tilted in the same direction, like a string of enormous satellite dishes in the middle of the ocean.

It takes a while for us to close in on them.

"Are these really naturally occurring?" I say, as we finally get close to one.

"They really are," Timoteo says, reading from his glasses. "Each bowl, or 'outland' of the Jutting Archipelago is actually a complex of several organisms with symbiotic relationships. The upper organisms are photosynthetic, but the lower organisms draw energy from a long trench of volcanic vents deep beneath the sea, and their waste is cycled through—"

"I'm going to get closer and fly over one," I say, and angle the pod down toward the nearest of the bowls. Umberto's map didn't show an exact location for the Outlanders' base, just directions to this long chain of outlands dozens of miles long. "Keep an eye out for any signs of the Outlanders. Like, I don't know, buildings or something." Close up, the bowl's surface is brown and gnarled, like hundreds of tree roots woven together in a thick, rough tapestry. Purple sheaths fill the gaps between the gnarl of roots, like canvas stretched across a frame.

I skim the pod over the vast bowl, the vegetation getting thicker. A flock of the helicopter-like birds fly by, and a group of creatures swing across the upper level of the branches below—like Hoshans, but smaller and with longer limbs.

"This doesn't exactly look like a secret Outlander base," Timoteo says.

"I'm going to fly us over the whole area. Turn all your thoughts to the fact that we're looking for Ferus and that Umberto was our uncle, and maybe they'll sense our thoughts."

"This is your plan?" Timoteo says. "Hope they catch us on their telepathic radar?"

"Let me know if you come up with something better," I say.

We fly over more than twenty outlands in a chain that goes on as far as we can see—all nothing but dense forest. But these Outlanders don't want to be easily found, so it's no surprise we can't see them from the air. Our best hope is for them to find us.

Hopelessness winds its way into my thoughts, even as I try to focus my mind on Ferus. Timoteo glances over at me, raising his eyebrows in a typical Timoteo I-told-you-so look.

But then Checkers' voice cuts through the quiet desperation of my thoughts, announcing an incoming transmission: "It's a welcome relief to see the currents of your mind, Valiant One. I never doubted you would find me." It's the same as the voice from the hologram.

"Ferus!" I shout. My plan actually worked.

Ferus asks us to turn control of the pod over to them, and as soon as I do, the windows darken. Timoteo taps on the darkened glass. "I really hope you're right about this, Val ..."

It is unnerving, not being able to see where we're going. The pod makes a gentle landing. The hatch opens, and Timoteo and I climb out into a hangar with a bunch of other pods. I'm surprised to see pods here. I'd pictured the Outlanders as more ... rustic.

From behind me, there's a series of clicks. I turn and see a slim Hoshan male with shortly trimmed orange fur, wearing a shiny yellow amulet around his neck. It must be Ferus. He scurries toward me on all six legs. "It's an honor to meet you in person, Valiant One." He kicks up onto his hind legs, and surprises me by stretching up to paw my face instead of just scratching my forearm. "The scratch-greeting may be shared with any stranger," he explains, "but Umberto was family to you and me alike, and so we are family to one another."

I reciprocate the gesture, crouching over to touch my palm to Ferus's face. My hands are trembling again—not with fear this time, but with gratitude. I've met dozens of sentients on Hosh, but this is the most warmth anyone has shown me. And it's coming from someone that Umberto called friend.

"A true friend," Ferus says. "I still mourn his loss, and I see in your mind that you do as well."

Ferus turns to Timoteo. "I am indeed Ferus, and you are Timoteo." Ferus reaches up to paw his face, but Timoteo is too tall—and stays standing upright, out of Ferus's reach. "Ah. You're desperate for help to solve the mystery of Umberto's murder. You've read of my history with the Hosh-Unam Front, and so a dark wariness tinges your hope that you might trust me as Umberto did. Your thoughts are two opposing waves crashing against each other."

Timoteo looks down at the ground. "That pretty much covers it."

"It's true then?" I ask. "You were in the Hosh-Unam Front?"

"Thankfully, my career in insurgency was short-lived," Ferus says. "And largely unsuccessful."

"So what did you find?" Timoteo says. "What's hidden beneath Tumasra?"

"I found the sample," Ferus replies. "And will share all I can in due time."

"We don't have time for this cryptic stuff," Timoteo says. "We need to know what your deal is, and we need your help figuring out what Umberto knew."

"It's not my intent to be cryptic," Ferus says. "I'm as desperate as you to save the peace. But there is much debate among the Outlanders as to what course to chart next—and whether we can trust you as we chart it."

"So you have to test us before you'll help us," Timoteo says.

"I would not say 'test,'" Ferus says. "I trust you just as I did the Bright Warrior. But there are others among us who would know you better first."

"That makes sense," I say, before Timoteo has the chance to say something else. His impatience is no help, not when our only hope is to win the Outlanders' trust.

"Come," Ferus says, dropping to all six legs. "You must meet the others."

We follow Ferus through a corridor, its walls and floor made of a slick polymer. Soon the slick floor gives way to a ground of gnarled roots, and the walls give way to tall trees and shoots of luscious purple forest. Ferus navigates the gnarled ground with ease, but Timoteo stumbles in the dim light.

Soon we come to a clearing in the woods. A group of Hoshans is gathered around a table that just reaches the height of their middle limbs when they stand on their hind legs. Some are stirring bowls, and others are chopping egg-shaped red fruits. Beyond the table, a Hoshan is tending a stove that's split into four shelves, each with a pot or pan mounted on it. He stands on his hind legs, stretching to his full height to reach the pot on the top shelf, then drops to five legs to stir the pot on the lowest shelf. It smells like stew and onions and something bitter, like vinegar. A sense of ease comes over me as I take it all in. There's nothing alien about this: a group of friends and family cooking together.

The Hoshans look up as we approach. The chopping suddenly stops, and even the Hoshan tending four flames abandons his steaming pots. They all stare wide-eyed at Timoteo and me.

"It's rare we host guests here," Ferus says. "And even rarer that we host aliens."

The Hoshans leap away from the table and scurry toward us. In moments, they're circling Timoteo and me, reaching up to paw at us, examine our clothing, stare at our smooth furless hands. One of them scrambles up Timoteo's clothes to touch his face. "Whoa," Timoteo says, "don't mess up my hair."

The two of us stand quietly, letting the Hoshans satiate their curiosity about us. It's awkward at first, but then feels more natural, like the way little kids get to know each other. I hope it builds some trust with them.

One Hoshan hasn't joined the circle and is still sitting at the table, looking at us with a frown. She's short and stocky, sitting on the bench with quiet confidence—almost regal. I can tell she's important. I extricate myself from the circle and sit next to her.

Hi. My name is Valeria Vega. I'm honored to meet you, and I appreciate you hosting us.

Her eyes squint beneath her unkempt fur, then she lets out a harrumph. Ferus paces over to us on six legs. "This is Kettle," Ferus says. "And she's pleased to meet you too. She was born here in the Outlands, far from any mind-deaf. She grew up communicating only with telepathy, unaccustomed to the languages taught us by the Etoscans and Levinti."

Kettle turns her head toward me, but not her body. She speaks in slow clicks. "Foolishness. You allow them play with you like giant dolls. But your existence not dolls. Your existence aliens. Aliens always bring problems, violence." A note from Checkers flashes across my arm-screen: *Kettle speaks North Hoshan with nontraditional grammar. I'm attempting to interpret the unusual flow of her speech as best as possible into English.*

"Umberto was an alien too," Ferus says. "In time, he earned our trust—even yours."

"What result exists?" Kettle says. Timoteo joins us, and she looks at the two of us. "Now Bright Warrior dead. Hosh in greatest danger in generations."

"You must forgive Kettle's bluntness," Ferus says. "Speaking out loud is taxing for her."

Kettle harrumphs and says, "But Ferus love talk by any manner or language."

Ferus responds by nuzzling Kettle's neck with his nose. Hoshans are so affectionate that I'm not sure if it's a friendly gesture or something more romantic. They'd make an unlikely pair, Kettle so gruff and Ferus so smooth.

"Oh, yes," Ferus says, unhooking his face from Kettle's neck. "Kettle and I have been primary partners for many years now."

Timoteo and I trade a look, our eyebrows raised in unison.

Ferus snorts. "Yes, she is irritable, but the depth of her mind is as full of wonders as the vibrant seascape that stretches beneath the Outlands."

Kettle grunts. "Told you he liked to talk."

Ferus touches his paw to Kettle's face. "The treaty talks will determine Hosh's fate, and these two are among our few true allies. You see in their minds they mean us no harm."

"Virus means no harm," Kettle says. "Still virus makes you sick."

"We're not like the others," I say. "We want peace, the same as you."

"Look," Timoteo says, "if you give us the sample and tell us what you know, maybe we can figure out a way out of this mess."

Kettle sits unmoving on the bench, like a statue in a park.

"Perhaps they could join us for the midnight meal," Ferus suggests. "That will give us all a chance to get to know each other better."

Kettle grunts. I'm not sure if it's assent or refusal.

"You want to chat over lunch?" Timoteo says. "We need to figure out who killed our uncle, and who's trying to sabotage these talks!"

Ferus reaches up to gently touch Timoteo's arm. "We're fortunate Kettle is open to sharing a meal. And I sense your hunger. Even in crisis, you must eat at some point."

✧ ✧ ✧

THE DINING AREA is in a clearing, covered with wood planks, like a big deck. It's dimly lit by lamps hanging from the branches and by the light of Hosh's large copper moon. Across the deck, twenty tables are spread out, each low enough for Hoshans to eat comfortably while sitting on their four hind legs.

Ferus guides Timoteo and me to where Kettle and a group of others are sitting. We sit down cross-legged at the too-low-for-Terrans table. Smoke wafts from the Hoshan stew, its scent like burning grass. The stew isn't digestible for humans, so they bring us a simple bowl of fruits, which Checkers confirms is edible for us. I expect the fruits to taste like strawberries, maybe because they're red, but they taste more like avocados drenched in lemon juice. Who knows when we'll have the chance to eat again, so I eat as much as I can, and supplement mine and Timoteo's with some trail mix from my bag.

I was hoping to ask Ferus about the sample and if he can confirm any of our theories, but Timoteo and I are the ones answering questions. What's it like on other planets? What's it like being mind-deaf? Do you always worry about people lying to you? How do the mind-deaf avoid bumping into each other?

"Unfortunately, some of us bump into each other and all kinds of objects all the time," Timoteo answers, and the entire table titters with Hoshan laughter, probably sensing in Timoteo's mind his long history of clumsiness.

In the middle of the meal, one Hoshan stops eating and stares at Timoteo and me. The Hoshan's tail is like a female's—not naturally fluffy—but adorned with violet furry curls, almost like a wig for a tail. It makes me wonder if they're the Hoshan equivalent of trans or nonbinary.

The violet-tailed Hoshan lets out a titter and signs, "Yes, many Hoshans like me let our minds and bodies flow through waters both male and female. Especially here in the Outlands, where we are free to explore the deepest oceans of our minds.

"You're both so much like your familial, and yet so different," they go on signing. It's interesting that some of them are speaking the sign language of the South, and others the vocal language of the North. I guess they come to the Outlands from all over the planet. "It's an odd feeling we Hoshans experience sometimes. I've seen you both so often in Umberto's thoughts. I feel as if I've met you before, though we are meeting mind-to-mind for the first time. Yet you are not quite as I saw you in his mind, and so it's ... incongruous. We call this *vasek antrellus*."

Ferus nods as he lifts a ladle-like spoon to his mouth. "Yes, I've been experiencing *vasek antrellus* as well."

"How are we different from how Umberto pictured us?" Timoteo asks.

Ferus snorts. "For one thing, you're surprisingly large, but that's to be expected, since Umberto often pictured you as children. And I suppose any Terran would seem large to us!"

"*Vasek antrellus*," I say, remembering my conversation with Charism. "Does that have do with *vasek antom*?"

"Ah," Ferus says. "So Charism has told you of *vasek antom*. The root is the same—*vasek*, which means an encounter of the minds."

I try to remember how Charism explained it—an intense disagreement, but which brings you closer. I didn't quite understand it.

"Indeed, you do not understand," Ferus says. "It's much more than a disagreement. *Vasek antom* can only take place when you dive deep into the difference between your thoughts and those of another. It's only then that you can truly know one another's minds."

"Ferus expert," Kettle says. "He and I have *vasek antom* every day."

"Indeed, my love," Ferus says, nuzzling Kettle's neck. "Every day brings us into ever deeper union." I'm not sure if they're serious or joking or some ironic combination.

There's a moment of silence, and then the violet-tailed Hoshan makes a slow series of signs. "You've seen the brutality of the Hosh-Unam Front," they say. "They robbed you of air itself for a few moments. Your mind still rings with the horror of it."

"Jerana's mind has keen hearing," Ferus explains. "They can sense feelings with great depth—and from great distances."

"Marrow threatened another attack," I say.

Jerana looks down at their bowl of half-eaten stew. "Such wretched violence. And where will it carry us?"

"To further violence, of course," says a Hoshan with a pointy nose, who seems like an intellectual. "Violence: the only creature in the Galaxy that is its own parent as well as its own offspring."

"I don't know," says another, from the far end of the table. "Sometimes I'm not sure which is worse, the brutality of the Hosh-Unam Front or the complacency of the masses. The Etoscans and

Levinti have been exploiting us for centuries, and our brethren in North and South do nothing. Our complacency is our doom."

"But why do Hoshans just accept all this?" Timoteo says. "I mean why haven't Hoshans rebelled? It seems like your telepathy would at least give you a tactical advantage."

"It's not a matter of the tactics allowed by telepathy," says the intellectual with the sharp nose. "It's a matter of the culture created by telepathy. We're a pliable people. We sense others' thoughts and accommodate them. The Hoshan mind can adapt itself to any situation. Unfortunately, we have adapted ourselves to a situation that is wholly unacceptable."

"We don't all bend with every current," Ferus says, sipping his stew. "There were attempts at rebellion, when the occupation first began. And the Hosh-Unam Front still resists, however terrible their methods."

"The Hosh-Unam Front is not a relevant example," Sharp-nose retorts. "Their members are pathological, aberrations from the normal Hoshan mind—no offense intended, Ferus. Early in the occupation, there were pockets of resistance in the mainstream Hoshan population—a subset, perhaps, with tendencies toward boldness but without the pathological characteristics of the Hosh-Unam Front. But our occupiers have brilliantly culled these potential rebels from their Hoshan herds, recruiting the boldest of us to go off-world to join their telepathic legions!"

"A theory," Ferus says, his words slow and measured, "that is oft-repeated by the Hosh-Unam Front, whose members you dismiss as pathological."

The sharp-nosed Hoshan waves his spoon in the air dismissively. "A lunatic can count the stars as easily as the sane."

"So what about now?" I ask. "All of you are against being colonized, aren't you? Why not rebel now? Not like the Hosh-Unam Front, but with nonviolence. If millions of Hoshans rose up, the Etoscans and Levinti couldn't kill all of you, could they?"

Kettle snorts and sets down her bowl. "Millions not exist," she says. "Safer here, far from alien wars and alien politics."

"It's as Kettle says," Ferus says. "There are simply too few of us. Most Hoshans in both North and South see the occupation as benevolent— or are simply too fearful to resist. And you must not underestimate the brutality of the Great Powers. They have laid waste to entire villages in both North and South to remind us just how absolute their power over us is."

"That's horrible," I say. "But maybe there's another way. Umberto wanted you to be part of these negotiations. If the Outlands were recognized, if you could live out in the open, maybe it could help inspire other Hoshans ..."

Ferus turns his snout downward and shakes his head. "Ah, Valiant One, you are true to your name. But we both know you lack the power to bring us into the peace talks. And we would not risk jeopardizing them. At least now you seem to have some slim possibility of success, which would preserve the peace we know now, even if it is a peace without freedom."

Nearly all the Hoshans have finished eating. Timoteo looks at Ferus and Kettle. "Umberto figured out something so dangerous that it got him killed. If you give us the sample, maybe we can figure out what he knew. Maybe that will give us the leverage we need to push the Etoscans and Levinti to give Hosh more autonomy, to recognize the Outlands."

Ferus touches Kettle gently, paw to paw. "The violence may reach us here regardless, my dear."

Jerana looks at Kettle, lips trembling. "And what of the souls all across our world who will suffer if war should come again? Are they not our brethren too?"

All eyes are on Kettle, who returns their gaze with a silent frown.

"Kettle's really in charge here, isn't she?" Timoteo says.

"Kettle has long been our leader," Ferus says, smiling at his mate. "And she still has many reservations about the role of the Outlands in this conflict, and about the two of you. But she has reservations about most sentients she encounters." He turns to Kettle and says, "This whole time, their minds have revealed only good intentions. What more may they do to earn our trust?"

Kettle pulls herself up onto the table and stands on top of it so she's at my height. She clutches my shirt with her upper claw and pulls me toward her.

I gulp. "What do you—?"

"Words only confuse!" She leans over, the fur of her forehead pressing against mine.

The only noise is the quiet chirping of a distant Outlands animal. It feels like my mind is under a microscope.

CHAPTER 16

KETTLE'S FUR IS MATTED AND WARM. She smells like freshly fallen autumn leaves. Beads of sweat form on my face, which makes me self-conscious. It feels like she's deciding if I'm worthy.

I try what I did when Trimana interrogated me, to consciously share my thoughts. *I understand how hard it is to trust people. I think what you're building here in the Outlands is inspiring. I just want—*

She lets out abrupt clicks. "Not word-thoughts. Images. Feelings. Raw matter of the mind."

How am I supposed to share the raw matter of my mind? The first image to come to me is Umberto, and with it that gnawing feeling of grief in my gut. Then the pressure to live up to his faith in me, to maintain the fragile peace. I flash through all the memories of my investigation of Umberto's murder. For some reason my mind turns to the misting with the Etoscans, the image of a giant-sized Umberto in my locker, telling me not to miss the train. Whatever that meant, I'm worried I already missed it.

Abruptly, Kettle pulls away from me. "Your mind soft like putty," she says. "But deep like layers of soil." She lifts her snout toward Ferus.

"Kettle feels she knows your mind enough to begin to trust you," Ferus explains. "She's ready—" Ferus whips his head toward Jerana, as if she'd cut him off with a shout. "How far?"

"Twenty minutes away," Jerana signs.

"What's going on?" I ask.

"A swarm of bots," Ferus explains, "flying toward us from the mainland. We need to shut down all technology to prevent them from detecting us." To Jerana, he says, "Are any Hoshan agents with them?"

Jerana closes their eyes for a few moments. "I sense no minds approaching. Not for miles. Gerwyn has begun the transition to full stealth configuration."

"Good," he says. "We must gather in the central grotto." His upper and middle arms interlace with Kettle's, the two of them leading the way to the grotto.

✧ ✧ ✧

THE GROTTO IS DRY and nothing like caves on Earth. Buds and spindles of coral line the walls and ceiling. The floor is smooth, and dozens of lanterns hang from the buds all along the ceiling, casting a soft light.

The cavern is full of machines and computers and pods—all of which were powered down within minutes of the warning of the approaching swarm. It's surprising they have such advanced technology here in the Outlands.

"We're hardly primitives," Ferus says, approaching Timoteo and me. "We've done all we can to avoid detection. Now we must wait for the swarm to pass."

I hope it's not our fault the swarm is here, that our pod wasn't followed—I'd hate to have put the Outlanders in danger.

"That's unlikely," Ferus says. "Our net of sensors showed that the swarm was following a standard search pattern across the archipelago. If they did follow you, they didn't do a very good job of it. The search-swarms have been through these parts regularly for months now. They may not even be searching for us. More likely it is the Etoscans or Levinti making ready for war should the treaty fail."

"You do this every time?" Timoteo says. "Power down, hide here in the grotto?"

"Not always here, but, yes," Ferus says. "We must be ever vigilant to avoid detection."

"They really can't find you?" Timoteo says. "With all their technology?"

"We have keen telepaths like Jerana, who give ample warning when any organic mind is approaching. And the Outlands are filled with nooks and crannies, no shortage of places to hide beyond the easy reach of bots and mind-agents. But those are not the only reasons we've remained in hiding so effectively." He drops to all six legs and beckons us toward a corner of the grotto where the ceiling is lower. "Come. Kettle has asked me to show you something."

Timoteo and I follow Ferus, Timoteo ducking to enter the low-ceilinged passage. Ferus holds a lantern in his upper-left claw, its light guiding our way. The passageway opens up, leading to a smaller chamber that branches off from the central grotto. Ferus lifts his lantern to cast light on the chamber and says, "This is where we learn."

The room is lined with low tables designed for Hoshan arms—no higher than my knees. Each table is strewn with lenses, scopes, centrifuges, and dozens of other devices. Beneath those scopes, under the magnification of those lenses, are bots. Each bot has been pulled apart in various phases of disassembly—and maybe reconstruction.

"Oh, yes," Ferus says, leading us further into the laboratory, "most definitely reconstruction. You see, my friends, whether in the North, where the Etoscans deny us the Galaxy's wondrous technologies, or in the South, where the Levinti pamper us with all technology's benefits but none of its secrets—all across Hosh, it is the same. Why have any curiosity about the laws of mathematics when the Levinti have solved every equation? Why ponder the deeper truths of creation when the Etoscans can give us a pre-packaged God that weds science and mysticism? Our colonizers have stolen many things from us, but I daresay their greatest crime may have been to steal our sense of wonder."

"So you're, like, trying to reverse-engineer Etoscan and Levinti tech," Timoteo says.

"Yes," Ferus says, "and we've come up with some of our own innovations as well. We've dozens of laboratories like this, hundreds of scientists working every day, all across the Outlands. We sync our minds as we investigate. I can't tell you how inspiring it is, when one Hoshan's discovery ripples across our minds and a wave of understanding washes over us all. Legend says that's how it used to be across all Hosh, before the first invasion." He waves a claw at the air, and clucks his lips. "But a million things are said about how it was before the first invasion. Who knows what's true and what's myth?"

"So how far have you gotten?" I say.

Ferus lets out a grunt, a sound eerily like one that Kettle might make. "Not nearly as far as we'd like. But far enough that we can detect a bot coming from hundreds of miles away. Far enough that we know a dozen ways to keep them from detecting us. We've even found at least one way for bots to communicate with one another unlike anything developed by the Etoscans or the Levinti. Perhaps our telepathic way of thinking grants us insights into possibilities the mind-deaf have not yet imagined."

Ferus stands on his hind legs and holds the lantern up as high as he can, so that it almost reaches my shoulder. The three of us stand in its gentle glow, and Ferus goes on, "Until you, Umberto was the only off-worlder who knew of this. He knew we weren't just a bunch of antisocial eccentrics. Umberto told me that we represented something far greater than our numbers. He said we represented a new path for Hosh—proof that Hoshans need not be dependent on our masters."

"And that's why he wanted you to be part of the treaty negotiations," I say. "To represent the Outlanders as a fifth party."

"Precisely. Though I never believed even Umberto could accomplish such a feat. I show you all these, because I want you to know all that Umberto knew." He pulls something out from a sealed compartment at one of the tables. It's a small vial containing a translucent blue fluid. "Your familial's last request of me was to attain this sample. He traced that odd energy surge to somewhere just near—and under—Tumasra. He knew I knew those caves well from my brief time in the Hosh-Unam Front, and asked me to investigate. Those caverns are still the haven of the Front—and are routinely patrolled by Etoscan swarms. It took all the guile and resources of the Outlanders to infiltrate them, but at last we found this unusual compound near the source of the energy surge. Half a mile beneath Tumasra and the Etoscan Citadel. I failed to deliver it to the Bright One before he died, but by giving it to you now, I at last complete my mission."

He places the vial in my palm, and suddenly my hand feels lighter, as if the vial has weight that works in reverse.

"Indeed," Ferus says. "It has many odd properties, but even here in the Outlands I lack the proper instruments to analyze its composition. But you do, at the Terran Embassy."

"Finally," Timoteo says, reaching out to me. I pass him the vial and moves it up and down like a helium balloon with its strange reverse-weight. "Do you have any idea what it is?"

"It goes far beyond my knowledge," Ferus says. ""But given that we found it so close to the Etoscan Citadel, it made me wonder if the Etoscans are developing a secret storehouse of weapons there—some kind of weapon outlawed by interstellar law."

Timoteo shakes his head. "I thought that too. But I've been reading up, and what Charism told Val is true. The Etoscans are building up weapons all across the North, and everybody knows it. Nothing in interstellar law stops them from building as many weapons as they want in territory that belongs to them."

"I know little of interstellar law," Ferus says. "But I sensed in Umberto's mind that he believed something was hidden beneath Tumasra. On his last visit to Hosh, Umberto came here to the Outlands. His mind was far from its usual state of calm. He asked many questions about the caves beneath Tumasra, their layout and depth. He even had me draw him a map from memory! Then he asked if I could help him find out more about the suspicious energy surge. He hoped that would provide the proof he needed."

"But proof of what?" I say.

"He never said," Ferus says. "He managed to keep that crucial fact far from his mind. I only sensed vague suspicions—of Listener in particular. That's why I thought the Etoscans must be hiding a new weapon in their Citadel."

"I've been researching too," I say. "Even if there is some weapon prohibited by interstellar law, there's another gap in that theory. On Earth, there's only one sentient who's sympathetic to the Etoscans: Wasala. And she's not even allowed on Hosh. She'd have no way of communicating with Listener and Speaker, not without the Interstellar Subway security systems detecting it."

Ferus scurries over to one of the research tables and picks up a tiny bot no bigger than a pinhead. "*We* found a way. We call this a seed." He holds the bot up to the soft lamplight. "It's a software program that's a blueprint for a much more complicated program. Once activated, it can even develop into a simple AI. Nothing as complicated as swarm-technology, or the Synthetics. But capable of building simple constructs like the squirrel we sent you—and of sending recorded messages. But as long as it's in seed form, it appears innocuous, much easier to hide from the Interstellar Subway security systems. The Etoscans could be communicating with Wasala using something like this."

Timoteo takes the tiny seed-bot and holds it in his fingers, peering at it through his glasses. "That's an interesting possibility. But it still doesn't give us the goods on what the Etoscans could be hiding. Charism's theory about the Levinti spying from an outpost just beneath Tumasra seems more plausible."

"There's one other possibility," Ferus says, "of a deeper conspiracy—involving more than one faction. There's one more secret I confided in Umberto. The Etoscans—and the Levinti—have been arming the Front for decades."

"What?" I say. "But why?"

"Their relationship is insidiously symbiotic. The violence of the Hosh-Unam Front helps justify their endless occupation."

Timoteo gives the seed back to Ferus and folds his arms. "That's not surprising. It's not that different from what colonizers on Earth do. And maybe Umberto hid his real theory from you because he didn't fully trust you." He glares at me and adds, "We're getting intel from a killer."

I grit my teeth. "Umberto trusted him, Timoteo. You're literally insulting one of our only friends on this planet—"

"It's all right," Ferus interrupts. He sets the lantern down on the ground and sits on his four hindmost legs. He looks up at us, his somber face lit by the lantern's orange glow. "It's reasonable to question my history. I was young. Bright. My telepathic sight—it's nowhere near Jerana's talents, but well above average. Traits that made me an ideal candidate for the Etoscans' Brigade of telepathic agents. The Brigades were alluring, with all the Etoscans' propaganda about that adventurous lifestyle. But I couldn't bear the thought of never coming home again. That price made the adventure too expensive.

"The Hosh-Unam Front found me only days after I'd received my draft notice for the Brigades. I felt so relieved to have an escape hatch. I thought I'd found the best of all worlds—a life of intrigue and adventure, without having to leave my world.

"Then I went on my first mission for the Front. Marrow knew I still had doubts. He promised me that no Hoshans would be killed. Only occupiers. I was several hundred meters away when the weapon discharged. We were supposed to kill more than a dozen Etoscans, but our timing was off, so we ended up hitting only one.

"It happened so fast. In one moment, his mind was there. The next, it was not." Ferus looks up at us in the dim light, his lips quivering. "I left the Hosh-Unam Front that night, and, thankfully, found my way here. I understand your wariness toward me. I feel wary toward myself, toward the person I was that night when I robbed the world of a mind. Ever since, remorse has been a constant companion of my thoughts."

I sit down beside Ferus and touch my palm to his face. He reaches up to cover my hand with his paw, his lips still quivering.

Timoteo stares at us, his eyes darting between sympathy and judgment. "Okay. At least we have a couple viable theories."

Ferus stands up, calmer now. "I wish I could be of more help. Perhaps your analysis of the sample will allow you to complete the puzzle, as Umberto hoped."

"Maybe," I say. "I guess that's our only hope at this point."

"The swarm has passed," Ferus says, leading us back toward the central grotto. "Timoteo, if you find Jerana, they can give you more food for your journey."

Timoteo leaves, and Ferus tugs me gently by the sleeve. "When Kettle looked more deeply into your mind, I saw your memory of seeing Umberto in the Etoscan mists. Dig deeper there. Perhaps he left you some other clue that you missed. Sometimes the mind reveals things in unexpected ways."

"Okay," I say, not sure what to make of that.

Ferus holds the lantern up to me, searching my face. "Yours is truly a fascinating mind. You're almost like a Hoshan, the way you bend your mind to accommodate the thoughts of others. Yet you're also so different from us, so utterly un-Hoshan."

"How is that?"

"Hoshans are not merely adaptable to the thought-streams of others. We're also boldly open with our own thoughts, unashamed of sharing who we are. If we weren't, we'd be like an empty corridor of mirrors, light bouncing back and forth, but ultimately reflecting nothing. You're not like us. You hold back your thoughts. You hold back your very self."

When did I do that?

"Quite frequently," Ferus says. "Most recently, just now, when I first began speaking about being a member of the Hosh-Unam Front. A wave of harsh judgment passed over your mind, but you pushed it away, fearful of hurting my feelings should I sense your critical thoughts."

So what am I supposed to do? Just think terrible things about you?

"Yes!" Ferus says. "Think terrible things about me, think them right to my face! Share with me your judgments, your anger, your fear, your you! That is *vasek antom*!"

I just stand there in silence, not sure what to say, or even what to think.

"You've been gone too long already," Ferus says. "You must return to the mainland."

✧ ✧ ✧

TIMOTEO SITS NEXT TO ME in the pod, holding the vial up close to his glasses, squinting at it. We're still passing over the Hoshan ocean, just a few minutes away from the Northern mainland. "Majel says this has exotic matter," Timoteo says. "That's the only thing that explains this weird reverse-gravity thing."

"So what would that mean?" I say.

"It's definitely not something you can get from a Hoshan bodega. Maybe this will answer all our questions once we do a full analysis. Or maybe it's another dead end, I don't know. I'm a political scientist, not a physicist, damn it, Jim!"

We both chuckle. "I can't believe you watched all those ancient *Star Trek* shows from, like, last century."

"Those are classics!" Timoteo carefully puts the vial in the inside pocket of his purse. "But seriously, Val. I'm sorry. You were right about coming to the Outlands. You were right to put our trust in the same people Umberto did. Ferus did something terrible, but people—sentients—can grow. Tío Umberto taught us that, and I should have listened when you reminded me. I still can't believe he's gone—that all this is real. I'm so sad and angry and it's making me bonkers and I'm at my worst. Like lashing out with the Etoscans—that was so stupid. I'm sorry."

"Wow, this is historic. An apology from fancy Harvard political scientist great wise big-brother Timoteo." I take out my phone and hold it up to him. "Can you say that one more time? I need to record it for posterity."

Timoteo swats the phone away, playfully. "For the record, I

apologize routinely!"

I'm about to put my phone back in my bag when I see something approaching. Three somethings. Bots.

"Oh shoot, are those Etoscan bots?" Timoteo says.

"It looks like it," I say, as the bots zoom toward us. They're the size of grenades, glowing red lenses pointing straight at our pod. Lenses for cameras—or weapons? Even if they're just cameras, if the Etoscans catch us here, the peace talks are doomed.

I do the only thing I can think of—I open the Set to Stun app on my phone. If it would work on Johnny, it's got to work on these things. I activate the neutralizer and aim it at the bots. There's a brief flash of light, and abruptly the bots' red glow disappears just a few feet from us. Their velocity slows, but momentum carries them toward us, all three of them bouncing harmlessly off the front window of our pod.

Timoteo lets out a lungful of relief. "How did you do that? I thought they had us for sure. Um, is our altitude dropping?"

The lights of our pod's control board have all gone dark. We drop faster and faster, falling straight toward the Hoshan ocean.

CHAPTER 17

WE'RE CAREENING TOWARD THE OCEAN and can't have more than a minute before we crash.

"We have to find the emergency eject!" I shout. "It's probably mechanical, it may still work!"

Timoteo is pressing his hands against the wall and ceiling of the pod. "I don't see any levers, any buttons! All the controls went dark! How is this even happening? I thought you knocked out those bots before they got to us!"

I'm searching my side of the pod and can't find anything either. "I think I caused it! When I knocked out the bots, the neutralizer took out our own pod too! Wait—we're thinking like humans. We reach up and to the side with our hands, but Hoshans have six prehensile claws."

I reach below my seat, to where a Hoshan's hind claws would easily reach. I find a knob the size of a Hoshan claw. It won't budge clockwise, but when I twist to the left, it gives. Then I yank it upward.

Suddenly Timoteo and I are surging into the air, the entire middle section of the pod ejected upward. My stomach lurches and I suppress a wave of nausea. A material of bright green inflates like a line of bumper cushions all around our seats. After rising a few hundred yards into the sky, we start falling again—gently at first, but then faster.

"Um," Timoteo says, "is it just me or are we still accelerating? Where's the frigging parachute?"

"Maybe it works on antigravity," I think out loud. "That must have got knocked out too!"

Timoteo presses his back against his seat, avoiding looking down. "Shoot. But wait! We have antigravity!"

Of course! "Checkers," I say. "Can your antigravity work on this whole thing we're in?"

"I'm afraid the mass is too large for my capacity alone," Checkers says. "But I could manipulate such a large mass by extending my antigravity field in tandem with that of Timoteo's suit."

"Majel, do it!" Timoteo says, talking to his suit at the same time.

We stop accelerating and gently descend. Below us, the rest of our pod has already crashed into the ocean, split into pieces.

Timoteo still has his back pressed against the chair, breaths heaving. "Please let's never do that again."

✦ ✦ ✦

OUR RAFT BOBS in the waters of Hosh's ocean. With two bright moons lighting up the sky, the nighttime isn't as dark as on Earth. It's been about 30 minutes since we reactivated the transponders in our suits and called Pash-Ti. They sounded pretty angry—even for Pash-Ti. And I can't blame them. We ghosted them and then asked if they could come rescue us from this mess. It's like that time I stayed out past 2 am and then had to call Mami to pick me up from some sketchy parking lot. Only ten times worse because Pash-Ti is way scarier than Mami.

Finally, near the edge of the horizon, something approaches—a bright red fin cutting through the water.

"Oh God," Timoteo says. "I really hope that's not a Hoshan shark or something."

"I ... don't think that's organic." The fin has a shimmer to it, and

I've seen that same exact shade of red before on a motorcycle, a pod, and a racing jacket. But I'm not sure until it gets closer, and a gleaming red submarine rises to the surface of the water. "Johnny? Is that you?"

"Hey there, Val, long time no see!" comes Johnny's familiar voice from the submarine as it pulls up beside us.

"Is that you, Johnny?" says Timoteo. "I'm so glad you're okay!"

"The one and only," Johnny says, his human body emerging from a hatch, followed by Pash-Ti's wiry gray form.

"Pash-Ti," I say. "It's a relief to see you, too."

Pash-Ti folds their long arms. "I'm relieved you both appear unharmed."

I stand up. "Johnny, are you okay? The Southland Hoshans finally let you go?"

Johnny extends a hand to help me cross from our makeshift raft to his submarine. "Not exactly. They're still interrogating me, actually. Oh, how they love interrogation! But I sent off a little seed-bot small enough to fly under their radar. Then I just whipped up a dupe of my fab bod, which is what you see standing before you now." He turns to Timoteo and winks. "Welcome to the team, BTW, Timoteo."

"Um, so there are two of you now?" Timoteo says, struggling to balance as Johnny helps him onto the sub.

"Two bodies." Johnny does a jazz-hands splay. "Only *one* Johnny."

Pash-Ti stands unmoving atop the submarine, long spindly arms folded together. "One Johnny is quite enough for the Galaxy. Ambassador, your record of getting yourself into dreadful situations remains unblemished. What did you possibly hope to accomplish commandeering the pod of the leader of Northern Hosh and venturing so far from the mainland, endangering yourself, Timoteo, our mission, and any semblance of order in the Galaxy?"

Timoteo and I have been preparing for this. We still can't trust them enough to tell them everything—especially about the sample—but we have to tell them at least part of the truth. "I found Umberto's notebook," I say. "And it had these notes about that energy surge ... about Ferus and the Outlands. It seems like Umberto trusted Ferus, like Ferus might know more about whatever secret got Umberto called. So we borrowed Charism's pod and tried to find them."

"A little Outlands field trip, huh?" Johnny says. He holds up a grenade-sized bot that looks like the ones that nearly attacked us. "I had some of my own bots check all the waters in this vicinity and found three of these. *This* is a problem."

"Etoscan scout-bot," Pash-Ti says, then extends their eyestalks toward Timoteo and me. "How did you manage to disable it?"

"Um, Charism gave us this neutralizer thing," I say. "But I think we ended up knocking out our own pod too."

Pash-Ti's eyestalks blink at me, clearly skeptical, but then quickly turn back to Johnny. "How much did the scout-bots transmit before being disabled?"

"Nothing dangerous, luckily. The problem is that they *stopped* transmitting so abruptly. More bots will be here to investigate soon." A thin red goo seeps out of Johnny's hand and seeps into the bot, then throws it back into the water. "These things are pretty rudimentary. I'm reprogramming all three of them with false memories. This part of the ocean gets electromagnetic storms every couple days—that's our most plausible cover for how they got knocked out. Anyway, we'd better get out of here before more of them show up."

Johnny climbs down the ladder under the submarine's hatch. Timoteo and I follow, ducking away from the judgmental gaze of Pash-Ti's eye-stalks. Pash-Ti comes down last, descending arms and head first, their long limbs nimbly alighting the submarine floor without even using the ladder. "You're one step away from dooming these negotiations. All it would take is for one observant Etoscan bureaucrat to look at this too closely, and they'll see that the scout-bots' signal loss didn't coincide with any real storm here. You've risked everything to find these Outlanders, who undoubtedly evaded you as easily as they've evaded the Etoscans and Levinti for decades. If the Etoscans uncover this, they would have every right to demand your dismissal as mediator, destroying any hope for the peace talks to succeed. You're not going to win the peace by playing Terran detective games."

"I think my memory tinkering bought us at least a few weeks," Johnny says. "But Pash-Ti's kinda right. This Scooby Doo stuff is only going to get you in trouble."

My ears pop as the submarine descends and accelerates across the ocean depths.

Pash-Ti squats spider-like on their stool. "Diplomacy is our only path forward."

Timoteo and I both nod. "I understand," I say, and hope Johnny's fake memory implants work. But now that I know the Levinti might be the ones hiding a secret outpost beneath Tumasra, I can't help but wonder. Is Pash-Ti worried about us getting in over our heads? Or are they worried we'll find out the truth?

We sit in awkward silence as the submarine takes us back to the mainland. Exhaustion rolls across my body. I must have gone another full night without sleeping. "Wait, what time is it?"

"Two and a half hours until dawn," Pash-Ti says.

"No, what time on Earth?" I say.

"Saturday, 8:17 a.m.," says Johnny.

No wonder I'm so tired. Another sleepless night—wait, Saturday?

"The big game is today!" I say. "I'll never make it home in time for it. And Mami is going to kill us!"

Pash-Ti's eyestalks extend toward me. "Tardiness for your athletic ritual is yet another consequence of your reckless actions today. Nevertheless, we will need to develop a credible cover story for your long absence."

✧ ✧ ✧

KATE HITS HER BAT against her cleats, knocking the dirt out from between the spikes. She leans back against the bench behind home plate. "I still don't get it."

"I told you," I say, my eyes on the other team's pitcher. "I was at this internship thing and one of the people who works there fell, so we had to take her to the hospital, and it was just this horrible night where everything went wrong."

From Kate's other side, Des leans forward to shoot me an incredulous look. "And that took you from last night until this afternoon?"

Kate walks to the on-deck circle. "Maybe your Mom bought that story, but there's no way that BS is going to work with us. We might actually be winning this game if you hadn't missed half of it. What kind of team captain misses half a game?"

"Haven't you ever had a totally horrible night?" I say "Like, hospital horrible?"

"What were you even doing at your internship on a Friday night?" Kate says.

"There was this deadline. And this internship is helping me, like, work through stuff."

"Look, Val," Kate says, taking some practice swings, "everyone feels bad about your uncle, but—I only say this because you're my friend—

that doesn't mean you can go around missing games and lying to people."

I'm trying to figure out how to convince them when our hitter swings and hits the ball deep into left field. The outfielder makes a diving catch.

"Damn," Des says, "that's two outs, and we're down by three."

Kate walks toward the plate. "We've still got a shot. Chrissie's on first, and I'm our strongest batter." I walk to the on-deck circle, watching Kate out of the corner of my eye. Kate *is* one of our strongest hitters. Much better than I am, even though I'm team captain, which Kate obviously still resents. But Coach says that being captain isn't about being the best player; it's about helping the team work together. Not that I've been great at that lately either.

On the first pitch, Kate swings and makes direct contact. The ball goes flying out towards the deepest part of center field and sails far over the fence. I've never seen Kate hit one so far. Chrissie and Kate jog triumphantly around the bases.

I walk to the plate. Kate's given us a chance, now I just have to keep us in the game. If only I'd gotten more sleep. These short naps on the Interstellar Subway just aren't enough. Even at my best, I'm no homerun champ like Kate, but I'm the master of the solid line drive. That could give me a single and at least partial redemption for missing half the game. But if I don't get a hit, then I'll be the deadbeat captain who came late and made the final out.

The first pitch comes. I swing and miss. Two familiar voices chant, "Go Val-Val, go Val-Val, go!" At the bleachers, my brothers are doing a two-man wave, alternately bouncing up from their seats with ridiculous speed. Timoteo catches my glance and winks at me. Thank God he's here to help with our ridiculous cover story.

I turn my focus back to the pitcher. The second pitch is a ball.

As the pitcher winds up, I catch sight of something in the corner of my eye. It's my mother, sitting on the bleachers near Timoteo and Miguel. She's surrounded by Johnny, Wasala, and Pash-Ti in their human disguises. When did they get here?

The ball whizzes by. "Strike two!" the umpire calls. I didn't even see the pitch. I grip the bat, trying to focus. But I can't stop looking to the bleachers, where Wasala, in her disguise as a human little person, is patting Mami's knee. That close, she can sense Mami's every thought.

I swing, but too late. That's it—game over. The other team bursts into cheers, and my teammates sag their heads. But my attention is still on the bleachers. I run over to where Mami is unknowingly sitting with a group of aliens, one of whom murdered Umberto.

They all look up at me as I stop in front of them, still holding the bat in my right hand. "Um, hey," I say. "What are you all doing here?"

"We came to support you," Wasala says, in Spanish.

"And to thank your mother for the assistance that you and Timoteo provided with my injury," Pash-Ti adds. They gesture toward their leg, which is in a cast, propped up on the bleachers. A pair of crutches lies beside them. The crew is going all-out to back up our cover story.

"What you did for Umberto's friend was very kind," Mami says. "You were right to help her get to the hospital."

"Yeah, we couldn't have done it without them," Johnny says, gesturing at Pash-Ti. "What with Patrece being extra extra tall, it was def a four-person job."

Wasala looks up at my mother. "Don't worry, Ms. Vega, our work isn't dangerous at all. It's mostly just shuffling papers. Patrece just tripped on the stairs." Wasala must be reading Mami's mind, assuaging her unspoken worries. Wasala seems so gentle, but seeing her next to

Mami reminds me how dangerous she is, how she might have been probing Umberto's thoughts.

"Well, thanks for coming," I say. "You can go now, really, no need to linger ..."

"Vega!" Coach waves her clipboard at me. "First you show up late. Then you play with your head everywhere but the game. Then you run off before things are properly done. Get your butt over here and shake hands with the other team. Act like team captain for a minute!"

"Yes, coach." I run back to the field where everyone else is already lined up, each team in single file. Kate and a few other teammates shoot me dirty looks as I run by them to take my place up front. "Good game," I say to the other team captain, shaking her hand, and then do the same for every player on down the line, my teammates following suit behind me.

After the good-game chorus, Kate and Des stand shoulder to shoulder, blocking my way.

"You totally should have hit those last two pitches," Kate says. "Where's your brain?"

"Are you okay, Val?" Des says.

"I'm sorry," I say, feeling under attack from every side. "I'm just ... distracted." Beyond Des, Pash-Ti is still sitting with their "broken" leg stretched on the bleachers. Wasala, Johnny, Mami, my brothers, Will—all of them are standing, in animated conversation. Wasala is right next to Will. "Sorry," I say to Des and Kate. "I have to take care of something."

Kate follows my gaze to the group by the bleachers. "More nonsense with those weirdos from your uncle's office? I'm out of here." She runs toward the locker room.

I ignore Kate and jog to the bleachers. I can't stop thinking about Wasala reading all their thoughts. *Wasala!* I think, the words loud in my mind. *I need to talk to you in private.*

Wasala raises her eyebrows. In her true form, her ears must be pricking up. She walks over to me. "No need to shout," she whispers. "What's wrong?"

"Nothing," I say. "I just don't feel comfortable with all of you being here. I'm not ready for my worlds to collide like this."

Wasala smiles. "Is this about Will? Their feelings for you run deep, and they—"

"Stop!" I say. I'm dying to know more about how Will really feels about me—but not like this! And why is she even telling me these things? To manipulate me? I ball my fists, trying to contain the anger welling up inside me. "It's one thing when you do this with me, it's another thing with my family and friends. You can't go invading people's thoughts."

"I'm not invading anything," Wasala says. "You know it's just how I'm built. What's really wrong?" I try to steer my thoughts, but know I've failed as Wasala's eyes widen. "You still think I may have killed Umberto!"

I don't know if it's you, I think.

Johnny and Pash-Ti approach, Pash-Ti taking long strides on their crutches, just like they do when running in their true three-legged form. I wonder if the two crutches are actually two of Pash-Ti's legs holographically disguised.

"What's all the tea, fam?" Johnny says.

"Val thinks one of us killed Umberto," Wasala says. "She was already suspicious, and then Charism told her the Etoscans are hiding something, and that one of us is a double agent."

"I didn't say that!"

"You thought it," Wasala says.

"Her conclusions are reasonable," Pash-Ti says, pointing at me with one crutch. "We all suspect Umberto was murdered. Since he died here, it's likely there was at least an accomplice to his murder here on Terra.

And there are only the three of us."

"Well, which of us does she think it is?" Johnny says to Wasala.

Wasala looks up at Johnny. "You're the one she least suspects. She most suspects Pash-Ti and medium-suspects me. But she doesn't trust any of us. Really, Val ..."

Pash-Ti leans forward on their crutches. "You're making suppositions based on your instinctive emotional reaction to each of us, a major attribution error. If indeed the spy is an Etoscan agent, I'm the least likely suspect, given my known antipathy for their superstitious culture. In contrast, Wasala's parents served in the Etoscans' Brigades. Furthermore, both Johnny and Wasala have capacities for covert surveillance that I simply lack."

Johnny gapes at Pash-Ti. "Wow, not you throwing all the shade back at your years-long co-workers, Pash-Ti."

Everyone falls silent as Mami and Timoteo approach. "Está todo bien?" says Mami.

"All's well, Ms. Vega," Pash-Ti says. "The long night simply took a toll on all of us."

"I'm exhausted, Mami," I say, avoiding contact with Johnny, Pash-Ti, and Wasala. "Let's get home."

✧　✧　✧

THE BROKEN-LEG STORY WORKS, but the whole drive home Mami still yells at Timoteo and me for not finding a way to call her when she was up all night, preocupadísima con ansiedad.

Timoteo holds his purse tight against his lap—he hasn't let it and the vial out of his sight since we got back. We decided we have to wait until nighttime to analyze it. Hopefully no one else will be at the interstellar consulate at that hour.

We both crash into a deep sleep the second we get home.

I wake up at three a.m. I can't believe I slept that long. Timoteo is still snoring on the floor. I flick his ear.

"Ow!" he says, eyelids heavy. "Just a little more sleep."

I pull on my jeans and a clean t-shirt. "It's already 3.a.m."

"Really?" he says. "This interstellar jetlag is the worst."

"Welcome to my world," I say. "Get dressed."

We sneak out of the house and bike to the Jersey consulate.

We walk into the science lab I've seen Wasala use, and Timoteo and I both stop abruptly at the entrance. Timoteo and I look at all the equipment and then at each other with raised eyebrows.

"Um," says Timoteo, "do you have any idea how to do this? Because I have no idea how to do this."

"Let's ask our suits," I say, tipping my newsie cap at him. "Hey, Checkers? We need to test that vial we got in the Outlands to find out what's in it. Can you help us? And can you make it so that no one except Timoteo and me can see the results?"

"At your service, Madame Ambassador," says Checkers. "And as ambassador, you may compartmentalize information as you see appropriate."

"Perfect," I say. "And you can project your voice so Timoteo can hear all this too."

Timoteo pulls the vial out of his purse and passes it to me. It has that same eerie lightness, as if a helium balloon were tugging it away from me. "So where do we start?"

"I already have," Checkers says. "My sensors indicate the sample includes exotic matter. Your human senses should be experiencing it as inverted gravity."

"Yeah, my suit told me that a while ago, BTW," Timoteo says.

"We'll need more sensitive equipment to analyze the composition in more detail," Checkers goes on. "There's a quantum analysis panel on the table to your right."

We go to the table and find a transparent tray that's filled with a dark red liquid. If I didn't know better, I'd think it was a baking dish filled with jello. "This one?"

"Indeed," Checkers says. "Any substance that contains exotic matter is likely to be unstable, so it's important that the sample not make contact with the air. I'm taking the liberty of providing you with gloves to protect your hands." A black liquid oozes across my hands, then congeals itself into two form-fitting gloves. "Place the vial in the tray, then close the lid."

I follow Checkers' instructions. Even through the gloves, the gooey red liquid feels cold. "I assume you'd like a full spectral quantum analysis?" Checkers asks.

"Um, yeah," I say. For a split second, the tray crackles with energy, like ripples of lightning trapped in the clouds.

"The analysis is complete," Checkers says. "The sample contains 73 percent exotic matter, 16 percent common Hoshan minerals, 10 percent entangled quantum threads, and less than one percent graphotons."

I remember the Tumasra storm is graphotonic, but I'm not sure what to make of all the rest. "Checkers, could you walk us through what each of those is—what they're used for?"

"Exotic matter is an essential component of much advanced technology, including anti-gravity, the creation of traversable wormholes for the Interstellar Subway, and the complex cybernetic systems used for military bots. The Hoshan minerals are unremarkable, likely the result of sample contamination. Entangled quantum threads are also used in much interstellar technology, particularly observation and communication across great distances. Graphotons are rare, naturally occurring only in the Tumasra storm."

"That seems like it could fit any of our theories," Timoteo says.

"Yeah," I say. "Okay, Checkers, I'm going to give you three theories about what this sample could mean, and I'd like you to tell us how feasible they are." I explain all three theories: the Etoscans building a secret weapon, the Levinti spying on Tumasra, and the Hosh-Unam Front building more advanced weapons, maybe with the help of the Etoscans.

"All those theories seem plausible," says Checkers. "The exotic matter and entangled quantum threads would allow the Hosh-Unam Front to create war-bots that would be faster and more advanced than any they've possessed before. The entangled quantum threads could also be Levinti technology to study Tumasra—and the presence of the graphotons could support that theory. The Etoscans could also be using these components to construct weapons, such as highly advanced swarms."

Timoteo presses his glasses against his face. "Majel," he says to his suit. "Can you think of any weapon of this composition that the Etoscans would be prohibited from building within their own territory on Northern Hosh?"

"None," Majel says, projecting her soft voice for me to hear as well. "And there are public records of both the Etoscans and Levinti amassing large quantities of military swarm technology across Hosh in recent months."

"Well," Timoteo says. "At least we've eliminated one possibility."

"I guess," I say. "So either Pash-Ti is helping the Levinti spy on Tumasra, maybe set up a base there. Or the Etoscans are secretly arming the Hosh-Unam Front with weapons way more advanced than before.

If that's the case, Johnny or Wasala might be helping them. Or both. But most likely Johnny. I don't think Wasala would ever help the Hosh-Unam Front."

"I still can't imagine Johnny hurting Umberto," Timoteo says. "But it is suspicious, the way he disappeared for so long, then came back so easily. And he did have that map."

I slump against the table. "All this effort to get to the Outlands and find Ferus and get this sample, and it's all been for nothing. We still just have a couple theories, and the negotiations start next week. Without knowing who's trying to sabotage them, it feels like there's no way we can succeed."

"Madam Ambassador," says Checkers, "I've just received a transmission for you via the Interstellar Subway. I believe it has some relevance to your discussion."

"Play it for us," I say.

"Ambassador Vega," comes Marrow's voice. "You have one week left to respond to my demand for a voice in the fate of my world. If you continue to be complicit in my people's oppression, we will not allow your so-called peace talks to continue. We will raise a horde of destruction on our Etoscan and Levinti oppressors with a merciless precision that will at last win freedom for the Hosh-Unam."

Timoteo and I stare at each other, eyes wide with horror.

CHAPTER 18

MARROW – threatened to derail treaty negotiation with violence again today. The usual, but tone was different — more confident. Could he have stolen tech to get past advanced security bots guarding the talks? Seems impossible, but Marrow always has a stratagem.

- From the notebook of Umberto Olmeda

TIMOTEO AND I STUFF HIS PURSE and my knapsack full of trail mix, protein bars, and plantain chips. There'll be food we can eat on Hosh, but the final treaty talks will last at least three days, so it will be good to have some Terran comfort-food snacks.

"I just hope I made the right call ignoring Marrow's threats," I say.

"You did," Timoteo says, trying on a different vest. "And the Etoscans insist their security at Tumasra is impenetrable."

"For whatever that's worth," I say. "Let's go, Johnny'll be here any minute."

"Right behind you," Timoteo says, switching for yet another vest.

I roll my eyes because I know he's going to try on at least three more vests, then grab my knapsack and bound down the stairs. At least we already said good-bye to Mami when she left for work this morning.

That should save us 20 minutes.

I get downstairs, surprised to find the couch populated by all my friends—Will, Des, and Kate sitting in a row, plus Miguel in the armchair in the corner. I guess they want to send me off before my trip to "Istanbul." Though I really don't have time for long good-byes.

Kate pats a spot next to her on the couch. "Come sit down, Val."

I stay standing, a nervous flutter running across my skin. "Uh, what's going on?"

"We know your uncle's death was hard on you, but it's been a month now," Kate says.

"We all care about you a lot," Will says, their hand on Des's knee. "But you need help."

"What are you talking about?" I say.

"You haven't been yourself," Des says. "Skipping practice. Falling behind in school."

"Hanging out with your uncle's weird friends all the time," Kate interjects. She presses her palms together as if she were praying. "You can't run away from your grief, Val. We want you to pay attention to the things that matter—like school, softball, and us. We don't think you should go on this trip."

I look from serious face to serious face. "So this is like a grief intervention? So I'm doing an internship where my uncle used to work. So softball doesn't seem as important as it used to. So what?"

"We know, Val," Will says, "but it's not just softball or the internship. It's the way you never talk to any of us, and even when you do your mind is like a million miles away." Probably because my mind literally is on things millions of miles away. "You need therapy. That's why Kate thought we should all get together and, yeah, do a bit of an intervention."

I look at Kate. "This was your idea?" I'm feeling more defensive by the second. If Will or Des had organized this, I'd believe it was out of concern. But if this was Kate's idea, then it's just her latest manipulation, some weird way to boost her ego. "You've got one thing right. It has been hard on me. Let me deal with it my own way."

"Val," Kate says, "all we want is for you to get counseling. And to delay this trip until you've had more time to heal."

"I can't delay this trip," I say. "It's too important."

"What makes it so important you have to go now," Kate says. "It's *just* an internship."

My mind races for a reasonable-sounding explanation, when I hear footsteps coming down the stairs. "Okay," Timoteo says, modeling a purple vest, "now I'm ready." He looks at the couch and sighs. "Oh, God, I told you guys not to do this."

"You knew about this?" I say.

Timoteo swivels his head back and forth. "Sort of. But I told them they were blowing things out of proportion."

"You're as bad as she is," Miguel says from the armchair, his usual relaxed smile replaced by tight-lipped anger. "The two of you have been acting nuts. Staying up late. Running around with weird old people. Talking about nonsense like Levitiri and whatnot. You think I can't hear? Are you in a cult or something? You guys both need help."

From outside comes the rev of Johnny's motorcycle. Timoteo and I exchange an exasperated look.

"I know you guys are doing this because you care," I say, "but none of you get what's happening. You have to trust me. But I swear I'll be back soon. And if you want, I'll do this therapy thing when I get back."

Timoteo hugs Miguel and salutes the others. "I promise I'll take care of her."

I go over to the couch to hug Miguel and my friends goodbye. It's awkward, but they all hug me tight to let me know things are still good. Except for Kate. She shrinks back from me, her face stone. "Stay, Val."

Without answering, I walk out of the house.

✧   ✧   ✧

IT'S NIGHT ON HOSH when we arrive at Tumasra. Our vehicle crests the hill, and the swirling fiery tower comes into view, lighting up Hosh's evening sky with a gentle orange glow.

Timoteo coughs and covers his nose. "Ugh, I forgot how harsh the smell is."

"The scent will be minimal once we've entered the Citadel, even to your delicate Terran noses," says nose-less Pash-Ti. "We'll exit momentarily. Guard your thoughts."

We step out of the vehicle. Thousands of Hoshans are crowded around the stone Etoscan Citadel towering above us. They're here because the fate of their world is at stake today. My shoulders tense under the weight of it all.

As we approach the entry, dozens of small grey machines fly toward us, circling each of us. Though far fewer in number, they're similar to the swarm of weapons at the border between Northern and Southern Hosh. "Standard security measures," Pash-Ti says. "Scanning for weapons." That makes me think of my phone, but I quickly steer my thoughts to the negotiation.

"Standard culture of paranoia," Johnny mumbles. Several bots hover in a circle around him. He looks up at them. "Hey, I'm as powered down as I can get! It'd take at least ten seconds for me to make anything dangerous." Most of the bots whiz away, but three mosquito-sized bots stay in orbit around Johnny. "Fine. Keep a detail on me."

The high level of security reminds me of airports on Earth. But part of me feels relieved to have the protection. Maybe Marrow's threats have all just been bluster.

When we enter the Citadel, we're met by several low-level Hoshan and Etoscan administrators. The others go directly to the negotiating chamber, but they escort me to a waiting area just beyond the main entrance for the entry processional. After a few minutes, from within the main chamber of the Citadel comes the trumpet-like sound of an Etoscan chant, signaling that the processional is starting. The Etoscan ambassadors enter first, followed by Charism and the Northern Hoshans. An elderly Hoshan leads me toward a stone archway that towers dozens of meters above us. I'm up next. My heartbeat accelerates as I walk through the enormous entrance. I remember what my brother Miguel always says: "Stage fright isn't bad, it just means your body's ready to put on a hell of a show."

I follow my prescribed path, walking at a slow, deliberate pace, like a wedding processional. I stifle a gasp of awe as I enter the chamber. The ceiling is the highest I've ever seen—at least triple the height of St. Patrick's Cathedral. But somehow the room still has that grounded feeling of Etoscan architecture. The walls and ceiling are made of brown stone, the surfaces rough and jagged. The walls are inset with life-sized sculptures of Etoscans molded so gracefully that they look like they weren't chiseled, but grown. At first, it seems like there's no wall on the far left of the chamber, just open air. But several Hoshans are pressing their noses against a nearly-invisible surface, looking out at the view of Tumasra's flames. This close, Tumasra is like the surface of the sun. It's like being in a cathedral inside a volcano.

"Valiant One?" says a familiar voice—that's my cue to greet the Etoscan ambassadors. I turn to my right, where Speaker stands, flanked by another Etoscan I've never seen before. Where's Listener? Part of me is relieved—Speaker is by far the more reasonable of the two—but it also worries me. Why would Listener not be here?

Behind them is a Hoshan wearing a headpiece. All my thoughts are under observation. I bow to Speaker and her comrade. "It is an honor to see your eyes, and an honor to be with you in this sacred space."

Speaker's wearing a taller headpiece than before, adorned with orange jewels. She lets out a gentle rumble with her trunk. "It's an honor to see your eyes, again, Valiant One. Many welcomes to you. Alas, my second could not attend today, but I'm joined by his alternate, Listener." Speaker points her trunk to her right, and I wonder again how Etoscans keep track of each other when so many have the same names. I bow to both.

I walk forward, to where Charism stands waiting on his hind legs. As leader of Northern Hosh, he's technically a co-host of the talks, though the Citadel is run by the Etoscans, with only token involvement of Charism and the North Hoshan government. "Madame Ambassador!" he says, four upper arms spread wide. "Such joy to see you again." He extends an upper arm toward me. I reach down, and we give each other a gentle scratch along the forearm.

It's great to see you, too, I think—a thought that comes easily and authentically. Charism lifts his nose with a smile, and I continue walking.

I'm supposed to take my seat now. Along the wall closest to the door are at least a dozen Hoshans, seated in the typical circular, papasan-like chairs. The Southland Hoshan support staff. Opposite them is another group of Hoshans in the same circular chairs—the Northern delegation. In the large space between the two, closer to the window, is a small cluster of Terran-style chairs, where Johnny, Timoteo, and Pash-Ti are seated, just behind the single empty chair for me. I walk over to them and nod a silent greeting as I take my seat. It's a simple wooden armchair, made for my exact height, so my feet can rest comfortably on the ground when I sit up straight. Other than one pillow for comfort, it's unadorned, but its back stretches six feet high, needlessly high above my head. The combination of simplicity and height was Pash-Ti's suggestion. It's important, they said, for everything I do—from my choice of words to the aesthetic of my chair—to convey humility, but not submission.

Trimana enters next, walking on her hindmost legs and holding her head high. On her upper left arm, she wears two armbands like the ones I've seen on Southland police, but more similar to Levinti rings—they glow with a pattern of phosphorescent red and gold colors. Checkers flashes a note on my arm: *Trimana's armbands are ceremonial garb indicating she has attained two of the Scholocracy's degrees in colonial governance.* She lifts her snout in polite greeting to me, then takes her seat at the head of the Southern delegation.

The Levinti enter last. Kantroponar glides into the chamber, her enormous body dwarfing everything else in the room. She hovers close to the ground as she makes a round of cordial greetings. Thankfully, the entrance sequence was easy to negotiate: as hosts, the Etoscans have the honor of entering first, while the Levinti have the honor of entering last—the most valued placement in their respective cultures.

Close behind Kantroponar comes Guiyomar, her mentee, followed by four more Levinti—each a pair, a large adult Levinti followed by a smaller *kiromakee*. The Levinti group glides across the room toward the Southern Hoshans. Their long tendrils dangle just above the Hoshans, and the massive forms of six jellies floating above them makes the vast chamber seem less empty, like a giant tank suddenly populated by a herd of whales.

With all four parties in the room, I feel a pang of guilt that the Outlanders aren't represented. But even Ferus said that was impossible— and even the thought of them could be dangerous, so I push it away from my mind.

The entry procession now complete, Charism takes his seat with the Northlanders, and the Etoscans walk up the long ridge that winds its way along the far wall. They come to the top, joining several other Etoscans in an alcove just below the ceiling.

This had been a trifling, but thorny point of contention, something tío Umberto worked out just before he died. The Levinti had insisted on a space large enough to allow them to float freely in the air, but the Etoscans found the idea of the Levinti floating above them an offensive assertion of Levinti superiority. The Levinti had then suggested the Etoscans make use of antigravity to float as well, which the Etoscans scoffed at—since that would make them half-deaf, the mechano-receptors of their toes out of touch with the ground. Umberto organized the compromise that the Etoscans could stand on solid ground in an alcove close to the ceiling, so that the Levinti could never rise above them.

From the alcove, the two Etoscan ambassadors look out over the chamber, like royalty on a castle balcony. Speaker lifts her reddish-brown trunk and lets out a mighty trumpet. "Welcome, honored guests," comes the translation, "to this hallowed site of Tumasra. Let us begin with a ritual of welcome, to name the echoes of history that dwell here still.

"Let us honor the first caretakers of Tumasra, the Hoshan priests whose names be lost to history, who protected this sacred site with their wise minds, who welcomed the brave Hoshans who made the pilgrimage here to bathe their minds in Tumasra's fires. We honor all those ancient Hoshan pilgrims who made that long journey, at a time when they had no power cells, traveling only on the back of a charo-beast or their own six legs."

Dozens of Levinti tendrils twitch in irritation. This was why the Etoscans wanted to host the talks here. They wanted to open with the sacredness of Tumasra not as a matter for discussion, but a presupposition.

Speaker goes on, "Let us honor Sage, that great Etoscan prophet. Millennia ago, Sage shocked the Etoscan worlds, when late in life he— the wisest of priests—experienced a spiritual crisis. He was overcome with profound loneliness, with the certainty that it was impossible for one being to ever truly know another. We are all of us, he said, trapped in the tyranny of our own subjectivities. He abandoned his home and loved ones, setting off for the stars in a small vessel for one. The emptiness between the stars mirrored the emptiness in his soul, and in this he saw the quiet whisper of Synchronus. He hibernated, seeking solace in prayer.

"Years passed before Sage awoke, his vessel plummeting toward an unknown planet. He crashed less than a mile from here, where he was met by Hoshan priests, who offered him shelter. When he realized that these creatures could look within his very mind, he knew that Synchronus had answered his prayers. He gazed for the first time upon Tumasra, and as he bathed in its fires, surrounded by loving Hoshans who could see his soul, he realized he had never been alone. So began the great tradition of Hoshans and Etoscans praying together at Tumasra. Just as those ancient Hoshans welcomed Sage, so I welcome all of you to Tumasra, that we may pray and learn together."

Speaker lets her trunk rest upon the ground, and the vast chamber is silent. Kantroponar inflates to slightly greater size, rising a few meters higher. A stream of colors dances across her skin, followed by the translation: "Thank you, Ambassador Speaker, for welcoming us warmly, and for sharing your quaint story." A note appears on my arm: *The Levinti word for "story" also means "folk legend," often used in reference to a myth held among primitive people as the explanation for a natural phenomenon not yet understood by local science.* I'm sure the Etoscans won't love *that*. "We can all learn from the spirit of openness embodied by the character of Sage and the Hoshan natives. May we all be equally open in the sharing in the study of Tumasra, which offers much knowledge to all those who pursue the scholarly method."

Speaker touches her trunk to the ground and lets out a rumble so strong I feel the tremors in my feet—even without mechanoreceptors. I can easily see this exchange of passive-aggressive insults escalating into an irreconcilable argument before the negotiations even start.

Pash-Ti has told me dozens of times that I have no real power—that my only authority comes from the agenda that all the parties have agreed to. I stand up. My hands are trembling, so I clasp them behind my back. "Honorable Speaker and Doctor Ambassador Kantroponar, thank you both for your wise words and for the spirit of openness you bring to these negotiations. With our welcome ritual complete, I'd like to begin our agenda as planned—turning to the many matters of substance we must cover today." I hope that last bit will discourage them from arguing over symbolism, reminding them to save their arguments for bigger concerns.

Speaker slowly rolls her trunk away from the floor, and Kantroponar deflates slightly and sinks a few feet. I figure that's as close as I'll get to agreement. I take a deep breath. My opening script is super verbose, but I've rehearsed it so much I have it memorized. "Whereas Article 17 of the Third Treaty of Centron will expire on Galactic Standard Date 43A4.25, and whereas the Etoscan Fellowship and Levinti Scholocracy seek continued peaceful shared stewardship of Hosh in accordance with the principles of the Interstellar Declaration of the Rights of Primitive Worlds, and whereas I as ambassador of the planet Terra am designated mediator of these talks, I call this meeting to order. The first agenda item is the Misreni borderlands, and Doctor Ambassador Kantroponar of the Levinti Scholocracy has five standard minutes to speak."

I sit down, my body still tense. If everything goes well, that might be the hardest thing I have to do. As Kantroponar inflates herself and speaks, a message lights up across my arm. *Good save, Val-Val! –Tim-Tim.* I smile. From just behind me, Timoteo is using super-advanced alien tech to text me. I bring up my holoscreen keyboard and write back, *Thx.*

The Misreni discussion goes on for hours. Every 80 minutes we take a scheduled break to rest, confer with colleagues, and attend to the various bodily needs of various species. Timoteo and Johnny give me encouraging advice in whispers and texts, and even Pash-Ti is helpful, keeping track of the allotted times to the second. Everything is going well.

Still, two things bother me. First, the Etoscans and the Levinti are talking three times as much as their Hoshan counterparts, whose fates they're deciding. But it's always been clear the Etoscans and Levinti are the ones making the real decisions. Even this imperfect process is better than the violent alternative.

My second worry that there's another meeting—a sort of shadow meeting of unspoken thoughts. Just behind Speaker and Listener stand three Hoshans in Etoscan headwear. Another group of Hoshans wearing armbands stand just beneath the Levinti, literally in their shadows, continuously typing into small handheld devices, transmitting messages to their Levinti bosses. The delegations of both Northern and Southern Hosh exchange meaningful glances throughout the talks, undoubtedly in constant telepathic communication. Of everyone in the room, my small team is the only group excluded from the thoughts being shared in parallel to the words spoken aloud.

After more than five hours, we wrap up the borderlands discussion, with all sides agreeing to a division of territory that basically maintains the status quo. After a brief break, I reconvene the group for discussion of a more difficult issue: Tumasra. I stand again, relieved that my hands finally seem capable of not trembling uncontrollably, and give the floor to Speaker.

Speaker approaches the edge of the alcove above us and lifts her trunk to speak. "Since Sage first came to this land, guided by the hand of Synchronus, Tumasra has been a sacred site not only for the people of Hosh but also for Etoscans across the Galaxy. It must remain inviolable. A temple cannot be made a laboratory.

"But Synchronus teaches us the importance of fluidity. So we offer the Levinti the opportunity to study the physical aspects of Tumasra through limited and monitored visitations. Visitations may take place only during the daytime, when fewer of our nocturnal Hoshan brothers come to Tumasra to pray. They must be limited to a duration of one nine-day-period per cycle, and the Levinti may leave no permanent equipment of any kind in place at Tumasra. Only representatives of the Levinti's Meteorological and Geological Academies will be permitted visitation, and no Levinti with any affiliation to the Academy of Military Studies will be admitted. Finally, all Levinti visits must be observed by surveillance bots."

That's about what we expected as an opening offer from the Etoscans. Now the Levinti will push for more—the question is how much more.

"Thank you, Ambassador Speaker," I say. "Doctor Ambassador Kantroponar, you now have seven minutes to respond."

Kantroponar inflates and rises several feet higher, gesticulating with her enormous tendrils, decorated by dozens of rings. "Your offer is appreciated, Ambassador Speaker, as is the religious meaning that both you and the primitive North Hoshans ascribe to the Tumasra phenomenon. We have no military interest in Tumasra. We seek only knowledge, the ultimate goal of the Scholocracy in all things. The Tumasra phenomenon is unique in the Galaxy, and yet remains poorly understood, because you allow no others access to it, and you yourselves have devoted more resources to worshiping the phenomenon than studying it. For this reason, we continue to demand a permanent scientific base at Tumasra."

Kantroponar inflates to a greater size and rises higher, so that she's near the ceiling of the cavern, her many large eyes at the same level as the Etoscans standing in the alcove. "However, in the spirit of mutual compromise, we are open to a visitation model on three conditions. One: the period of visitation must be at least ten nine-day periods per cycle. Two: scholars from the Academy of Neurology must also be permitted entry." That means the study of Tumasra's effect on telepathy, which the Etoscans will probably see as military. This is not going to be easy. "Third, in accordance with the basic rights of all sentients, we ask that the children of Hoshans who have served in the interstellar Legions for both the Scholocracy and the Etoscan Fellowship be permitted homecoming to Hosh."

The chamber erupts in a cacophony of languages in the wake of this unexpected announcement. The South Hoshan delegation exchanges hurried glances, gesticulating wildly to one another. The Northern Hoshans let out a torrent of clicks. Charism and Trimana gaze at each other from across the room, as if an offer is being made and considered. In the alcove above, the Etoscans huddle, their Hoshan agents whispering in their ears. Only the Levinti hover in unperturbed silence above the clamor.

I twist around in my chair to face my team. "What's going on? I thought the Levinti were completely against homecoming. Isn't it as bad for them as for the Etoscans?"

"Most unexpected," Pash-Ti says. "The Levinti may believe homecoming would be even more harmful to the Etoscans, since they've shared less technology with the Northern Hoshans, a policy which would be threatened by the return of Hoshans with interstellar experience."

"Or maybe," Timoteo says, "the Levinti just want to look like the benevolent one?"

Pash-Ti's eyestalks extend up and to the right, which means they're looking at the clock on their eye-screen. "More than a minute has passed, Madame Ambassador. You must call the meeting back to order and move discussion forward."

It's not just my hands shaking now, it's my legs too. I have no idea how to get this back on track. But I stand and try to hold my body steady. "Order!" I say, projecting my voice theater-style. "Order!" The room quiets. "Thank you, Madame Doctor Ambassador Kantroponar," I say more quietly. "Ambassador Speaker now has the right of response."

A Hoshan agent is still standing at Speaker's side, murmuring to her as her red trunk twitches in agitation. Before Speaker can speak, Trimana leaps up and stands on her two hindmost legs, stretching her body to maximum height. She signs with her claws, "I must speak on this proposal with great urgency."

According to the complex rules of the talks, the Levinti and the Etoscan delegates are each permitted to speak out of turn on three occasions, but the two Hoshan delegates are never allowed to. Trimana looks at me from across the room. My proper role is to stop anyone from speaking out of turn—but doing that now would mean silencing someone with less power in favor of those with more, and there's no way I'm doing that.

Trimana quickly resumes her gesticulations. "On behalf of Southern Hosh, I applaud the bold proposal on the part of Doctor Ambassador Kantroponar calling for homecoming for the children of Hoshan Legionnaires. We recognize homecoming as an essential right of all Hoshans. I call for all parties to embrace this proposal immediately."

Across the chamber, Charism stands on his hindmost legs, stretching out his upper arms as if to embrace everyone present. "For too long the children of our Legionnaires have been orphans of the Galaxy. Their parents choose to join the telepathic brigades, to embrace a life of interstellar service and exile from their homeworld. But their children do not choose to be born in exile, a life of isolation among the mind-deaf. I wholeheartedly support this proposal."

The Etoscans and their Hoshan agents are still huddled together, whispering, looking desperate. Whatever the Levinti are hoping to accomplish, it might be working. Trimana and Charism must sense the surprise in the minds of the Etoscans and are taking full advantage.

Finally, Speaker steps forward. "We appreciate your concern for the children of Legionnaires and share it. We're open to consideration of this proposal, but the matter has been raised prematurely, as discussion of homecoming is not scheduled until tomorrow, and was never to be tied to negotiations for visitation of Tumasra. Moreover, our ersatz mediator has allowed this discussion to range far beyond agreed parameters. We urge that we return to our agenda rather than jeopardize these talks with wild deviations from protocol."

That last bit is clearly a stab at me for losing control of the meeting. With everyone else supporting homecoming, the Etoscans have lost the

moral high ground on substance, so they're shifting focus to process—
and me.

If I let the group discuss homecoming now, the Etoscans could
balk and say the talks have become a farce, all because of my failure as
"primitive" mediator. But if I delay the discussion, the Etoscans and
Levinti could get stuck in a stalemate, which could also derail the talks.
A message flashes across my forearm: *When faced with unexpected
complications, form a committee. –Pash-Ti.* They can be so helpful when
they're not berating me.

I clear my throat. "Ambassador Speaker's point is well taken, and
adherence to our agreed agenda is of great importance. However, given
that we've completed today's primary item of the border territories, and
the unexpected, um, energy, around the homecoming issue, I suggest we
adjourn for today, and that a committee of representatives of all parties
meet tonight to adapt the agenda for our remaining two days."

A dance of lights flashes across Kantroponar's skin. "I support
this proposal."

"As do I," says Trimana.

"The motion has been supported by two of four parties. Do any
wish to block the motion?" No one speaks. The Etoscans can't object
without appearing unreasonable. I feel a wave of relief. We've made it
through the first day. Now I just have to officially adjourn ...

The Etoscans are the first to prick up their ears, followed by the
Hoshans. A few seconds later, I hear the buzzing too.

"What is that?" Timoteo says.

"Oh, no," Johnny says, looking toward the window. I follow his
gaze, but can't see anything yet.

Then it comes into view. First, a speck in the distance. Then many
specks. Then a swarm.

Chapter 19

THE BUZZING GETS LOUDER as the swarm approaches the Citadel. Just outside the window, hundreds of bots—shaped like miniature medieval shields—rise up from beneath the building. The shields form a perimeter around the Citadel, interlocking so every inch is protected.

The Etoscans rumble to each other, the Levinti's skins are kaleidoscopes of fast-flashing lights, and the Hoshans all stand up on their hindmost legs, looking to one another in shock and confusion. Fear fills my body, my heart racing. Should we run out of the room? Is there some sort of bunker we can go to?

Speaker lets out a roaring trumpet, and for a moment the room is relatively quiet. "Remain calm. Our defenses will block this attack by the Hosh-Unam Front."

Speaker's words are little comfort as thunderous booms echo outside, like hundreds of fireworks exploding in chaotic chorus. Outside the Citadel, it's a battle of two swarms—the attacking swarm of the Hosh-Unam Front against the Etoscan defenses—though it's hard to tell which bots are on which side.

I've never felt so utterly helpless. What can I do against a swarm of super-advanced machines? I turn to my right to look at Timoteo. At exactly the same moment he's turning to look at me. It's like a mirror, the fear and helplessness in his eyes the same as mine.

"We might not make it through this," Timoteo says. "We could die here, and no one on Earth would even know where we went."

It's a relief to hear his voice, even if it's just to articulate his anxieties. I push my own fears to the background of my mind, and bring the needs of Timoteo and everyone else to center-stage.

"We can't think like that," I say. Behind us, a bunch of Hoshans are running for the exit, while others stay in place, huddling together. All the Etoscans and Levinti seem to be staying in place. I turn back to Johnny and Pash-Ti. "How bad is it? What can we do?"

Pash-Ti's eyestalks extend warily toward the window. "Those bots are far more advanced than any the Hosh-Unam Front have been known to possess before."

What if the Hosh-Unam Front did get advanced weapons from the Etoscans? What if that's what this has been about all along? Marrow said flat-out they were planning a deadly attack—I should have done more, found a way to stop this!

"They're going to get through," Johnny says. "And I may be the only thing here that can stop them." Three guard-bots still hover just a few feet from Johnny's head. Johnny points a finger up at them and says, "Y'all better help or get out of my way." The guard-bots hover for a moment, then glide away. To us, he says, "Get behind me, I'll protect us as best I can."

Is Johnny sincere or has he been working with the Hosh-Unam Front all along? What if he turns on us as soon as they break through? I can't count on him to get us through this. Dozens of Hoshans are scurrying for the door—maybe we should do that too. "Can we evacuate?" I shout over the buzzing and explosions of the battle outside.

Pash-Ti is staring out the window, eyestalks darting back and forth as if counting the tiny warring machines. "There's nowhere to go. The Citadel is undoubtedly surrounded by that swarm on every side."

I follow Pash-Ti's gaze to the window. The shield-bots that had blanketed the entire surface of the glass are fewer—now they only cover a few patches. I've been trying to steer my thoughts clear of it, but I do have a weapon—the app Umberto hid on my phone. The neutralizer setting for Johnny worked on those scout-bots over the ocean, so it should work on this swarm too. I pull my phone out of my knapsack and open up the app, ready to use it as soon as I have to—whether on the swarm or Johnny—or both. Hopefully, in all the panic, none of the Hoshan telepaths will notice.

Suddenly, the window explodes, sending shards of the thick transparent material flying through the air. The Etoscans and Levinti are high up enough to be beyond range of the flying debris, but a few Hoshans get hit, falling and clutching their limbs in agony. The pungent scent of Tumasra breaks into the chamber. A swarm of buzzing spheres streams into the Citadel.

The room erupts in total panic. The Etoscans let out desperate trumpets, lifting their massive forelegs high into the air. The remaining Hoshans let out high-pitched squeaks and scurry toward the exits on all six legs. The Levinti inflate themselves to their maximum size, hovering up near the ceiling, their skin ablaze with panicked patterns of lights.

"Everyone, get back!" Johnny shouts. His entire right arm is gone, replaced by dozens of tiny red droplets. The rest of his arms and torso follow, transforming into a sea of seething red goo, coalescing into thousands of tiny red ant-like bugs. Johnny's human shell is left emaciated and armless. If I didn't know how Johnny works, it would seem like his body was being consumed by a horde of red ants—but actually he's transforming himself into an army of bots. I clutch my phone, my finger primed on the trigger.

Johnny's transformation only takes a few seconds, but already the swarm of invading spheres has multiplied in size, hundreds more pouring into the chamber. Johnny's horde of flying red ants engages the invading swarm of spheres, hundreds of them meeting in a surreal miniature combat. Johnny's horde overwhelms the spheres, dozens of which drop to the floor like lifeless marbles. The phone trembles in my hand, my spirit walking a tense tightrope between hope and desperation. Maybe Johnny *is* on our side, and maybe he is powerful enough to protect us all from this attack.

But the spheres keep streaming in the window, an endless supply of reinforcements. Johnny's red ants get overwhelmed by sheer numbers, and several of the spheres get past them to attack what's left of Johnny's human form.

"No!" Johnny shouts. Strands of his hair uproot themselves from his scalp, transforming into shimmering threads of sharp silver, which slice through the invading bots like a needle piercing silk. But one sphere evades the threads and zips toward Johnny, flying into his right ear. Johnny's human body shakes violently, as if in a seizure, then falls motionless to the ground. Simultaneously, all his red bugs abruptly halt, crashing to the stone floor with clinks, like a sudden hailstorm of metal pebbles.

"Johnny!" Timoteo shouts, rushing toward him. Pash-Ti reaches out with a wiry arm to grab Timoteo's vest and hold him back.

"There's nothing you can do," Pash-Ti says, pulling him toward the door. "You'll only endanger yourself."

"Will he be all right?" I ask, desperation cracking my voice.

"Uncertain," Pash-Ti says.

Pash-Ti and Timoteo move toward the crush of Hoshans rushing for the exit, but I hang back. I lift the phone, aim at the densest part of the swarm, and fire. Dozens of the spheres come to a sudden stop, falling to the floor in another hailstorm of metal clinking on stone.

I aim at another dense pocket of bots and fire again. This time nothing happens. I fire again, and still nothing. The bots must be in communication with each other, must have learned to defend against the weapon after my first attack.

The swarm spreads out, dozens of spheres flying toward the alcove, where the Etoscans are stampeding toward a rear exit on the upper floor. Nearly a dozen of them are bottlenecked at a doorway only wide enough for one of them at a time.

One by one, the spheres fly into the folds of the large flappy ears of the Etoscans. One of them lets out a moaning trumpet tremoring with pain. The floor quakes as his weight hits the ground. There's a succession of keening trumpets as other Etoscans fall. The floor trembles with each fall, a series of minor quakes. Three of the Etoscans are trying to escape down the stairway instead of the alcove, and they fall too, their massive, lifeless bodies tumbling down the stone steps.

At the edge of the alcove, Speaker is one of the last to fall, the only one who hadn't sought escape. She stands motionless, her eyes sullen with a stony gaze that might be sadness—or betrayal. She doesn't even moan as her body falls to the ground.

From directly above, there's a tremendous, high-pitched hissing sound, like a bomb from an old war movie. A Levinti is rapidly deflating, its massive body careening toward the floor.

"Look out!" I shout. I race to get out of the path of the plummeting Levinti. All around, Hoshans are scurrying to escape as well, their short six legs unable to keep up with my relatively long strides. With each hand, I grab a Hoshan by the back of the neck, picking them up like you would a cat. My arms strain with the weight, running as fast as I can. Right behind me, the Levinti lands, its slimy body hitting the floor with a massive wet slap. One of its tendrils splays out from the fallen body, and I duck to avoid being hit across the head. I gently set the two Hoshans down on the ground.

"Sorry," I say. "Are you okay?"

One of the Hoshans looks up at me, his eyes wide. He makes a gesture that moves from the chest to an out-stretched claw. "Thank you," comes the translation.

Above, the bots attack the five remaining Levinti, flying into the mouths at the base of their bell-shaped bodies. There's a cacophony of hissing and crashes as the Levinti fall to the ground. I shudder, helpless and horrified as another adult Levinti lands on the floor with a thud, crushing several Hoshans beneath its massive body. Other Hoshans get knocked to the ground by its splaying tentacles.

I brace myself for the spheres to continue their deadly attack. Next they'll strike down the Hoshans, and Pash-Ti, and—oh God— Timoteo—just as easily as they did the Etoscans and the Levinti. Where is Timoteo? In a panic, I whirl around searching for him. If he got crushed by one of the Levinti's falling bodies—

No, there he is, over by one of the fallen jellies near the exit, pushing himself back up to his feet with help from Pash-Ti. He got knocked to the ground but looks okay.

Something else is odd, but it takes me a second to realize what. The buzzing of the spheres has stopped. Not a single sphere is in sight. Have they finished their work and left? Why did the spheres only attack the Levinti and the Etoscans? Could this be what Marrow meant by "merciless precision"—that he could target an attack only at Etoscans and Levinti, not at other Hoshans?

If only I'd done more, figured things out faster, I could've prevented all of this ...

But there's no time to wallow in regret. If the bots are gone, maybe that means there's a chance to get everyone else out safely. I run over to Pash-Ti and Timoteo. "We need to evacuate quickly," Pash-Ti says, "but both exits are blocked." Pash-Ti is right—an enormous jelly is sprawled across the floor directly in front of the main entryway. There are Etoscan bodies blocking the upper exit at the rear of the alcove, but there's enough space to crawl past them. Pash-Ti goes on, "The only way out is to move the bodies or climb over them. The latter may be less respectful, but is far faster and more practical. We need to direct the Hoshans to the alcove exit and help the injured make their way out. With all the Levinti and Etoscans dead, we're the only ones left here with antigravity, so we'll be able to maneuver with far greater—"

Pash-Ti is interrupted by a loud popping sound. It's followed by several more pops, each accompanied by a brief flash of flame lighting up the air, then quickly dispersing.

"It's the hydrogen from the Levinti, from when they deflated," Timoteo says, reading something on the inside of his glasses. "The gas is igniting with the atmosphere. And the Citadel's fire safety systems were disabled in the attack."

"We need to get everyone up to the alcove immediately," Pash-Ti says. "It's the only exit and is further from the Levinti bodies and the trail of flammable gases they've left behind."

Near the windows, there's another series of pops, closer to one of the fallen Levinti. Another trail of flame sparks in the air, and this time the Levinti's skin catches fire. The flames spread across that corner of the chamber, and a group of Hoshans rush away from it.

By the main exit, dozens of Hoshans climb over the fallen Levinti blocking the way, not realizing another fire could ignite at their feet any moment.

"Pash-Ti," I say, pointing toward the main exit. "Can you round up the Hoshans over there and get them up to the alcove? Timoteo and I can help the ones who are injured."

Pash-Ti nods assent with their eyestalks. They dash toward the main entry in long three-legged strides and direct the Hoshans to the alcove. Timoteo is staring at the flames on the far side of the room, his face stricken with panic. He's hyperventilating. "Tim-Tim," I say, clutching his hands in mine. "I need you to stay calm. We have to help these people."

"You're right," he says, leaning over to rest his hands on his knees, as if he just finished running a long-distance race. Adjusting his glasses, he says, "Majel, increase oxygen levels." His breathing calms. "I'll get Johnny, and then come back for the others." Favoring his right foot, Timoteo walks to where the remainder of Johnny's body lies on the ground. He cups Johnny in his arms, struggling with the weight at first, and then levitates up to the alcove.

I look around and see a Hoshan struggling to carry another Hoshan who's lost consciousness. I run over to them and take the unconscious Hoshan into my own arms. "Thank you," says the other Hoshan with a few quick clicks and whistles. When he stands up on his hind legs, I see that he's bleeding on his side.

"You're not in such good shape yourself," I say, and gather him up in my other arm. "Checkers, bring me up to the alcove." I levitate up and find a stream of Hoshans scurrying from the stairway to the exit at the alcove's rear, crawling over and around the maze of Etoscan corpses that lie lifeless across the floor. The Hoshans are surprisingly orderly in their mass exit, proceeding in single file, helping one another or clearing the way for others. Even in all the panic, they're moving as one, their minds synchronizing their motions. At the exit itself, Charism is helping other Hoshans climb over an Etoscan corpse blocking the way. Nausea crashes across my stomach. These are the dead bodies of real beings, who just minutes ago were alive, and these Hoshans have to climb over them to survive. But there's no time for squeamishness, so I push that thought from my mind, and try to think of the bodies only as obstacles.

Levitating over the maze of obstacles, I carry the two injured Hoshans over to Charism. "Can you help these two get out safely, Charism? I'll try to help all the others down there who are too injured to get up here on their own."

"Fret not," Charism says, taking the unconscious Hoshan into his arms, and directing one of his comrades to help the one who's bleeding. "We'll get them to safety."

I fly back down to the lower level. The fire has spread. The scent of smoke is mixing with the scent of the Tumasra storm, and the heat of the flames is getting through the protective membrane of my suit. Most of the Hoshans are proceeding up the stairs, and all have gotten away from the main exit, which is now completely blocked by a Levinti's enflamed body.

One Hoshan has her foot caught under the weight of a Levinti tentacle. I lift the tentacle so she can get out, then carry her to the safety of the alcove. I fly back and forth from the lower level to the alcove, helping every injured Hoshan I see, Timoteo and Pash-Ti doing the same.

The room has nearly been cleared out when I see a group of Hoshans clustered around a Levinti body, dangerously close to the flames, making no move for the exit. Four of them are crouched at the side of the Levinti corpse, as if trying to burrow beneath it. "What are you doing?" I say. "We need to get out of here, fast!"

One of them stands up on his hind legs and signs. "She's still alive," comes the frantic translation. "We hear her desperate thoughts. She's trapped under there, and we can't get to her."

Now I understand—the Hoshans are trying to get underneath and push up a portion of the body. I crouch and try to help, but it's hard to get a grip on the Levinti's slimy skin, and it's surprisingly heavy, even deflated. I expected it to be like an empty parachute, but it's more like a giant tire, its empty hide thick and bulky. Between all four Hoshans and me, all we can do is lift the edge of the Levinti's body a few inches off the ground.

"Checkers," I say, standing up and catching my breath. "Can we use your antigravity to lift this Levinti?"

"I'm afraid I lack the power for an antigravity field for such a large mass," Checkers says. "However, if you were to gain appropriate leverage, I could generate an antigravity field to augment the force of your own strength over a limited portion of the Levinti's body."

I think for a second. "I guess that means I'd pretty much have to get under it."

"Correct, Madame Ambassador."

Shoot. The flames are everywhere now and soon there'll be no way out. But if someone is alive under there, there's no way I'm leaving her behind.

"All right," I say to the other Hoshans. "I'm going to try to get under there and lift up more of it. As soon as you have room, I need you to pull out the Hoshan who's under there."

The Hoshans nod agreement. I get into crawling position and slide myself under the Levinti's body. It's slimy, and surprisingly clumpy. Could those be its internal organs? Another thought I have to push from my mind. I imagine I'm just crawling through a moist cave. I push myself further long, so that my entire upper body is beneath the Levinti. The weight is overwhelming, like crawling under a mountain of slimy rocks. But I keep going, drawing in my legs as well. With all my strength,

I push myself up on all fours, taking even more of the Levinti's weight onto my back.

"Checkers," I grunt, "can you give me a hand now?"

"Of course, Madame Ambassador," Checkers says, and suddenly the weight on my back lightens a bit. I lift my arms above me and push the Levinti's body up, then lift myself into a crouching position. All around me, the Levinti's skin forms a slimy tent, one of its edges just a few inches above the ground, letting in a ray of light. The trapped Hoshan is right there, lying on the ground beneath me, her lower legs still caught beneath the Levinti's body. In the dim lighting, it takes me a few seconds to realize it's Trimana.

Even with Checkers' help, I've reached the limits of my strength, and I still haven't gotten the Levinti's skin high enough for Trimana to get out. All my muscles groan in pain as I push them even further, extending my arms to push the Levinti's skin up just a few inches higher. With the weight lessened, Trimana digs into the floor with her front claws, dragging herself out from under the Levinti. Two of the other Hoshans scurry under the tent that I've created. My arms tremble beneath the Levinti's weight as they help Trimana struggle out from beneath the giant jelly's skin.

As soon as they're out safely, I collapse, my body sinking to the ground, the weight of the Levinti's body still heavy on my back. Slowly, I crawl my way back out from under the Levinti, too physically exhausted to even think. I'm drenched in sweat and Levinti fluids.

One of the Hoshans helps me up as I make my way out into the light. We're surrounded on all sides by thick smoke and crackling fires.

"There's no way out," one of the Hoshans says. "We're completely trapped."

I look up wearily toward the alcove, but can't see anything through the smoke. I pick up Trimana, cradling her in my arms. "Grab onto me," I say to the other four Hoshans. "I don't have the strength to lift any more of you, so you're just going to have to hold on." I can only half-feel the sensations of my own body, claws digging through my clothes and into my skin as two of the Hoshans climb onto my back. The other two grab hold of my legs.

"Bring us up to the alcove, Checkers," I say, panting for air. "And I need you to guide us right up to the exit, because I can't see a thing."

"Of course, Madame Ambassador," Checkers says, and then I'm soaring through the air, five Hoshans clinging to my body. The entire chamber is filled with smoke, and even the alcove is engulfed by the flames. But Charism is still there, waiting at the exit.

Checkers sets us down right next to Charism. My legs can't hold me up any longer. I collapse on the floor panting and coughing. I don't have any control of my body anymore, it's just this useless thing that happens to house all my senses. I lie helplessly as one of the larger Hoshans lifts up Trimana and carries her to the door. Without speaking a word out loud, Charism and the remaining three Hoshans each take me by one of my limbs and carry me. My eyes flutter closed, and when I open them again there's less smoke. The ceiling looks different, the walls closer together. My body bounces along, much too heavy for the Hoshans, even four of them, and half the time they drag me instead of carrying me.

As consciousness leaves me completely, all I can think of is Timoteo, and Johnny, and Pash-Ti, and all those Hoshans who were hurt. I pray they all got out in time.

CHAPTER 20

I WAKE UP TO WHAT SOUNDS like a dozen showers running. My body aches all over. Then Checkers' gentle voice: "Judging by your elevated blood pressure, I believe you've regained consciousness, Madame Ambassador, and I'm much relieved. I'm terribly sorry I wasn't able to protect you properly. The co-factors of smoke, Tumasra fumes, and Hosh's lower oxygen level forced me to shift from filtration to direct molecular production of O2, but that process is cumbersome, and I fear my slowness caused you to suffer oxygen deprivation—"

"Thanks, Checkers." I'm still too groggy to open my eyes. "You saved my life."

"I'm honored to be of service," Checkers says. "I've deployed med-bots to repair the damage to your lungs and other minor injuries. They're at work as I speak."

"Val?" It's Timoteo's voice. "Are you talking to your suit? You okay?"

My eyes flutter open. Timoteo's a friendly blur. "Hey, Tim. I'm okay." My vision comes into focus. Timoteo's face is covered with grime, his hair disheveled. "The others," I say, lifting my head to see. "Are they okay?"

Timoteo cradles my head in his arms. "Take it easy, Val-Val. You got quite a workout. Pash-Ti's fine, they're talking with some other diplomats. Johnny ... I'm not sure." He looks to his right, where Johnny's body is lying a few feet away. His torso is armless, an oddly emaciated trunk bridging his legs and his head. "I mean, he's Synthetic. He's got to be fixable, right?"

"I hope so." It's startling to see Johnny helpless. I think of him as a Synthetic Superman.

A Hoshan pads up to us on all six legs, raises her two front arms in the air and looks at me with concern. As she signs with her claws, the translation comes, "The patient has awoken."

"This is Leresta," Timoteo says. "She helped get you to safety."

"Only after the Ambassador saved all our lives," Leresta says. "I'm relieved you're well, Madame Ambassador. Too many souls have left us today."

The med-bots must be working, because my aches are easing. I pull myself up to a sitting position, leaning back against a stone bench. We're in a park near Tumasra, a field of purple grass dotted with cylindrical stone benches. All around, Hoshans are lying on cots, and others are treating them with bandages and ointments. In the valley below, the windows of the Citadel are shattered, its walls blackened, billowing plumes of smoke. A net of thick ropes hangs along the sides of the Citadel. A dozen Hoshans climb nimbly along the ropes on all six legs. Cylindrical canisters are strapped to their backs, releasing what looks like a spray of snowflakes into the remaining fires. That's the sound I've been hearing.

"I'm glad to see you're well, Ambassador," says a Hoshan on a nearby cot. It's Trimana, one hind leg bound in a yellow bandage. I don't think Etoscans have shared med-bot tech with the North Hoshans. How much faster could these Hoshans recover with that technology?

Charism scurries toward us, apparently unharmed. "You have all our gratitude, Valiant One. You have proved your parents to be skilled in the art of naming."

It's hard to hear any praise when I've failed. I could have—should have—prevented all of this. I should have paid more attention to Marrow's threats.

"The fault for this disaster lies not with you, Valiant One," Charism says. "We all received the threats from Marrow and had intelligence of increased activity from the Hosh-Unam Front. But they've never had weapons so advanced before ..." He frowns in my direction, whiskers pointing toward the ground. He's had the same thought as I have—the energy surge. I try to steer my thoughts, though I'm not sure there's any point in that now.

Trimana looks toward me and Charism, ears pricked up. She leans forward in her cot. "All of us bear the burden for this tragedy. Our intelligence warned us as well, but there's always chatter of another Hosh-Unam Front attack. We'd no reasonable way to predict ..." She looks at the destruction around us, then buries her face in the fur of her shoulder. I've never seen her so emotive. "And the devastation is not only here. The Southern Capital was attacked as well. A swarm of bots attacked every Levinti in their path, killing hundreds."

"The bots must have been engineered to target the Etoscan and Levinti genomes," Timoteo mutters, half to himself.

"Yes," Charism says. "Marrow has put out a statement taking credit for the attack. He says that the bots were used only to attack our so-called oppressors, that not a single Hoshan was killed."

Trimana stands up on her uninjured hind leg. The Hoshan tending her wounds clutches her shoulders, gently trying to ease her back onto the cot. "Marrow well knows the consequences when a Levinti dies and deflates on a world like Hosh, with so much oxygen in the air! In the South it was even worse. A rain of Levinti corpses falling all across the city. Explosions everywhere, the city in flames. Thousands of Hoshans were injured or killed!"

"This is the worst act of mass violence Hosh has seen in a generation," Charism says, walking toward Trimana on his two hindmost legs. "Marrow cares nothing for the death of ten thousand Hoshans, so long as he advances his objectives."

"The only objective he's achieved is the certainty of war," Trimana says. "From the moment the treaty expires, both North and South will be consumed."

"Too often," Charism says, "our thoughts have flowed in opposing currents, but in this our thoughts flow as one. Our hearts are emptied of hope. War is upon us."

Pash-Ti comes over and helps me to my feet. I'm still sore and light-headed. Timoteo isn't in great shape either—his sprained foot is in a makeshift splint.

"The two of you should rest for a few hours," Pash-Ti says. "Then we must discuss our options, limited as they may be."

Timoteo looks down at Johnny's motionless, emaciated body. "What about Johnny?"

"He requires a specialist familiar with Synthetic medical engineering," Pash-Ti says. "With no such specialist on Hosh, his care will have to be deferred until after the more immediate crisis. His body will keep in the meantime."

"His body will keep?" Timoteo says. "How can you talk like that?"

I look at the ground, wishing Pash-Ti had more tact. Crawling through the purple grass is a red ant-like creature. Behind it is another ant, and behind that, another. A long trail of red ant-like creatures crawling from the Citadel to Johnny's body.

"Hey, guys," I say, "I think Johnny might be okay."

The horde of ants is overrunning Johnny's torso, one by one re-integrating themselves into his body. His half-formed body sits up.

"Whoa. Anybody get the number of that truck?"

"Johnny!" Timoteo says. "Thank God you're okay."

Pash-Ti's eyestalks extend toward Johnny. "Indeed. What an unexpected relief."

✧ ✧ ✧

A FEW HOURS LATER, I feel more rested, but still sore. I'm sitting at the edge of a bed, drinking water and munching on a protein bar. My "bed" is actually three circular Hoshan mattresses pushed together to make a human-sized bed. Pash-Ti took us to this Hoshan guest house for visiting dignitaries, just outside Tumasra, so we could sleep and treat our injuries, particularly Timoteo's foot, which is taking time for the med-bots to repair.

In the corridor outside, there's the pitter patter of Hoshan footsteps. Trimana enters, walking uncomfortably on five legs. Her left rear leg is still in a cast. "I hope I'm not disturbing you, Ambassador?"

"No, please, sit down," I say. Just looking at Trimana's injured leg makes me wince. She and the South Hosh delegation came here for treatment too.

Trimana climbs onto the chair by my bed, curling up in it so that all her weight is on her right side, favoring her uninjured leg. "I owe you both my thanks and apologies, Ambassador. I treated you with suspicion and hostility when you came to Hosh. But despite my mistrust, you have responded with nothing but respect and *unam*. Today you saved my life."

"Thank you," I say. "But I'm sure anyone would have done the same."

"If you could see others' minds, you would know that is not so. It's not simply that you saved my life that moved me. It was the shape of your mind during the attack. You barely gave a thought to your own survival.

Your thoughts dwelled upon your familial, yes. But you thought barely at all of yourself. Indeed, much of the time your mind was unclouded by thoughts. You were simply acting, courageous compassion flowing across your mind. And your compassion was not bound by your species or your world. Your compassion for me and my fellow Hoshans was as great as your compassion for your fellow Terrans. That is something I've rarely seen."

My cheeks flush. The intensity of her praise is overwhelming, especially when I don't deserve it.

"In any case, I must leave for the South while I still can. We'll likely never see each other again, and so I came to share my thanks, and my farewell."

"But what about the talks?" I say.

"The talks have been suspended, indefinitely," Trimana says. "The Etoscans and Levinti are preparing for war. Soon the border will be closed completely. I must be with my own people now, to do all I can to protect them from the destruction to come. My deputies are already evacuating the border towns. Perhaps we can minimize the initial casualties."

"But there must be something we can do," I say. "We still have three days before the treaty expires. If we can get the Etoscans and the Levinti back to the negotiating table—"

"They were always only feigning interest in peace," Trimana says. "Now, the Hosh-Unam Front's devastating attack has given them all the pretext they need for war. They've proved we're as primitive as they say."

"There's got to be someone who'll listen to reason," I say.

"The most reasonable of the Etoscans and Levinti died in that chamber last night. Speaker is dead. Kantroponar is dead. I'm not even dealing with the Levinti Academy for Colonial Governance anymore. The Academy of Military Studies has assumed control of Southern

Hosh. I've dealt with them before, but they've never been in charge, not in my lifetime. They've spent centuries making a science of war. I assure you, Ambassador, they've no interest in peace."

After the attack, I felt so relieved that Timoteo, Johnny, Pash-Ti, and Trimana had all survived, that we saved all but a handful of Hoshans. I thought we could continue the negotiations despite the Hosh-Unam Front's attack. I've been so naïve.

"Yes," Trimana says. "It was somewhat naïve of you. But it is only natural that you, having such a noble mind, yet being mind-deaf, should assume that other minds are as noble as yours. I wish it were so." She climbs down from the chair, walking on her five uninjured legs. "Farewell, Ambassador. I suggest you return to your own world, to your own problems. There's no more you can do for us here. Thank you again for saving my life. If ever I may reciprocate your kindness, I assure you I shall do so." With those words, Trimana limps out of the room.

✧   ✧   ✧

MINUTES LATER, PASH-TI is at my bedside. The ceiling is too low for them to stand, so they sit on a circular Hoshan chair, long legs tucked in a spider-like squat.

"Can't I do something?" I ask them. "As mediator?"

"I've already attempted to contact Listener on your behalf, as well as the newly assigned Levinti Professor of Military Studies. None have replied. After the attack, all are focused on preparations for war." Pash-Ti leans their spindly grey torso in close. "Listen, Ambassador—Valeria—there is another option. You know there are other forces at work here, something else that Umberto discovered, something important enough that he was assassinated. Our only hope now is to find out what he knew. That information might allow us to turn the tide for peace."

That's what I've been trying to do from the start. "I agree, but how?"

Pash-Ti leans back again. "Johnny is the key. I still believe it was he who betrayed Umberto. Wasn't it convenient that—for the second time—he was disabled so easily by primitive insurgents? That he then recovered so quickly after the attack? It's improbable that the Hosh-Unam Front attained such advanced technology so quickly without assistance, and even more improbable that an advanced Synthetic warlord like Johnny was so easily overpowered. The simplest explanation is that Johnny feigned being incapacitated—and indeed has been working with the Hosh-Unam Front all along—including providing them with more advanced swarm technology for the attack."

That all makes sense, but Pash-Ti doesn't know about the sample from beneath Tumasra. Maybe the energy surge happened because the Hosh-Unam Front was experimenting with the new interstellar technology they used in the attack on Tumasra, and maybe they did get that from Johnny. But I can't tell Pash-Ti that—there's still a chance they could be the traitor too. "But does even Johnny have the capacity to create a swarm of that scale and power so fast? He can't create exotic matter or quantum threading and all that stuff by himself, right? Wouldn't they have needed all that?"

Pash-Ti's eyestalks extend, apparently surprised at how much I've learned. "Indeed. Which may be the secret Umberto uncovered. Perhaps some source or faction within the Etoscans or Levinti secretly assisted Johnny and the Hosh-Unam Front in procuring the technology required for the swarm, in order to pave the way for war. That may be the secret Umberto uncovered—and that Johnny killed him for."

That was our other theory. And after today's horrible attack, it seems more likely. "So what are you saying we should do?"

"Johnny is dangerous," Pash-Ti says. "I saw your weapon, the one you used against the Hosh-Unam swarm. You must use it to disable Johnny. Then we can contain him, and, if necessary, use invasive software to search his memory banks for the answer."

"Invasive software? That sounds like torture." I stand up, my muscles straining. "Your whole case is conjecture, and we can't attack Johnny just because you're suspicious. We've got to find another way. Gather the others. I want to go see Listener."

"I told you, Madame Ambassador, they simply will not answer my calls."

"Then let's show up at their doorstep."

✧　✧　✧

IT'S MIDDAY, SO THE STREETS are quiet as we drive to the Etoscan embassy. The nocturnal Hoshans are home asleep—or trying to sleep. I wonder if, like me, they're having trouble sleeping after the trauma of the attack. Do they share their dreams too? All around us, in those flat stone homes, are Hoshans dreaming a collective nightmare of swarms and flames?

A massive flock of birds flies across the grey sky above—but then I realize they have no wings. "Are those bots?"

Johnny—now back in his human form—looks up through the car's windowpane. "Yeah, the Etoscan swarm isn't just at the border anymore. They're deploying them everywhere." A soccer-ball-sized bot is hovering over every Hoshan home. I shudder at the realization that we're inside a war zone now.

Pash-Ti, Johnny, Timoteo, and I all step out of the vehicle as we arrive at the Etoscan embassy. The Hoshans at the gate don't lead us to the grand misty chamber where I met the Etoscan ambassadors last time. They lead us to a small room with five Hoshan-style chairs and two Etoscan stools. Timoteo, Johnny, and I sit on Hoshan chairs, and Pash-Ti takes their place on the larger stool, saying, "This is futile, Madame Ambassador."

Ten minutes later, a small Etoscan enters the room. His headpiece is unadorned, and his thick reddish hide is rough with age. "Salutations. I am Greeter. How might I assist you?"

"We need to speak to the Etoscan ambassadors," I say.

Greeter's trunk trembles slightly as he speaks. "I'm afraid the ambassadors are indisposed for the foreseeable future. It's a busy time, with much to do to protect Northern Hosh after these terrible attacks."

"That's why we need to see them," I say. "We can't let the attack stop the peace talks."

"Come on," Timoteo says, "Listener, or the new Speaker, can spare a moment to see us."

"Even if they could, they're not here at the embassy. They're busy elsewhere making ready the swarms," Greeter says, turning away from us. "And you should know that Listener has taken a new name this season. His proper name is Commander of War."

Chapter 21

I close the door behind Johnny after he walks into our room at the guesthouse. He leans against the door, his eyes darting between Timoteo and me. "So what's up?"

There's a moment of tense silence. I'm not ready to use "invasive software" like Pash-Ti said, but that attack was ... devastating. There's no way the Hosh-Unam Front got that tech without help. And Johnny's the one most easily able to offer it.

"Why did you have a map of Hosh-Unam Front bases in your office?" I say.

Johnny chuckles, almost with relief. "Is that what this is about? Umberto asked me to make that for him. He was getting super paranoid, so he asked me to make it paper instead of digital."

I grip my phone inside the pocket of my jeans, ready to press the neutralize button if I have to. "Then you led me right into their trap. You *knew* one of their bases was right beneath the Southern capital."

"Well, yeah, obvi," Johnny says. "I guessed the spy we were chasing was Hosh-Unam Front. But I figured I could take them. I didn't know they had a frigging positronic pulse."

Timoteo looks up at Johnny from his seat in the corner. "But you can defend against a positronic pulse. That's not hard for a Synthetic warlord."

Johnny throws both hands in the air. "If I know it's coming! If I know vaguely what frequency it might be, so I can modulate my shield for it. But the Hosh-Unam Front have never had access to that kind of tech before. I just wasn't ready for it."

"So you're not the one who's been helping the Hosh-Unam Front get these more advanced weapons?" I say.

"No!" Johnny says. "I hate the Hosh-Unam Front! I hate violence! You're totally right that someone got them a major power upgrade, but I swear it wasn't me. And even if I wanted to, I couldn't arm them with a whole swarm like that all by myself. Only someone high up in one of the Great Powers could do that. Did you notice Listener—Commander of War—wasn't at the talks? That he survived the attack as a result? He must be the one who's been arming the Hosh-Unam Front."

"Hmm," Timoteo says, scanning the inside of his glasses. "Listener's official communiqué says he was praying on the talks and had a vision that he shouldn't go. Does that sort of thing really fly with Etoscans? I guess it does, because some other Etoscan leaders praised his piety. And Listener getting his name changed to Commander of War was sort of like a promotion."

"Exactly," Johnny says. "Commander gave the Hosh-Unam Front the weapons to attack his own Citadel, taking out all his enemies in one blow—and now he wants control of all of Hosh."

Timoteo and I exchange glances. Johnny's corroborating all our theories—except the part about his own involvement. And if Johnny were really threatened by these accusations, he could probably take Timoteo and me both out before I pressed the trigger on my phone.

"Timoteo and I have some things to figure out," I say. "You can go."

"Guess I'm dismissed," Johnny says, walking out the door. "I'm here if you need anything."

Timoteo gets up and paces. "I didn't think it made sense before, because I thought supplying the Hosh-Unam Front with weapons wasn't really an issue of interstellar law. But now that I've seen how terrible this attack was ... maybe that *is* what they were hiding."

Finally, a theory that makes sense. "If Umberto found out that Commander was conspiring with the Hosh-Unam Front, even against Speaker and other Etoscans—that seems like the kind of secret Commander would kill him for. But if not Johnny, then I guess Wasala was his agent. That's hard to imagine too."

"I know," Timoteo says. "But something's missing. It's still the Levinti who have the strategic advantage in a war on Hosh. Why would Commander manipulate things like this just to start a war he's likely to lose?"

"It could be the Levinti who armed the Front," I say. "Which would make Pash-Ti the most likely agent. Maybe that's why they're trying to deflect our suspicions to Johnny."

Timoteo lifts his glasses, rubbing a finger and thumb on his eyes. "Maybe, though that doesn't explain the weird sample, or Listener being the only one to conveniently avoid the massacre."

The massacre. My entire body trembles. Over a dozen Etoscans, Levinti, and Hoshans died, right in front of me. Speaker is dead. Kantroponar is dead. They were hard to negotiate with, but they seemed like good people—good sentients—and now they're gone. Just like tío Umberto.

A sob wrenches out of me, my body convulsing so hard it shakes the round Hoshan chair I'm sitting on.

"Please don't lose it, Val," Timoteo says, tearing up too. "I'm about to lose it, so I can't have you lose it. How could tío Umberto do this to us? How could he leave us alone like this? Didn't he tell you anything else? Didn't he leave you a fricking clue?"

"No!" I shout. "He didn't leave us with anything! Just a giant mess of a Galaxy!"

Timoteo falls to the floor, taking off his fogged-up glasses and hiding his face in his hands. I have to stay strong, for him and for everyone.

I take a deep breath to steady myself. Why did Umberto leave me alone like this? He knew they were trying to assassinate him, why didn't he leave me more clues?

Ferus said maybe Umberto had left me a clue, and I'd missed it, that maybe that's what my vision of him in the mists meant. "You don't want to miss the train!" If that was a message from my subconscious, it was a pretty useless one.

Then I remember the most random thing. I wipe away my tears and grab my phone from my knapsack. My phone chimes to life. I'm obviously way out of range, but I can still scroll through old messages. The one I'm looking for is way down in my inbox, but there it is, from Umberto Olmeda. It came into my phone a few hours after Umberto died, but the time-stamp of the email is from two days *before* he died.

Tío Umberto left me a virtual message in a bottle. Of course he found a way to tell me his secret—something so subtle that no one else could guess what it was. How could I have mistaken it for a stupid joke-email forward? But then, how could I have known? I got this email before I even found out about all the secret-ambassador stuff.

I re-read the email, word by word. I think back on everything I've learned—and what was in that vial. It's like a stuck window suddenly being flung open, the sounds of the outdoors rushing in.

"Oh my God," I whisper aloud. I'm still trembling, but now my trembling is tinged with hope instead of despair.

Timoteo looks up, his eyes red with tears. "What is it? Are you okay?"

I stand up. "I know what's hidden beneath Tumasra. And I know who killed tío Umberto."

CHAPTER 22

TIMOTEO AND I WALK through the corridors of the transit station on Hosh-tor, an uninhabited, gaseous planet—the sixth from Hosh's sun. We've never much time here before, just used it as a transfer station on trips back and forth from Earth to Hosh. It's a massive transit center. The walls, floor, and ceiling are all transparent, exposing the corridors and rooms beyond, a maze of interconnected passageways. Etoscans, Levinti, and at least a dozen other species stampede or fly or swim through the station's corridors. Everyone is rushing to leave after the Interstellar Council's order for all non-Hoshans to evacuate the system. Everyone is expecting war to erupt as soon as the treaty expires in just a day and a half.

Checkers guides us through the throng of aliens racing through the station's Oxygen Section. I take the longest strides my short legs allow, trying not to let the fear all around us infect me. These panicking aliens don't know what I know. We can stop this war. We have to.

✦ ✦ ✦

WE FIND PASH-TI AND JOHNNY standing at the far end of our meeting room in awkward silence. Pash-Ti points a spindly finger at me. "Why have you called this meeting here on Hosh-tor? We must evacuate immediately, as every sensible sentient is doing, before the inevitable war."

There've been so many layers of tension between Pash-Ti and me this past month. Some of it is because they never really thought I was qualified to be ambassador, and some of it's because they're so by-the-book and I tend to be more seat-of-my-pants. But a lot of it has been because I didn't know if I could trust them. It's a relief to finally be able to confront them directly. I step up to them so that we're barely a foot apart, my eyes at the level of their elbows. "It's not inevitable. You may have given up, but we haven't. And, look, I'm sorry I haven't been fully up-front with you. I wasn't sure if we could trust you—either of you. This whole time I've been ambassador, it's been impossible. I've tried to work with all three of you while still staying prepared for any one of you to be the traitor. I've had to keep secrets from all of you, which I hated doing. But all that's changed now."

"Are you saying you figured out who killed Umberto?" Johnny says. "Wait, if you're here talking to the two of us, does that mean it's Wasala?"

"We'll get to that," I say. "You both should take a seat."

Pash-Ti's eyestalks bend down at me, blinking. "Very well."

"Um, hey, room," I say to the air, "we need a meeting table and four chairs of appropriate heights for each of us." We all step away from the center of the room as one large mass and four smaller objects rise up from the floor and shape themselves into a table and chairs.

I take the seat across from Johnny. Timoteo sits down next to me, and Pash-Ti sits last, in the taller stool beside Johnny. I take a deep breath, my confidence shaky. I just have to be direct, unravel the facts one by one.

"I think I know the secret that got Umberto killed," I say.

"Whoa," Johnny says.

Pash-Ti lets out a sharp whistle. "How might you have attained such information?"

I take the vial out of my messenger bag and pass it across the table to Pash-Ti. "It started with this." I explain to them how we actually did find the Outlands and Ferus, how he gave me the sample that Umberto had asked him to get.

Pash-Ti grasps the vial in two thin fingers, moving it up and down, taking note of its odd reverse weight. "This appears to contain exotic matter," she says, passing it to Johnny.

Johnny holds the vial up to the light. "Yup. Also entangled quantum threads and graphotons."

Pash-Ti stands up and takes a step back from Johnny. "That composition could be used to develop advanced swarm technology of the type used by the Hosh-Unam Front in their attack on Tumasra. Particularly if they had the assistance of a Synthetic former military command unit."

"Hold up, Pash-Ti," Johnny says, palms in the air.

"Think about it," Timoteo says. "If the Hosh-Unam Front were the culprits, why didn't Umberto report it? They've got no clout with the Interstellar Council."

Pash-Ti shifts their weight back to their third leg. "True. But if they were conspiring with one of the Great Powers—if he believed the Etoscans intentionally allowed their technology to be stolen by the

Hosh-Unam Front—that would have made Umberto more reluctant to report his suspicions until he had proof."

"We thought that too," I say. "And Ferus confirmed that both the Etoscans and Levinti have been arming the Hosh-Unam Front, which is probably how they got the technology for that super-advanced swarm. But Ferus says he saw in Umberto's mind that Umberto was suspicious something the Etoscans were hiding beneath Tumasra, where the storm and the caverns would block both sensors and telepathy."

Pash-Ti leans over the table, their long torso casting a shadow over my face. "I see no logic in this line of thinking. The Etoscans are undoubtedly hiding a plethora of weapons beneath Tumasra, but nothing about that would violate interstellar law."

"We also thought that too," Timoteo says. "But weapons aren't the only things that matter in war. Which is the clue Val realized from her vision in the Etoscan mists."

"You claim you've solved the mystery of Ambassador Olmeda's murder based on a hallucinogenic vision?" Pash-Ti says, still leaning.

I wish Timoteo hadn't mentioned the vision thing. This is hard enough as it is. "The vision isn't important, it just helped me remember something. A clue Umberto left behind. When I used the mists, I saw Umberto, and he told me not to miss the train. It all just seemed like a trippy vision, but Ferus told me I should pay attention to it, that it might be my unconscious trying to tell me something."

"Ferus is a former insurgent and wanted criminal," Pash-Ti says.

"He's reformed," Timoteo says. "We think."

"The vision and Ferus aren't the point," I say. "On the night of Umberto's funeral I found an email from him in my inbox. It was just a stupid joke email, and I hadn't looked at it closely before. I figured he'd sent it just before he died. But a few hours ago I looked at it again and saw it had been written a few days *before* he died but wasn't sent until the day after he died. Which made me think he was trying to send me a message in a way no one else would notice."

"That would be pretty smart," Johnny says. "By sending it through a primitive channel like email, the Great Powers and their spies would never detect it."

I stand up and pace around the table, like moving my legs will help me get the words out. "Right. So this email is just a joke-article. Umberto always used to send me stupid joke articles and memes. But the article was about a train station being built right under a volcano. A *Subway* station."

Pash-Ti finally stops leaning, straightens their long spine in surprise. "Are you implying ..."

"Yes," I say. "The Etoscans are building an unauthorized Interstellar Subway Station beneath Tumasra."

Johnny gapes. "If that was what Umberto figured out—"

"It would definitely freak out the Etoscans," Timoteo says. "Since the Interstellar Transit Authority is maybe the most powerful body in the interstellar bureaucracy."

"Indeed," Pash-Ti says. "The ITA rigidly regulates the construction and control of each Subway station, which has tremendous strategic consequences. It's the *only* way to travel faster than light, making it essential for all transport of arms, personnel, supplies ..."

I finish my loop around the table, unable to contain the energy building up in my body. "Exactly! And the fact that the Levinti control the only Subway on Hosh itself is their main strategic advantage. So if the Etoscans had their own station on Hosh—plus the element of surprise—they could defeat the Levinti and take control of the planet."

Johnny holds up the vial again. "Actually, the exotic matter and entangled threads are exactly the right proportions for constructing the quantum shield arrays required for an Interstellar Subway. And Subway stations are hard to hide from sensors, but under Tumasra would be the perfect place to do it."

"And because of its alleged sacred status," Pash-Ti adds, "no one has been permitted to inspect Tumasra for decades. It certainly would be typical of the Etoscans to abuse their rhetoric of sacredness for political and military gain."

My theory's right, I'm sure of it. I smile at the thought of Umberto communicating with me in such a clever way, like a message in a bottle from beyond the grave. "I'm sure this is what Umberto was saying with that email. It's exactly how he thinks."

But then my mind turns to the last thing, the thought that makes me shiver. "So the only question left is who the Etoscans' agent on Earth was. And unfortunately only one answer makes sense. Wasala. Her parents were telepathic agents from Northern Hosh who worked for the Etoscans. It's clear she has a personal stake in Hosh's fate. And even with her short-range telepathy, she could've read Umberto's thoughts, and sensed he'd figured out the Etoscans were building an unauthorized Subway station. And eventually killed him."

Pash-Ti sits back down, interlacing their long fingers. "Your case is surprisingly compelling, but one flaw remains. Wasala is not permitted to set foot on Hosh—and hasn't even left Earth in months. She had no way of communicating with the Etoscans without detection."

"The Outlanders found a way, which means the Etoscans could have too," Timoteo says. "They must be transmitting messages to Earth using a seed—a blueprint for a more complex program. A seed is innocuous enough that they could have hidden it in, I don't know, Umberto's luggage, or even in part of the Subway itself. Then, once it was through, it could develop into full form—a long message, or even a fairly simple AI."

"Wasala knows the Subway security protocols better than anybody," Johnny says. "I'll bet she could have helped them come up with that."

"Your theories are sound," Pash-Ti says, rising from their chair. "We must return to Earth at once and confront Wasala with this information."

"Actually," I say, "I don't think there's time for all of us to do that. We only have 36 hours to stop this war, which means we have to split up." I take the vial from Johnny's hand and pass it back to Pash-Ti. "I was hoping Pash-Ti could take this vial to the Interstellar Transit Authority, use it as evidence to get them to investigate a potential violation by the Etoscans on Hosh. If we can do that, it could stop the war, or at least delay it."

"I'm willing to try, Madame Ambassador," Pash-Ti says, "but this vial is not incontrovertible proof. The ITA does not launch investigations lightly, and, while I believe you're correct, we may still lack sufficient evidence to move them to action."

"I know," I say, "and that's why at the same time I want Johnny and Timoteo to go to Tumasra to find definite evidence of the unauthorized Subway."

Johnny stands up and puts his arm around Timoteo. "I think we can handle that. And it's been years since I tried an Etoscan look." As he speaks, Johnny's free arm begins transforming into the long trunk of an Etoscan.

"In the meantime, I'm going back to Earth," I say, "to confront Wasala. Maybe I can get some evidence directly from her."

"Madame Ambassador," Pash-Ti says, "I'm uncertain your delegation of tasks is prudent. Even though Wasala is telepathically nearsighted, she was raised on a military base for telepathic agents and their families. She's well-trained in combat, not to mention her sophisticated knowledge of interstellar technology. It may be wiser for me to accompany you before proceeding to the nearest office of the Interstellar Transit Authority."

"No," I say, hoping I sound more confident than I feel. "We're running out of time, and I need someone to talk with the ITA right away, otherwise they'll never get to Hosh on time. You have the most political skill and connections to get them to pay attention with the minimal evidence we have. Am I wrong?"

Pash-Ti stands a moment, wiggling two sets of spindly fingers against one another. "Your deployment of our resources is well-reasoned. But you need to be armed appropriately for your confrontation with Wasala."

"Actually, um, this is awkward," I say, pulling my phone out of my bag. "Uncle Umberto put a stunner in my phone to use on—on whichever of you turned out to be the traitor. That's how I'll disable Wasala. Hopefully I can catch her by surprise."

"Be ready to use the other setting, too, the one for me," Johnny says. Timoteo and I trade looks of surprise. "I was paralyzed but still conscious when you used it on the swarm during the Tumasra attack. Clever of Umberto to hide it in your phone—I'd never noticed it before that. Glad you didn't use it on me, but you may need it for something else. Wasala may have an AI working with her, remember?"

"Right," I say. My relief that Johnny's on our side is weirdly mixed with my rising anxiety at confronting the reality that Wasala is the traitor. "Thanks, Johnny."

"It was prescient of Umberto to take such precautions," Pash-Ti says, apparently unfazed that Umberto gave me a weapon to disable them, too. "We should all depart immediately."

"I'll need about ten minutes to finish changing," Johnny says, his body surrounded by miniature scaffolding as an Etoscan form gets constructed all around him.

Timoteo takes my hand and squeezes it. "Be careful, Val-Val," he says.

I give him a squeeze back. "You too, Tim-Tim."

I look at the three of them, my only allies on a mission that's a total longshot. "All right. We have 36 hours left until the treaty expires. Let's stop a war."

✦   ✦   ✦

As the Subway approaches Jupiter, I try to quell the unease in my stomach. How much of the nausea is my anxiety about confronting Wasala, and how much is the psycho-tropic effects of interstellar travel? It's the first time I've taken the Interstellar Subway alone. Just like all interstellar technology, the interface is super-intuitive, but it's disquieting to ride the massive tower alone, through the endless empty space between space. At first, when I figured out what the Etoscans were doing, my confidence surged, but now all my doubts are back. How can I confront Wasala alone? I still can't believe she killed tío Umberto. She may even have watched his mind fade away as he died.

The Subway comes to a stop, my skin tingling as it re-materializes in normal space. Jupiter, last stop before home. I take my phone out and open the stunner app. I point it at the Subway doors, in case Wasala's waiting right outside. My best hope is to catch her by surprise.

"All right," I say to the Subway, which I've set for audio interface, "make the final leap to Earth." There are a few seconds of the usual time distortion, and then the Subway tower re-materializes on Earth. The door opens onto an empty platform.

"I'm not detecting anyone on the platform, Madame Ambassador," Checkers says.

I step out onto the platform, slowly, scanning for any movement, in case Wasala has found a way to cloak herself from Checkers' scanners. But no one's here.

I step into the elevator. "Ground level," I say, and the elevator ascends.

The elevator door opens onto the familiar offices of the Terran embassy in Istanbul, and I cautiously step out, holding my phone in front of me, my finger on the trigger. All is quiet, and there's no sign of Wasala. One of the cabinets has been knocked over—and behind it, there's a tuft of fur. Could it be Wasala crouching behind the cabinet, hiding for an ambush? No—she's collapsed on the floor, the fur of her face matted with transparent Hoshan blood.

Who could have done this?

I walk down the corridor, toward the cubicles and offices. As I approach my own office, I see someone through the glass plating, sitting with sneaker-clad feet propped up on the desk. Along with the sneakers is the familiar bright yellow of my high school softball team's uniform.

It's so incongruous—so impossible—that it takes me ten seconds to realize that it's Kate. "Hey there, BFF," she says. "Have you been having lots of fun in outer space?"

CHAPTER 23

"KATE?" I SAY, MY JAW GAPING. "What are you doing here?"

Kate kicks away from the desk, rolling the office chair backward. "Oh, Val. Is this all part of your phony act or are you really this slow on the uptake?"

"You knocked out Wasala?" I say, my mind racing to work through what's happening. "You can't be the real Kate. You're a Synthetic disguised as Kate, or a clone, or something."

Kate stands up and nudges a soccer ball out from under the desk. She dribbles over to me, smoothly passing the ball from one foot to the other. "Nope, just me, your frenemy since ninth grade."

It *sounds* like Kate. "Listen, Kate, I'm not sure what's going on, but someone's been manipulating you. If you'll just sit down and talk, I can help you work this out."

Kate punts the ball into the air and catches it in her arms. "That is so typical of you. 'Let's talk it out, *I* can help.' Do you realize how patronizing you are? I just *can't* with you." She pulls the soccer ball back and hurls it at me.

I twist sideways and tighten my stomach, but still get the wind knocked out of me. I crouch over, clutching my stomach. She's already knocked out Wasala and now she's attacking me. Whatever's going on, I have to stop Kate before she does something worse. I pull out my phone and fire the stunner, releasing a thin streak of electricity at Kate's body.

Kate lets out a slight shudder. "Wow, I felt that a bit. Did I mention how awesome Etoscan drugs are?"

"You're on drugs—from the Etoscans? It must be affecting you—altering your mental state."

Kate saunters toward me. "Technically, I'm not sure drug is the best word. It's like some sort of nano-biotechnology thing. Whatever it is, I'm like a superhero on it! Faster, stronger. Invulnerable to loser stunners. Plus it comes with a nice little high. But here's the thing you're not getting, Val." In seconds, Kate's right on top of me, slamming into me with a sharp punch to the stomach. "You don't *deserve* to be ambassador of Earth."

It takes all my effort just to breathe in. "Checkers," I gasp, "take me up to the ceiling, so she can't reach me."

"Of course, madam," Checkers says, and I feel the familiar sense of weightlessness as I float up to the embassy's ceiling.

Kate cranes her neck toward me and shakes her head. "Ah, Val, always trying to get away from the hard conversations." Looking over her shoulder toward the desk, she shouts, "Yo, Stripe, I need an assist here."

A dark green snake with copper stripes slithers out from beneath the desk, its tongue tasting the air. "Oh my God," I say, still hovering in pain just below the ceiling, "it's the snake from your party." All at once, dozens of memories reconfigure themselves in my mind, and I finally understand what's going on. "Checkers, get me out of here, anywhere, just as far away as possible!"

"At your service, Ambassador," Checkers says, gliding me toward the window.

"Knock out whatever's letting her fly," Kate says to the snake. The snake's eyes light up with a bluish glow, and suddenly gravity takes hold of my body, and I crash to the floor.

I try to get to my feet. My left arm is throbbing. I think it's sprained. "Checkers?" I whisper. "Checkers, are you there?" But there's no answer.

By the desk, the snake climbs up Kate's body and curls itself around her neck. It's bigger than it was at the party, but the pattern of its scales is identical. Kate pets it just below its head. "Good boy, Stripe. I did get nervous when he showed up at my party. Sometimes he gets confused when a new seed-message comes in. And of course *you* would have to be the one to pick him up and bring him outside. But I caught up with him a few minutes later."

"My God, Kate." I stand up, gritting through the pain, determined not to let the tears find their way to the surface of my eyes. "*You* killed tío Umberto?"

"I feel so bad about that," Kate says, walking toward me, her voice softer. "Honestly, I'm really really sorry, because he seemed like a nice guy. But it all kind of escalated. At first, I was just taking photos of his notebook and stuff. I didn't know the Etoscans were going to need me to—hurt people. But I had to stop him. If I didn't, the Levinti were going to take over Hosh and then the whole Galaxy for their evil empire."

I stare at Kate, trembling in disbelief, applying pressure to my injured arm to relieve the pain. "You killed my uncle!" My skin gets hot with anger, so intense that the pain in my arm fades into the background. I charge Kate and slam her with a sharp right hook.

But Kate's way too fast. She catches me by the wrist and holds me in a rock-hard grip. "Did you miss the part about the super-strength and super-speed?" Kate says. "Or did I stutter?" She tightens her hold on my wrist. It's like being crushed by a vice, the pain so unbearable that I fall to my knees. "And I *said* I'm sorry. I had no choice!"

My right arm is caught in Kate's vise-like grip, and my injured left arm is useless, but my legs are still free. I pull my leg out from behind me and sweep the floor with a wide kick, but Kate easily jumps out of the way.

"You are so annoying," Kate says. "Stripe, hold her legs." The snake slithers down Kate's soccer uniform and onto the floor. I try to squirm away, but Kate's grip holds me tight. The snake winds itself around my legs, clasping them together. I'm helpless at Kate's feet.

"It's been you this whole time?" I say, wishing my voice didn't sound so weak. "Is this why you pulled that stupid intervention on me?"

"Yeah," Kate says, "that one was extra credit. The Etoscans had written you off at that point, thought you were a totally incompetent kid just like they'd hoped, but I figured it couldn't hurt if the mediator was stuck on Earth during the big-deal negotiation. But I have to say, other than pretending I could actually stand you, the hardest part was staying away from your freaky alien telepath friend."

Of course, that's why Kate ran away so abruptly at the game. She was making sure to stay outside Wasala's telepathic range. "But how do you *know* all this?" I say.

"Stripe here is a great messenger. Commander of War and I friended each other way back, when he still went by Listener."

"I don't understand," I say. "Why are you doing this?"

"The better question is why do *you* get to be ambassador of Earth? Is it fair for you to speak on behalf of the entire planet just because of your uncle's nepotism? *I'm* the one who's done Model UN! *I'm* the one who's proactive and politically strategic! Why should you get to be ambassador *and* captain of the soccer team *and* the softball team? Why should someone with no ambition get to have so much power? But after this is all over, the Etoscans will make me ambassador of Earth, someone who's actually qualified."

"Did you even take the xenoreactive test?" I say. "Kate, stop and think. Killing people is not okay. Being violent like this isn't normal.

You're not yourself. The Etoscans are using these drugs to control you or something. Half the things they told you were probably lies. They want to start a war! Millions of Hoshans will die!"

"Unlike you, I do my research, Val. The *Levinti* are the ones who want war," Kate says. "You'd get that if you had any real political savvy. This treaty you and your uncle were trying to broker was just going to give them a license to use their Hoshan legions to conquer the Galaxy."

"There probably are Levinti who want that, but there are others who want peace," I say. "No species is monolithic. This is why you've been acting so nice lately? You were using me to spy on tío Umberto?"

"Kinda yeah. Sorry." Kate lifts me into the air with one hand. "You can let go now, Stripe." Stripe loosens his hold on my legs and slinks back to the floor.

"Oh, Val Vega," Kate says, "how do I hate thee, let me count the ways." She grabs me by the torso, lifts me above her head and flings me into the air. My back slams into the wall, and I fall to the ground, trying to land on my good side.

"Reason number one why I hate thee," Kate says, stomping toward me, "you're the most totally two-faced person on this planet of totally two-faced people. When you're with Des and she trash-talks me, do you defend me? No. You just go along with it because all you care about is making everybody like you. Yeah, I'm not an idiot, I know you've done that like a million times. And now you're flinging the same BS all across the Galaxy! Lying and manipulating, everywhere you go!"

Despite the pain, I manage to get myself up onto all fours. Before I can get to my feet, Kate grabs my ankle and rotates my leg one hundred eighty degrees and then snaps it upward.

I scream. The pain is overwhelming. I think Kate just broke my leg.

I collapse on the floor, barely able to move. My leg hurts so bad it makes my sprained arm seem mild by comparison.

Kate steps across my body and stands over me, one foot on either side of me. "Reason number two why I hate thee: you're a total invertebrate. When was the last time you were proactive or took a stand on anything? You knew how everyone was making fun of Des and you never did a thing about it. For a while I thought it was because you were a coward, but then I realized that's not it at all. It's worse than that. You're just *lazy*. You're not willing to do the work of making tough choices, of picking a frigging side. That's why I'm a better person than you, even if nobody realizes it except for a bunch of aliens who look like elephants! That's why I'll be a better ambassador than you could ever be. I'm smarter, I'm more proactive, and I'll actually represent the Earth with some authenticity."

"Please, Kate." I look up at her from the floor, struggling for the strength to talk. "Don't do this."

Kate finishes stepping over me and looks down at me with a mixture of pity and disgust, as if she were looking at a dead animal on the side of the road. "Reason number three!" she shouts, and kicks me in the side, hard. "And this is the big one, the one that took me a long time to figure out. You know what people always say about you, whenever they babble about how great you are? 'Val's such a good listener.' But is that really such a great thing? I mean when do you ever *talk*? Beneath all the phony listening and lies and being-all-things-to-all-people BS, who is the *real* Val? But I figured out your secret, Val. I know who you really are."

Kate bends over so her head is hanging just above my face, bits of her long blonde hair falling into my eyes. "You – Are – Nobody!" As she shouts the last word, she grabs my hair and slams my head against the hard tiled floor.

The pains all across my body blur together into one massive, throbbing sensation of numbness. The room turns into a blur of colors. Then everything goes black.

✦ ✦ ✦

ICE-COLD WATER SPLASHES across my face.

"Wakey-wakey," Kate sings. "No time for sleeping! I'm not through with you. I've gotta say, this is really cathartic!"

I let out a soft groan. I've never been in such excruciating pain. There's no way I can beat Kate. With the Etoscan power-boost, she's too fast, too strong. I can't even get up off the floor. My only hope is that the others might come through, that Johnny and Timoteo can find evidence of the Etoscans' unauthorized Subway Station, that Pash-Ti can get help from the Interstellar Transit Authority in time.

My vision gets clearer. I look up and see Kate walking away from me. "Hold that groan," Kate says. "I've got a DM."

A single tiny bot flies across the room, entering the snake's waiting open mouth. From its eyes, the snake projects a miniature holographic image of Commander of War.

Kate sits down to watch the message, propping her feet up on the desk.

"We've confirmed our initial intelligence," says Commander of War, letting out a series of long brays with his trunk. "We've captured the ambassador's brother and the Synthetic warlord attempting to infiltrate the Citadel. She's deduced that we're building an Interstellar Subway Station beneath Tumasra. The Terran ambassador must not be allowed to leave Earth with this knowledge. Deal with her the same way you handled her predecessor. If possible, make it look like an accident, something feasible with primitive technology—but ultimately, use whatever means you must. Within 36 hours, the new Subway Station will be operational, the treaty will have expired, Hosh will be saved from the Levinti aggressors, and you will be the new Ambassador of Earth. Report back on your status immediately."

The message flickers out. "Aw, they got your brother, too," Kate says. "Sorry, that's rough. I'm sure he'll be fine though. Maybe. Stripe, record my response. 'Greetings, Commander of War. I've taken care of Valeria Vega, the so-called ambassador. Mission accomplished. I look forward to meeting you face to face soon.' End of message. Stripe, send it back the usual way, hidden and coded as a seed through the Interstellar Subway communications thing." A tiny bot emerges from Stripe's mouth and flies away toward the Subway platform.

Kate gets up and walks toward the window on the far side of the room. "Oh, Val, as much as I hate you, I wish I didn't have to do this. It's for the good of the Galaxy, though. But how to make it look like an accident? The window, maybe? That could work ..."

I only half-listen as Kate wanders around the room, pondering different ways she can kill me. They've caught Timoteo and Johnny. There's no hope. What will happen to them? I can't imagine losing Timoteo too ... Timoteo, Johnny, the entire Hoshan people—they'll all be massacred by Commander of War within hours. And I'm here lying on the ground, helpless. Why did Umberto trust me with all this? Why did he ever think I'd have the capacity for this? I can barely manage to pass the SATs and get through a full day of school, much less solve an interstellar crisis. I'm a nothing, just like Kate said.

But Umberto did trust me. He believed in me, always. I hear his voice echoing in my mind, one of the last things he said to me: *The problem is not that you're two-faced. You're able to imagine yourself behind the eyes of the other person, to see the world from their perspective and meet them there—even when that perspective is vastly different from your own experience. But our greatest gifts can also be our greatest liabilities. The problem is that you too often take the path of least resistance. And that path, though the easiest one to follow, is often not the one that will get you where you need to go.*

The memory of Umberto's gentle voice rescues a sliver of courage from my heart. I am *not* going to let him down. Timoteo needs me! Johnny needs me, and Hosh needs me! And I'm not going to just lie here. I'm *not* going to take the path of least resistance. One way or another, no matter how hard it is, I'm going to find a way to save them. I summon every last bit of strength and pull myself to my feet.

But as soon as I put just a bit of weight on my leg, the pain is searing. I lie on the ground, my determination insufficient to heal my broken leg, sprained arm, and possible mild concussion.

Willpower isn't enough. I need something else, something that will give me an edge. But what advantage do I have over a super-powered Kate? That's when it hits me—Kate has never been off Earth. All she knows is whatever the Commander of War and the synthetic snake have told her. That's my advantage—everything I've seen and learned these past four weeks.

Kate's still on the other side of the room, and the elevator's maybe fifteen feet away, if I can just get to it. "I don't know, maybe we should just go with the window. It seems cleaner than a fire. Val, are you listening? This is important."

Kate turns back toward me—now is my only chance, while she's still on the far side of the room. With my good arm, I roll myself toward the elevator. The pain pierces through my body every time my weight rolls onto my left side. As I get close, I say, "Elevator, open!"

"What the hell are you doing?" Kate shouts, racing for the elevator.

I finish rolling my way into the elevator and say, "Elevator, close! Take me down to the Subway platform!" The door closes just seconds before Kate reaches it, and the elevator descends. I clutch my left leg, which hurts even worse than before. But I tune it out. Focus on the goal, like at the end of a game.

The elevator opens onto the Subway platform. "Elevator," I say as I crawl through the elevator door, "stay here on the platform. Don't return to the upper levels of the office without explicit permission from me."

"Confirmed," the elevator responds. That should hold Kate off for a few minutes, though I'm sure Stripe will find a way to help her get down the shaft.

I crawl to the Subway tower and collapse on the fleximatter floor of the Subway, which automatically contours itself to fit the curves of my body. I lie there a few seconds, catching my breath.

The Subway isn't equipped with any weapons—the ITA doesn't allow that—but Wasala told me it has basic first aid and repair functions. "Computer," I say, "I've been injured badly. I'm pretty sure my right leg is broken, and I think my left arm is sprained, and I've got bruises all over. And a bad bump on the back of my head that might be a concussion. Can your med-bots take care of all that?"

"Affirmative," the Subway's computer replies. "My first-aid bots are fully capable of repairing such superficial injuries in a Terran human. Med-bots are being deployed presently."

The med-bots are microscopic, but I feel tiny pricks in my neck, leg, and arms as the bots puncture my skin. I lie on the floor of the Subway, letting them do their work. The med-bots aren't instantaneous, but they should work quickly on injuries like bruises and broken bones. I just hope they'll be fast enough.

"Computer," I say, "My synth-suit was disabled. Can you repair the damage to that too?"

"Yes," the computer replies. "However, it will take several minutes to reboot the system."

"Do it."

I lie there, letting myself heal and thinking through my options. I could take the Subway all the way back to Hosh, just leave Kate here at the Terran embassy. But as soon as Kate sees I'm gone, she'll send another message to Commander of War, and the Etoscans will be ready for me on the other side. And Wasala looked badly hurt—I can't leave her behind.

Poor Wasala. I can't believe I thought she was the one who killed Umberto. I was right about the Etoscans, about the Subway, about everything *except* that.

I can't believe it was Kate all along. She's always been egocentric, but I never imagined she'd be capable of murder. The Etoscans convinced her of their cause, appealing to her self-righteousness. And those drugs must be affecting her mental state.

I have to be as prepared as possible to stop her. "Computer, I'm going to need to make the jump to Jupiter quickly. Can you be ready to do that? And to make adjustments to other systems, like the gravity adapter, on my verbal command?"

"Confirmed, Madame Ambassador."

Another idea occurs to me. I slip off my jacket and hold it in my good arm. Just then, there are sounds from the direction of the elevator, like a laser slicing through metal. Then feet pounding on the floor.

The med-bots haven't finished yet, but I already feel a bit better. The ache of my right arm is completely gone. The other arm and my broken leg still hurt, but at least I can move them now. I stay lying on the floor, letting the med-bots finish their work, hoping Kate will think I'm still almost totally immobilized.

"There you are!" Kate says, walking toward the Subway. "Trying to take a little get-away trip without me? Sorry, Val—no more outer space adventures for you!" She steps into the Subway and pounds a fist into the palm of her other hand. Then she lunges at me.

"Computer," I say, "close door and make the leap to Jupiter."

The Subway exits normal space and I feel that familiar leap in my stomach, the usual time distortion—but I'm used to it now. Kate is moving toward me in what seems like slow motion. Wincing through the pain, I push myself to my feet and slip out of Kate's path. Kate careens past me and slowly turns to look back at me, her face contorted with a mixture of rage and paranoia. It's just what I planned—Kate is experiencing the intense temporal and psychological effects of subnormal space.

Kate dives for me again, fists flailing wildly. Again, I step aside, and this time I catch Kate in my jacket. I pull it tight to her face and tie it around her head with the sleeves. Kate's growl is muffled by the jacket and by the hum of the Subway making its interdimensional jump.

The flow of time goes back to normal. We've finished the leap to Jupiter. Kate rips the jacket off her face. "Now I'm really gonna kill you," she shouts, and charges at me.

I try to dodge, but I'm no match for Kate's speed now that the time distortion is gone. Kate slams into me with the full weight of her body, knocking me to the floor. The pain returns to my arm—the injury was barely healed and Kate's blow must have undone whatever progress the med-bots had made.

Where the hell is Checkers? The timing is so close ...

Kate grabs me by the shirt and pushes me up against the wall. "Nice try, Val," she says, through gritted teeth.

But then I hear a soothing voice in my ear. "Madame, I'm fully operational and ready to assist you."

"Computer," I say, "shut down the gravity adjustment system, now!"

"Confirmed," the Subway's computer replies. Suddenly, Kate drops to the floor as if someone just piled 140 pounds on top of her.

"I assume, Madame," says Checkers' voice, "that you'd like me to continue adjusting your personal gravity to normal Terran levels?"

"That's right, Checkers," I say. "It's good to have you back."

Kate slowly pushes herself to her feet. Jupiter's gravity is two and a half times Earth's, which was enough to knock her down, but maybe not enough to keep her there with her augmented strength.

"Checkers, Kate's on some sort of Etoscan drug that's increasing her strength. Can you augment the power of the stunner in my phone so it will knock her out in spite of that?"

"Done," Checkers says.

I pull the phone out of my pocket and open the stunner app again.

Kate pushes herself upright. "Va-a-al!" she shouts.

"How's this for proactive, Kate?" I say, and fire. There's a crackle of energy, and Kate slumps to the floor.

CHAPTER 24

INTERSTELLAR WEAPONS COMMITTEE

Subspace Observation Log

3

**Level:
ELEVATED**

Estimated number
of Etoscan warbots
armed for immediate
deployment on Hosh:
247 BILLION

3

Estimated number
of Levinti warbots
armed for immediate
deployment on Hosh:
305 BILLION

29:42

Countdown to
Article 17 expiration:

29 Terran hours
and 42 minutes

THE ELEVATOR PINGS OPEN at the main floor of the Terran embassy.
I limp out the door, headed to where Wasala was lying on the ground
before, hoping she's all right.

Something rustles. "Wasala?"

The snake! It shoots out from behind the wastebasket, slithering
toward me with astonishing speed. I yank my phone out of my pocket.
The snake springs off the floor, its fangs only seconds away from my
face. I press the neutralizer and fire. The snake goes limp, momentum
carrying its lifeless body forward until it falls at my feet.

I let out a long sigh. At least something is working the way it was
supposed to.

But then the snake lets out a hiss as its head lifts off the floor.

Why didn't the neutralizer work? I back away from it, looking for something—anything—I can use as a weapon.

The snake slithers toward me, its mouth wide open, fangs sharp. I break into a run, ignoring the lingering pain in my leg. I knock over a desk behind me, spilling office supplies on the floor, creating an obstacle course for the snake, but that will only buy me a few seconds.

Then there's a sudden blur of brown fur. Wasala pounces on the snake and digs into it with her claws, ripping its scaly skin. With a final hiss, it falls to the floor.

"Wasala!" I say. "Thank God you're okay. Is that thing really dead now?"

"I'd say so, dearie," Wasala says, licking a bead of blood from her claws.

The snake's scaly skin is shredded in places, blood pooling around it. "How can a synthetic snake bleed?" I say. "And why didn't the neutralizer work?"

"Etoscans mix biotech with nanotech," Wasala says. "Cybernetics that also use genetic coding and grow real organic parts."

"So it was like a snake-cyborg," I say.

"Something like that," Wasala says. "Your neutralizer knocked out the cybernetics, but not the biological components, which followed through on their last command—to kill you."

"Well, thanks for saving me," I say. "Are you okay?"

"Thank Synchronus," Wasala says. "I woke up and activated my emergency med-bots. Your friend did quite a number on me. Where did she ..."

"Downstairs. Checkers says she should be out for at least an hour."

"We'll need to get her in a containment field," Wasala says.

"They have Timoteo and Johnny," I say. "We have to save them—and Hosh."

Wasala stands to her full height on her hindmost legs. "I know. First, we need to take care of Kate."

◇ ◇ ◇

WASALA PUNCHES IN A CODE to activate a containment field around one of the bedrooms on the embassy's residential level. The room is like Checkers, an AI that will make sure Kate has food, water, and other basics. She's lying on the bed, still unconscious.

We turn away from Kate's makeshift cell, back toward the elevator. "I just can't believe it," I say, still breathless and shaky from my battle with Kate—from everything. "I feel like I never even knew her. She tried to kill me. She *killed* tío Umberto."

"Her resentment for you was palpable," Wasala says as we enter the elevator. "I could sense it the moment she was near me. Sometimes an intense emotion can be—like a fire, feeding off itself, becoming larger than the spark that started it."

"So all that was just her?" I say. "They weren't using mind-control or drugs or anything to manipulate her?"

We exit the elevator and walk to the conference room. "Not quite mind control," Wasala says, "but those biotech enhancements have horrible side effects. The drugs amplified her aggression, distorted her thinking—as did Commander of War's manipulations. But that flame of hatred toward you—that existed before. Commander of War just fanned it for his own purposes."

I stop mid-step. "Then it's my fault Umberto is dead. If I hadn't made Kate hate me ... none of this would have happened. He might still be alive. And Timoteo and Johnny wouldn't be prisoners ... and everything wouldn't be falling apart."

Wasala stretches up to her full height and takes my hand in her two upper claws. "You mustn't think that, dearie. You didn't make Kate hate you. She did that, with help from Commander's manipulations. I wish *I* had foreseen that. Since I was a child, I was raised to have faith in Synchronus. And with that, in a way, came a certain faith in our Etoscan stewards. I failed to see that some, like Commander, preach the path of Synchronus, but care nothing for its practice. But it's not our fault. We can't blame ourselves when others betray our faith in them."

"Yeah," I say. "I just wish I could convince myself that was true."

The six fingers of Wasala's soft furry hand stroke my arm with a gentle assurance. How could I have thought Wasala was the traitor? *I'm so sorry I didn't trust you, Wasala.*

Wasala nods. "I can't imagine how hard it must be to trust someone, when you can't read their minds. In my family, we shared all our thoughts with each other. Trust was always there, all around us, like air. But as I interacted with sentients outside the family, I saw how great the gap was between speech and thought. They kept secrets, betrayed one another with fleeting thoughts and lifelong masquerades. With all that uncertainty, how can you ever trust anyone?"

"That's for sure," I say, collapsing in one of the office chairs. My exhausted body tingles all over. I hope that's the med-bots healing the last of my wounds. There's no time for rest. "Did you sense anything else in Kate's mind? Anything that might be useful?"

"Mainly confirmation of what you've already guessed," Wasala says. "Commander of War—how I hate that name—is not only building an Interstellar Subway beneath Tumasra, he also provided the swarm to the Hosh-Unam Front for the attack on the Citadel."

"Timoteo and I thought maybe that was what happened. But that means they knew the attack was coming. That's ..."

"Insidious," Wasala finishes. "Speaker was a noble sentient, a true follower of the path of Synchronus. She was open to a peaceful resolution for Hosh—so Commander eliminated her."

My memory is invaded by images of the carnage at the Citadel, a dozen Etoscans falling with keening trumpets, Speaker falling in silent dignity. "I can't believe they'd do that to their own people." I pause and think for a second. "You sensed all this in Kate's mind. Can we use that? Take it to the Interstellar Transit Authority as evidence?"

"I doubt that would help," Wasala says. "Kate's a primitive whose mind is corrupted by biosynth enhancements. The truths in her mind are worth little more than the evidence we already have. It won't move the bureaucracy of the ITA any faster than Pash-Ti can now."

"There has to be another option," I say.

Wasala walks up to my chair and kneels on her four hind legs. "Our best hope is for Pash-Ti to succeed in their efforts. Sometimes there is no option, no good answer."

Absurdly, my thoughts roam to the SATs, to all the questions where I saw how every answer could be right, and how every answer could be wrong, depending on your point of view. Sometimes the answer isn't on the list they give you. Sometimes the answer is none of the above.

Wasala's ears prick up. "What are you thinking, Valiant One? What answer?"

I stand up. It's like I'm on the soccer field, letting my body take me to where the ball is going next.

"Val, where are you going?" Wasala says, dropping to all six legs and following me to the nanotech supply closet. "Your mind is moving too quickly to follow your thoughts."

"Back to Hosh," I say.

"To confront two interstellar armies and a band of telepathic insurgents? Do you even have a plan?"

"The plan is a work-in-progress," I say, scanning the closet. "We need supplies, primitive supplies that will work even after a positronic pulse. In Kate's last transmission, she told Commander of War that I'd been 'taken care of.' So he thinks I'm dead. At least that gives us the element of surprise."

Wasala reaches up to clutch me by the wrist. "Val, you can't do this alone."

"I'm not," I say, surprised at the certainty in my own voice. "You're coming with me."

"My dear, you well know I'm not allowed on Hosh. The Treaty of Centron forbids it."

"The treaty that's a day away from expiring?" I say. "What good is that if Hosh is a war zone? You're right. I can't do it alone. Johnny and Timoteo are prisoners. Pash-Ti's making our case to the ITA. That leaves you. I need you, Wasala. And so does Hosh."

"The current of your mind is strong, drawing my own thoughts to flow with yours," Wasala says. "You're right, my dear. I'd rather die in prison than abandon Hosh in its moment of greatest need. It's time for me to go home."

✧   ✧   ✧

WASALA PILOTS THE SUFRI STEALTHCRAFT. Trimana was happy to secretly help us any way she could—and called in a favor to get us access to it. It hides us from sensors but not from telepathy, so we enter Hosh's atmosphere on the outskirts of the Outlands, far from the minds of the mainland.

As we fly across the Hoshan sea, Wasala's lips tremble. "Earthlings have legends, don't you? Of places that have come before—of where you came from? Places too perfect to be real?"

Eden, I think.

"Yes," Wasala says. "Imagine Eden was a real place, that you knew exactly where Eden was, but all your life you'd been forbidden to go there. Then one day, to your shock, you land there. The place you've heard tales of since you were a child, that you've seen in the minds of others but never for yourself—suddenly, you're there. And it's as beautiful and as fragile as you'd imagined." I nod. I felt a bit like that the first time I went to Puerto Rico, looking out the window of the airplane with tío Umberto.

We get to the Outlands. Just like last time, I let the Outlanders take control of the ship, steering the stealthcraft into the hangar beneath their settlement.

Ferus greets me at the hangar. "I didn't expect to see you so soon, Valiant One."

"I'm afraid it's not a social call," I say, as I climb down the ladder on the side of the craft. Wasala is still inside, completing the shutdown of the ship.

From behind Ferus, Jerana comes rushing forward, scurrying toward us on all six legs. They sign excitedly with four claws at once. "You've brought one of the lost children home to us!"

Ferus says, "You're as prone to surprising actions as your uncle was, Valiant One. It's well that you brought her here. In the North or South, they'd have arrested her immediately."

A crowd of Hoshans scurries around Ferus and me, headed directly for Wasala, who's taking her last step off the ladder. They surround her, reaching out to scratch her forearm, to palm her cheek, to touch her anywhere they can. Wasala's lips tremble, and so do the lips of the Hoshans around her. I can't hear the conversation of their minds, but I can tell what's happening. They're welcoming Wasala back to the home she's never known.

✦ ✦ ✦

KETTLE HASN'T SAID A WORD out loud, but her resistance is visible in every gesture. She sits cat-like on the floor, her lips tight, making her whiskers point downward in a frown that extends beyond the boundaries of her face. Ferus stands over her, gesticulating with all four upper limbs, like an impassioned lawyer pleading to a skeptical judge.

Jerana, Wasala, and I watch the wordless argument from afar. "You're right," Jerana says. "She doesn't want him to go. She's quite stubborn. Ferus is equally passionate but knows it's her decision. They're working through *vasek antom*."

"Why doesn't she want him to go? Or you?"

"A number of reasons," Jerana signs. "She still thinks the affairs of the mainland and the Great Powers are all petty politics and violence. She thinks we've almost no chance of success, since we're far outmatched in technology and resources, and only have a matter of hours. But most of all she knows it's dangerous and is terrified of losing Ferus."

"Well that's basically all completely true," I say. "But we're running out of time." I walk over to Kettle and Ferus and kneel on the ground in front of Kettle.

I'm sorry for interrupting, I think. *But I'm part of this, too. We all are. Kettle, your worries—all of them—are well-founded. The odds we face are almost insurmountable. You've looked in my mind. You must know that sometimes I can be ... too slow to act. But my uncle taught me that the easiest path is not always the best path. It will be dangerous for Ferus, for all of us. But doing nothing would be even more dangerous for everything and everyone you know and love.*

Kettle looks back at me, her lips puckering even more tightly. Slowly and with great care, she lifts herself up to her hindmost legs. Ignoring me, she turns to stand face to face with Ferus. For a full minute they stand silently, looking at each other. Their eyes are like blocks of ice, slowly melting into one another.

At last Ferus looks up. "Kettle has decreed that Jerana and I shall join your mission. But she has one condition."

Kettle clutches me by the forearm. "You protect him," Kettle says, holding up a single claw. "Or I kill you."

I gulp. "That's ... clear."

✧ ✧ ✧

WASALA, FERUS, JERANA, AND I take the stealthcraft to a secluded outpost the Outlanders use for excursions to the mainland. It's about 30 miles north of Tumasra—as close as we can get without risking detection by the patrolling swarms and telepathic sentries.

Jerana's far-sighted telepathy allows them to serve as lookout. Ferus's knowledge of the caves beneath Tumasra will help us find a back-door into the clandestine Subway Station. Wasala has knowledge of interstellar technology that no planet-bound Hoshan has ever been allowed to possess. I've nearly finished assembling my team.

We huddle around a hologram displaying the whirling Tumasra storm, the Etoscan Citadel beside it, and the surrounding city. The three Hoshans point at the hologram, exchanging looks and nods so quickly that I'm completely lost. This must be what Mami feels like when my brothers and I slip into English.

"My apologies," Ferus says. "I was just thinking that the feat before us is beyond our capacity. We simply need more resources if we're to succeed."

Abruptly, the ears of all three Hoshans prick up, and a few seconds later I hear the humming too. Ferus turns to Jerana, his furry face scrunched up in confusion.

"I don't sense any thoughts," Jerana signs. "Whatever it is, it must be automated."

The humming gets louder, and there's the sound of a craft alighting. I smile. "That would be our extra resources."

My hopeful smile spreads to the three Hoshans as they read my thoughts. Ferus punches a code to open the base's main door. Johnny Excelsior stands in the entryway. "Miss me? No need to fuss. I know you did."

Ferus looks from Johnny to me in confusion. "I still don't understand. He escaped from his prison?"

I laugh and run up to hug Johnny.

"Sometimes there are two of me," Johnny says, lifting me into the air. It's such a relief to finally be able to trust him, to know that his friendship is authentic. "The real question is, how did you get Trimana to release me?" Johnny says.

"Val can be very convincing," Wasala says, scurrying over to join Johnny and me. Johnny lifts her up as well, holding one of us in each arm. "And ever since Val saved Trimana's life, she's willing to do anything for her."

"Sounds hot," Johnny says. "So what's the plan? How are we going to rescue Timoteo and the other me and save Hosh from certain doom?"

We renew our planning, huddled around the holomap.

"Timoteo and my other half found out quite a bit before they got caught," Johnny explains, pointing at the Etoscan prayer center directly adjacent to the Tumasra storm. "The shaft leading to the Etoscans' secret Subway station is right here, inside the prayer center.

"Inside the prayer center?" Wasala says, eyes wide. "The sacrilege!"

"Ya think?" Johnny says. "And, as a religious site, the prayer center is off-limits to interstellar authorities, and the Tumasra storm makes everything there undetectable. The perfect hiding place for an unauthorized interstellar transit station."

Ferus asks, "I found the exotic matter sample about a half mile beneath the Citadel. Is that where the station would be?"

"I'm not sure," Johnny says. "We'd just found the entrance to the underground loading dock leading to the Subway when they captured us. That's when I lost touch with myself."

I let out a breath. "I just hope Timoteo's okay."

"I'm sure he is," Wasala says, gently scratching my forearm. "They won't kill him so long as there's a chance he may be useful to them." I try not to think about it, to stay focused on the plan.

"If they captured you the first time," Ferus says to Johnny, "there's no sense trying that way again."

"Not necessarily," Johnny says, "Now that I know what I'm up against, I think I could do it. A lot of shipments are still coming into the station. If I could pose as one of those, I might be able to get in."

"No," Wasala says, "you might get inside, but the telepathic sentries will detect our thoughts. We won't get within a mile of Tumasra, dearie. Better to go in through the caves, as we were planning before."

Listening to Johnny and Wasala, I can see a good argument for both of their plans. "Let's do both."

"Hmm ... yes, that just might work," Ferus says.

"Want to clue me in?" Johnny says. "Psychic is the only language I'm not fluent in."

"Johnny disguises himself as a truck to get in the main entrance," I say. "The rest of us sneak in through the caves, once Johnny's disabled their defenses. We go in the back door, and he goes in the front."

"I like it!" Johnny says. "It'll be easier for me to get into the station without any organic minds for them to sense. Once I'm in, I can deactivate their defenses with a positronic pulse. I've got a new variation on a super-narrow frequency they won't be ready for. But my other half already knows this frequency, so he'll be able to shield himself and Timoteo's suit from it."

"Then," I say, "we sneak in from the caves, and all we have to do is rescue Timoteo and the other Johnny, disable the Subway, get evidence that it exists to make our case to the ITA."

The three Hoshans exchange glances and let out a collective titter.

"What?" Johnny says. "What?"

"We're merely noting what a motley team our honorable ambassador has assembled," Ferus says. He gestures toward Wasala and Jerana and says, "A half-blind exile, an anomalously far-sighted pan-gender Outlander."

"And a former terrorist," Jerana signs, returning Ferus's nod.

"Only briefly!" Ferus amends with a snort.

"And a quirky Synthetic iconoclast," Wasala says, looking up at Johnny.

"I resent that!" Johnny says. "Actually, that's totally accurate."

I let out a nervous laugh. "Don't forget the rookie ambassador from a primitive backwater planet." I look at their faces. Beneath the laughter, they must all be as nervous as I am. I try to project more confidence than I feel. Even if the Hoshans can see through it, they'll sense the truth of my words. "I can't imagine a group of people I'd rather save a world with."

CHAPTER 25

INTERSTELLAR WEAPONS COMMITTEE

Subspace Observation Log

4

Level: HIGH

Estimated number of Etoscan warbots armed for immediate deployment on Hosh:
295 BILLION

4

Estimated number of Levinti warbots armed for immediate deployment on Hosh:
392 BILLION

88:88

Countdown to Article 17 expiration:

3 Terran hours and 31 minutes

THE FOUR OF US CRAWL through the darkness of the cave. Ferus shines his glow-beam in a circle, getting his bearings. "We're ... roughly where I thought we would be. This way, my friends."

So far, things are going as planned. Johnny disguised himself as an Etoscan delivery vehicle on the road running through the Short Mountains, while the rest of us snuck into a remote entrance to the caves a few miles from Tumasra. It'll take us time to make our way through the caves, but it's as close as we dared get without risking detection.

We hike through the darkness, following the light of Ferus's glow-beam. I'm carrying the bulk of our supplies in the knapsack on my back. The Hoshans easily slip through the narrow passages with their spry frames, but I keep having to unstrap my knapsack and crawl to squeeze my way through, pushing my bag ahead of me.

"Careful," Ferus says from up ahead. We crawl through the narrow tunnel until we reach the edge of a shaft that points directly downward. We all stop to catch our breath, leaning against the mossy sides of the tunnel. I shine my light into the shaft. It's so deep I can't see the bottom.

"Yes," Ferus says. "It's a long drop. But if your suits can do as you say, then this is the fastest way for us to get to the deeper caverns, near where I found the sample."

Wasala looks down at the shaft and then up at me. "Ferus is lighter, so I'll take him."

"All right," I say. Jerana climbs onto my back, wrapping all six limbs around me, and Ferus does the same with Wasala.

"Ready, Checkers?"

"Of course, Madame Ambassador," Checkers says. I step off the ledge and feel the familiar non-falling of anti-gravity.

Slowly, our bodies sink downward through the narrow shaft. As we descend, I shine my light on the walls of the shaft around us. The edges are smoother than most of the caves, which makes me wonder if it's not natural, but constructed.

"It is indeed Hoshan-made," Ferus says, answering my unspoken thought. "The Hosh-Unam Front have dug shafts to facilitate their movements underground. Though they're not able to move about quite this easily." Still clinging to Wasala's back with five claws, he points his glow-beam at a column of knobs running up the side of the shaft, in a zig-zag pattern spaced perfectly for a six-limbed Hoshan to climb.

Within minutes, we're back on solid ground, winding our way through another narrow tunnel. A half-hour later we find our way to where the underground Subway Station should be.

Wasala stands on her hind legs and grips the cave wall with her four upper paws, then scans it. "Hyper-carbonation should work. It'll only take a few minutes to set up."

I bring my knapsack to Wasala, who takes out components and assembles them. Ferus and I assist, following Wasala's instructions—though Ferus has the advantage of telepathy, anticipating Wasala's needs before she voices them. Jerana sits at the edge of the small grotto, keeping telepathic watch.

Once it's assembled, Wasala turns it on, and a clear liquid gushes from the device. As the liquid makes contact with the wall, its stone surface fizzes, releasing a yellowish-green gas.

Wasala says it should take 20 minutes to cut through the rock and get to the outer hull of the Etoscan base. Jerana and Ferus maintain their telepathic lookout while Wasala does the tunneling, making me the only one with nothing to do. Waiting is impossible when every minute means more danger for Timoteo—and for Hosh. To distract myself and make myself useful, I do a final supplies check.

My knapsack is lighter now that it doesn't have the equipment for the hypercarbonation machine. We have three dozen packets of small chemical explosives, which look like tiny squares of chewing gum. They're like C-4, Wasala says, but more compact. They're exclusively chemical—no electronic parts, not even for the detonator. Which means they'll work even after Johnny's positronic pulse. But that also means there's no way to detonate them remotely. You just remove the security seal, unwrap it, press it against whatever you want to blow up, and 30 seconds later, boom. I hope we don't have to use them—I hate explosives almost as much as I hate guns. But if we have to, we could use these to destroy the Subway Station before the Etoscans activate it. I divide the packets between Ferus, Jerana, Wasala, and me.

Then I check both oxygen masks to make sure they still work properly even after crawling through all those caves. If Johnny's positronic pulse knocks out all advanced tech, Checkers will be down too, and I'll need one to breathe. The Hoshans will be fine, but Timoteo might need one—though his suit should still work, if Johnny Number Two is with him and can shield him from Johnny Number One's pulse.

We have a notebook and pen and four gas lamps, for when the lights go out. The boson scanner is the last item in my knapsack. That will get us the evidence that the Etoscans built the Subway before the expiration of the treaty. Even if we can't disable the Subway, if we can escape with definitive evidence of its existence, that might be enough. It would be an interstellar embarrassment to the Etoscans, forcing them to renew negotiations for peace to save face. The Levinti—I hope—would choose a lopsided negotiation over a costly war.

Finally, Wasala says, "We're almost through. I'm going slowly now to make sure I don't trip any alarms along the base's outer perimeter." She adjusts the controls, and the liquid's flow thins from a gush to laser-thin jet, then to nothing at all. At the end of the newly created tunnel, there's a thin crack of light. "To the Etoscans' sensors, that should look like a naturally occurring fissure," Wasala explains. "It should let us do an initial reconnaissance." With her upper paws, Wasala waves Jerana toward the newly formed tunnel. "I'm fairly sure you're better suited for this than I."

Jerana scratches Wasala's arm as they walk toward the tunnel. "Near-sighted or far-sighted, our thoughts and our hopes flow in one stream." They climb into the tunnel and crawl on all six legs to its end, until their whiskers graze the newly created crack in the wall.

"You're sure they won't be able to sense us through that crack?" I ask.

"Not unless they were to get very close to it, as Jerana is doing now," Ferus says. "It's like a telepathic peephole. So narrow that you can only see through it if you're standing directly in front of it."

Jerana sits silently in the dim light of the tunnel, eyes closed. Our glow-beams create large shadows from the signals of their claws as they speak. "There are two Hoshan guards not far from here. They're well-trained in the telepathic martial arts. Their thoughts are calm, so Johnny hasn't arrived at the main entrance, at least as far as they know. And ... there are six more guards, and another twelve sleeping. We're fortunate it's daytime or more of them would be awake and on duty."

"And Timoteo?" I say.

"I'm not sure," Jerana signs. "Wait ... yes. He's exhausted, but alive. He's being held in a containment cell with the other Johnny."

Thank God. And that means Johnny can protect his suit from the pulse. "What about the Subway? Do you sense anything about it?"

"Most of the Hoshan guards know very little about the base's activities, other than what's required for their duties," says Jerana, their eyes still closed. "There are five Etoscan minds as well. They're guarding their thoughts, but ... yes. The Subway is here, and it's complete. Oh, my. It's as we feared. The moment the treaty expires, they'll activate the Subway. Incalculable swarms await on the other side. Millions will die."

"Where's Johnny?" Wasala says. "He was due to send out the pulse minutes ago. We need to get in there!"

"Wait!" Jerana says. "I'm sensing alarm from the Hoshan guards. They discovered Johnny as he entered the lower levels. They've deployed guard-bots against him. So many minds now, all racing. They've raised the alarm and the off-duty guards are waking."

"If Johnny made it to the lower levels," Wasala says, "he should be deep enough inside to release the pulse." I pull my oxygen mask out of my knapsack and strap it to my face—if all goes well, I'll lose Checkers at any moment.

Jerana gasps. "Oh, no. Not now!"

"What?" I say. "Did they take down Johnny?"

"No, not that," Jerana says. "Several minds. Nearby, and coming toward us."

Already? But how could the guards have found us so fast?

"No, not inside the Etoscan base!" Jerana's claws sign with urgent motions. "Here, on our side. In the caverns."

Ferus closes his eyes in concentration. "I sense it too. A mind I know too well."

"And others too, not far behind him," Jerana signs. "They're quite close—I couldn't see them coming, with my attention focused on the base, and with all the twists in these caverns."

"He's racing toward us," Ferus says, his whiskers upturned in horror. "I feel the heat of his anger approaching." He turns to Wasala, a silent stream of thoughts passing between them.

Wasala squeezes in beside Jerana. "I just need a few seconds to break through the final layer to the Etoscan citadel," she says. Whether Johnny manages to release the pulse or not, this is our only chance, especially with the Hosh-Unam Front nearly on us. We have to break into the station even if it means dealing with the Etoscans' fully operational defenses.

Ferus walks away from us, toward the far end of the grotto. I shine my glow-beam in the direction of his gaze, toward an opening about forty feet away from us. The shadow of a sharp nose is visible first, followed by a long neck and a slender body scuttling nimbly across the stony floor on all six legs. Marrow emerges from the aperture and stands on his hind legs to stretch to his full height, holding a baton-shaped weapon in his upper-right claw.

Chapter 26

"Ambassador Vega," says Marrow. "What interesting companions you're keeping."

"Leave this place, Marrow!" Ferus shouts, standing on his rear four legs like a centaur-soldier, placing himself directly between Marrow and me.

Marrow looks toward Wasala and Jerana, the fur of their backs visible inside the small tunnel leading to the station. "So the Etoscans have built an illegal Interstellar Subway right here under Tumasra! Typical treachery. They'll easily take control of the entire globe, with their militarized swarms flooding Hosh. And people question the Hosh-Unam Front's methods, when this is the kind of vile violence we're up against.

"And you, Ambassador Vega. Bringing an exiled child of Legionnaires with you, no less! I approve. We must defy every bankrupt law of our oppressors! But your strategy is misguided. Your naive attempts to renew diplomacy will only further legitimize our colonizers. Only mass uprisings led by the Hosh-Unam Front can save our world now. And, with access to this Etoscan base—and an Interstellar Subway Station—we'll finally have the tools to win back our home. The oppressors will no longer control our access to the stars!"

From the aperture behind Marrow, another Hoshan emerges, followed by several others. Soldiers of the Hosh-Unam Front, each carrying a baton-shaped weapon.

We're outnumbered and outgunned.

"So you are," Marrow says. "But stand aside peacefully and we'll spare your lives."

There's an explosive bang, and Wasala shouts, "We're through!" Light shines through the tunnel now, opening the way to the base. Wasala leaps into the hole, falling out of sight and into the Citadel. Jerana is only seconds behind her.

Marrow opens fire. The blast narrowly misses Jerana as they crawl through the newly-made hole and drop out of sight. Jerana and Wasala have made it through, but there's no way Ferus and I can escape Marrow.

"Indeed not," Marrow shouts, and points his baton at me. I race toward the hole, moving erratically and ducking, but there's no way I can dodge his shots for long.

Ferus dives at me, knocking me just below the path of Marrow's blast. "Go," Ferus says, pushing me toward the tunnel. "I'll handle Marrow. Seal the way behind you."

"No! I won't leave you."

Marrow fires again, but Ferus easily sidesteps it, sensing the shot before it comes. His speed and agility are incredible, but I can't abandon him. Ferus pushes me into the tunnel and leaps toward Marrow. "You leave me so that you may save my world. That is not abandonment."

Ferus is right—if I don't go with Wasala and Jerana, we have no hope of stopping the Etoscan swarms. As I turn toward the fissure, I see Ferus knock the baton from Marrow's claw. Their bodies meet, a blur of limbs slicing through the air. They dodge each other as if it were a dance, anticipating each other's movements in telepathic combat.

I crawl through the tunnel toward the hole. I steal one last glance behind me. Ferus is surrounded by a half-dozen Hoshans, moving with incredible speed as he blocks them from getting to the tunnel. I force myself to crawl to the tunnel's end, where I leap down to join Wasala and Jerana inside the Etoscan base.

Wasala is clutching one of the explosive packets in her claws. As soon as I land beside them, she breaks the seal and unwraps it, then slaps it to the inside of the hole.

Jerana looks toward the tunnel and signs, "I wish there were another way."

"We've no time," Wasala says, and tugs us both down a corridor, away from the hole. Seconds later, there's a loud boom and the sound of debris crumbling, sealing the way we came.

Everything is happening so fast. Is Ferus all right? Is there any way he could possibly be all right?

"We can't think about that now," Wasala says. "We have to focus on the mission."

Jerana buries their snout in the fur of their shoulder. "This is what Ferus wanted—the shape of his mind was clear."

Then all the lights flicker and everything goes dark.

"Finally!" Wasala says. "Johnny's positronic pulse must have worked."

I reach to get our gas lanterns from my knapsack, when the hallway is relit with a dim glow from the ceiling. Have the Etoscans already gotten some sort of emergency power system running? Wasala lets out a series of clicks and snorts, but no translation comes. Of course—I've lost all of Checkers' functions, including the translation software.

But we expected this. I get the notebook and pen from my knapsack and pass it to Wasala. Her physiology is too different from a human's to articulate the words of Terran languages, but she's been on Earth long enough that she understands the words—and can write them. And we still have telepathy—so I can communicate my thoughts to them, at least.

Wasala points with three fingers at the dimly glowing ceiling. Then she scribbles on the pad: *Phosphorescent fungi for back-up lighting. Johnny's pulse knocked out power, but all the Etoscan biotech still working.*

I nod. That means that even without power, the Etoscans could still have a lot to throw at us. Wasala scribbles again. Her handwriting is scrawling, but the letters are big and easy to read. *YES. Viruses, genetically engineered weapons—and the Hoshan guards. Be wary.*

Jerana's and Wasala's ears prick up and they trade grave looks.

Wasala writes: *Jerana says guards sense us. Several on way here.*

Then we'd better move, I think. *You need to get to the Subway. Which way is it?*

Jerana gestures toward the right.

And Timoteo and Johnny?

Jerana points in the opposite direction.

Wasala scribbles quickly: *Etoscans will get power back up soon. We only have 15 minutes.*

All right, I think. *Jerana—guide Wasala to the Subway platform and deactivate it if you can. I'll get Johnny and Timoteo and meet you there.*

Jerana clutches my wrist and shakes their head. They don't want me to go alone.

There are only three of us now, I think. *We need Wasala's tech knowledge to disable the Subway. And you need to guide her and help her steer clear of the guards. So that leaves me to find Timoteo and Johnny.*

Wasala and Jerana exchange a series of looks, two furry faces furrowed with concern. Then Wasala writes, *You're right. Jerana says follow this corridor and take a left at the eating area. The holding cells are at the end of that hall. She says Timoteo is OK.*

Seeing the word OK makes my breathing ease. *Thank you,* I think. I trade scratches with both of them. *See you at the Subway platform. Good luck.*

I turn and run down the corridor under the dim glow of the phosphorescent fungi. I pass several rooms, and one that might be a medical center. How far is it to the mess hall? Without slowing down, I adjust my oxygen mask and think of Timoteo. If Jerana sensed his thoughts, hopefully Johnny was able to protect his suit from the pulse.

Finally, the hallway comes to an end, opening up into a large mess hall with six low, Hoshan-sized tables. One wall is almost completely covered with a large viewing screen. Entertainment for the soldiers during meals? Training? Propaganda?

I'm about to exit through the doorway on the left, when I hear dozens of scurrying footsteps approaching from another corridor. It must be the Hoshan sentries, following my thoughts like a beacon. I look around for a place to hide, but wherever I go, they can follow my mind.

The footsteps are getting closer. I have to do something, but what? All I have is the explosives, and even if I were willing to use those on a living being, these telepathic sentries could anticipate any attack. My eyes settle on the screen. Hoshans always leave their claws bare, since all six claws are prehensile.

I grab one of the explosive packets, break the seal and unwrap it. I slap it against the view-screen and dive for the corridor on the left.

As I race down the corridor, there's a loud boom behind me, followed by a hail of shattered glass on the stone floor. The scurrying footsteps stop, and in their place is the sound of slow and careful padding, interrupted occasionally by the sound of glass sweeping across stone. That should slow them down for at least a few minutes.

I keep running, hoping that Timoteo and Johnny's cell isn't much farther. But then I hear bounding footsteps behind me. They must have gotten past the broken glass. They're gaining on me. How can creatures with such short legs be so fast?

There's a loud plucking sound, like a bow releasing an arrow, and something sharp presses into my shin. Some sort of pliable wire loops itself around my legs and then tightens, squeezing my legs together. I lose my balance and fall to the ground. I pull out my pocket knife and cut the wire.

I've barely managed to get to my feet when the Hoshan sentries reach me. The four of them surround me. One grabs my ankle and another grabs my wrist, forcing me back down to the ground. A third holds up a canister-shaped weapon and aims it at me, releasing a stream of sticky, silken material that looks like a spider's webbing. Within seconds, I'm covered with the thick webbing, gluing me tight to the floor.

The lead Hoshan soldier lets out a series of aggressive-sounding clicks and barks at me. Beneath the webbing, the pocketknife is still in my hand. I twist it around, trying to saw off a portion of the webbing so that at least my hand will be free. The lead Hoshan lets out two clicks and holds me down. There's no way to escape.

Then all four Hoshans prick up their ears and swivel their heads toward the door. A bright light flashes, blinding them—and me too. There's the sound of a struggle, of several bodies thumping to the floor in fast succession.

In a few seconds, my sight comes back, and by then the four Hoshan sentries are lying unconscious on the floor. Johnny Excelsior is standing over them, arms akimbo.

"Johnny!"

"Hey, Val," Johnny says. "I've got somebody here who's excited to see you."

From behind Johnny, Timoteo comes running toward me. "Timoteo!" I say. "Oh my God, are you okay?"

Timoteo leans over me, touching the side of my neck. "I should be asking you that. You really need to work on your rescues, sis. I give this one a B-minus, max."

"Hey, I'm not doing too bad," I say.

"Sure," Timoteo says. "Other than being tied down to the floor with weird bio-engineered web things. Johnny, can you ...?"

"I've got it," Johnny says. A ray of light shines from his palm, and the webbing heats up, then melts into a gooey liquid. I wiggle out of it and spring up into the air. I wrap my arms around Timoteo, and he hugs me back, clasping me tight.

"Thank God you're okay," I say, pressing myself against my brother's chest. Hugging him is a relief, as if I need physical contact to confirm the reality of his existence.

Without letting go of me, Timoteo pulls back slightly. He pats my arm, his fingers sticking to the slimy residue that's soaked my clothes. Through tear-filled eyes, Timoteo says, "You do realize you're still covered in bio-engineered spider-web-goop, and it's pretty gross."

"I have to say I'm feeling a little left out of this tearful reunion," Johnny says.

"Me too," says a second, identical voice, "but we need to get down to the Subway platform right away."

I look up from my embrace with Timoteo and see two Johnny Excelsiors standing before us. The first, like Timoteo, is wearing what look like white pajamas—that must be the one the Etoscans had been holding prisoner. The new arrival is wearing Johnny's trademark leather jacket—which must be the one I saw just a few hours ago.

"Oh," Timoteo says. "The other Johnny found us. He, um ..."

"I know," I say. "And he's right. We have to get to that Subway right away. Johnny—er, Johnnies, can you fly us there?"

"No problem," says leather-jacket Johnny, offering me his back. I climb on, piggy-back style, while Timoteo does the same with the other Johnny.

"Timoteo is having trouble containing his excitement at the sight of two of me," says white-pajamas Johnny. "Who can blame his imagination for running wild?"

"Hold on tight, kids," says leather-jacket Johnny. "And try not to mind my double, he got the short end of the interpersonal programming split, and we're still working on re-integration of our higher functions."

Then we're in the air, two Johnnies flying Superman-style, Timoteo and I clinging to their backs. We soar through the corridors of the base, passing quickly over the mess hall and its floor blanketed with shards of glass.

"The armored-transport ploy worked like a charm," explains

leather-jacket Johnny as we fly down the corridor. "It got me past all the checkpoints and the first perimeter of the base's defenses. But then they caught me."

"While the Etoscans held me captive, they hacked my systems," says the other Johnny, "which was not fun. They figured out some pretty smart ways to detect me, which is how they discovered my dupe here."

"I'm not the dupe," says leather-jacket Johnny. "You're the duplicate. So thanks to my dupe, as soon as I got into the base, there was a swarm surrounding me. But luckily I was already inside their defense perimeter. I released the positronic pulse and took down all the advanced tech defenses at once. And by then twinsie and me were back in touch."

"So Timoteo's suit is still up?" I say.

"Yeah," Timoteo says. "My Johnny protected the two of us with a modulated positronic field. Once the tech systems shut down, it was easy to escape from the brig."

"Any chance you can fix Checkers?" I ask.

"The pulse did a bad number on him," Johnny tells me from over his shoulder. "I did reactivate your Salfren translation software, so you at least have comms back. But it'll take a while to restore enough power for his other systems."

"And time is one thing we don't have," says the other Johnny. "The Etoscans are already rebooting their own systems and they should have things back up in seven minutes. And then this entire base will be crawling with some nasty swarms."

"Hopefully, Wasala and Jerana already got the evidence, maybe even disabled the Subway," I say. "Oh, Tim. Wasala was never the traitor. It was Kate the whole time."

"I know," Timoteo says, nodding toward the Johnny who's carrying me. "Johnny Dos filled me in. That's crazy about Kate. Are you okay?"

"What does okay even *mean* at this point," I say.

"We're almost to the Subway platform," white-clothed Johnny says, slowing down. "I'm detecting a whole bunch of Hoshans in there. And elevated bio-signals."

"That's not good," I say. "The Hoshan sentries must have overpowered Wasala and Jerana."

We land just outside the entryway to the Subway platform, the two Johnnies gently setting Timoteo and me on the floor.

"Synthetics first," Johnny says. "Stay behind us—we can handle the sentries." Both Johnnies stride through the entryway, Timoteo and I hanging a few steps behind them.

"Not one more step, war machine," comes a familiar sharp voice. Marrow. Both Johnnies come to an abrupt stop. Timoteo and I edge into the room to find Marrow and five agents of the Hosh-Unam Front. Four Hoshan guards are lying on the floor, puddles of clear Hoshan blood pooled around them. The autonomists hold guns that look like Terran pistols, but with knob-shaped handles fitted for easy grip by a six-fingered claw. Wasala's lying on the ground, all six limbs tied behind her back, Marrow standing over her, his gun an inch from her head. Jerana is tied up too, another of Marrow's agents looming over them.

"That's right, Ambassador," Marrow says. "These are primitive pistols, just gunpowder and steel, of the sort found even on Atomic worlds. It's been a while since we've made use of these, but we learned long ago the necessity of using whatever crude tools are within our reach."

I breathe in deep through my oxygen mask as I take in the scene. As with the other Subway Stations I've seen, just beyond the platform, an enormous chasm stretches upward, bordered by towering walls of circuitry.

"Drop your bag, Ambassador," Marrow orders. I don't see any options, so I do what he says. "If any of you move even a millimeter without my permission, your friend will die." He turns to Johnny and says, "Your mind may be silent to me, Synthetic, but your thoughts are not hard to guess. In only a second, one of your bots could render me unconscious or dead. But a second is all I need to pull this trigger."

"He *will* kill her," Jerana signs from entangled limbs, lips trembling. "He's killed Ferus—and hundreds of others."

I feel a shudder of anguish hearing Jerana say aloud that Ferus is dead. I was still holding out hope that he managed to survive. But I bury those feelings deep, deep down with my grief for Umberto. I'll grieve for all of them later, if I survive.

"It doesn't matter if he kills us," Wasala shouts. "Don't do anything he says, Johnny."

Both Johnnies hold their hands up in the air in acquiescence. They look at me, as if seeking my guidance.

"What do you want, Marrow?" I say.

"What I've always wanted," Marrow says, making a fist with his free middle claw. "Freedom for Hosh. Help me take control of this Subway Station in the name of the Hosh-Unam Front!"

I look into Marrow's eyes and sense his sincerity. For all his intelligence and skill as a military strategist, on some level, Marrow doesn't understand what he's up against. Is it narcissism? "I don't think we could even *do* that," I say. "Johnny, could even *you* do that? Turn control of this base and its swarms over to Marrow?"

"No," Johnny says. "Temporarily knocking them out is one thing, but re-programming the base and all the swarms ... Maybe I could do it if I had a few weeks."

"Convenient lies!" Marrow says.

"Marrow," I say. "You can't see Johnny's thoughts, but you can see Wasala's. She knows as much as anybody when it comes to interstellar tech. Look into her mind and you'll see it's true. Even if we wanted to, we couldn't do what you ask."

Still hovering over her, Marrow drops to all six legs. He lets his head droop so that his eyes meet Wasala's, his gun still pointing squarely at her head. Wasala looks back, unflinching, thoughts passing between them. Marrow strums his hind claws on the floor.

"Listen, Marrow," I say. "The only way for you to achieve your goals is to work with us. Help us destroy the Subway so that the Etoscan swarms on the other side can't invade your world and decimate your people. Then we'll reveal what they've done. The Etoscans will be forced to negotiate on our terms. We can get more freedoms for Hosh, take steps toward autonomy."

"Steps are not enough!" Marrow says. "We've waited for centuries. The Hosh-Unam must be free, unified, and independent! I will accept nothing less."

I suck in air through my oxygen mask. Even if I trusted Marrow, how could I deliver on a promise like that? If we disable the Subway and get out of here alive, with evidence that the Etoscans violated the treaty, then the Etoscans will be humiliated and would have to make concessions. But the Levinti would have no reason to give up control of Hosh ...

Marrow's ears prick up and his eyes widen. "Right you are, Ambassador. You'd be a shrewd negotiator if you were not so pliant. The Levinti will never surrender to our demands, and they'll never back down to the likes of you. That is why *I* must have a place in the negotiations, representing the Hosh-Unam Front, the one true voice of a free and unified Hosh."

"Any minute now, the Etoscans will have their systems back up, and then we're all as good as dead," I say. "And a few minutes after they kill us, they'll send a thousand swarms hurtling through that Subway, an army of machines that will decimate all of Hosh. Do you want your ego to be responsible for the destruction of your planet?"

"My ego is nowhere to be found in the matter," Marrow clicks. "I'm fighting for the freedom of my people!" He stretches four arms up as if reaching for freedom in the air.

"It's not worth it, Val!" Wasala shouts, lifting her head slightly from the floor.

Not worth it to save a planet? I think.

"Indeed," Marrow says, "You're out of choices and out of time, Ambassador."

I imagine Marrow participating in the negotiations. He's taken so many lives—he killed Ferus only minutes ago! If I even try to give him a place at the negotiation table, I could be destroying any possibility of peace. But he's right that there are no good choices.

"I can't do it, Marrow," I say. "Even if I wanted to, I could never get you a place at the negotiations. But help us and you can be a hero. You can be the one to stop the war and expose the Etoscans for their crimes. Think of what a victory that would be for the Hosh-Unam Front."

Without loosening his grip on Wasala, Marrow stretches his long neck toward me, scrutinizing me. "You'll give me credit? You'll tell everyone it was I who incapacitated these collaborators and seized this station in the name of Hoshan freedom?"

"Yes," I say. "I'll tell everyone how you helped us."

"And then I'll insist on my rightful place," Marrow says. "Do not forget this. I will hold you to your word."

"I'm sure you will," I say. "Now stop pointing those guns in my friends."

Marrow lifts his gun away from Wasala and releases her with a nod at his comrades. The agent holding Jerana frees them as well. Jerana and Wasala scurry away from their captors, joining Johnny, Timoteo, and me on the other side of the room.

I turn to Wasala and the two Johnnies. "What now?"

"We only have a minute before the Etoscan systems are restored," Wasala says. "We don't have time to disable the station. All we can do is get the evidence." She reaches into her bag and pulls out the boson scanner. The small metal box looks primitive by interstellar standards— it's analog technology, unaffected by Johnny's positronic pulse.

Wasala flips a switch on the boson scanner, and it makes a loud series of clangs. She holds it up so that it points at the lower part of the Subway chasm, then slowly rotates it upward. Then she presses another button to turn it off. The clanging stops, and Wasala walks over to me on her four hind legs. With her upper limbs, she holds out the scanner. "Here it is, Madame Ambassador. Evidence that the Etoscans illegally built an Interstellar Subway station before the expiration of the treaty."

"Thank you," I say, taking the scanner. Timoteo and I look at each other, letting out a breath of relief at the same time. "Hey," I say to him. "Let me have your phone." Mine was disabled by Johnny's pulse, but his was protected by Johnny's shield. He takes it from his purse and I take a few seconds of video of the Subway, scanning it from top to bottom. It never hurts to have a back-up.

"We gotta get out of here, fast," one Johnny says, a thin lattice extending between his arm and the other Johnny, beginning to form a small pod. "I can get us back out through the tunnels in just a few minutes."

Abruptly, the soft glow of phosphorescent fungi is replaced by far brighter lights all throughout the station. The curved wall of the Subway chasm comes to life, lighting up with a rainbow of glowing nodes like a giant circuit board. A background hum comes alive, like a refrigerator turning on in the night.

The trumpeting sound of an Etoscan booms out. "A few minutes is more than you have," says Commander of War. I turn. Commander and another Etoscan enter the Subway platform from an upper entrance, surrounded by a dozen Hoshan soldiers and dozens of guardbots.

In unison, Marrow and his soldiers lift their pistols. There's a cacophony of bangs as they release a hail of bullets at the Etoscans and their Hoshan guards. Moving at blurry speeds, the guardbots intercept each bullet, which disappear harmlessly as the bots make contact with them.

"Marrow," Commander of War says, "I owe you my appreciation for assuring the treaty negotiations failed horribly and claiming full credit for it." To someone else, Commander says, "Activate the signal."

Wasala, Jerana, Marrow, and every soldier of the Hosh-Unam Front all twist their faces in agony and fall to the floor. They lie completely still.

Timoteo and I rush over to Jerana and Wasala and kneel over them.

"They're still breathing," Timoteo says.

"For as long we wish them to be," Commander says. "Every inch of this base is coated with a virus. You were all infected the moment you set foot here. The virus is harmless until activated by a radio signal. One signal triggers the virus to cause immediate paralysis in its host. Another signal causes instant death. It was bothersome that the temporary crippling of our power systems prevented us from sending either signal until now."

"But we're still okay," says Timoteo, looking at me. "And the guards too?"

With his trunk, Commander gestures toward the Hoshan guards that surround him. "Our own soldiers are routinely vaccinated. As for the two of you ... I confess we've never bothered to design a virus that affects Terran physiology. Why expend resources on such an inconsequential species?"

"No virus affects me," says Johnny. He and his double position themselves in the path of the Etoscans, blocking them from reaching Timoteo and me.

"Indeed," Commander says. "That positronic pulse of yours caught us by surprise. We won't make the same mistake twice."

Both Johnnies suddenly go as still as statues, then fall to the floor with two heavy thuds.

"The Synthetics are such a demure lot, one rarely gets the chance to analyze them," Commander says. "It's a wondrous piece of technology. But we found a weakness to exploit."

Timoteo and I exchange wary glances.

"Get that boson scanner," Commander says to one of the guards. One of the guards approaches and takes the boson scanner from me. I steer my thoughts, focusing on my frustration.

"I must admit, Ambassador," Commander says, slowly walking toward us, his trunk hanging low to the ground, "you're more brazen then we'd expected. We'd received reports that you'd reached a rather sudden end. So we certainly hadn't expected this dubious—and utterly illegal—raid. You even brought an exile. The penalty for that is life imprisonment, you know.

"You don't understand how the Galaxy works. This isn't a matter of rocks and sticks against gunpowder, as happens on so many primitive worlds. This is a matter of rocks and sticks against gravity itself. You can't help but come crashing to the ground. There are only three things that matter in contemporary interstellar conflict: software, transport, and the illusion of moral authority."

Commander is only a few feet away now, his large pale body casting a shadow over us. "For centuries, we've been roughly matched with the Levinti when it comes to software. They have a slight edge in synthetic technology, while we're superior in organic design, but that's an arms race both meaningless and endless. So the conflict here on Hosh, as with so many other conflicts, will be determined almost entirely by *transport*."

"What about moral authority?" I say. Maybe if I can keep him talking, I can think of a way to escape, or at least stay alive.

"The illusion of moral authority?" Commander corrects. "Irrelevant the moment the treaty expires. In just sixteen minutes, this station will become a legal interstellar gateway."

On the far side of the platform, a hatchway opens. On the other side of it is a long tunnel leading up to the surface. Natural sunlight shines through. Even from this far underground, I catch the faint whiff of sulfur from the Tumasra storm above.

Commander goes on, seeming to take pleasure in the horror on our faces. "Yes, primitives. On the other side of this manufactured wormhole is a large, barren world. Unsuitable for life but perfect for the construction of one of the largest swarms in Galactic history. The first wave of the swarm is about to arrive." Commander of War gestures toward the hatchway that leads to the surface. "The Levinti will be utterly unprepared for an attack of this scale. All of Hosh will soon join the Etoscan Fellowship!"

There's a flash of light and a thunderous boom, and inside the Subway chasm an enormous tower materializes, larger than any other Subway tower I've seen. A tremendous buzzing sound fills the air, like a thousand chainsaws ready to take down a forest. The walls of the tower yawn open, revealing a mass of bots from floor to ceiling, filling every inch of the tower, writhing like a horde of ants the size of a mountain.

My stomach contracts, and I taste acid in my mouth. I thought I knew the meaning of the word *hopelessness* before, but I never did. Not until now, standing before this endless swarm.

CHAPTER 27

INTERSTELLAR WEAPONS COMMITTEE

Subspace Observation Log

Level: EXTREME

Estimated number of Etoscan warbots armed for immediate deployment on Hosh: **1.2 TRILLION**

Estimated number of Levinti warbots armed for immediate deployment on Hosh: **502 BILLION**

88:88

Countdown to Article 17 expiration:

0 Terran hours and 14 minutes

THE SWARM EMERGES FROM THE SUBWAY, the writhing bots filling the massive chamber, their buzzing filling the silence. I gape in horror as the horde surrounds Timoteo and me.

I look over at Timoteo. His eyes meet mine, and he gestures toward his mouth and nose. I nod, immediately understanding. Unlike mine, his face is not covered with an oxygen mask; his synth-suit is still working. Which means Timoteo still has anti-gravity as well as oxygen. Johnny protected him from the positronic pulse, and the Etoscans haven't noticed. We're only a dozen yards away from the hatchway leading to the surface. If we can get away, even just for a few minutes, maybe we can get help, from Charism, the Levinti, anybody.

From the corner of my eye, I see several Hoshan soldiers prick up their ears in alarm—they've already sensed what we're thinking. I lean over and pick up Wasala, cradling her motionless body in my right arm. Timoteo picks up Jerana with his left.

"Commander!" one of the Hoshans shouts, darting toward Timoteo and me. "The Terran male—his suit still works!" In a single beat, an entire line of Hoshan guards drop to all six legs and race toward us.

Timoteo wraps his free arm around my shoulders and under my armpit, and I clutch him by the waist. Together, we take three long strides and leap toward the hatchway.

"Up, Majel, up!" shouts Timoteo.

I hold on tight to Timoteo as his suit drags the four of us upward. The suit's anti-gravity field extends to encompass all four of us, easing the burden of Wasala's weight, but my shoulder still stretches awkwardly as I drag Wasala along with us. I pull myself up onto Timoteo's shoulders, wrapping my arm around his neck.

We emerge from the tunnel's mouth into a high-ceilinged room with ornately patterned walls and ceilings, its floor crowded with loading trucks and enormous canisters, like a make-shift cargo bay set up inside a cathedral. We're back on the surface level of the Etoscan Citadel. But there are Hoshan soldiers on this floor too, more than a dozen of them scurrying toward us, readying their batons to fire.

"Majel, evasive!" Timoteo shouts. The suit takes us farther up, toward the high ceilings in a zig-zag pattern, narrowly dodging a barrage of blasts from below. I hold tightly to my brother, while still clutching Wasala.

I nudge Timoteo to our left, toward a tall archway leading out of the chamber. "Timoteo, over there! A way out!"

We fly toward the archway, jostling left and right to avoid more salvos as the Hoshans shoot at us from below. If not for Timoteo's suit, the Hoshans would easily have hit us, and the Etoscans won't allow us that advantage long. If we're going to get out of this alive, we need more time and more help.

The suit brings us through the archway, taking us into another high-ceilinged room, filled with the sculpted trees that mark an Etoscan prayer center. One entire wall is transparent, the view occupied from edge to edge by the whirling flames of the Tumasra storm, its sulfur scent strong in the air.

From the next room, the sound of scurrying Hoshan paws draws closer. "Take us to the ceiling," I tell Timoteo, "right at the top of the archway. And hover there a second."

Timoteo takes us up. "What are you doing, sis?"

"Buying us some time." With no free hands, I turn my body slightly so Timoteo can reach my knapsack. "Open the front pouch of my bag. See those tiny packets that look like chewing gum?"

"Yeah," Timoteo says, reaching into the bag with the hand that's not holding Jerana.

"Those are explosives. Pull one out and take off the wrapping, then slap it onto the arch. Then tell Majel to get us out of here. We'll have thirty seconds."

"Got it," Timoteo says. There's a rustling sound as he unwraps it, then a loud smack as he slaps it onto the arch.

"Majel, now!" Timoteo shouts, and we fly across the prayer center. A boom echoes throughout the chamber, followed by a low rumble as the arch collapses, blocking the way we came.

"We just blew up a wall in a prayer center," Timoteo says.

"The Etoscans are launching an invasion from a prayer center," I say.

We land in a corner of the empty room. Timoteo looks around, still cradling Jerana's motionless body in his arm. "We're lucky. I think we drew all the guards up here into that room."

"Not that lucky," I say, pointing toward the rubble where the archway had been. Dozens of bots are crawling out from beneath the rocks, cutting through the wreckage with scalpel-like lasers. "I think that bought us a few minutes max. Try calling Charism."

"On it," Timoteo says, eyes scanning back and forth on the inside of his glasses. "I can't get through. Not to Charism, not to anybody. They're blocking the signal, and—" Timoteo gasps and falls to the floor. He clumsily manages to set Jerana on the ground beside him, his arms shaking. He chokes for air, clutching his throat with both hands.

The Etoscans must have shut down his suit—he doesn't have enough oxygen! I grab the other oxygen mask from my knapsack. I lean over Timoteo and strap it around his head.

Even with the mask on, Timoteo heaves for air. His asthma! Anxiety makes it worse. Over by the archway, dozens of bots pick through the rubble, like an infestation of termites eating through stone. We're running out of time.

"You have air now," I tell Timoteo. "Try to breathe normally." I gesture to my own chest, breathing steadily. Timoteo nods, his eyes watering. He takes a small breath, then another.

"I'm okay," he says, though his voice is weak. He leans down to pick up Jerana.

I wish I could give him more time, but we don't have any to spare. "This way," I say, breaking into a run toward the nearest exit. From beyond the rubble, I can make out the buzzing of the gathering swarm. "If we can get out in public, we'll be safer."

"Okay," Timoteo says, still short of breath but close behind. "But it's daytime. Everyone on this side of Hosh is fast asleep."

The swarm's buzzing gets louder. As I exit the prayer center, I look over my shoulder. In a matter of minutes, the bots have not only created a path through the rubble, they've constructed a new doorway. Not nearly as large as the archway had been, but large enough to accommodate an Etoscan.

"Run!" I shout, though despair sinks into me. There's no way to outrun a swarm of war machines. I run anyway, my brother just a step behind.

Outside, the Hoshan sun shines high overhead. The scent of sulfur is stronger here. Instantly, my head splits with pain, the familiar side effect of Tumasra's strange gases. Timoteo must feel it too, pressing a finger to his temple to relieve the pain. In my arms, Wasala twitches, as if she can feel Tumasra's proximity even in her paralyzed state.

If any Hoshans are awake at this hour, they'll be at the Tumasra storm.

"This way!" I say, leading Timoteo around the side of the Etoscan Citadel. A group of Hoshan soldiers emerges from the Citadel, the ones that had been chasing us before. Another group of Hoshan soldiers joins them—now there must be nearly forty chasing us as Timoteo and I race toward the Tumasra storm. And close behind them is the buzzing of the swarm, growing in intensity with every second.

We turn the corner of the Citadel and Tumasra comes into view. The flames swirl in a spiral pattern, like a giant tornado made of magma. We run toward it, the scent of sulfur getting stronger. Finally we come to a stop at the foot of the storm itself, at the short fence that surrounds it. I feel its heat on my skin. It looms above us, as tall and imposing as New York's highest skyscrapers. I've never been this close to it. A million embers flow across the storm's dense, grainy surface, as if the wind itself had caught on fire.

My heart sinks. Only a handful of Hoshans are here, lying on the ground at the foot of Tumasra, in the Hoshan manner of communal prayer. Several sit up on four legs, tilting their heads to one side, looking at Timoteo and me with curiosity. Non-Etoscan aliens are an unusual sight, and they probably sense our distress.

The buzzing of the swarm grows louder. From around the side of the building, dozens of Hoshan soldiers scurry toward us on all six legs. Within seconds, a semi-circle of Hoshan soldiers form around Timoteo and me, blocking every path, save for the Tumasra storm at our backs. A swarm of warbots circle the air above us, like a flock of miniature vultures ready for a carcass.

Commander of War approaches, the ground tremoring with each landing of his massive feet. Instinctively, I hold Wasala tight, her fur pressing into the skin of my neck.

"Ambassador Vega," Commander says. It's not the tone he used underground, but the gentle tone he's used so often in diplomatic meetings. "You have illegally raided the most sacred of sites, not only for Etoscans, but for the good Hoshans of the North. You've brought an exile to this world in violation of interstellar law. You've colluded with terrorists and Outlanders.

"It saddens me that our attempts to make peace have failed," Commander continues, hundreds of warbots buzzing in the air around him. "And now I see that perhaps you were never suited to play the role of Mediator. Through all our talks your true sympathies lay with the brutal ideology of the Hosh-Unam Front. With such treachery at work, our pursuit of peace was doomed to fail. In four minutes, Article 17 shall expire. With little choice before us, the Etoscan forces shall seek redress for our grievances with the Levinti on the field of war. We shall do all we can to protect innocent Hoshans from harm. But for you, Ambassador Vega, and your companions, we can offer no such protection. You deserve none, after committing such treacherous crimes."

"He's covering his ass," Timoteo whispers. "In four minutes, the rest of that swarm is going to come busting through the prayer center and they're going to tear us apart. All it takes is one bot breaking a tiny hole in our oxygen masks and we're dead."

"And he's waiting until the treaty expires so he has a clean cover story," I say.

"We've lost," Timoteo says. He takes my hand and laughs through his tears. "At least being killed by a robot swarm in front of a mysterious lava-storm on an alien planet is an interesting way to go."

The despair in my brother's voice sinks into my skin. There has to be something else we can do. I look up at the flames of Tumasra and wipe sweat from my brow. The stench of sulfur is overpowering, and my head is throbbing. I remember when I first came to Tumasra, how Charism brought me here so that the mysterious storm could amplify my thoughts, revealing them for all of Northern Hosh to see. Beyond the swarms and the soldiers, the small group of praying Hoshans look on, their faces frightened and confused. I realize something then. I have no weapons, but I have my mind—which, to Hoshans, is also my *voice*.

People of Hosh, I think, *I'm Valeria Vega, Ambassador of Earth, and I'm calling out to you for help! The Etoscans have betrayed us all, building an illegal Subway here beneath the sacred grounds of Tumasra. Right now an endless swarm is streaming through the Subway, ready to decimate Hosh the moment the treaty expires. Help me defend this world from war!*

The Hoshan soldiers surrounding Timoteo and me exchange glances and snickers. Beyond them, the handful of praying Hoshans look up, but remain unmoving.

"She thinks she can call our brethren to her aid," one of the soldiers says.

"The Etoscans have taken care of us for centuries," says another. "Why would anyone so much as climb up from their pillows for the likes of you and your anti-social conspirators?"

I look down at Wasala's small form, still cradled in my arms, at Jerana's body in my brother's arms. They lie motionless, but their eyes are open, and I wonder if their minds can still hear and share thoughts with the Hoshans all around us. Can the Hoshans sense Wasala and Jerana's fear, trapped in their unmoving bodies? Or does their fear of the exile and the Outlander surpass their empathy? How can I convince anyone of anything, when every side in this conflict has been so complicated, when every choice has so many uncertain consequences?

I need more than words. I tighten my grip on my brother's hand. "Open your mind," I whisper to Timoteo. "Let them see everything." Timoteo looks at me quizzically, but then nods and squeezes my hand.

I look down at the motionless forms of my Hoshan friends. *If you can hear me, Wasala and Jerana, I need your help too.*

I close my eyes and summon everything that's within my mind and heart. The first thing that comes to the surface is my grief for tío Umberto, how even now the thought of him makes a chasm open up inside my chest. Then comes my fear and excitement the moment I first stepped off the Interstellar Subway, the fear I feel this very moment, not only for myself and Timoteo, but for all of Hosh, only seconds away from war.

I let them see how overwhelmed I felt as I careened from ambassador to ambassador, a different set of lies from each, like a kid drowning in deep ocean waters. I let them see my envy the first time I imagined what it must be like to be Hoshan, to truly know another's thoughts, to experience a kind of trust that the mind-deaf can only mimic. I let them see my horror at the violence of the Hosh-Unam Front, and that, yes, I feel sympathy for their cause, but not one iota for their methods. I let them see my wonder at the Outlands, those gorgeous islands that hang above the sea, and my deep respect for the kind of world the Outlanders are trying to build.

I open my eyes. On the hill overlooking Tumasra, a handful of scattered Hoshans have gathered. They stand on two legs, gazing down in my direction, their fur unkempt and their large eyes blinking, recently awoken from their daytime slumber.

The Hoshan guards surrounding us aren't scowling or laughing now; instead they're looking at each other in confusion. They step toward me, closing in around me, raising their weapons in an unspoken ultimatum.

At Commander's side, a Hoshan stretches up to whisper into his ear. Commander glares at me, his trunk letting out a low rumble. "Whatever you think to accomplish, Ambassador Vega," he says, "your efforts are futile. Time has expired, for all of you. The Treaty of Centron no longer holds, and a swarm as vast as a planet awaits my command."

From the Etoscan Citadel comes the buzzing of the swarm, so loud that it's deafening. From the prayer center the bots come flooding out, a swarm so thick that no gaps are visible in the writhing mass of black and grey. They stream in all directions, north, south, east, and west. Within seconds, they blacken the sky, creating the illusion of an early dusk.

Beneath the shadows of the swarm, the brightness of Tumasra's flames sharpen. For the first time, the scent of sulfur doesn't bother me. I again reach within myself—and find there's some force pulling me even deeper than before, as if I've heaved myself over the peak of a mountain and momentum is carrying me forward at an ever faster clip. My fear, my hesitations, my doubts ... all of it suddenly comes bursting to the surface of my mind. The fires of Tumasra burn through the clothing of my psyche to reveal a naked, helpless soul beneath.

But the fires burn on, melting away my psyche's skin to find another layer deeper yet. The empathy I feel for all no matter how different they may seem. The serenity I can find in the midst of adversity. The courage to put the lives of others before my own.

I'm surprised to find courage inside me. I've never thought of myself as brave. Tumasra's fires continue to burn within my mind, but they can't burn up my courage. The burning flames transform into a shining light. I let the light shine within my mind until my inner self is a sea of illumination.

I call to you, my Hoshan friends, I think, and feel my mind's voice booming out across the hills. *I call on you to stand with me against this war. Here in the North and in the South and even in the Outlands, several of you have told me that my mind is unusual for a mind-deaf, that it has an almost Hoshan quality to it. I bend easily to the thoughts of others, adapting myself to better understand them. I have opened my mind to you and so you know that this is so.*

But from the wisest of Hoshans I've learned that it's not enough to bend one's thoughts to listen. There comes a time when you must share of your own mind, when you must not bend, but hold firm. Now the Etoscans and Levinti are on the brink of a war that will devastate this world. We must not bend to violence! We must stand firm for peace!

Atop the hill, a Hoshan looks on, her lips quivering. She drops to all six legs and marches down the hill, toward the throng of Hoshan soldiers and the swarm of warbots. Another Hoshan onlooker does the same, then another, and another, until two dozen scattered Hoshans are marching down the hill toward us.

From over the hill, a speck of fur comes into view, the ears of another Hoshan, followed by her entire body as she crests the hill. She's followed by dozens more, a row of Hoshans scuttling over the hill from one end to the other. Behind them come still more Hoshans, rushing over the hill.

Among those in the front of the pack is Charism, his face haggard but his legs full of energy as he bounds down the hill. "We answer your call, Valiant One!" he shouts. "We stand with you for peace!"

Still more Hoshans come pouring down the hill, a teeming mass of fur and scampering legs. The soldiers raise their weapons, but the crowd of Hoshans scurries onward, pushing past the soldiers. The ones in the lead come to where Timoteo and I stand holding Wasala and Jerana, and then they turn around and stand on their hindmost legs, staring back defiantly at the Hoshan soldiers standing with weapons at the ready. More follow, until Timoteo and I are surrounded up to our waists by a crowd of Hoshans standing at full height.

As the throng of Hoshans surges around us, the soldiers look up at Commander, his massive white form standing tall above the crowd of furry creatures.

"Charism!" Commander bellows, his trunk rolling high into the air. "This primitive has conspired with the Hosh-Unam Front, betraying us all. Stand aside."

"No," Charism says. "It was you who betrayed us when you made a military base on this most sacred of sites. The Valiant One's only conspiring has been for peace. And as you can see, the conspiracy for peace has become a vast conspiracy indeed."

"Self-righteousness will do you little good against this swarm," Commander says.

"There's no way we could resist your swarm," I say. "But what are you going to do, Commander? Kill us all?"

"These are unarmed Hoshans," Timoteo says. "These are the people you say you're here to protect."

"We mean the Northern Hoshans no harm," Commander says. "Our swarm will easily pass over these crowds to take the South."

"But every Hoshan here knows of your crimes, Commander," Charism says, gesturing toward the growing multitude approaching from the hill. "And not just those here. The word is spreading across the *unam*, neighbor waking neighbor with urgent thoughts. They know of your subterfuge here beneath our sacred Tumasra. They know we've gathered here to oppose you. Their minds listen now, waiting to hear of what happens next."

"Will you wipe out half a continent to hide your crimes?" Timoteo says.

Commander of War charges toward us, his massive feet pounding. The ground quakes and the Hoshans in his path leap back to avoid being trampled. He gets within a few inches of me and lets out a rumbling trumpet. I stand unmoving, looking up at the angry Etoscan.

"He considers it!" shouts a Hoshan from the crowd.

"His mind is more twisted than Marrow's!" shouts another.

Commander looks out at the crowd, the muscles of his pale face taut. "Arrest the Terrans and the terrorists and clear away the Hoshans," he orders his soldiers. "Detain as many of them as necessary, but use no lethal force." He turns and bends his trunk toward me. "You have only delayed the inevitable, Ambassador Vega. War will soon begin and you will be among its first casualties."

The swarm hovers overhead, still blocking the sun from view. But from above the swarm, an even larger shadow approaches, looming larger with each passing second. Beyond the thick clouds of buzzing warbots, a massive ship draws closer.

From far above, a voice booms out, louder than a stadium's sound system. The words come in three languages simultaneously: the trumpeting sounds of the Etoscans, the clicks and chirps of the North Hoshan tongue, and the familiar cadence of English. "We are here on behalf of the Interstellar Transit Authority." It's Pash-Ti's voice! They must have convinced the Interstellar Transit Authority to come to Hosh! "Ambassador Vega, we understand that you possess evidence that the Etoscan Fellowship has constructed an Interstellar Subway Station on this site, in violation of the Treaty of Centron and without proper authorization of the Interstellar Transit Authority. Do you possess such evidence?"

"Yes, I do," I say, smiling. "And it's great to hear your voice, Pash-Ti."

"It's a lovely surprise to find you among the living, Ambassador," Pash-Ti says, "Commander, stand down and we'll land to begin our investigation."

Commander of War rears up on his hind legs, then batters his front legs down upon the ground. "The Interstellar Transit Authority has no basis for these outlandish accusations, nor does this savage Terran! Tumasra is a protected site under exclusive domain of the Etoscan Fellowship. The Transit Authority has no jurisdiction here."

Another voice answers from above, one I don't recognize. "The Transit Authority has jurisdiction anywhere that an unauthorized Interstellar Subway Station is constructed."

"We have hundreds of witnesses ready to testify to the construction of the illegal Subway," I say.

"Thousands of us!" Charism corrects. "We see the criminal intent in the mind of Commander of War, and we see the Subway in the minds of the Valiant One and her comrades."

"Telepathic hearsay!" Commander replies. "And the Treaty of

Centron has expired, making this an authorized zone of war. The construction of an Interstellar Subway is legal at all times in zones of war."

"That'd be a fast construction job," Timoteo says, "building a Subway in 15 minutes."

I take out Timoteo's phone. "Also, I have a video recording time-stamped prior to the expiration of the treaty."

Commander of War glares at the phone. "Surely, the ITA is not going to admit evidence from a Terran youth recorded on a primitive communications device."

"Commander of War!" booms the voice from above. "There is ample evidence to warrant investigation. We now declare Tumasra under our jurisdiction as an Ad Hoc Investigative Commission of The Interstellar Transit Authority. Order your forces to stand down."

Commander lifts his trumpet, as if he's about to voice his defiance again. But then his head drops down, his trunk falling limply to the ground. "All forces, stand down," he says with a soft rumble.

The Hoshan soldiers lower their weapons. The swarms of warbots part like two dark clouds, revealing the Hoshan sun and the enormous ship of the Interstellar Transit Authority. The ship lowers toward us, passing between the two columns of warbots.

As the ship lands on the hill beside Tumasra, the crowd of Hoshan citizens erupts into wild cheering hisses, bounding upon one another and scratching each other everywhere. Charism reaches up to scratch Timoteo and me, and we both return the gesture. Timoteo and I hug each other, then scratch each other in the Hoshan manner, causing the Hoshans all around us to burst out in tittering laughter.

When Pash-Ti comes down from the ship, I hug them too, and am surprised when they reach out with their long arms to pull me in close to their bony chest. They clutch me by the shoulders and say, "You've done well, Ambassador. Umberto would be proud." I beam as if tío Umberto himself had said so.

The Hoshans are celebrating all around us, but there's still work to do. It takes an hour to revive Wasala and Jerana and the other paralyzed Hoshans, and even more time to re-activate Johnny. Then the ITA investigators interrogate all of us.

Technically, Commander of War was right—we did commit crimes, particularly by trespassing on the Citadel and bringing Wasala home. But Pash-Ti defends us with a rarely used clause in the First Treaty of Centron—allowing an interstellar ambassador to take "extraordinary actions in response to extraordinary circumstances." Commander of War's crimes—assassination, attempted assassination, arms-smuggling to insurgents, and construction of an unauthorized Subway—are pretty extraordinary circumstances.

Shortly after the sun sets, Pash-Ti gathers Timoteo, Johnny, Wasala, Jerana, and me to update us. "The Interstellar Transit Authority has formally opened an investigative file on the unauthorized Interstellar Subway Station beneath Tumasra. Commander of War is in custody, and the Etoscans have already dispatched two new ambassadors. They're quite eager to renew the peace talks. The Levinti have forestalled military action as well. They know that with these revelations, the talks are likely to skew heavily to their advantage."

"Then we did it?" Timoteo says. "It's done?"

Johnny puts a hand on Timoteo's shoulder and says, "Nearly every culture in the Galaxy has a saying about how it ain't over till it's over. But pretty much yeah. It's done."

My friends and I join the crowd of Hoshans. Beneath two rising moons we celebrate a day that's brought a planet from the hopeless certainty of war to the unexpected possibility of peace.

CHAPTER 28

MARROW'S EARS PRICK UP as I approach the holding cell. He lifts his front legs from the circular Hoshan pillow. He treads slowly toward me on four legs, coming to a stop just before the thick transparent wall that contains him.

"Ambassador Vega," he says, looking up at me. "I assume my current circumstances are a result of a misunderstanding that will soon be corrected."

No, I think. *No misunderstanding. Although a lot of people are fighting over who gets to put you on trial first. The Northern Hoshans, the Southern Hoshans, the Etoscans, the Levinti, the Tribunal of Interstellar Crime …*

Marrow rises to stand on his hindmost legs. "I'm not to be tried. I'm to be vindicated."

No, I think, *you'll be tried for murdering Ferus and Speaker and hundreds of others.*

"You gave me your word," Marrow says. "You vowed you'd give me full credit for the exposure of the Etoscans' crimes."

I gave you credit, I think. *I told them how you helped us, just like I promised. But no one, including me, thought that made up for all the lives you've taken.*

"I am to stand as the leader of the Hosh-Unam Front in the final phase of negotiations. I demand freedom and unity for the Hoshan people!"

Hoshan autonomists will be represented in the final negotiations, I think. *But not by you. You nearly cost this planet everything. You must have known that swarm came from Commander of War, even if it was through a middleman. You played right into his hands. In your own way, you've been complicit with your colonizers.*

Marrow places his upper paw on the glass as if to silence my thoughts. "You have no right to such sanctimonious thoughts toward me. You are nothing but a mind-deaf deceiver! You swore to it! I saw in your mind the truth of it! You are ill-named, Valiant One! You're the worst kind of traitor! Even the fragments of your mind betray themselves!"

Two-faced. That's the word for it on my planet. Sometimes I can be two-faced. I'm working on it. Good-bye, Marrow, I think as I walk away. More to myself than to Marrow, I think, *There's another promise I broke that was much more important.*

✦ ✦ ✦

THIS TIME, THE SHADOWS OF the Outlands forest seem heavy with gloom. Jerana leads the way along the dim path. They say that when Kettle heard the news, she fled deep into the forest, far from all other minds. It's an ancient Hoshan ritual, when in a state of extreme grief, to retreat from all thoughts but one's own. Only Jerana's farsighted telepathy gives us any chance of finding her in the depths of the forest.

"Are you sure she'll want to see me?" I ask.

"Oh, yes," Jerana says. "Her ritual retreat cannot end until she has seen the body and shaved it of its fur."

I felt shocked when they found Ferus's body in the caves. Part of me had hoped he was alive somehow. I've been carrying his body through miles of forest. It seemed light at first, but now my muscles are aching from the weight of it, and the scent of preservative chemicals is making me nauseated. My stomach twists in guilt for whining about my tiredness, even if it's just in my own thoughts. My aches are trivial compared to this brave being who gave his life for his planet—and for me.

"We're almost there," Jerana says, pushing their way through a thicket of purple vines, into an open clearing.

Kettle lies with all six legs on the ground, facing away from us. She's so still that her stout body almost looks like a furry stone in the middle of the forest floor.

"Does she know we're here?" I whisper.

"Of course," Jerana says. "She sensed us coming several minutes ago." Jerana stands on their hindmost legs and turns to look up at me. "You must go to her alone."

"Why only me?" I ask.

"Because you are the one she is angry with," Jerana says.

My shoulder blades tighten. I want to run back into the forest, far from Kettle and Hosh and death and consequences. But I can't. Carefully cradling Ferus's body, I stride across the clearing to Kettle.

I look down at Kettle. I have no idea what to say or think. "Um, hello."

Kettle says nothing, doesn't even look up at me.

"I've brought you Ferus," I say. With great care, I lay his body on the ground in front of Kettle, as Jerana instructed.

Remaining completely still, Kettle lifts her eyes to look upon her lover's body. Her lips quiver, softly at first, then erupt into a tremble so violent that her entire face is shuddering.

Finally, Kettle looks up at me, our eyes meeting. "His fur!" she shouts. "You promise me you bring him home, and all you bring me is his fur!"

I kneel down on the ground and touch Kettle on the shoulder. "Kettle, I'm so sorry."

Kettle stands up on her four hind legs and jerks away. "Sorry a mind-deaf word that mean nothing and do nothing! I lose my love! For what? To end occupation? To stop war? I rather live through a hundred occupations and a thousand wars than live without Ferus."

I want to apologize and defend myself at the same time. *It wasn't just me who wanted to stop the war,* I think. *Ferus did too. He chose to come with me. He chose to sacrifice his life because he knew millions could die if he didn't. I could never have forced Ferus to come against his will—he had a mind of his own, a strong mind, no one knows that better than you.*

"You do not understand," Kettle says. "He say my thoughts better than I say my thoughts. He know my thoughts better than I know my thoughts. His mind went with my mind, like two vines all tangled up so you can never untie them. Now he is dead. What does living vine do when all tangled up with dead vine? Where can it go? This is why I made you promise! This is why you had to bring him back!"

I'm sorry! I'm sorry that Ferus is gone! I'm sorry that you're in pain! I can't stop the tangle of anger and grief bursting from my mind. *But you're not the only one who's lost someone! I lost my uncle, the man who was like a father to me, the only person in the world who understood me. I lost him for your world before I even knew it existed!*

Kettle responds with a grunt, but doesn't look away. Her lips still quiver but the rage has faded from her eyes. I wonder if I should ask her now or if it's better to wait, then realize the thought is in my mind and Kettle has sensed it, so I've already half-asked. *I'm so sorry,* I think. *I know this will be hard for you. I've already gotten the other parties to agree to it. I need for you to represent the Outlands in the final phase of the talks.*

"No!" Kettle shouts. "No, no, no! I will not go and talk with those mind-deaf!"

You have to! I think. *This is a chance for the Outlands to be legally recognized! You won't have to live in hiding anymore. You can show the Hoshans of the North and the South that your people can live on your own, free, without the Etoscans or the Levinti.*

"Jerana should go," Kettle says. "They good with words. They good with mind-deaf, sense their lies from far away. They represent Outlands in mind-deaf talks."

"But Jerana is not the leader of the Outlands," I say. "You are."

Kettle rolls back onto her hindmost legs. Again her lips tremble. "I cannot go. With Ferus I could. But alone I cannot." With her nose, she points at her lover's dead body, lying in the purple grass. "I exist like him now, only empty fur."

I know, I think, and suddenly I'm crying—not just crying, my lips are trembling too. *I know about the emptiness. I still feel like empty skin every time I think of Umberto. But you're not alone. You are not alone.*

I open my arms to Kettle, and Kettle falls into them, her soft fur pressing into my skin, two lonely bodies from different worlds, in a weeping, trembling embrace.

Later, I realize I'm starting to understand the meaning of *vasek antom*. The definition from Checkers and even from Charism weren't even close. *Vasek antom* is so much more. It's something that can only happen when you dive deep into difference, when you make a path through the thicket of pain, when you find your way through grief and rage to love.

CHAPTER 29

AMBASSADOR VALERIA VEGA

AMBASSADOR VALERIA VEGA – The 79th ambassador of <u>Terra</u>, a primitive world in the Orion Belt. Despite the insignificance of her homeworld, she attained some renown due to her unexpected success as mediator for the <u>New Hoshan Treaty</u>, which altered the course of Hosh's future and of interstellar relations among the <u>Great Powers</u>.[1]

Excerpted from **WIKI GALACTICA**

I FILL IN THE CIRCLE marked "C" and look up at the clock. I've managed to finish the entire test—with thirty seconds to spare. Not enough time to check my work, but I can at least glance back at my answers. Only a couple erased and re-scribbled out answers, and not one left blank.

"Pencils down," says Ms. Papio, and everyone stops   except for one boy in the back, who scrambles feverishly to fill in a few more circles. I feel a pang of empathy for him—that was me a few months ago, when I could see a way for A, B, C, and D to all be right. I don't think I aced it or anything, but I did a lot better than last time. Well enough to get into a decent college. What would it be like to be a college student and the ambassador of Earth? A lot cooler than being a *high school* student and the ambassador of Earth, that's for sure ...

I pull my knapsack over my shoulder and turn in my answer sheet, then walk out into the hall. The school is oddly empty, but then it is a Saturday afternoon in June.

Will is waiting outside in their hand-me-down Toyota and gives a friendly honk as I walk out the doors. It's still weird that Will is driving now—though, objectively, in the grand scheme of my life, my best friend getting their driver's license is probably the least weird thing.

"How'd you do?" Will asks as I get in the car.

"Oh, I think I got a few questions right," I say.

Will smiles and starts up the car. "I'm sure you rocked it."

I shrug and stare out the window. With the test behind me, my mind is on the treaty signing. Pash-Ti says the real work is done, that it's only a ceremony, but it'll still be a huge relief for the signing to be done, for my duties as mediator to be officially complete.

"Where are you?" Will says, stopping at a light. "What are you thinking about when you space out like that?"

"Just … thinking," I say.

"Were you thinking about Kate?" Will says. "Because I can't stop thinking about Kate. I wish we knew if she was okay—or not okay—or anything. I just can't deal with not knowing."

"I know," I say. "It's hard." I hate not being able to tell them the truth. But even if could, what would I say? Actually, Kate is hundreds of light years away on the planet Centron being tried by an interstellar tribunal for multiple violations of interstellar law? Just hearing Kate's name makes my body flush with a mixture of anger and betrayal and grief.

Will shakes themself, as if trying to physically escape the specter of Kate's disappearance. After a minute of silence they say, "So you going to the party tonight?"

"No," I say. "Remember, tonight I head to Istanbul."

"Oh, yeah, that's right. This is your last trip, right?"

"Yeah," I say, "for a while, anyway."

Will takes their eyes off the road for a second to look over at me. "I can't believe you've gone to Istanbul, like, five times or something. You have the sweetest internship ever."

"Yeah," I say, "nice consolation for losing my uncle."

"I'm sorry," Will says, then goes quiet. Lately, I just mention Umberto whenever anyone seems suspicious of a lowly intern getting to take frequent trips halfway around the world. The topic of death is an astonishingly effective deflector in human social interactions.

Did I really just think that? I've been spending way too much time with Pash-Ti.

Will pulls over to the curb in front of my house and gets out of the car to hug me good-bye. "Have fun in Istanbul," they say. "And come back soon. New Jersey needs you too." They tighten their embrace, and I do the same, my heart rate accelerating. They're still with Des, and I wish I could just make my crush disappear, but I don't think it ever will.

✧　✧　✧

JOHNNY EXCELSIOR WAVES HIS SPOON in the air dramatically. "I must say, tía Ana, this crème brûlée is amazing!"

"Gracias, Johnny," says Mami. "You're such a sweet young man."

Pash-Ti puts down their spoon, having emptied their own dish. "Indeed, Ms. Vega. I'm impressed by your mastery of the cuisine of so many of the planet's regions."

"World," Miguel corrects, rolling his eyes as he helps himself to another serving. "In Spanish we say *world*. You guys are nice but I still think you're all weirdos."

"Miguel!" says Mami. "Don't be rude to our guests. Spanish isn't their first language. Why, it's not even their second language. Johnny, how many languages do you speak?"

Johnny lifts his eyes toward the ceiling as if counting. Timoteo elbows him and says, "Many. Johnny speaks many languages and let's leave it at that. No need to brag, Johnny."

"This has been simply lovely, tía Ana," says Wasala. These regular dinners were her idea. The regular phone calls home from a computer simulation of mine and Timoteo's voices just weren't enough to stop Mami from worrying during our long trips to "Istanbul."

"Your mother's mind works based on relationships," Wasala said. "If she trusts the three of us then she won't worry so much when you're away with us." Even without telepathy, Timoteo and I knew that was true. These dinners have become a near-weekly tradition.

Pash-Ti rises from the table. Even with the holographic technology that makes them look human, their head nearly touches the low ceiling. "Thank you again for hosting us, Ms. Vega. But I'm afraid we must leave now to catch our flight."

"Of course," says Mami, reluctantly. The farewell hugs and kisses begin, each of them accompanied by the same whisper from my mother. "Take care of my children, bring them home safe, God willing."

✧ ✧ ✧

I'M STANDING WITH HANDS CLASPED behind me on the hover-platform, with Timoteo, Johnny, Pash-Ti, and Wasala just behind me. The Etoscan contingency is on my left, the Hoshans to my right, and the Levinti ambassador and her *kiromakee* are floating just beside the platform. On the floor far beneath us, the tentacled shadow of the Levinti is nearly as large as the one cast by the dais itself. This Levinti conference center in Southern Hosh is the only facility on the planet large enough to hold such an enormous crowd. Apparently, it's the standard layout for a multi-species interstellar gathering: a super-sized arena with a central open space for the speakers, surrounded on all sides by a multi-level globe to accommodate the spectators. But unlike any arena on Earth, this one is segmented into dozens of sub-sections, accommodating species of all sizes and atmospheres.

The Levinti section is the largest, so crowded that some Levinti have to float above and below each other, which, in their culture, is unorthodox. The other sections—even the aquatic and ammonia levels— are just as crowded. I've heard there was a waiting list for seats. No one in the Galaxy expected the peace talks to succeed, making this treaty the biggest news story in a century—literally. Sentients from across the Galaxy have travelled hundreds of light years to witness Galactic history unfold.

The official treaty is displayed in the center of the platform, more than twice my height. I've seen the draft before, but there's something awe-inspiring about seeing the original in all its rich complexity. The document is filled with the full text of the treaty in eight languages: Northern and Southern Hoshan, the standard dialects of all five of the Great Powers, and Centronian. The phosphorescent colors of the Levinti-language column run alongside the Sufri column, whose tactile language is rendered in contours, like a topographic map of a mountainous land. The treaty has even been translated into the coded language of the Synthetics, which, though not visible, is included in the digital file embedded in the document. Even the digital file is stamped with a unique code so it can never be precisely duplicated; this is the one true original for posterity.

Peltiquinas, the new Levinti ambassador, is assigned to speak first, and to sign the treaty first—which is apt, since the Levinti have pretty much dominated the final phase of the negotiations. After Commander of War's subterfuge was revealed, the Levinti happily renewed negotiations—knowing that they now had the leverage to get nearly everything they'd wanted, while maintaining their strategic advantage of controlling the planet's only Interstellar Subway Station—without a long and costly war.

Peltiquinas's skin glows with a dance of color as she addresses the crowd. "Honored colleagues, we are here today not merely to sign a historic treaty. We are here today not merely to maintain peace. We are here today to celebrate a victory for scientific inquiry! No longer will Tumasra be sequestered beyond our reach, where none can study its unique properties. No longer will Tumasra be merely a shrine dedicated to folk rituals and the worship of primitive deities. Today, the Tumasra storm becomes a beacon for scientific learning, not only for the Levinti, but for all species—for we have won the right for all who come in the name of scholarly inquiry to enter Tumasra."

The entire Levinti section of the arena lights up in a glowing cascade of lights, and there are eruptions of noise and motion from other sections in various gestures of applause—except, notably, the Etoscan section. I join in, clapping my hands, knowing my actions are on display for all to see. Deep down, some part of me wants to laugh. It was my idea to open up Tumasra for other species, not just the Levinti, though I was happy to let Peltiquinas claim it as her own.

Peltiquinas basks in the applause for a few moments before gliding over to the side of the platform. "On behalf of the Levinti people, it is my honor to certify the Treaty of Hosh." She lifts a single tendril and releases a thin layer of phosphorescent fluid onto the over-sized document. It looks more like a painting than a signature, its glowing colors still fluctuating even after the ink has dried.

Next, Reconciler, the new Etoscan ambassador, strides toward the imposing document. His skin is a shimmering dark black, like obsidian crystal. The Etoscan Fellowship says Commander of War was acting alone, a rogue leader who violated not only interstellar law but Etoscan tradition. It does seem like Commander's actions were never officially endorsed by the Etoscan leadership, but some were also happy to look the other way—right up until Commander got caught. Then the Etoscans sent in Reconciler to finish the treaty negotiations and salvage the Etoscans' reputation in the interstellar community.

Reconciler raises his trunk, like a priest lifting his arms to the heavens. "In the language of my people, the word for treaty is said to originate in prehistoric times, before we had ventured from our homeworld to explore the stars, and even before the great Seeker revealed the sacred truths of Synchronus. Thus, 'treaty' is said to derive from two ancient words, meaning 'sharing' and 'gods.' For in ancient times, when two rival villages would form an alliance, they would consecrate that pact by sharing their gods, by recognizing that the gods they worshipped were but two faces of the same divinity. In so doing they foreshadowed the truth that Seeker would one day reveal to our people: that all gods are but faces of Synchronus in all Its splendor.

"What we do here today is much the same. We recognize that many of you do not share our understanding of Synchronus. But you all share our awe of the universe, our pursuit of truth in all its wonderful varieties, and so you also pursue Synchronus by a different path, just as our ancient tribes prayed to It by different names. In recognition that we have more in common than we know, we proudly sign this historic treaty. In that spirit, we warmly open Tumasra for all peoples, so that we all may learn and grow together, to better understand the Tumasra storm and the wondrous mystery of Synchronus it represents."

"Wow," Johnny whispers from behind me, "unlike some Etoscans, Reconciler lives up to his name. You'd never guess they only opened up

Tumasra because they've become an object of interstellar ridicule."

"I thought it was a nice speech," whispers Wasala.

"I did like the historical allusions," Timoteo says.

"All of you, hush," Pash-Ti says.

"On behalf of the peace-loving Etoscan people," Reconciler goes on, "it is my sacred honor to place my stamp upon the Treaty of Hosh." He places his front left foot on the slab before him, creating a massive footprint in the clay-like substance. Gently gripping the slab with his trunk, he lifts it up and affixes it to the treaty. The slab's clay sinks into the rigid document, Reconciler's footprint merging into it, not a single seam visible.

After a brief, polite applause from the arena, Trimana steps forward, remaining upright on her hindmost legs. "I ask my fellow Hoshan leaders and friends, Charism and Kettle, to step forward with me." Charism glides forward with his usual ease and smile. Kettle totters close behind, her steps heavy and firm.

I smile. We'd talked about doing it this way, but I wasn't sure if they could work it out.

"We stand side by side in the spirit of the *unam*," Charism says, "in the name of the shared siblinghood of the Hoshan people."

"Hoshans of North, of South, and of Outlands," Kettle says.

"For the first time, this treaty recognizes the Outlands as a legitimate, self-governed region of Hosh," Trimana says. Their speech flows so smoothly from one speaker to the next that they must be syncing with each other.

"And," says Charism, "it grants greater autonomy to both Southern and Northern Hosh. For although our Etoscan and Levinti stewards shall remain with us, this treaty recognizes that one day it must be—and can only be—Hoshans ourselves who rule Hosh." From the Hoshan section of the arena, there's a massive collective hiss of applause. It's amazing how hard we had to fight for that simple clause! After Commander got caught, I was hoping we could get full independence for both North and South, but it was immediately clear there was no way the Levinti—or even the humiliated Etoscans—would concede that much. But we did win a handful of symbolic gestures toward autonomy, and the clause recognizing that eventually Hoshans must be granted self-rule—which Pash-Ti says is no small victory, since Hoshan autonomy is now a matter of interstellar law, however vague and open-ended.

The hissing subsides, and Kettle speaks. "And now our children, our lost children, can come home. All Hoshan children welcome in Outlands with arms wide open." With that, there's an even more overpowering hiss from the Hoshan section.

Goosebumps dance down my arms as I join in the applause with both a hiss and a Terran hand-clap. The open existence of autonomous Outlands can prove to the Galaxy—and, maybe just as importantly, to Hoshans themselves—that Hoshans are fully capable of self-governance. As the lost children come home to Hosh, they'll bring with them stories and experiences from across the Galaxy. And what Trimana, Charism, and Kettle aren't mentioning—for political reasons—is that any Hoshan can now move to the Outlands at any time, creating a refuge for Hoshans seeking independence for their world, without joining the Hosh-Unam Front or risking arrest.

As Trimana, Charism, and Kettle finish their speech, they speak simultaneously in each of their languages, which Checkers interprets: "We sign this treaty together, as the leaders of Hosh's three peoples, in the unity and spirit of the unam, and with the hope that one day all of Hosh will be free."

With that, Trimana signs the treaty with a pen that leaves a phosphorescent signature much like that of the Levinti, and Charism and Kettle stamp their claw-prints on a slab of clay, much as Reconciler had done. Even today, as they take such an important step toward autonomy, the most basic rituals reveal the legacy of their colonizers ...

Now all that's left is for me to certify the treaty as the official mediator.

I step forward to stand before the treaty, the enormous document towering over me. My hands are trembling, but instead of clasping them behind my back, I lift them up toward the crowd. Long speeches aren't my style, but I've known for a long time now what I have to say.

"I sign this treaty today not only for myself, but for my predecessor, Ambassador Umberto Olmeda. Umberto had a dream that *all* sentient beings, whatever our origins and whatever our limitations, should have the opportunity not only to live but to explore, to stretch beyond the things that are easy for us to reach, to discover the infinities of the universe and the infinities within ourselves. He died for that dream. And today, with this treaty of peace and possibility, we make his dream more real."

I love you, tío Umberto. I promise I'll never stop fighting for the dream.

With that, I sign the treaty in big, swooping letters: Valeria Vega, Ambassador of Earth.

Acknowledgments

This book was years in the making, and I am so appreciative of the many writing partners, teachers, friends, family, and chosen family who have supported me and my writing in so many ways.

I'm eternally grateful to my Cake writing group, a team of superpowered writers who critiqued the first draft of this novel chapter-by-chapter, month-by-month as I wrote it. Daniel Braum, M.M. De Voe, John C. Foster, Nicholas Kaufmann, Sarah Langan, Chandler Klang Smith, and David Wellington—thank you for teaching me to be a better writer and for the unforgettable dinner conversations.

Fifteen years ago, I got on a plane and flew for 24 hours to Brisbane, Australia, for the Clarion South writing workshop, where I learned to get a story from inception to completion in seven days or less, made life-changing friendships, and played too many games of mafia. Thank you to my classmates, teachers, and all the people who made that workshop possible.

I'm also appreciative for The Taos Toolbox workshop (I'm promiscuous when it comes to writing workshops!), which was equally formative and introduced me to yet another brilliant set of people, who gave insightful notes and guidance on the early rough outline and opening chapters of *Secret Ambassador*.

Through these workshops, I've been blessed to have some instructors who are not only great writers but also gifted teachers—and all-around wonderful people. Thanks especially to Kelly Link, Gavin Grant, Margo Lanagan, Walter Jon Williams, Lee Battersby, and the late Gardner Dozois for offering me so much wisdom.

I am also appreciative of my extended writing community, all of my writer friends who have shared critiques, resources, and comradery, especially Steve Berman, Rick Bowes, Chris Green, J.J. Irwin, David Levine, Will McIntosh, Nathan Long, Chris Lynch, Charles Rice-Gonzalez, Cindy Rizzo, and Charlie Vazquez.

A special thanks to Peter M. Ball for being a great friend and publishing coach, especially in the final sprint to the finish line.

It was an unexpected blessing to connect with Luis Carlos Barragán Castro, who not only created a gorgeous cover, but is also a kindred spirit and brilliant writer of queer Latin American fiction.

Many thanks to Todd Cooper for his lovely design for the cover and interior, especially the awesome science-fictional realia.

Thank you to all my writing buddies and dear friends who read various drafts of this novel in its entirety and offered thoughtful, insightful feedback: Jennifer Lauren Brown, Corey Datz-Greenberg, Janice Gallagher, Lyle Matthew Kan, Matthew Hro Lehosit, Omri Navot, Marcus Pereira, Dashboard Yaron Schweizer, and Daniel Tamulonis. I am so appreciative of the time and love that all of you gave to this novel—and that you've given to me.

Thanks to all my other friends and chosen family who have supported me throughout the long journey of writing this novel: Gaby Garcia-Vera, peter panZy, Marco Antonio Quiroga, Felipe Sousa-Lazaballet, and Isabel Sousa-Rodriguez.

And thank you to the siblings I was born with but would have gladly chosen—Dave, Val, and Jo—and to my parents, who have nurtured all our creative spirits with affirmation and love.

Finally, to my partner, my husband, mi amor: mil gracias, Juan, por siempre empujarme a perseguir mis sueños.

About the Author

Ben Francisco (they/them) is a queer Puerto Rican writer born in the Bronx and raised in New Jersey. They encountered the original *Star Wars* movie in the womb and remain convinced it left a permanent imprint. Ben grew up watching *Star Wars* and *Star Trek: The Next Generation* and reading space adventure novels by authors like Isaac Asimov and Robert Heinlein. They thrilled to the possibilities of science fiction, but rarely saw their mixed Latinx family or LGBTQ lived experience reflected in those imagined futures. *Val Vega: Secret Ambassador of Earth* is the book their younger self longed for, affirming that the wonder of the stars belongs to all of us.

Ben's short stories have been published in *Strange Horizons*, *PodCastle*, and *From Macho to Mariposa: New Gay Latino Fiction*. They won the *Indiana Review* 2022 Fiction Prize, and their work has been featured in several year's best anthologies of LGBTQ fiction. *Secret Ambassador of Earth* is their first novel.

Outside of writing fiction, Ben has two decades of experience in nonprofits and philanthropy working for immigrant rights, LGBTQ rights, and racial justice. They've also worked as a church receptionist, middle school teacher, and highly unsuccessful gardener. They live with their husband, Juan, in Brooklyn.

www.benfrancisco.net

Printed in the USA
CPSIA information can be obtained
at www.ICGtesting.com
LVHW040742100424
776895LV00007B/25